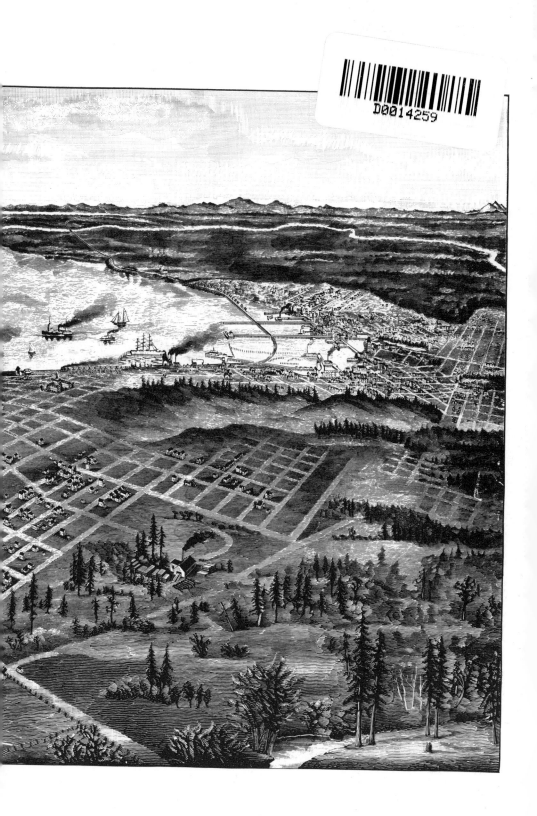
D0014259

THE LIVING

BY THE SAME AUTHOR

THE WRITING LIFE

AN AMERICAN CHILDHOOD

ENCOUNTERS WITH CHINESE WRITERS

TEACHING A STONE TO TALK

LIVING BY FICTION

HOLY THE FIRM

PILGRIM AT TINKER CREEK

TICKETS FOR A PRAYER WHEEL

THE
LIVING

ANNIE DILLARD

HarperCollins*Publishers*

Part of *The Living* appeared in *Harper's* magazine and *Elvis in Oz*.

THE LIVING. Copyright © 1992 by Annie Dillard. All rights reserved. Printed in the United States of America. No part of this book may be used or reproduced in any manner whatsoever without written permission except in the case of brief quotations embodied in critical articles and reviews. For infor- mation address HarperCollins Publishers, Inc., 10 East 53rd Street, New York, NY 10022.

HarperCollins books may be purchased for educational, business, or sales promotional use. For infor- mation, please call or write: Special Markets Department, HarperCollins Publishers, Inc., 10 East 53rd Street, New York, NY 10022. Telephone: (212) 207-7528; Fax: (212) 207-7222.

FIRST EDITION

Designed by C. Linda Dingler

Library of Congress Cataloging-in-Publication Data

Dillard, Annie.
  The living: a novel/Annie Dillard.—1st ed.
    p. cm.
    ISBN 0-06-016870-6 (cloth)
    1. Bellingham Region (Wash.)—History—Fiction. I. Title.
PS3554.I398L5   1992
813'.54—dc20   91-58376

92 93 94 95 96 ❖/HC 10 9 8 7 6 5 4 3 2 1

for Bob

CONTENTS

AUTHOR'S NOTE

Historically, there were four linked communities on Bellingham Bay—Whatcom, Old Bellingham, Sehome, and Fairhaven, which incorporated with each other in various combinations throughout the second half of the nineteeth century. It was not until the events in this story had long passed—not until 1904—that they consolidated to form the city of Bellingham. Whatcom was the first settlement, and had the lumber mill; Sehome had the coal mine. Fairhaven expected the Great Northern Terminus, and it saw the most dramatic boom. Jim Hill actually decided where to locate his Great Northern Railway terminus two years before the '93 panic.

The Living is fiction, and all of its characters are imaginary save Chowitzit, the Lummi chief, and Hump Talem, the Nooksack chief; James J. Hill and Frederick Weyerhaeuser, the railroad and timber magnates; Seattle political leaders; Tommy Cahoon, the scalped Pullman conductor; and George Bacon, the lively little mortgage agent.

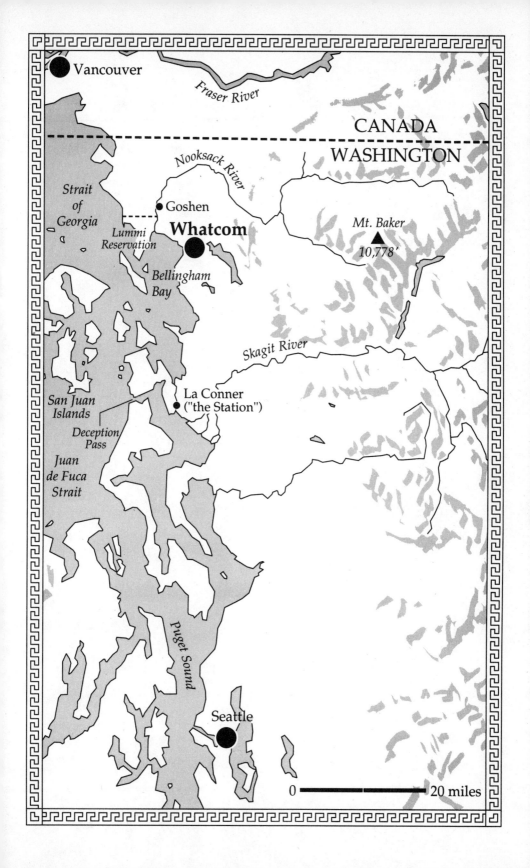

Vancouver

Fraser River

CANADA
WASHINGTON

Nooksack River

Strait
of
Georgia

Goshen

Whatcom

Mt. Baker
10,778'

Lummi
Reservation

Bellingham
Bay

Skagit River

San Juan
Islands

La Conner
("the Station")

Deception
Pass

Juan
de Fuca
Strait

Puget Sound

Seattle

0   20 miles

BOOK I

FISHBURNS

CHAPTER I

The sailor put down the helm and Ada Fishburn felt the boat round up towards the forest. She stood in the bow, a supple young woman wearing a brown shawl and a deep-brimmed sunbonnet that circled her face. She carried her infant son, Glee, in her arms.

Without a sound the schooner slipped alongside a sort of dock that met the water from the beach. This dock represented the settlement on Bellingham Bay. Ada Fishburn had been sailing in Puget Sound and along this unbroken forest every day for almost a week. The same forest grew on the islands they passed, too: the trunks rose straight. She had seen enough of this wall of forest to know that even when the sun and all the sky shone full upon it, and the blinding sea glinted up at it, it was always dark.

From behind her on deck Ada heard her older son, Clare, singing a song. Clare was five—a right big boy for five, long in the leg bones like his father—and life suited him very well, and he found his enjoyment. She glanced back and saw her husband, Rooney, moving their four barrels, their five crates, their four kegs, and the rolled feather-bed to the rail. Young Clare climbed up on everything barefoot, as fast as Rooney set it down on the deck. Rooney tied the two cows and gave the ropes to Clare to hold, and the boy sang to them, half-dead as they were. Neither man nor boy glanced up to see where he was getting off, which was a mercy, one of few, for she herself scarcely minded where she was since she lost her boy Charley on the overland road, but she hated to see Rooney down-hearted, when he staked his blessed being on this place, and look at it.

Ada and Rooney hauled their possessions off the dock. The baby, Glee, stayed asleep, moving its lips, and missed the whole thing. The schooner sailed on north and left them there.

It was the rough edge of the world, where the trees came smack down to the stones. The shore looked to Ada as if the corner of the continent had got torn off right here, sometime near yesterday, and the dark trees kept on growing like nothing happened. The ocean just filled in the tear and settled down. This was Puget Sound, and some straits that Rooney talked about, and there was not a thing on it or anywhere near it that she could see but some black ducks and humpy green islands. Salt water wet Ada's shoes if she stood still. Away out south over the water she made out a sharp line of snow-covered mountains. From the boat she had seen a few of such mountains poking up out of nowhere, including a big solitary white mountain that they had sailed towards all morning, that the forest now hid; it looked like its sloping base must start up just back there behind the first couple rows of trees. God might have created such a plunging shore as this before He thought of making people, and then when He thought of making people, He mercifully softened up the land in the palms of his hands wherever He expected them to live, which did not include here.

Rooney inspected the tilting dock. He folded his thin body double and studied the pilings and planks from underneath as if a dock were the wonder of the world. When he stood up again, Ada tried to read his expression, but she never could, for his bushy red beard seemed to grow straight down out of his hat, and only the tip of his nose showed. She watched him tear off some green grass blades at the forest edge and feed them to the spotted cows. Then he disappeared partway up a steep trail near the dock, returned, and set off up the beach.

Ada stayed in the silence with their pile of possessions. Her feather-bed was on top, on the barrels, to keep it dry. She poked one of its corners back in the roll so it would not pick up sand from the barrels. Deep inside the bonnet, her bow-shaped mouth was grave. Her dark brows almost met above her nose; her eyes were round and black. She made herself look around; her head moved slowly. The beach was a narrow strip of pebbles, stones, and white old logs laid end to end in neat rows like a necklace where the beach met the forest. Young Clare got right to breaking sticks off beach logs and throwing them in the water. Then he ran along the logs, and every time he stopped, Ada saw his bony head looking all around. It was October. The layer of cloud was high and distant, and the beach logs and the quiet water looked silver.

Ada said to herself, "For we are strangers before thee, and sojourners, as were all our fathers: our days on earth are as a shadow, and there is none abiding." The clouds overhead were still. There were no waves. A fish broke the water's sheen. It was not quite raining, but everything was wet.

A while later she saw a few frail smokes and some cabins under the trees back of the dock; she missed seeing the cabins at first because they were down among the roots of the trees, and she had been searching too high, thinking the trees were smaller. In all those days of sailing past the trees, she had nothing to size them by. Rooney came back beside her and said nothing. While Ada stared at glassy water and the dark islands near and far, here came an Indian man.

The Indian man, in a plug hat, was paddling a dugout canoe in smooth water alongshore. He had another canoe trailing behind him, and no one in it. He was a smooth-bodied, almost naked man, whose face had a delicate, modest expression. The plug hat sat oddly high on his head. He held a paddle low in one hand, and he pushed its top lightly with the other hand; his round, bulging shoulders moved. The silver water closed smoothly behind his path. Little Clare must have caught sight of him, for he came flying down from the logs to the shore.

The man beached the log canoe. Rooney took the few long-legged steps to the water. Clare marched directly into the water to try to help, and the man looked down at the boy and his wet britches with a trace of smile. He brought the other canoe alongshore and, wading, lifted the tan grass mats that decked its red interior. What was in this second canoe was feathers. It was white goose feathers, just loose under the mats. Ada looked out at Rooney; his mouth behind his red beard showed nothing, but she could see that he glanced at her from under his hatbrim.

The man came forward and said his name was Chowitzit. They knew he must be a Lummi Indian, for the schooner man said the local people were Lummis, and "right friendly." He had said, in fact, that the settlement at Whatcom "would have starved to death a dozen times" without the Lummis. Now the Lummi man and Rooney shook hands. He had a wide face and a small nose; he wore an earring made of something pale and hard. He indicated, speaking English in a tender voice and making gestures, that he was selling the feathers. Ada saw that around one of his wrists was a tattooed bracelet of black dots. He said that the price of the whole canoeload of feathers was "two cups of molasses." If they needed less than the whole canoeload, they could just take what they needed. He barely moved his lips when he spoke. His voice lilted.

They had just debarked from a schooner full of molasses; they had two kegs of molasses right there on the beach; everybody in their wagon train had molasses. They had molasses when they had no water. Molasses was plenty cheap for them, that is, but on the other hand, they needed no feathers. Rooney told the fellow no, and thanked him. He added that they could use fresh fish or meat or vegetables if he could get them. He could. Rooney thanked him again, and his high voice cracked. It was all coming home to Rooney here, Ada thought, where one powerful effort was ending, and another was beginning.

They tied the cows and left their outfit on the beach. Chowitzit led them up the hillside on a short trail through the woods by a creek. From behind Rooney, Ada watched Chowitzit's sure feet on the steep trail. In the past six months she had engaged in a great many acts of commerce with a great many native men of many tribes, and had accustomed herself to the sight of grown men's buttocks. Clare ran on ahead, ran back, and said, "Here's a house," which she could plainly see, a log house across the creek from what she knew was Felix Rush's sawmill.

The log house was low in the forest, and there were stumps and slash smoking all around it in the dirt. The door was open. Chowitzit walked straight inside, and the Fishburns hung back on the bare ground. Ada glimpsed a blue apron, a white woman's face. She heard the woman greet the bare-legged Chowitzit with glad sounds, and they started talking. Then the woman came out, all smiling and showing her long gums, and caught hold of Ada, hauled her inside, and began to weep. She put her arms around her, and Ada gave in to weeping too. The baby woke up and commenced to bawl. Rooney went out to have a look at the mill.

Chowitzit had taken off his hat in the house, and Ada saw that the top of his head was flattened into a wedge, so his forehead sloped back. He and the woman, who was Mrs. Lura Rush, made a stir over puny Glee equally, as if neither had ever encountered such a thing as a baby.

CHAPTER II

That night, Ada lay on her feather-bed on the Rushes' floor. Rooney slept in a blanket beside her. She thought Clare was likely sleeping in the corner with the Rushes' children—they had a striking black-haired little girl named Pearl, and a baby boy. Felix Rush had come in for dinner at dusk. It was Felix Rush who had bought the land and obtained Chowitzit's permission to build the mill the settlement grew up around; he owned the schooner that brought them. He turned out to be a stocky, animated fellow from Ohio who walked in jerks. He wore an opened vest, and kept saying "shirr" for "sure." He passed his boyhood on a Great Lakes schooner, he told them, shipping lumber to Sault Sainte Marie. That very night he gave Rooney a job at his sawmill, and they seemed fairly launched. Ada reflected that at daybreak this morning she had never clapped eyes on any Lura Rush nor Felix Rush either, and tonight they were all her world. They acted decent, more than decent, and they looked almighty glad to have company, which was just as well, for they had it.

Ada opened her eyes and saw black darkness over the room. There was a bit of color, a burnt red, that spread from the dying fire, and by its glow she made out a log stool by her head. Nothing stirred. Whenever things calmed down like this, Ada's mind became aware of the prayer that her heart cried out to God all day and maybe all night, too, that He would lend her strength to bear affliction and go on. She was not aware that underneath she prayed another prayer, too, as if to a power above God or at least to His better nature: that He was finished with the worst of it.

Her boy Charley was the worst of it, for she had not braced herself for life back then, a few months ago; she did not know how life could be, how it could dish you between one step and another. She had been a merry girl, and although traveling the overland road was hard most of the time, she had a head for adventure. Clare was five years old and Charley was three, and the road was taking their big train along the Sweetwater River. Charley fell out of the wagon and their own wheels ran him over, one big wooden wheel after the other, and he burst inwardly and died. There was no time to stop the oxen up ahead, though she shouted out and Rooney turned around and said, "What?" while the wheels ran straight over Charley's middle, before he could get away.

He was such a well-favored boy, people used to say he would be breaking hearts someday—when what they meant was, he was breaking their hearts right now, the way his green eyes sized up a person, and his mouth was so wide and dark, and his hair stood up in front. He was a little bucktoothed, and he had big teeth. She knew she should not love a child for being so pleasing to look at; she knew it at the time. There could be a statute about Thou shalt not go looking at a child every minute, and certainly there was Thou shalt have no other god before me: that might have been why he got run over, but it was harsh. Charley had never been a god to her, but just a boy, a beloved son that God of all people should know about, and know that a person's beloved son was not a god like God's was, but just an ordinary human child, which is how life goes on, if He will let it.

On the floor beside Ada, Rooney started to snore. The red firelight was gone, and the darkness was complete. Ada reckoned that intervening between her and the heavenly bodies there was her blanket, the house's log purlins and its shake roof, the stiff boughs of the forest, and the cover of cloud. She wished there were a sight more.

Charley had been riding with her in the front wagon; the back wagon held all their tools, grain, and furniture, and bacon and molasses and water in barrels. Clare was larking off somewhere up ahead in the train, and Rooney walked ahead with the oxen. When Charley got too lively in the wagon, Rooney carried him, although he was three years old and Rooney's curly beard tickled his neck. Some of those men in their train carried their little ones in their arms most of two thousand miles; they were good farmers who understood about carrying live things. That morning Charley was riding in the wagon right beside her, and she was looking at the neat curve of his forehead—he had a narrow forehead that curved so, it looked like you could cup it in your hand like a ball—and he stood up, and over the board he went, and into the rut.

Their train had eight hundred head of people and three thousand head of stock; it took a week just to cross it all over the Missouri River. They outspanned, bunched up waiting, crossed, inspanned, and spread out again, and the oxen pulled two yokes to a wagon. Oxen were slow, but they were strong, and they took one step after another. Oxen proceeded at the same steady walk boosting up a mountainside or traveling a plain; they were like locomotives that ran on grass and turned wheels.

"The oxen are bearing the brunt of it," people said every day. "The oxen are meek, and patient, and strong, and we thank God for their strength and pray they hold out." The day Rooney first bought the teams, Ada walked around the four beasts and looked into their eyes and found nothing there—just shine and brown, like wet boots. When Rooney was busy she drove the team herself. She sat on the wagon and called out, "Up, Maude" and "Up, Bright," and tapped them with the whip—"Up now, up. Up!" She tapped all four of them on their white hipbones, which looked like shifting mountains. Whether she tapped or not, when the cow column ahead moved, the teams all down the line started up, and the wagons rolled, and there was no stopping them.

When they buried Charley under an arching cottonwood tree by the Sweetwater River, the spade turned up big bones and worse, for it was a good tree to be buried under, if you had to be buried, and the emigrants who came before them on the road picked it, too. Rooney held his hat and bowed his thin head and said a few words over the hole, and they rolled on, lest they hold up the train. A few days later Glee was born, and they were still pegging along the Sweetwater River. Rooney thought of naming the baby Wyoming for the territory where he was born on the overland road, but although she, Ada, did not then care about a thing in this world, she rose up on her white feather bed and said no, so they named him Gleason after her side. He was so small she kept him in an empty bacon barrel, and she took no great personal interest in him; she knew it.

He woke now, on the Rushes' floor, and Ada burrowed down in the shifting feather-bed to find his face. This feather-bed had turned into a sorry joke.

She and Rooney had carried the white feather-bed over the emigrant road with them in the wagon for six months. When the oxen turned up lame, they abandoned the other wagon and lightened their load by the Snake. Rooney wanted to keep the feather-bed, because a man could sleep on the ground but a lady needed a feather-bed, and Ada agreed. It had been her mother's, back home in southern Illinois. Her mother had brought it from Pennsylvania, and it was the finest thing in the farm-house—white muslin stuffed with expensive goose feathers from the Chesapeake. Her mother gave it to her as a wedding present. The feather-bed was a frill that took up half the wagon and was a caution to keep dry on river crossings, but she was a lady, and she could continue to live like a white woman in Washington Territory. She and Rooney hauled the feather-bed in the wagon from Council Bluffs, Missouri, over two thousand miles of desert and mountains. They walked the feather-bed over country so poor, Rooney said, "There's just a thin sheet of sandpaper between this country and hell." They rushed the feather-bed over the Elkhorn River's quicksand; they dragged the feather-bed in the wagon over the Rocky Mountains, which they could see for a month before they got there. They floated it in the caulked wagon across the same river eight times, which took the fun out of it. She lay on it breathless and bashed when Charley was taken. She gave birth to Glee on it. She and Rooney ferried this feather-bed over the Columbia River, and they winched and pulleyed it up and over the Blue Mountains in Oregon, which were the living worst; they had to yoke up the heifers to help.

Then today on the shore, that man Chowitzit offered them a canoeload of feathers for two cups of molasses. At that price, Ada thought, she could whipstitch up feather-beds for every mother's child in the world.

Rooney and Ada stayed at the Rushes' all winter, mending from the trip. They ate dried salmon and dried peas, and got used to the trees. The trees were mostly Douglas firs. A big fir was seventeen feet through the trunk, and they all grew right close together, so you needed to turn sideways and tamp your skirt to pass between them. Among the firs grew some cedars the size of silos. Ada marveled to see robins the size of ducks, ivy leaves the size of plates, maple leaves the size of platters. Glossy shrubs and thick grass sprang up everywhere, and grew all winter, grew through the log walls and in the door and up through the floor; Ada and Rooney never saw the like.

During their first weeks on the Sound, they studied the settlement as sightseers, and said to each other wonderingly, "Look at these people: they just live here on salmon and clams, as their children will too, for whole ages; they live and die on this isolated coast like gulls, as if there were no other place in the world." Soon they both forgot this view, and joined the life, which now seemed purposeful, and even central. Their own Lummis, as they put it, revealed their separate natures like anyone else, and the Fishburns began to pride themselves on their good fortune, to have taken up with amiable people.

Rooney filed on a beachfront claim of 320 acres a mile north, but he could not work on it as much as he wanted to. The U.S. Army and the Nisqually and Yakima tribes east of the mountains were heating up for a war. The territorial governor reckoned it was cheaper to feed the Lummis than fight them, and so he made the big Lummi winter village on Goose-berry Point a reservation. The Lummi reservation abutted the bay settle-ment to the north. At the same time, northern warriors were paddling down from Canadian lands; they were raiding tribal and immigrant hous-es indiscriminately, and stealing, shooting, and beheading folks. "Some-times around here," Felix Rush remarked to Rooney, "it gets almighty western." Rooney spent his days with the other Whatcom men, building a stockade to shelter the settlers from the northern raiders. He had to.

Work on the stockade ended with darkness at four o'clock. When Rooney came in there were twigs in his bushy beard, and sawdust all over him. He went out again directly after dinner and walked up the beach to their claim, taking Clare—the long, steady, light-limbed man and the bony boy. He tried cutting trees on his claim by lantern light, but it was no go; the Lummi men he worked with had gone home and it took two men to stand on the platform six or eight feet up the trunk and swing axes. A single ax swung from the ground did nothing; it just gummed up in the pitchy, foot-thick bark near the ground. Rooney could, however, adze a scaled log by lantern light, so he did. Rooney adzed logs; young Clare held the light. Clare's arm hurt, but he loved to keep company with the motionless, live tree trunks, and he loved to watch pale chips curl and fly off the log and into the dark. Clare and Rooney carried armfuls of bark back to the Rushes for fuel. A flake of fir bark was the size of what Rooney used to call, back in Illinois, a log; it burned hot, wet or dry. It was always wet.

When he was a boy in southern Illinois, Rooney worked with plows and cows. He had just spent six months on the overland road working with oxen. Here he saw he was going to spend the rest of his life working with logs. It was not work a man could hurry, though he looked forward to getting out of the Rushes' laps and establishing himself on his own claim. His nature fitted him for living frugally and biding his time. He had become a man when he learned the chief fact of life, which is to take it slow and steady. Few things amazed him more than the evidence that other men had failed to grasp this.

Ada and Rooney learned the local politics quick, which were that the northern Indian tribes from the Canadian and Alaskan coast were wiping the Lummis out. They had already wiped out the Semiahmoo people from the Sound. There were about six hundred and fifty Lummis living here along Bellingham Bay, which lands they stole from the Nooksacks because it was safer living on the mainland than on the islands where they lived before. These were skilled, peace-loving canoe people who ate salmon, venison, camas bulbs, and clams. They had no chiefs until the whites needed chiefs to sign treaties. Like the other seven or eight thousand Indian people on Puget Sound, they lived in dread of the northern Haidas, the Kwakiutls, and the Stikeens.

The northern tribes carved big totem poles; they were so rich they burned food for show. Russian traders had armed them with rifles and powder. Summer was their raiding season. This past summer, as every summer, the northern warriors had swooped down the Strait of Georgia in fifty-man seagoing canoes and ransacked the Lummis for slaves. Chowitzit told Rooney that five hundred Lummis lived captive with northern tribes, as slaves. The Lummis were exposed on the beaches wherever they lived, for they netted and dried the summer chinook salmon that ran in July, and the sockeye that peaked in August. The beleaguered Lummis built houses underground and concealed their entrances; there they fled when northern raiding canoes appeared on the bay. Chowitzit and the other big men, like Old Pollen, Whilano, and his brother Yellow Kanim, welcomed the Fishburns, as they had welcomed the Rushes, bachelors like Jay Tamoree, and everyone else: they had guns and ammunition.

Indian men from many coastal tribes worked in the lumber mill or the coal mine. Their languages were mutually unintelligible, so everyone used the jargon—Chinook, the trade language people spoke on the coast from California to Alaska. Lively little Clare picked it right up, and chattered to everyone in sight. The language comprised only three hundred words, so it was simple to learn; on the other hand, Ada complained, it was difficult to say anything the least bit interesting. The coastal natives called all the white settlers the "Bostons," except for those up in the Canadian colony, whom they called the "King Georges." Ada and Rooney marveled at the vivid and amusing names that the settlers stuck on the locals: Napoleon Boom was a Skagit; the Duke of York and his wife, Queen Victoria, were Clallam Indians who lived on a big rancheree at Port Townsend. There was Black Moses, King Frisi, the Jack of Clubs, and Billy Clams. Most men were Jim. Very few settlers knew by what names, with what meanings, the Lummis referred to them.

One November night after a supper of dried salmon and potatoes, the Fishburns sat in the Rushes' dark cabin drinking coffee made from burnt toast. Their son Clare was out roaming the windy beach with little Pearl Rush in the dark. Inside, Lura trimmed the rag in the oil lamp they called the "bitch light." Felix and Rooney fed the fire and smoked pipes full of tobacco the schooner had brought.

They had seen nothing of Chowitzit for a few days. Other Lummis were always in and out, mostly in; Ada had spent the past few weeks protesting in vain when three or four men picked up baby Glee, unwrapped him, and examined him all over. They made fun of Lura, she told Rooney, when she sang to her own baby. Neither she nor Lura could turn around in the house without bumping into a Lummi. The men walked in and without a word watched them cook and clean; they watched little Pearl, three, sweep the floor as if she were a play on a stage. Ada could not fully reconcile herself, she said, to working all day among a crowd of curious, half-naked men, God's creatures though they may have been, which she sometimes doubted. One—Billy Tom—wore a leather breechclout and a felt top hat. He was a warm and confiding man who loved most everyone he knew, but still, it unnerved her. Some old-timers wore nothing but a woven waistband.

Not only that, Lura put in, but the Lummis were Catholics, and they crossed themselves left and right. Felix and Rooney listened, exchanging a glance, and Felix stirred the fire. The possibility of war was real. The Lummis had been their good friends so far, and the women knew it. What they wore did not pertain.

Ada Fishburn looked at Rooney's wild red beard in the firelight. He was usually asleep by now. One of his galluses had slipped off his shoulder. She knew that, whatever she said, she was in fact getting used to the Lummis, and altering her views to fit the living people at hand. She was getting used to their flattened skulls; at first she thought all the high-class Lummis looked like woodpeckers. She was getting used to their soft, liquid voices, and their habit of conversing with their eyes closed. It seemed like a person could get used to anything, except having Charley run over before her eyes and being still gone every morning and all day.

"They mean no harm on earth," Lura went on—she smiled her gummy smile—"but sometimes they are right queer outfits."

Ada listened, tilting her round head. She was wearing the tight-waisted, square-bosomed dress of checked green flannel that she wore all winter, and a sooty white apron.

"Two summers ago," Lura said, when the Lummis filled the house daily as usual, their spotted dogs "used to spree around" her garden. Lura expressly told the Lummis that she did not want the dogs spreeing around the garden, but nothing changed. One day the Lummi dogs were "ripping up" her flower patch, and she mentioned it rather forcefully to the solid man they knew as Striking Jim, who was sitting by the stove with the other men in a clump, watching Pearl sweep. Striking Jim rose, laughing, and all the Lummis went outside. They called the dogs to them, shouting their names and bending over, "the way anyone would call dogs."

The four or five spotted dogs came bounding to the Lummis, who commenced to beat them all to death, laughing with "So sorry, ma'am!" expressions. Lura and little Pearl tried to stop it, but the Lummis carried on. They clubbed all the dogs with sticks and logs, and threw their bodies on the woodpile.

"That is not what I meant," Lura explained again to Ada and the men. Ada nodded. It was going to take some more getting used to. Of course, she expected some differences of custom; the Lummis were Catholics, after all.

CHAPTER III

The children came in from the beach ruddy and chilled. Clare was dragging a dozen bull kelps by their bulbs. He was thin as a switch, five years old, a live beat; his bony face glowed with vitality. He pulled the bull kelps happily right back outside as requested, and left a trail of sandy water on the floor. Pearl, who was a tearing brown-eyed beauty at a very tender age, warmed her hands at the fireplace, and blocked the heat; Lura sent them all to bed in the corner. The low flame lighting the cabin flared fitfully, and illumined first one face, then another.

Lura was reminiscing about Ohio when a scream came from the woods behind the cabin. They all knew it was a pig; it was screaming blue murder. All the pigs screamed like that, when bears picked them up.

The children popped up in their bedding; the men got their rifles. The Rushes let their pigs loose to scratch out their livings in the woods, for they had nothing to feed them. The bears learned which woods had pigs, and came down to cart them off. You could not keep a pig to save your life; this was the Rushes' last pig in the world.

Rooney and Felix tore out like sixty; they found the bear in moonlight, twisting into the trees, running away on two feet. It carried the screaming, kicking pig under one arm. The men routinely lit out after stolen pigs with rifles, but this was the first night they were quick enough. Felix took aim and shot the bear in the back and head with his Henry repeating rifle. The dark bear ran on for a while, then hauled over dead by a mossy trunk. Rooney was quick enough to catch the pig the bear dropped. They dressed the bear out by lantern on the fir-needle forest floor where it fell. They cut out the acorn gland in its knees, which made the good meat taste awful. Ada stuffed the meat into sacks to hang out overnight. She knew that tomorrow morning the adults would post the children to invite the Lummis for a bear-meat feast on the beach—for the Lummis loved it so dearly, and there was always so much. Some coastal women dried long bear-meat muscles, separated strands into hanks of three, and braided them for snacks; the men carried the braids around in bags like—Clare thought—scalps. Everyone on the beach invited the Lummis when someone killed a bear.

Before dawn the next morning Chowitzit walked into the Rushes' house barefoot. Chowitzit's wide face was serious above the straight column of his wrapped red trade blanket. Ada had recently decided there was an air of greatness to the man. She had never seen any human being so plainly attached to all his family—and him a chief, a *tyee*. Even undercutting a cedar with an ax, even joking in a kind voice with Rooney, or bringing to the door a bag of salmon, he seemed to move and speak deliberately, as if he had clouds of power in there he let out just a speck at a time, as he judged fitting. Now he touched hands with the men in their beds. He brought a message: The territorial governor was calling for volunteers to hold the country east of the mountains against the Indian tribes until army regulars showed up. All the "Bostons" from here to Olympia were signing on. The Lummis naturally hoped the Bostons on the bay would join, too. So saying, Chowitzit gave a kingly nod, unwrapped his blanket, relaxed, smiled, opened a skin bag, and produced two rattling strings of dried clams. Lura heated up the peas porridge.

Rooney joined the volunteers, Company H, Second Regiment. He drew the happy assignment of staying in Whatcom to guard the coal mine; it was the only coal mine on the northern coast, and steamers needed coal. That winter, the settlers moved into the stockade. Later Clare would remember this time as a frolic, for the stockade concentrated children like a whirlpool, and they spun with excitement. Many children were there with their Lummi or Nooksack mothers. In Rooney's spare time he started rolling up a cabin. The Lummis helped. When the war east of the mountains cooled off, and when it was clear that Chowitzit and the Lummis would not join the uprising, the Fishburns moved out of the stockade and onto their claim.

They had built on the low bank behind the beach. Chowitzit gave them seed potatoes, which Ada planted in the dooryard where the sun came in straight over the water. He gave Ada dried salmon every winter, and sides of halibut the size of horses, and berries to ease their cravings, and duck eggs, as Ada gave the Lummis cane syrup when they had it, and bread whose dough she mixed in a gold pan, and cash for labor, and iron tools, and old shirts.

Rooney cleared trees. One year he swung an ax with Striking Jim, and the next year with Clallum Chaz. Falling the enormous firs was the easy part, if they missed the cabin; it took two good men four or five hours. The hard part was chopping through the same trunk again and again, to make pieces small enough to move with oxen or burn, and then fighting the stumps. Rooney kept fires going year round. He and the other settlers did not have land; they had smoking rubble heaped higher than their heads. Surely, Rooney thought, soil that grew such oversized trees could grow boss wheat and corn, or anything, if a man could just claw his way down to it. The country needed more men.

Pretty soon the Harshaws joined the settlement via San Francisco. They were squinty little folks from Virginia, who held their expressions down all day and seemed like they laughed all night. They had a horse that drank hot coffee, and people liked to give him some, if they had any, so the Harshaws' coming was a whole sensation on the bay. The horse had learned to drink hot coffee in the Utah desert, where the alkali water was so bad he refused it.

Some nights Ada and Rooney walked two or three miles up the beach to visit the Rushes, the Harshaws, or Jay Tamoree, to hear the news and tell their stories. Chot Harshaw had watered and protected, on the thirsty wagon road all the way from the Mississippi River, a fir tree in a barrel of dirt—a Douglas fir tree—, thinking it might be worth something out here. On the lumber boat on Puget Sound he saw it was not, and he kicked it overboard half a minute before his wife, Louetta, did. They could go off into regular gales of laughter, men and women alike, and tip over benches, and feel better for it. The oldest among the white families was Felix Rush, and he was twenty-six. He and Ada Fishburn were the only ones who could read.

bitters, and anisette. A printing press rolled off a ship on a dolly, ...ers and editors disembarked, rented rooms, and began publishing ...aper. Building lots sold for five hundred or six hundred dollars. ...Harshaw made three hundred dollars just darning socks.

...and Rooney had their one durable cow. A parade of men in dark ...followed young Clare when he went to milk her. The first men ...privilege of paying a dollar for a gallon of milk, as long as it last- ...re was eight years old now. His jaw was squaring off at the chin, but ...med small. He dearly loved the ships, the boats, the men, the ..., the cows, and the campfires on the beach every night. In his ...e spilled half the milk. Ada sold pounds of butter for a palmful of ...st each. She said one miner poured his gold dust from an elk-scrotum ...very settler who had a cow up in the farm settlement called Goshen ...that cow down the swampy wagon road into town, lived beside her ...beach, and rowed out to greet incoming ships with buckets of milk ...e. From all over Puget Sound, from the island farms and mountain ...sts, and from all over the Pacific coast, from Portland and Humboldt ...Sacramento, people converged on Bellingham Bay, where the beach ...white with tents, and so were the woods above it. By July, Whatcom ...three hotels, fourteen grocery stores, two drugstores, twelve saloons, ...bakeries, eight eating houses, six metalsmiths and a blacksmith, and ...agencies for drays, carts, and wagons.

...Whenever Rooney got to bed, he slept so hard, he said, he nearly ...e his neck. He worked on the big hotel, and he enjoyed new friends ...everal saloons without ever buying a drink. Pretty soon he was bossing ...ew that was building a road to the gold fields.

...For there was no road. The Fraser River mouth was only eighteen ...es north, and the gold fields were only thirty miles northeast as the ...w flies, and still a man could not get there. The town hired idle ...spectors to grub out a trail they could call a wagon road, and paid them ...scrip it hoped the army would honor, for the town itself had no cash. ...adbuilding was cussed toil, the men said. There were trees as big ...und as buildings, growing close as grass. It was just barely easier to chop ...tunnel through the forest with axes than it would be to hew down a ...ountain. Rooney knew a man who set off with a mule and a compass to ...ushwhack. The timber was so thick, he said later, and the cross-piled ...eadwood so high, it took a day to walk half a mile. He got lost, found

* * *

In late August, 1857, on a hillside on his claim, Rooney and a Lummi called Jack Pain falled a Douglas fir over two hundred feet high. It hung up dangerously, about 180 feet high, on another fir. When it got too dark to see, they had to leave the bad job.

The next day, Nettie was born. Early that morning, Rooney and Jack Pain set about whacking cautiously into the other fir—the one whose crown supported the widow-maker. As always, each man began by cutting himself a path through the underbrush on which to run away. Rooney and Jack Pain were good falling partners, because Rooney was left-handed. Just after noon, the kerf started to open, the hinge bent over the under-cut, and the men jumped off their springboards and ran. "Tree!" Rooney shouted. Both trees came groaning down at once. They cracked a score of other trees, smashed the earth, and the earth rebounded. Rooney could feel the impact hit and the rebound rise through his boot soles. Splinters, bark, and sunlit dust spun where the trees had stood. When it was all over he stood still in the stunning, expanding silence to listen towards the cabin, and he heard, distant and high and frail, what he was listening for: a baby's cry. On his way down to the cabin he glanced back at Jack Pain and saw him crossing himself, and smiling from earring to earring.

Nettie was their first girl. Clare and Glee struggled over who got to hold her. She looked to Rooney just like the others—impossible. Rooney had forgotten how they looked; so had Ada, really.

Two or three times those first summers, Ada and Rooney paddled out into the bay in the evening, to get out from under the trees. The sky widened above their canoe and soaked them in its colors. From there, from out on the gleaming bay, they could see Mount Baker. Mount Baker was pretty as a picture, Ada used to say, for its glaciers shone almost all night in summer, when snow was the last thing you expected to see any-where, let alone halfway up the sky. Its snowy peak was always higher than they expected—the conical summit, and a lesser sharp peak nearby, both slicked up in layers of ice that shed more light than the moon. Its glistening tonnage seemed to float loose above a layer of sky, and it gave Ada the willies.

The mountain showed how far north they were, that snows lay so thick on it all summer long. On the map back in Illinois, they had seen that the northernmost tip of Maine was south of this territory, and so was

Nova Scotia. Mount Baker was useless, and they all needed so much. It was too high to climb. It was out of scale the way this whole country was, if you let yourself think about it—pretty as a picture, and fit for bears. Who could believe the United States would find its way out here? After their first few years, however, Ada and Rooney grew proud of living so far north, and so far west, as everyone there was proud. They declared it was the best country in the world, as everyone there declared; they said Mount Baker was the noblest and fairest mountain in the world, which it was.

CHAPTER IV

1858, Whatcom

Rooney Fishburn was tall and light. His bushy red beard frizzed up and hid his face, covered his expression, and made his pale blue eyes look tearful, so his enterprise and application startled people. He did what a man has to do to live: he compared prices, dealt hardly but fairly in his transactions, and took care. The cost of moving here made him reel. He started out in southern Illinois with eight oxen, eight head of dairy cattle, and four hundred-some dollars cash money. He paid out for ferry crossings. A man had to cross the rivers. He paid out for barges, for two steamers, and the schooner. Almost all the expense came near the end, and he sold off his surviving stock to pay it. When he washed up in Whatcom he had two cows, one of whom died immediately. Winter was coming, and he had no house or land. He had thirty dollars, and a pain behind the eyes from the schooner, a set of back muscles tight as a bowstring, and gums that bled when he sucked his pipe. He moved his family into the stockade the first year, and out of the stockade the second year; he worked on and off in the mill and scratched out a farm.

Back in Illinois, Rooney loved a grove of old pines that stood about three miles off his parents' place. He used to travel out of his way to stand in the blue light under those evergreen boughs, and to cool his arms in their shade. He thought of that grove from time to time ruefully, for now he wished he would never see another growing tree. Formed of drips, trees dripped. They seemed a condensation and embodiment of the rain and

the crushingly heavy rank growth a man foug day of his life, and hated with all his sore hea this country needed. His task was to crack the sunlight down.

One morning of his third year, in April, 18 new schooner anchored in the bay. He thou toward the mill, which was also the post offi There he discovered a crowd of strangers, all m midst of them. He learned what it was; it was gol

There was gold up on the Fraser River, i Columbia, just eighteen miles north. The Huds eight hundred ounces of gold to the mint in Sar panned it out of the Fraser gravels. These rough- heard about it, hired a boat out of San Francisco, ham Bay, the last American outpost. They were h set out for the Fraser River gold fields.

The next day Rooney saw another schooner in later, another. All that spring they kept coming, e made it or lost it in the California gold rush, and ev lawyer, real estate agent, gambler, merchant, and mu find a boat. At the Blue Moon Saloon he heard that were selling land for nothing; they were dredging up caulking them. Minerals on open land were free to first, except Chinese men. Miners appeared in What sands. Between 75,000 and 100,000 people landed on said most of these landed in Whatcom. Dark masts stripes. One day Rooney counted thirteen square-rigge steamers. The newspaper said miners were panning from lars to fifty dollars a day, every day, up the Fraser River; t women to pan, too. Cash in silver coin and gold beg Rooney's pockets.

A city of tents arose on the beach. Mr. E. H. Langtre Bankers bought lots and started construction. Two merch first brick building in Washington Territory, a warehouse. N boned stakes into the mud of the tide flats, called them them. Saloonkeepers, lawyers, and blacksmiths operated u there was a dance hall in a tent. Downtown, a man willing his money—a man unlike Rooney—could buy claret, m

three other lost men, and the four of them found the body of yet another lost man with a note pinned to his blanket: "July 6. Three days without food or water. J. R. Dillerson, of Sacramento City." The lost four who found the body were too famished and weak to bury it, but they crawled into an outpost and reported it. Beyond the forest, on the route to the gold fields, lay the mountains, where the average snowfall was fifty-four feet a year. Up there, Rooney heard, miners were eating horseflesh, and selling it for fifty cents a pound.

The stampede began in April; by August, there was still no road. Rooney worked at clearing—alongside every sort of man, he tended to think, on earth. When he came home, he liked to have Ada read to him from the Scripture. It all sounded so grand. "I believe that I shall see the goodness of the Lord in the land of the living," she read, and Rooney believed it, too.

All summer, the miners killed time on the Whatcom beach and spent money. Some hunted deer on Lummi Island; some took building jobs, or worked on the road. Ada said she dreaded the brutality and lawlessness so many rough, idle men would inflict, but Lura Rush fed a great many of them, and reported them to be calm, intelligent men who—as perhaps the hallmark of their intelligence—treated white women as species of gods. As the summer wore on without incident, Ada began to believe this was true. Greedy dogs they may have been, like everyone else, but they were not dangerous. When a miner got to spreeing, he shouted in the streets, "I am a true American!" When the roaring boys had their back teeth very well afloat, they tried to hoist the Stars and Stripes in the middle of the night. And when they got banged up clear to the eyes, when they were so drunk they could not see through a ladder, they leaned against each other at a campfire and sang "Three Blind Mice."

In the fall, while Rooney's Whatcom crew was still trying to push the wagon road ahead, British Columbia got smart: Whatcom was making slathers of money off the miners, and British Columbia had the gold. The government at Victoria passed a simple law: Fraser River miners needed a license. Licenses were obtainable in the island city of Victoria, British Columbia, colony of Canada.

The schooners pulled out of Whatcom. Those miners who elected to wait out the winter in Whatcom changed their minds when a cold spell stayed. The tide rose on the wind, and a log boom broke. The logs poked in on the tide and wrecked their tents. The mud froze black. The sky looked crystal all day, and at night Orion was so full of stars he looked like Apache warriors shot him. On the horizon, the water in the passages between islands was cracked and brittle with mirages.

The miners left; they rolled up their soaked tents and vanished. The merchants left; they knocked down their storefronts and carried the lumber and canvas with them down the wharves and onto the schooners. The muleskinners and lawyers, bankers, gamblers, doctors, real estate agents, whores, dray agents, and purveyors of dry goods and groceries left; the purveyors of madeira and anisette vamoosed. The newspaper publisher dismantled the printing plant and sold the press. In a few weeks, there was no town at Whatcom at all, but only the old sixty smokes from settlers' cabins back from the shore, as before. A building lot Chot Harshaw bought for five hundred dollars as an investment was not worth a nickel. The only improvements remaining were two new wharves, the fine empty brick warehouse, and half a road, ending in the mountains.

Rooney knew that his family was down to dried salmon, and the baby Nettie's belly was swelling up. He saw that Ada's face was losing its roundness; she sifted about with her apron untied. The town was overbuilt, and no one milled logs or bought lumber. The coal mine was on fire, so no one could work it. Chowitzit came by with a young elk over his shoulders, and he carried a bag of fresh salmon; they scratched along. "I believe I told you," Ada had the afflatus to say, "The loftiness of man shall be bowed down, and the haughtiness of men shall be made low … for Jerusalem is ruined, and Judah is fallen, and instead of sweet smell there shall be stink." She could find the worst things to put into talk.

Some of the miners returned to settle in Whatcom, or to farm on the sunny islands beyond it, for having seen a summer full of the million-dollar, slow sunsets in which the region specialized, men of a certain disposition tended to return and drop anchor. Rooney suspected, however, that a few settlers with a taste for the sublime do not make a city. The boom had busted, the rush had rushed away, and proud Whatcom, whose citizens like Rooney had intemperately boasted of its good fortune, was brought low.

Rafts of dark scoters, goldeneye, brant, and oldsquaw ducks floated the water, as before. They rose up suddenly, crying out. Rooney had forgotten the ducks on the sea and had not heard them all summer. Now he

saw them again and heard them, and their mournful, familiar voices settled him down. By spring, deer appeared on the beach where the tents had
been; they bent to lick salty rocks at low tide.

CHAPTER V

1859, Whatcom

That spring, Chowitzit died. As he was dying, he called for Felix Rush.
Ada was at the Rushes', and she went along. With her she toted her
daughter, Nettie, who was almost two and pert as a rabbit. She paddled up
the blue bay with Felix and Lura.

They visited Chowitzit in his lodge downtown, as the Rushes had
done many times, even during the worst of the last epidemic. Ada saw
Chowitzit's big housepost, taken from the old ceremonial longhouse, and
decorated with his vision powers: a carved design of circles, representing
the fiery sun which was carrying two valises of costly goods. They found
Chowitzit in the dark, split-cedar lodge, lying mirthless on his blankets.
A month before he had been vigorous and keen. Ada saw him rebuilding
the houses that the sea ice smashed on Gooseberry Point, and in silhouette on the beach he looked long in the torso and supple, like a man in a
statue that could move. Now the skin on his broad face hung slack, and
his delicate lips were parted. His eyes opened a bit. In the lodge were
many Lummi women, beating drums, telling rosary beads, and praying.
One of the women was Margot, who had made friends with Ada the year
they all lived in the stockade; she came up to Ada now, and her face was
stiff with tears. Ada proudly watched her look at Nettie sideways out of
her eyes. She noticed Margot's bracelet of silver dollars, and another silver dollar she wore upside her nose. The women stood back, and the
drumming let up.

For a stout man, and an old Great Lakes man, Felix Rush had a jerky
way of stepping, and he busted right up to Chowitzit's there and offered
the usual greeting.

"*Kah mika chahko?*" What have you been up to? Felix could speak
with the Lummis in their language, but he used the Chinook jargon.
Chowitzit did not give the usual response—"Oh, I've been out there for a

while"—for he had not been out there. He lay straight, dressed in a striped shirt and other finery, composed. A Cowichan Indian man, he said, keeping his eyes closed, possessed a lock of his hair, and he would now die—*melamoose*. He barely moved his lips. He spoke in his usual gentle, musical voice. The Cowichan was back in his village on Vancouver Island, among Lummi slaves. It was *hyas mesachie*—very bad. There was no help for it.

Felix brought up the news that Chowitzit's fine daughter, Clara, was marrying an enterprising settler, John Tennant, who was "shirr a true-blue man." Felix sounded like he wanted to steer the talk to this happy prospect, but Chowitzit declined.

Ada stood, holding Nettie's hand, with Margot and Lura by the foot of the pallet. Nettie's bow was sliding off the round top of her head, and her black stockings puffed in front where her knees poked them, though when you saw her naked fat legs, she appeared to possess no knees at all. Nettie looked out at the people in the world as if they amazed her beyond speech.

Ada watched the dust in the light shaft fall. It must have purely shocked Chowitzit when, only three years after the Rushes first came and built the mill—in '55, when she and Rooney came, while the Lummis outnumbered the settlers five to one, even after the cholera epidemic the wagon trains brought—, presto, he found his people driven off the good bay banks and creeks and confined to a reservation on Gooseberry Point. They were not allowed to make long visits to their relatives in other tribes, either. Yet in the Indian War the Lummis stood by them. Chowitzit had welcomed the settlers from human goodness, in ignorance, and with the hope of their help against the northern tribes. Chowitzit or Striking Jim warned them whenever northern canoes appeared in summer raiding season, and offered men to stand them off. In fact, the settlers helped the Lummis against the northern tribes by and by, as the Lummis helped the settlers, Ada reflected, but the northern tribes were not the Lummis' worst problem, come to find out.

Chowitzit lay calm, his black eyes fixed on the sooty shadows under the eaves. He did not have cholera, smallpox, or lung fever, so far as Ada could tell. A man with cholera turned chalk blue and doubled over; a man with smallpox showed spots like birdshot; a man with lung fever grew a red dot on each cheek and coughed the brightest blood you ever saw. If Chowitzit died, Ada knew, Davy Crockett would succeed him as chief. The Lummis called Davy Crockett "Whilano."

The lodge door darkened, and a young man in overalls entered, carrying a musket. The man ignored Felix and the women: he spoke over Chowitzit. He raised Chowitzit's shirt and passed a piece of white paper over his muscular, wrinkled chest. With a cry, he pounced on something, wadded it into the paper, rammed the paper down the muzzle of the musket, and fired it out through the smoke hole. Nettie jumped a mile, and her hair bow fell out. The burnt powder smelled; dust rose up and whirled in the smoke hole's shaft of light; Ada's ears rang. The man left. The women started drumming again.

"I am *melamoosed*," Chowitzit went on to Felix factually as before. The Cowichan *melamoosed* him, by stealing his hair. Chowitzit had killed the Cowichan chief in a quarrel; the Cowichans stole—*capswallowed*—a piece of Chowitzit's hair and warned him that they would cause bad spirits to kill him in revenge, through this hair.

Well, Ada thought, Scripture warned against wizards that peep and that mutter. Here was Lura Rush right ready-to-hand in the lodge with real medicine in a grass basket, but Chowitzit seemed unlikely to submit. Lura was the settlement's doctor, nurse, dentist, and surgeon. She treated ailments and injuries in an orderly sequence that began with whiskey. If whiskey failed she used quinine. She continued, when necessary, down through camphor and, finally, turpentine. To prevent pneumonia, she plastered rib cages with chopped-up onions. For measles, she fed her patients a roasted mouse, and Ada herself had seen it work in Clare and Glee both. It was a pity Chowitzit was superstitious.

The Lummis buried Chowitzit the modern way, in the ground, during a drizzle that lasted two weeks. A hundred whites attended the burial but not the potlatch accompanying it. Felix Rush had been staying with Chowitzit's grieving family for five days, during which he grew a stubble of beard that offended them all, Rooney learned later, but they seemed to overlook it. Rooney stood by Felix at the graveside, with Ada beside him; the rain beaded on their black hats. When Chowitzit's casket touched the grave hole's bottom, Ada broke down, and Rooney knew she was remembering the boy Charley and his rushed burial on the Sweetwater River. Rooney was feeling pretty grim himself. He said to himself that he hated to see his valiant old majesty go, who had saved their bacon so many times.

When the French priest took over, however, Rooney hardened up. Father Chirouse was a good man, who loved the Lummis dearly, and was raising a half-breed orphan. He was, however, a foreigner and, in Rooney's view, growing crazier by the minute. When he was a boy of fifteen in France, Felix told Rooney, this Chirouse person read a translated account of Lewis and Clark's expedition, and vowed to be a missionary to the Indian tribes. Now here he was. The Lummis were wearing calico dresses, and cloth trousers, most of them. Father Chirouse, a powerfully built man, was wearing a blanket woven of dog and goat hair, and under that a soutane dyed with blackberry juice. It fit Rooney's impression that Frenchmen went overboard with things. During the gold rush Rooney saw a Frenchman disembark from a steamer with a carriage, a matched team, and a poodle dog. Felix said he was disappointed to learn, first, that there was no carriage road; then he learned that there was no wagon road; then he learned that there was no trail. He swore oaths. Now Felix whispered to Rooney that Father Chirouse had dissuaded Chowitzit's family from killing one or two of his slaves to be buried with him.

A few days after the burial, the sky cleared, and people's spirits rose. The frogs in the marshes were peeping in their thousands by dusk, cougars screamed by night, and early in the mornings the flickers called out, and answered. Mornings, the sun seemed to appear from anywhere at random, like a swallow. It rolled up the sides of mountains and down the sides of mountains, range after range around the world's east rim. Every afternoon it threw a new set of shadows and shine on the parlor wallpaper; every night it flew behind a different island. The sun is a creature who flits, young Clare Fishburn thought; the sun is a bee. Daylight pried the darkness open and poured in; the whole beach was drunk and reeling on it. The Lummis emerged from their frame houses on the reservation beach and inspected their sharp canoes. Rooney had neither ox nor horse, so he hitched himself to the plow, and turned the soil. All winter Rooney and Ada had lived half asleep in the dark, they understood now, while rain beat the south windows and their spirits dwindled like sinking wicks. Now all that was behind them, and the widening day threatened to wrap around the clock and drive them mad.

Soon the first salmon swam, fat and firm, over the Lummis' reef nets; they feasted and gave thanks. Every week, a different settler throughout the territory held a square dance; men and women danced all night and rowed home for breakfast. Rooney thought about building a schooner, and heading off to Alaska for halibut. Ada got hold of a magazine from Victoria and started wearing her thin hair in a chignon. She thought about a plot in the county, up in Goshen on the Nooksack, a cottage covered with sweet peas, and some sort of baby crawling around on the porch, or maybe they should try to get the boys at least a pony, or paint the doors. One noon, young Clare passed the millhouse and heard music; it was Lura Rush playing the melodeon for a hundred Indian people gathered on the lawn.

Ada wondered where the Lummis found the time, when the settlers were so busy. A Samish they called Plug Ugly showed up for cane syrup every day and called her his friend—his *tillicum*—and told her his troubles, which were many, and she told him hers, which were many. A Lummi youth sold lagoon pitch—pine kindling—from door to door and stayed all day. She remembered when she used to nearly scrub the hide off Glee every time a Lummi man picked him up; now she let Nettie take her chances in this world. She set Clare to entertaining the crowd by showing pictures in his two books; it kept them located. She no longer noticed when her visitors tucked extra meat in their shirts and poked rising bread. The Lummi people, for their part, had learned to ignore the Bostons' terrible smell—for the newcomers rarely bathed and never changed their underwear. They learned not to rummage through things uninvited, for it excited the Bostons unnecessarily, and not to wander off toting things or offspring without mentioning it, ditto. People could get along.

CHAPTER VI

1861–1872, Whatcom

Nettie died when she was four, of an earache that leaked into her brain. Lura Rush bade Rooney blow pipe smoke into Nettie's ear, for that was the only remedy they knew, and she had not squirmed, only looked off, but it failed. Ada dressed the child to meet her Maker in a dress cut out of her own wedding shawl. Rooney especially took it hard, for he was wild about the girl, and Ada still worried during the second or third year afterwards that Rooney would never find the heart to keep on and keep up.

Back in the states, there was a war. Once or twice a year, a letter came for Ada from Illinois; it took her several weeks to quieten down from the excitement. One of her cousins joined the Illinois volunteers and marched into Virginia, where a farmer, defending his family, shot him. One of her uncles died of malaria outside Baltimore. John Wilkes Booth shot President Lincoln.

Clare was an exuberant, bony boy who loved his world. He often woke exalted, his heart busting in its rib cage, thinking: "Today is the day!"—but he did not know what day.

He got his great height in just a year or two; by the time he was fifteen, people said he was the tallest human being on Puget Sound. The Lummis called him Sma-Hahl-Ton, the long one. He was so thin, a logger named Iron Mike said, "you couldn't hit him with a handful of dried peas." He himself told people he "took his bath in a shotgun barrel."

One June afternoon, the summer Clare was fifteen, he and Glee went fishing for trout in Lake Whatcom. The lake lay southeast of the settlement and deep in the unbroken forest of Douglas firs two hundred feet high, on hills six hundred feet high. Clare and Glee walked a trail three hours to get there; they carried fishing poles and a lard pail of worms. Clare's long face expressed his usual eagerness; he talked the whole way, and tried to pry some entertainment out of Glee. They walked another hour around the lake on a footpath between the dark trees before they came to the overhang where the big trout fed.

Sunset took the glare from the water, killed the wind, and brought out mosquitoes. The lake held the sky and forced it to lie low between the steep hills. Clare Fishburn thought he had never seen such red clouds in streaks before, nor the sky's blue so green, polished, and frail. The clouds turned colors as he watched, as if by distant sorcery. The lake doubled the flung sky, so the streaks seemed to meet behind a hill on the far shore.

The brothers were quiet. They stood side by side on the bank under trees, and Glee's brown head came up to Clare's elbow. These were the brothers their mother used to picket in the yard to keep them out of devilment. She staked them out, well apart, on tethers they were too small to untie. Glee was ten now—a soft-faced, careful boy, small-jawed—who liked asking riddles. Their mother taught them to read at home—there was no school—and Glee came by a riddle book, which he wore to rags. It was about nine o'clock at night. Glee caught a one-pounder, and a two-pounder, and said he was going home. He gutted the trout and rinsed them on the spot, which Clare never bothered to do.

Clare had caught nothing, so he stayed. He watched Glee, thin and sturdy in overalls, start to head back on the trail; Glee's felt hat bent towards his feet. Out on the water, there was no wind. The sunset was starting to close down. The lake and its forested shore made a bowl of still air where twilight colors caught. Clare folded a worm on his hook and threw it.

Something brushed his hatbrim, and he looked up. It was a strip of old rag; it came from something in a tree, whose darkness bulked in the corner of his eye. The something was a canoe. He turned around. It was an old *melamoose* canoe, wedged among the branches of an alder—a casket and grave for someone who was *melamoosed*. The cloth that brushed his hat was a grave rag. He saw a snouted, mean-looking animal carved in the canoe's cedar prow.

Clare loved any excitement; he climbed a branch and examined the canoe. He lifted some of the cedar shakes that decked it and found a dead Lummi facing him. It was no one he knew. Gold pieces covered the dead Lummi's eyes. His blackened lips drew back over his dry teeth, giving him an anguished, vicious expression; he seemed to grimace and strain to see through the gold pieces. Clare looked, still. The dead man's head had lolled back and stuck; its jaw loosed and lay on his breast like a beard. A mouse had built her nest against his hair, and black scat speckled the corpse's face and neck. He wore a trade shirt and a necklace of curved animal teeth.

The dead Lummi looked younger than his father. In the red light of dusk Clare could see the dark pores on the skin of his nose, and his soft nostrils, the hairs of his eyebrows and his delicate hairline at his temples—all the familiar and intimate marks of humanity, and all lacking its chief point. The fellow's desolate, howling expression was fixed. No howl would sound, and the howling expression itself would decay and fall away. The teeth would loosen and drop, and mice would breed in the mouth. This was one ignored Lummi.

At fifteen Clare had already learned and forgotten how dead people lie crooked and serene, monstrous, oblivious to the terror their stillness causes. He had no memory of his brother Charley's death under the wagon wheels or his burial on the overland road. When Nettie had died just four years earlier, she lay in a coffin propped between chairs in the cabin. She wore a white dress and looked something terrible. Clare's mother, although she now remembered herself as enduring Nettie's death composedly, had in fact keeled right over in her mourning dress on the floor below Nettie's coffin, where she roosted a night and a day. She had risen to take

Clare, who was eleven, by the hand and draw him to his sister's body.

"Remember her," she said. She planted him at the coffin's head and locked his hand in her wet one. "Never forget your sister!" she had said with a wild, haggard urgency—remember this moment forever, promise me, &c.—and Clare promised.

In fact, by the time he saw the dead Lummi buried in a canoe, Clare had entirely forgotten his sister and her death, as if he never had a sister. He had forgotten, as well, the way dead people revert to materials, how limply their weight obeys laws, and drapes like cloth or bags, so that whoever sees them asks, Why is he holding his head that way? or, How does she bend her shoulder like that?—until he recalls that this is a corpse now, the muscles of which no longer hold and direct its bones, and which lies like mutton wherever the living stick it, while the living move on.

It gave him pause, seeing the dead Lummi in the *melamoose* canoe, for the man looked so forgotten and sorry, and life was booming along very well without him, which he probably would not have believed. Clare brooded about it that night, all the way back on the trail.

That winter he built himself a smoky cabin on his parents' claim, for the enjoyment of it. The next summer he made several long rowing expeditions, taking sweet butter in tubs clear to Victoria, British Columbia, where a pound fetched twenty cents more than at home, and he sold otter skins he bought from the Lummis. He rowed back from Victoria with tobacco, contraband whiskey for family use, and gabardine for Ada to fix into clothes.

Out on the water, Clare used to see killer whales. They rose and dove in an easy rhythm, showing the white lobes on their sides, and their tall fins kept him company. Often he found himself rowing down Rosario Strait in the dark; he slipped between bulking black islands and steered home for Bellingham Bay by the smoldering heap of coal mine tailings, which had been burning as long as he could remember. When later Glee took up fishing in earnest, Clare helped him build a sloop and a smokehouse, and brought him cordage from Victoria.

Every year, a few settlers arrived. Lura and Ada welcomed them; they sent the newcomers off into the woods and up the creeks to try their luck. They told them the region was too far north to grow corn, and watched their faces fall—how could a farmer live without corn? "It can be done," Lura and Ada said. It was something for Lura, and for Ada, too, to come from being, personally, not so special, back home in Ohio and southern Illinois, to being part of a first family here, and they knew it. Lura, especially, who was in Ada's view nice as pie, really, could lord her old-timeyness sometimes over the new women who hauled in half dead from the wagon road. In 1867, the coal mine hired a Welsh engineer, who carried a pancake in his pocket and wore it on his head, over his hat, when it rained. Clare and Glee helped Rooney clear part of a field for hay. That year at Christmas Lura gave Ada a washbasin for the cabin, and Ada gave Lura some fresh meat—venison, which Clare had brought in.

Next to a creature named Ethelda Olney, Pearl Rush was the best-looking girl in the settlement, white of skin and black of hair; she wore her flannel dresses with an air, and trimmed their collars and cuffs. When she became the first white girl to reach sixteen, the settlers figured they had a schoolteacher—her father had taught her to read—so they taxed themselves for a school. The school ran three months in the winters, and Clare and Glee attended, though Clare was by then eighteen. Miss Pearl Rush had a good heart and a weak mind. She had trouble with her girl scholars; once she lost her temper and called Sarah Harshaw a redhead, and Sarah called her a puddin'head right back, and quit for three years, saying she had no shoes. Pearl told her parents that Clare and Glee Fishburn were helpful scholars, though they blizzarded each other with words and fists and came in tardy, looking like the devil. Clare was always halfway out of his clothes. He was taller than all the men in the settlement when he was still in school, but he was so thin he lacked a giant's gentleness. He flew out and gave thrashings and tannings to other boys when he felt he had to, a bang on the nose here and there with heedless gaiety. He was, in the words of Felix Rush, a fine broth of a boy.

In 1870 Mount Baker erupted, and sent black ash and white steam into the sky. Clare hoped the mountain would shoot red lava, so he could see it; the Lummis said it had done so once before. All his life, Clare had seen the mountain appear to advance and recede every few days, as if it were an enormous snail traveling on a sliding foot. Clare did not know it, but he loved Mount Baker; he checked it from those vantage points in town where he could see it, and noted the thickness of its snows in winter, and its exposed streaky crevasses in summer. Clare was twenty now; he took his loves hard. He worked three days a week for a dollar a day at the coal mine. That summer he built a wharf with a crew of Indian men. They came from all over the Sound; they camped at the mine. Only the older men possessed flattened heads. The muscles of their bare chests and shoulders bulged, from paddling canoes. Clare knew that many newcomers to the region despised all Indian people, without knowing any, and prayed for their speedy extermination.

Four or five times a year, Clare and Glee took to sailing ninety miles south to Seattle, where a town was rising into the hills, to cheer themselves at the Mad House. The Mad House was the brothel John Pennell built down on the tide flats made into land by dumping sawdust on it. The men called the sporting women "the Sawdust Girls." They were natives; Pennell claimed he bought them from coastal chiefs for blankets. The dance hall was popular, as was the entertainment as a whole. More bawdy-houses appeared on the sawdust, and business boomed all over Seattle as men converged from the wide territory. Pennell soon brought in a shipload of white prostitutes from San Francisco.

Clare and Glee got to spreeing sometimes and pronouncing the preamble to the Constitution. They drank blue ruin till their heads were heavy and their pockets were light. They played *vingt-et-un* through the sunrise with other farmboys for plug tobacco, and tangled their fists with roisterers, bamboozlers, and buffalo hunters. Clare had quick arms and feet, and he knew how to use his hands. Although he was slow to anger and quick to forget, he brooked no insult from tinhorn gamblers, enjoyed some smart slinging, and bested more often than he was bested.

The famous madam of one pretty sawdust establishment was Old Mother Damnable, and Glee fell for her bright-eyed niece, whose name was Grace. Accordingly, Glee took to sailing to Seattle once a month if he could. Glee fished salmon for a living, and salmon had a way of running in the summer months. Storms had a way of running the other ten months, and it was through storms that he sailed to court Grace.

On one occasion when Clare accompanied him, a storm held them up for a week; they pitched a tarpaulin on an empty island's beach and ate raw clams. Glee had grown up long-legged and barrel-chested. He had a wide smile and narrow jaws, so his line of teeth made a tight turn, and when he laughed his mouth showed dark empty triangles at the corners. On the last night camping on the island, as the brothers sat soaked and steamed by a fire, Glee told Clare that Grace was "a hard girl to win, for she was pinch-fisted." Glee possessed nothing but his fishing gear, and every white man in Puget Sound was pitching her woo by the yard. Glee told Clare that Grace "worked hard, and had a 'cute mind for business." She was also about the only unmarried white woman in five counties.

The next day in Seattle, Clare saw for himself. Grace lit up and shone when Glee walked into the kitchen. She was making berry pies for customers, one for each man. Grace had glowing, protuberant eyes and a forward chin. She was dressed in stiff checked cloth and a stained white apron. Primly she turned aside to a bowl on the kitchen table and cut lard into flour with two butcher knives. Above her narrow forehead rose a curly pouf of bangs the size of a squirrel's nest. Behind this carefully disarrayed sphere she wore a tall, mannish hat. She was seventeen.

"How's my darling?" Glee said. "When are you going to marry me?" Clare was surprised. He thought a man could take hold of a girl's mind by only the subtlest wizardry.

"Aw," said Grace, and she turned with a smile, "aw, go chase yourself." She slapped the rolling pin down into the dough ball and leaned into it, but not too hard.

Glee persisted, and for two years he courted Grace with his stubborn presence and plagued her with importunings and sweet talk, for which he had a rare propensity Clare envied deep in his mind. Only much later did the brothers learn that during this period, local pioneer women were giving Grace the benefit of their observations, cautionary dabs of wisdom that hurt Glee's cause.

At a summer camp meeting on the beach, a crowd of sunburnt newcomers from California joined Grace in serving pies from an adzed log. They did not know that her aunt was Mother Damnable, the madam, and that she worked in the house, so they talked with her as if she were just anyone. It was advantageous, these women told her, if a girl had a choice, to marry a man from New England, for New England men treated their wives right fine. This was part of the knowledge of the overland road, where women compared notes. A girl fares best with an older man who has already made his mark. And by all means arrange to become a man's second wife, at least: the previous wife will have accomplished the backbreaking labor of improving his claim. Grace kept these counsels to herself, and considered that Glee Fishburn, with his long legs and brown eyes, might nevertheless be her affinity—for after all, a girl has a heart.

Clare was no begrudger; he enjoyed observing Glee's urgency and distraction, and he loved his own life as a man among men. There were few women of any sort. Seattle had imported a cargo of New England orphaned ladies, but they were all snatched off the dock; some were engaged by the time their ship reached the isthmus at Panama. Back home in Whatcom, Clare and Derwent Rush rented a fifty-man canoe from the Lummis two or three times a year, and with all the young men of the settlement, and the few unmarried girls, paddled off to Whidbey Island, or to Fidalgo, for dances where they hoped to meet people. They slept on the beach with chaperones, and paddled back the next day, or the next. Clare did some surveying, worked scratching out a road to Goshen, and enlarged the clearing on their claim, tree by tree. He bought a fiddle by mail and hid himself in the woods every few days for many years, to torment the instrument loudly in the rain while he learned to play it.

Clare in his twenties "enjoyed," he liked to say, "enjoyment." He worked in a slouch hat; when he took it off indoors his big forehead was white and the thick brown hair on top of his head stood up wildly. His face was so long and hollow, and his eyes set so deep and his mouth cut so wide, people said he looked like Abraham Lincoln, without the warts. His activities had expanded and spread his sphere; he had friends, and business, all over the territory. Clare's was the first generation to rise in this wilderness. He believed that therefore some greatness lay in store for it, and some unnameable heroism would be his. He would achieve, he would do, succor, conquer, succeed.

He planted apple trees when everybody planted apple trees. Mad with enthusiasm, he tinkered with grafting plums on the trees, and pears. He took up taxidermy with Jay Tamoree, to his mother's disgust. One winter he started reading books, a habit that took hold seasonally, and excited his mind; he read the essays of Carlyle, Lambs' Shakespeare, and travels. Everyone prized books, which were scarce, and used them sometimes as cash. One summer he gaily crossed the mountains on Felix Rush's horse and visited Samuel Harshaw, his old childhood playmate on the beach, who now had a cattle ranch and lived like a Mexican. When at supper Clare reached for bread, Samuel took out a revolver and shot through the floor, saying by way of information, "We don't eat around here until we've asked the blessing."

He took up drawing with a steel pen on sanded boards; he tried to draw the Douglas firs, the way their trunks grew straight and close as rushes, and their black branches high above swooped like skirts. Mostly he worked with his father, clearing, building, planting, and fixing, on the place. He was tall, and he came to specialize in roofs. He left tools out to rust, he let mice tear holes in seed bags; he built a shed with cottonwood, and it warped so bad Rooney wanted to shoot him.

Lura Rush died in a carriage accident when a bear startled the horses on the Nooksack River bridge. The team tried to back, and, as Rooney told it, the whole rickmatick tipped into the water. The oldest Rush boy, Derwent, lost an arm to the revolving plane in the mill; he lived through that, but died the next spring of the putrid sore throat. Striking Jim died in a blowdown. Billy Tom, another Lummi *tillicum*, drowned in Sacramento harbor when the steamer on which he was purser hit a collier; he saved two passengers before the third one pulled him down. Chot Harshaw, who had hauled a Douglas fir sapling in a barrel two thousand miles on the overland road before settling among the Douglas firs of Bellingham Bay, had died in an accident a few years earlier. A fall of slate from the coal mine roof bisected him. His stimulating horse, who drank hot coffee, died too; it choked on an apple. Death mowed the generations raggedly and out of order; Clare did not notice that a generation was being cut off, and parts of another.

At times Clare questioned his own goodness, and for a few days he helped his mother spin wool, as Glee always did when he was home, and once he rebuilt the henhouse on the double, as though goodness lay in these chores, when in fact he had prevented a stranger from shooting himself, without knowing it, by drinking whiskey with him easily one night in the Blue Moon Saloon. His inborn welcoming, active nature soothed and flattered people; he was so tall he seemed to savor them from on high, and he laughed readily. Ada thought she had favored Charley, who died, of all her children, but in fact she never preferred anyone to this slab-sided giant who was her boy Clare, for his persistent innocence and enthusiasm, and his glad ways.

CHAPTER VII

1872, Whatcom

For new neighbors, Rooney and Ada had a hapless pair of newlyweds from London, England. George Judd was a footman turned coachman; his lugubrious face was red from shaving. Priscilla, his kindhearted, chinless bride, was a ladies' maid. These two had spent their savings inching across Canada, looking for aristocrats to employ them and finding none. When even the pretentious city of Victoria failed them, they decided to try homesteading, hauled up in Bellingham Bay, and began improving, or at any rate harassing, a claim behind the bluff. Ada gave them papers of seeds—specklike carrot seeds and pea seeds and grass seed for hay—as Lura Rush had given her seeds; she gave them seed potatoes, as Chowitzit had given her seed potatoes. Priscilla called them "tatoes"—"We loves our tatoes."

Rooney and Glee whacked up their tiny cabin for them in a marshy clearing, in the guise of helping George do it. Clare brought them roasts of fawn haunch. Clare got some reservation friends to help him ditch their marsh to drain a plot to plant, and made them, carelessly, a bed, a bench, and a table. He shaked their roof. When George received a two-hundred-dollar bequest, Rooney brokered for him a team of geldings from Anacortes, to sled logs. Ada and Priscilla walked out on the beach in deep, flat-topped bonnets. Ada taught Priscilla to recognize clam holes in the tide flat, which excited Priscilla beyond bounds, so her chinless lower jaw quivered.

When Ada had sized the outline of all that their minds lacked, she took to walking up to their place on the marsh. She brought them a wad of her yeast sponge for rising bread, and told Priscilla to take it to bed with her in cold snaps. She showed them how to lay a rail fence, keep hens, stick a hog, scythe hay—everything—and was rewarded to see how much she had learned in fifteen years without noticing it. She got Priscilla to belay the "Madam" and call her Ada. Priscilla had a baby; Ada brought her string and scissors, and assisted. The baby was supernaturally large, hardy, and developed; they named him Samson, and lived in superstitious awe of him.

One day, a week after Independence Day in 1872, when the men of the settlement had sobered off on buttermilk and finished the haying, Rooney was digging a well. Clare was away in Victoria. Ada was carrying buckets of cold water from the rain barrel to the washing trough, a twenty-foot log Rooney had hollowed out. She was as eager for the well as Rooney was, for in August every year they ran out of rainwater, and had to row barrels up from the sawmill creek. Just now she had forgotten to plug the bunghole at the trough's low end and lost a bucket of water to the ground. Now here came Rooney from behind the house, all over mud and tickled pink.

"It's coming," he said. "I can hear it." She always smelled his sour beard when he got near, no matter how clean he was, and the smell had become dear to her, though it was sharp as vinegar. Sometimes she noticed that he looked bent over now, from the tree work, although he was only forty-one years old. Rooney took the bucket from her hand and set it down. "Come on and see," he said. "About two more strokes, and we got ourselves a well."

Back of the house near the smoking slash pile, Rooney's well hole was ten feet deep. He picked up his spade, sat on the edge, and jumped in. Ada watched and thanked God for the well water, though she was premature, after all. Rooney whacked a slice of dirt at one side of the hole. "It's right here," he said. He made a deeper cut, and Ada heard a hiss when he pried it off. No water came out, just the hiss.

Then Rooney fell over on his spade. He lay in the hole. He had gone down like a tree, head last. Ada questioned him.

He lay still, with the back of his head toward the sky. Without knowing she did it, Ada pressed both hands to her jaws.

She ran off then, to get George Judd, which was her mistake, but there it was. Ten minutes later she found him trimming a log. He and Priscilla came down with Ada through the woods and over the bluff; Ada's chignon came out and down her back. She reached the well hole first. She looked down and saw Rooney just as she left him: his bare neck coming crooked out of his collarless shirt, and him rumpled up and his beard in dirt. She saw red-faced George take one look and start to jump down in there. "No, don't," she said. "It must be poison gas—" but George Judd was already in the well hole. He lifted Rooney's right arm, put it over his shoulder, and bent to heft the torso's weight on his back, when he, too, unstrung and fell.

From the scruffy clearing in the woods, Ada and silent Priscilla Judd looked down into the stinking dirt hole where Rooney and George lay flopped over. They studied their husbands' backs and shoulders for signs of breath, and tried to think what to do next. George's face was dark red; his mouth sagged open and his black mustaches hung free. He had crumpled into Rooney, and now mixed limbs with him, as if they fought or embraced. The woods were quiet this time of year, and Ada abruptly noticed the stillness, and the heat, and for a moment saw herself as if from behind, standing at the lip of the hole that was her husband's grave, as she had seen so many women stand.

They buried Rooney Fishburn and George Judd side by side where their lands met. The whole settlement turned out, and half the reservation. The Lummis wailed, but this was not the way of the settlers, who tried for impassivity. Priscilla wanted George's body returned to Worcester, England, but came to agree that it could not be done without cash to pay freight on the various mailboats, schooners, oceanic steamers, and railways such a trip required. Maybe, she told Ada, she could find a way later to have him moved. She stayed on their claim, as a widow was expected to do, rearing the boy Samson. She worked hard, and barely got by, like everyone.

Clare and Glee had hauled their father's body, and George Judd's body, out of the hole with a gaff hook through their trousers' waistbands. They filled the gassy well hole at once, that same day, and stamped on the dirt and hit it with the backs of shovel and spade. In September Clare dug a well on the claim's northwest corner, through sand under trees, and the water ran sweet. The next spring he covered the well and rigged a pitcher pump. From his cabin he could hear the pump handle screech and the leather gulp when Ada drew water, summer and winter, as she could hear it when he did.

BOOK II

JOHN IRELAND

CHAPTER VIII

August, 1872,
the upper Skagit valley, Washington Territory

One month after Rooney died in the well, in August, 1872, the boy John Ireland Sharp awoke to find himself rolled in a blanket next to a box of gear on the shore of the Skagit River. The Skagit River, with its singular steep scenes, was all new to him. Ordinarily he lived in the town of What-com. Now he was thirty miles away from home; he was up the Skagit River and into the mountains. He had slept that night in a summer vil-lage of Skagit Indians, and this was new, too. Pale grass-mat houses lined the riverbank and trailed away from the big grass-mat lodge. He sat up in the blanket. The sun heated his arms. His wide, sharp mouth turned slightly down. He shook his black hair back. It was all, he thought, almighty fine.

The river cut a highway through the forest; it bared above its gravel islands and bars a swath of sky across which low clouds ran like white hens across a road. The morning sun touched the cottonwoods and yellow alders that grew up in delicate stands—between floods—along the river-banks and bars. For the past few days, young John Ireland Sharp's party had camped in the damp woods, alongside their canoes. The Skagit sum-mer village seemed a sort of paradise to John Ireland, where men were wider than trees, and the sun was hot on his arms. The people had already bathed in the river, and their ponytails and braids dripped. Wet children straddled dry logs.

Nearby, a company of women in calico dresses or deerskin skirts were gutting and beheading fish and spreading them high overhead on drying racks; flies glittered from fish heads on the ground. Up the creek on the opposite bank, two young men tilted over the sparkling water from a lean-ing platform; they dipped nets into the channel the weir forced the salmon to run. Swallows flew above them. John Ireland could just make out, in silhouette, a basket on the platform from which something rose quickly and subsided—a fish's head or tail appearing as it jerked. He rose and found his shoes under the blankets.

In full silhouette before him on the water, a bare Skagit boy who looked to be about his own age—thirteen years old—appeared walking in the river itself; he breasted downstream into camp. He was leading four cayuses, two ropes in each hand; he emerged on the bank and tied them, heads up, to four trees.

John Ireland heard the sound of a bell above the rushing water. A vigorous old man appeared in the village center, in a littered clearing backed by the vaulting trunks of the forest; he was ringing a brass bell hard. The old man's bare legs were knock-kneed; his ponytail was white; he stood upright, and sunlight gleamed on his brown arm when it rose.

From the grass-mat lodges, from the drying fires, and from the riverbanks, naked or breechclouted men, women dressed or skirted, and naked children, gathered around the bell ringer in a circle. The old man silenced the bell. John Ireland joined his father, his grandfather, and the other Whatcom men by the canoes; they watched. The Skagit people made the Catholic sign of the cross on their chests, just as the Lummi Indian people did, and uttered at each touch something unintelligible. John Ireland was used to the Catholic Lummis, who waved metal crucifixes about—which seemed to do them worlds of good, the Whatcom settlers said, for they never made trouble, and warned the settlers when other tribes' warriors threatened, and offered even to help drive them off. Once on a trip to Goshen he had seen the Methodist Nooksacks praying. They knelt in a circle facing out. Embarrassed, he had not known which way to look.

These people prayed in a circle facing in. Over their heads, upriver towards the British Columbia border, John Ireland could see a fragment of Hozomeen Mountain spreading cracked stone pinnacles across the sky; its snowy glaciers crumbled. Before it rose another mountain, whose glaciers, streaked with crevasses, glistened yellow in the south light. His father had said the whole population of Whatcom could slip into one of those crevasses and not be seen from its lip. These siwashes were indeed brave, John Ireland thought, to bare their naked bodies so to the terrible world.

Now the old ponytailed Skagit spoke in a soft voice, incomprehensibly, looking to heaven, and the people ducked their heads. Then it was over, and the people glided apart. Tom Sharp spat a stream of tobacco juice.

The forceful ponytailed man approached them barefoot over the stones, as lightly as an angel; he wore a clean bone through his septum, and his face was red below the eyebrows with vermilion. His name was Elliott Yekton. He was *siat*—of wealth and high birth, according to Adolph Sharp. His cousin was Laxabulica, a woman, who was now, due to extraordinary circumstances, the Skagits' chief.

Elliott Yekton greeted John Ireland's grandfather with high emotion, although he had last seen him only the night before. When John Ireland had rolled himself in his blanket, his grandfather, Adolph Sharp—wearing a striped vest over his shirt and trousers, and his invariable Mexican hat—was sitting still as a turtle on a pale log with a row of bare Indian men, every one of whose faces was painted red. The red paint discouraged mosquitoes, his father told him; the mosquitoes mired in it. His grandfather and the other men were talking in slurred, caressing words that sounded all alike.

His grandfather had married—as the family put it—a Skagit girl long ago, after his real grandmother died. The Skagit bride was daughter of a *tyee*—a big man—and circumspect to the point of cussedness, according to the Sharp family; but Adolph, who presumably knew her better, called her Bright Eyes, and was "dead nuts on her." Her name was Evelyn; she died during her second confinement, when she was nineteen. Adolph had never married again. In the four years he had his wife, he learned the Skagits' language and visited for months with her people in summer camps and in their big winter houses; he knew many families in the band. He said that Indian people were all different, every one of them, just like everyone else, and John Ireland was just beginning to imagine that this might be so.

Elliott Yekton touched hands with everyone else in their company and led them to a lodge, where his two wives, his *klootchmen*, unrolled fresh mats for their seating and served them soft salmon and hard potatoes. Later the lodge filled with many men, women, and children. They conversed with the whites in Chinook jargon. Once John Ireland looked to his father's face and seemed to see his profile smoothed in feature, joyous, the way he looked when he sang. He brought out his tobacco pouch. John Ireland smelled oily salmon skin and human skin. Many of the men and women were missing teeth. John Ireland could scarcely bear to look at their faces, at any faces, whose closeness and vivid reality overwhelmed him. Why were there so many people in the world, living tucked away, so real in their bodies, and so real to themselves?

CHAPTER IX

John Ireland Sharp's mother considered Skagits beyond the pale, because she heard they set newborn twins under a tree to die, at least the ones on the Skagit River used to; his grandfather had erred by mentioning this vanished custom one day when he had the twins, Vesta and Viola, on either knee. She had not wanted to let John Ireland join this expedition at all. He knew, from the steady way she held his shoulders on the Whatcom wharf before they boarded the steamer, that she was afraid he would drown or break his neck. She had said, however, in his father's hearing—holding his shoulders and looking off—only that she feared his table manners would deteriorate in the woods and mountains with four men for a month. John Ireland, for his part, had not understood that so many Indian men and boys would clap eyes on him, or he would not have come. He believed, superstitiously, that they would locate the cowardice in him, and would see, as if in a spiritual vision, that his younger brother Frank could best him easily, any day of the week.

John Ireland's party had arrived at the Skagits' fishing village yesterday, utterly baked. The men were exploring, and informally surveying, a possible railroad route through the three Skagit passes over the Cascade Mountains.

Things were looking pert in the town of Whatcom again. The partners of a Whatcom land company hoped to persuade the Northern Pacific Railroad to extend its transcontinental line from Spokane across the wide Washington Territory to Bellingham Bay, where Whatcom lay. This prospect so smote the excitable editor of the new Whatcom newspaper that he referred to that prominent trade route "the Liverpool–New York–Whatcom–Yokahama run"—quite as if this were an everyday expression.

The Northern Pacific was going to cross the hundred miles of chaotic Cascade peaks somewhere on coastal Washington Territory and locate the rail terminus on a harbor, and that place would become a great city. To the good people of Seattle, ninety miles south up Puget Sound, Seattle made the most sense. To the good people of Bellingham Bay, their town, Whatcom, made the most sense. The bay harbor was wide enough for several fleets, the site offered one of the few coal mines on the west coast—to coal the ocean steamers the railroad met and served—and the Strait of Juan de Fuca gave ready access to the open Pacific. There was, however, only the guess of a talkative miner named Jelly for the railbed feasibility of the Skagit passes through the mountains and of the narrow Skagit Valley itself.

Accordingly, the Sharp men—father Adolph, who grew potatoes in Goshen, and grown son Tom, who worked at the Whatcom sawmill—had set out a week ago to map a Skagit route, for five dollars a day. They were traveling under Conrad Grogan, a slope-shouldered man who carried his back erect, even at mess. He had surveyed the wagon trail through the mountains to the Fraser River in the gold rush of 1858. With them was handy Jay Tamoree—a slim, bowlegged fellow who wore a blue forage cap—and the thirteen-year-old Sharp boy.

Taking the side-wheel steamer south from Bellingham Bay to the river mouth, they had to go through Deception Pass. All day John Ireland, standing on deck, heard the men talk about this narrow tickle on the coast between cliffs, where the current overpowered steam engines.

When their side-wheel steamer, the *Patty Robison*, approached Deception Pass, John Ireland, piloting the rail, saw that there were two passages between the forested cliffs. In both, white foam swirled in whirlpools; the current was against them. The captain chose the wider channel. From the rail John Ireland reckoned the channel looked too narrow for the steamer; he judged the young captain "cold-out crazy" to crank up steam. They entered the foaming slot, and the wind tore his hair. The gray and brown rock walls high overhead cast a chill shade. Gulls screeched and dove by the smokestack. The current was fast as the wind; it surged against the hull, rattled the deck, and splashed the passengers and freight. The captain tried to hug the south bank to catch the back eddy. Backwash rolled the boat and raised a wheel, whose spinning clattered in the air. Beside either rail, near enough almost to touch, the pitted rock walls, grown with green ferns, firs, cedar, and twisting red madrone trees, seemed to converge. When the walls crushed the steamer, the hissing whirlpools in the current would carry them under the sea. There yellow crabs as big as their faces would eat them alive, and their bones would swirl on forever.

At once, the deck's trembling doubled and the wheels slowed. The red madrone trees they had passed now reappeared, the cliffs loomed, and John Ireland saw himself sliding backwards, and the world receding. He looked up at Mr. Tamoree, beside him at the rail, and saw that the skin drawn over his cheeks was gray, and his expression frozen. The engineer, his father, and other men passed cordwood and slabwood into the firebox. In a brigade, shouting, they handed up every stick of wood on deck. In all the din he heard the bearded captain, with pleasure in his voice, roar for bacon: "Get me the bacon, the bacon!"

Someone rushed two sides of bacon from the deck to the house; John Ireland watched the captain seize them in both hands and throw them whole into the firebox to stoke the boiler. Black smoke billowed from the stack, and the boiler roared as if it would burst. The deck groaned; the wheels churned and bit in. The boy's heart pounded in the racket while the balance of forces shifted. Now the rock walls slid back over the stern and delivered them into the wide and lighted world in perfect silence, in a glassy calm, on water hushed and pale as the sky.

Over the broad and shining mud of Skagit flats, flocks of dunlin like specks of mirror glittered and darkened by turns as they flew. Skagit clam shanties and shanty frames spotted the stone beaches behind the row of driftwood logs. Bald eagles strode the mud flat like fish crows, and pulled strands from carcasses. Salt tides washed the delta, so nothing could grow on the rich silt but beach rye and tules. These gentle prospects did not at this moment interest John Ireland, who intended, when he was a steamboat captain, to steam through Deception Pass every day of his life.

They had journeyed upriver from the barren Skagit delta by so-called siwash packets. These were shovel-nosed cedar canoes that native men owned and poled, for forty dollars a canoeload of men and freight. That was a week ago. The Skagits' foreheads were flattened, so their brows jutted out, it seemed to the boy, like shakes on a roof. John Ireland stared at their knees and elbows, where the skin was thick and ashen. He stared at the thin creases on the back of his father's neck. The Skagit men poled, and the Whatcom men and John Ireland paddled, up the Skagit for twelve or fourteen hours a day, for this would be the easiest part of their trip. It took them three days to portage around a logjam. They traveled wide land between low hills and camas prairies, where Skagit women dug roots and cultivated potatoes. They passed a Skagit winter lodge made of lapped cedar planks one hundred and fifty feet long and forty feet wide. They passed an immigrant settlement where dingy children waved at them from a dock. These settlers, his grandfather said, hailed from the Carolina mountains, or Tennessee. They passed two isolated claims where working men and black-haired children gazed at them in silence. Upstream the forested riverbanks sloped and narrowed.

Their spirits rose, and in the morning the Whatcom men sang and the Skagit men slung jokes at each other. To the north they could glimpse Mount Shuksan: its black stone ramparts shone as mighty blocks, between which glaciers bore glistening down. They ate sandwiches of cold breakfast pancakes with sliced raw onions and fried bacon. Conrad Grogan measured the pitch of the banks with a theodolite and consulted an altimeter, whose readings varied with the weather. Grogan was fair-headed and wore black mustaches. John Ireland wondered: if a yellow-headed man grew black mustaches, might he himself someday grow a yellow beard? Grogan and Tom and Adolph Sharp unfolded two maps, and consulted the Skagits, when the Nahcullum River entered from the north, and when the Cascade River forked in from the east. For two days it rained lightly, on and off. John Ireland was collecting animal skulls for the benefit of science, and on the voyage upriver a Skagit named Pawquitzy found, and presented him with, a duck's billed skull, a squirrel's, and, best, a cougar's, with sharp front teeth and a brainpan flat as a brick.

They slept under a canvas awning on which fir cones popped. They woke and fed the fire at its mouth. The fire was just for companionship in the rain; no one expected trouble. The Skagits intermarried freely with the Nooksacks and other nearby tribes; their only inland enemies were the so-called Thompson Indians, who lived on a branch of the Fraser River in British Columbia, and who hunted the Skagit headwaters and Mount Shuksan.

On the last night before they reached the Skagit summer village, Adolph Sharp had stayed up smoking with the Skagit men long after dinner. John Ireland watched from his blanket roll as his grandfather approached later; he squatted with the Whatcom men by the fire, and mentioned what he had heard. The Skagits were still skirmishing with the Thompsons, as they had done in Evelyn's day. By firelight his grandfather looked wild in his Mexican hat and the striped vest of a banker; he wore fluffy white mustaches and a straight white goatee on his chin. From the corners of his mouth, two dark-haired stripes extended down his goatee like tobacco juice. Only in the past few years had John Ireland dared look him in the face.

The Skagits regarded the Thompsons as cruel, he said. They called them savage and primitive. The Thompsons kidnapped babies for slaves.

They decapitated Skagit men whom they found alone in the woods. They left the heads loose on the trail to scare and grieve their families; they did something else worse to Skagit women and children, and sometimes to men, about which his grandfather abruptly stopped telling. His voice was cracked and airy. The Thompsons skulked about by night like animals, he said, and trailed down the river to hunt on the Skagits' land south of Stetattle Creek without first checking in for permission at the nearest village: they were worse than cruel; they were rude.

John Ireland looked at the two dark stripes at the edges of his grandfather's goatee. The firelight jumped and streaked his face. The man seemed incalculably old, as old and alien sometimes as an immortal bear speaking from unimaginable caverns of experience.

For his part, Tom Sharp said, he believed about half of this, although he had heard such stories from many sources for many years, for people had a way of saying such things about foreigners. Tom Sharp cooked for the outfit—"stood bitch," they called it—and he always looked dark around the eyes, where the greasy fir smoke pooled and left lampblack. He was a patient man who conserved himself for the long haul, and he did not let smoke chase him around a campfire. He had neat, crisp features like the boy, and black hair, but he was stout.

Earlier this summer, Adolph said—and this was a known fact—a Skagit named Sylvester found a Thompson man down at the Station; he dragged him into the marsh, sailed into him with an ax, took him upstream in his canoe, cut him into twenty pieces on a beached log, piled up the pieces like kindling, and set the head on top. "You might say there was bad feelings on both sides." At this profundity, the men nodded slowly and looked up at the river beyond the fire, where the waxing moon had cleared the trees and lay sliced on the rough water like shavings.

John Ireland had got to be thirteen years old in part by believing what he heard about the world. That night he was wakened in his blanket by the dark force of something he had heard and neglected to consider: the Thompson people possessed a spirit monster of the mountains, which was a white human torso without limbs. It rolled constantly on the ground and cried like a baby. To see it was to die.

This morning they ate breakfast in Elliott Yekton's lodge in the Skagit summer village, and set out for the mountains. They traveled on foot well behind Conrad Grogan, who was leading four broom-tailed packhorses they had bought from the Skagits for silver dollars; the Skagits had bought them from the Tulalip for hides. Elliott Yekton led them, vigorous and bent-legged; he showed them the old trading trail that crossed the mountains on the passes Grogan wanted to survey.

They walked in the swift river itself for the first mile or so upstream. The Skagits dreaded the snarled forest, and found the going easier in the rivers, and even up in the mountains' snows. The horses had entered the water readily, which pleased Grogan; he would have preferred mules if they could afford mules, he said, but mules would have dished this stage of the journey, as they purely misliked wetting their feet. He had seen a man shoot a pack mule dead, at the edge of a ford, simply to win the argument for the side of reason. The man had to carry his own gear, his *itkus*, in the mountains for a week, but never repented.

John Ireland agreed with the mule. That time of year, in August, the river was chalky with glacial melt, and as cold as water could run. John Ireland splashed ahead of his grandfather, numb as iron from the waterline down.

"This current is too strong, and too high up on me," he said to his grandfather, turning his head. "It really grinds me," he added.

His grandfather showed no mercy. He caught up with the boy and informed him—rather overheartily, John Ireland felt—that a skillful Skagit band who lived along the Sauk River used trails which routinely crossed the rushing river underwater. To keep their footing on the riverbed trails, the clever people carried big stones on their shoulders. So saying, his grandfather handed John Ireland a fifteen-pound basket of dried salmon—the Skagits had given them all they could carry—and told him, "Hold it on your head and keep it dry."

The riverbanks steepened. They boosted out of the gorge to the mountains, where the expedition's main work lay. The Indian trail up through the forest was steep as an avalanche chute. The men slung their arms against trunks to check slips. The horses skidded on stones. John Ireland's father lured the rawboned Mexican buckskin with a pone of bread; Jay Tamoree kicked the pinto, his flat Union forage cap fell off, and Yekton gave him an incredulous look. They ate lunch leaning three to a tree trunk, and two hours later they were still climbing. Several times the men opened the trail with axes; the black horse blew, and the pinto sneezed.

John Ireland traced the buckskin's ropy veins along its belly and down one leg. After seven hours' climb straight up, at the top of a ridge, they stopped to drink water.

While they were stopped on the trail at the ridgetop, Elliott Yekton gave a cry, and pointed to an ax slash on a tree. He talked to the men rapidly. He cried out again, unsheathed his trade knife, and searched the ground. The Thompsons were around; Thompsons were poaching again on Skagit land. The ax slash was wet. John Ireland looked at the white ponytail as it lay like an ermine pelt on Elliott Yekton's dark skin along his spine's trough between muscular ridges. Elliott Yekton and Grogan conferred, facing up the trail; the horses rested on three legs and panted and coughed with their heads down.

They proceeded up the trail and kept a bright lookout. The trail bent to the north past a tarn where the forest thinned. Ahead they could see pitched and sliding green meadows above treeline, where only a few sharp firs and dead snags stood. Above the meadows, patches of gray mist moved across pebbled precipices and bare snowfields; the mist in streamers sailed wildly out over drop-offs, and blocked distant peaks. High to the west, the muddy snout of a glacier drove down a chasm. Elliott Yekton was leading.

They heard sounds like a bear's long groans and sighs. The pinto, leading, balked. The trail curved around trees to a clearing; there, on the trail in the sun, sat a naked young Indian man. He sat cross-legged; his arms rested limp on his knees. His head was bent as if he were thinking, sitting cross-legged in repose there on the ground—as if an interesting insight had overtaken him, and he had sat down to relax and consider it closely. Behind his head, from the back of his neck, protruded a bloody sharpened stake. The stake had been driven into the ground, and he had been driven onto the stake. The stake was higher than his head by about a foot; it was impossible to determine how far it extended into the ground.

The young man was still alive, and his open-mouthed breaths made noise. Blood wetted the dust and stones in a circle around him. Elliott Yekton squatted to look in his face; the young man's eyes moved up with a pleading expression, and his breathing sounds came louder. The skin around his navel was blue; his fingers and toes were also blue, and his face and neck were gray. He rolled his eyes upward, and they met John Ireland's eyes with a knowing, even tender, look. John Ireland felt a hand on his back as Conrad Grogan eased him downhill without a word and faced him down the trail by the trembling horses, the way they had come. John Ireland turned his head and saw Elliott Yekton kneel and hold the young man's two shoulders, in the steady way John Ireland's mother had held his shoulders on the Whatcom wharf—but Elliott Yekton, unlike his mother, began to cry. Blood continued to flow thick over the gray ground, without seeping in. John Ireland's father took a step back when it reached his boot, then after a pause stepped forward again, and John Ireland saw the blood run under the boot's toe.

Now the Skagit's eyes stilled and emptied of intelligence. Elliott Yekton spoke to him, kneeling; he addressed the drooping head in low tones. There was blood coming out of the slack mouth, remarkably bright, and dripping on his abdomen. John Ireland, his blood rushing in his ears, looked back down the trail the way they had come, towards the dark chasms, but saw nothing in particular that he could remember.

That night the Whatcom men made camp above treeline. John Ireland smelled the snows. They laid the canvas awning directly over their blankets for warmth. The glaciated peaks in the distance all around them shone blue in the moonlight. Shreds of mist raced up the slopes towards them like horses running uphill.

It had been necessary to remove the staked Skagit from the stake. There had been some talk about when to do this—before or after he died—just as there had been some low talk about whether to shoot him in the head with a revolver. His name was Wakashak, Elliott Yekton had said while tears coursed down his face, to John Ireland's wonderment—his name was Wakashak, and he was the well-known son of a hunter, Elliott Yekton's friend; his mother cooked in the logging camp downriver on the shore; he had been seeking his guardian spirit alone in the mountains, as was customary for young adults of both sexes; many Thompson people would feel very sorry for this. His spirit had already left him, Elliott Yekton said, and gone to the dreary village of dead spirits. John Ireland thought this meant that he was dead, but he was not then dead.

In the end Grogan had handed his revolver to Elliott Yekton, handle out, gravely, and at that moment the young man staked to the ground had died. His breathing stopped, and his mouth and shoulders gave way. Without noticing, John Ireland had turned around to see directly, and taken a step. Elliott Yekton leaned forward and pressed the side of his head to the young man's sunken breast. After a long moment, he bounded to his feet and sent up a shrieking that gave the Whatcom men pause; they applied themselves to examining the scenery. The black horse was so impressed she raised her jug head. Next Elliott Yekton grasped the end of his own ponytail, pulled it back so his neck strained, and raised his knife. John Ireland wished he had stayed home. The *tyee* sawed through his ponytail, and its rawhide thong slipped off and fell to the ground in the blood with the hair. Now his white hair fell wide to his shoulders unbound.

The Thompsons must have driven the stake three or four feet into the ground, for the men could not budge it. Should they slide the Skagit a bit up the stake—the stake entered at his anus—to chop the stake down and ease it out from the bottom, or should they slide him, seated as he was, all the way up and off? At this, his father forcibly led John Ireland back down the trail, and stayed with him there.

John Ireland and his father, who seemed to John Ireland "on the prod," sat straight-legged on stones and looked out over chasms at iced peaks and rock spires, some of which prospectors had named: Despair, Damnation, Challenger, Terror. It was no kind of country for farms. A railroad seemed as unlikely as a wharf. John Ireland heard an ax chopping. After a while, footsteps approached: it was a troubled Elliott Yekton, carrying the dead young man over his shoulders, come to wish his *tillicums* good-bye. He was taking the body back. He held a gray wrist in his left hand and a bloody calf in his right; the dead head with its shiny black ponytail hung behind his left elbow. "Good-bye," John Ireland's father said, and, as the man turned down the trail, more faintly, "Good luck."

Their company had continued up the trail, and eastward. Here on this strikingly steep ridge they made the first of many mountain camps. They slept on stony ground under squares of canvas, and clouds blew into their beds. The fatal, glittering peaks in every direction brewed storms that jumped canyons and blew through their clothes. Snow fell on them, slid above and below them, and concealed glaciers' crevasses. Once during a snowstorm they saw lightning, and heard thunder crack below them. Beneath their camps, precipices dropped several thousand feet to hanging valleys where trees killed by avalanches lay heaped. Dirty snowfields sank into melt pools, whose waters tasted like nails. They watched a white mountain goat fall from a cliff. The rest of John Ireland's life would seem an extension of these first bivouacs after he saw the staked Skagit; all his subsequent rented rooms and houses were mountain camps from which the lay of the land was forever plain.

The hobbled packhorses found good grass. Tamoree rounded them up in the morning. John Ireland ate and slept; nighthawks hove overhead. Every day they coursed upended slopes on elk trails beneath crumbling glaciers; their prospects were a black sea of peaks. In the chasms beside them, fog swelled, and morning sun cast their walking shadows into the fog, so they seemed to travel with looming and spectral companions who walked on air. They began shooting marmots to eat. Tamoree ran out of horseshoes. Almost every day clouds gathered, chilled, and rained or snowed. From the main pass, they saw a black tower to the north, protruding like a shark fin from its glacier. To the south, the massive overhanging glacier on an unnamed mountain dropped ice once an hour to the valley floor. They climbed a narrow arm over the pass and rose to see ranges of ice and spires, and a thick volcano beyond. John Ireland, hearing his heartbeat, kicked his shoe soles into snowfields. He stared at the pinto's dusty rump as its two pink-edged halves rose and fell when it lifted and set its dumb feet again and again. No one stole the horses, here among the peaks and passes, or on their return on the long Whatcom Trail by Tomyhoi Creek and Chilliwack Lake in the mountains, and they saw no more Thompson sign.

CHAPTER X

When they returned to civilization at the end of twenty days, they learned that a wire had come ticking into the telegraph office while they were gone. Tacoma, little Tacoma, which had paper piers and paper blocks, and one hotel and two saloons, had been awarded the terminus of the Northern Pacific Railroad. The Northern Pacific tracks would cross the Cascades well south of the Skagit, at Stampede Pass. Tacoma would batten on capital, and the other towns on the Sound would shrivel and die.

In the streets of Goshen, on the county road, and on the named streets of Whatcom along which they led the sore-footed horses, people greeted them, wild at the news. Some held that the railroad had deliberately destroyed Seattle from spite, from hatred of the town and its two thousand hardworking citizens. Others noted that overconfident Seattle had not felt the need to proffer the many financial inducements Tacoma did. For three years, after all, investors from San Francisco and Portland had been buying up Seattle; Seattle was a shoo-in. Tacoma was handy to the new pass, but it had nothing, barely a wheelbarrow. And shipping would have to ply north along the seventy-mile length of Puget Sound, to the Strait of Juan de Fuca, before it could head out to sea.

What about Whatcom? Well, it had never been Whatcom all along, it seemed, and everyone knew it but Whatcom. Of course, Olympia made the most sense to many, and Anacortes thought it would be Anacortes, and Port Townsend had hopes, and so even did Mukilteo.

The men and the boy heard all this, dazed. At the village of Goshen on the Nooksack River they spent their last night together, and their first night in three weeks under a roof, at Adolph Sharp's place; he lived there on sixty acres, and grew potatoes on five. They ate breakfast together in the Veseys' rooming house. Jay Tamoree said, "I could eat a folded tarpaulin." The men and the boy removed their hats indoors and revealed around each head a shining, rippling ridge of hair where hat brims pressed. Their foreheads were white. Adolph wiped his striped goatee on a cloth napkin. Tom seemed to study his son. Tom had visited a barber for a shave that morning, and every time he turned his head they all noticed.

Outside, by the tied grimy horses on the village street, Adolph extracted his blanket roll from a pack box, and stuck his revolver in it, and held his rifle. He pounded the jug-headed black horse's flank, which about killed it, and noted that it had been a pretty good, hardworking horse. He shook hands all around, and his Mexican hat bobbed. He looked at John Ireland and laid one hand on top of his head, fingers spread, like a claw; he gave a squeeze, and turned up the street. Tom Sharp and Jay Tamoree redistributed the pack load and fastened it down.

In Whatcom that evening, they unloaded the horses at the livery stable. The horses balanced unbudging on their legs like tables, hung their heads, and looked like they would never take another step in this world. Conrad Grogan and Jay Tamoree returned to their homes. Tom and John Ireland Sharp returned to theirs.

In the two-story house on the hill over the bay, the two washed and ate, and ate. The little twin sisters, Viola and Vesta, crowded the benches where they sat. The twins looked uncannily vivid, insensible, motile, detailed, like human birds. They wore long black dresses—curious garments, John Ireland thought. John Ireland's mother wore a dress, too, a green dress, and a stiff white apron; she carried them a pan of cinnamon rolls. The kitchen was close, and baking had heated its air and dark walls. John Ireland's brothers, Frank and Willy, looked him over awkwardly, and found nothing to admire in his skull collection, which he brought forth and displayed—in fact, the soiled skulls looked even to John Ireland more like trash here than treasure, and he swept them roughly back in their sack. Frank and Willy took their plates outside; they were eleven and nine. The cinnamon rolls were packed tight, and the pan was hot.

They wondered, John Ireland and Tom, what Adolph Sharp, and Conrad Grogan, and Jay Tamoree, were doing right now; for most of a month they had known what each was up to, always. They did not look at each other, nor had they ever, really. At home, John Ireland rarely saw his father, who was always working at the sawmill and often away; he himself roamed the town with Frank and Willy, read books, and investigated the beach or the wharf. Three months a year, they attended school. John Ireland went to a neighbor's house for lessons, and his brothers went to the town school. He looked at the toe of his shoe. All that would start up again, like a riptide, and sweep him away. He did not know if he wanted to step back from it, or step into it.

"Imagine Tacoma!" John Ireland's mother said, but he and his father could not.

She had twisted her yellow hair into a tidy knot at the back of her neck, behind her head, where her spine met her skull. Her eyes were enormous and round, like a horse's or an angel's. Her damp face shone. She studied him, John Ireland knew, when he bent or turned his head. Everything in the kitchen—the canning kettles, the long-legged sink, the stove handles, woodbox, window frame, floor—John Ireland recognized with surprise. His mother said land prices were already dropping in Whatcom, and people were leaving. His father said he did not know about the new southern pass, but the Skagit passes they had mapped made a fine series. On the far side the railroad could meet the old Indian path up the Stehekin River. There was good grazing for a road crew's stock. The route through the passes was wide as a highway, and the grade was no more than fifty feet to the mile.

CHAPTER XI

1874–1876, Madrone Island

John Ireland Sharp's father rolled belly-up in the panic of '73, just like everybody else. Before he left for their journey up the Skagit, Tom Sharp turned down an offer of ten dollars an acre for his land, land he had bought six years earlier for $1.25 an acre. After their trip up the Skagit, after Tacoma won the terminus, after Wall Street failed, after railway financiers got caught robbing the public till and depression hit, the land was worthless. Soon all of Whatcom was on the block, and no one was buying at any price. In the next few years, most people left. The boy John Ireland walked with Frank and Willy through the boarded-up town in a dream. They saw the wharf a storm wrecked, the wharf the town had no funds to repair; they saw ruined bridges and trails lost to blackberry hells. Tom Sharp hadn't "a feather to fly with," he remarked in one of his few statements, but he flew anyway. He took his time with things, but the time had come. He turned his small, dark head to imagine all possibilities, and found no good ones. He removed with his family to Madrone Island.

Madrone Island lay out in the San Juan Islands, in thirty fathoms of ice water in Rosario Strait. Tom Sharp bought a red gill-net skiff and loaded it with provisions and tools, with tied, squawking chickens, and a bred sow. He rowed with his yellow-headed wife, with John Ireland, Frank, and Willy, and with the yellow-headed twins, Viola and Vesta, who grew silly and almost swamped the boat. For three windy days they rowed from Whatcom, and bivouacked on shores when night fell. They scraped up on a stony beach where the sun shone, on Madrone.

On Madrone the Sharps found three busted prospectors from the Fraser River gold rush, who lived there with Lummi Indian brides. One of them had witnessed the northern Indians' massacre of Lummis in their settlement on Orcas Island; the northern raiders killed the local Lummis with Russian rifles. The Sharps found three hermits, who despised one another, and two Whatcom families like themselves, who had moved there in the panic to try again. Some lumbermen were cutting down a cedar grove on the north shore. They found the schoolteacher, Miss Arvilla Pulver, a sober, winsome graduate of Oberlin College, whom Tom had met in Whatcom; she had urged them to come with their five children, to enlarge the island school.

By the sweet rosebushes behind the beach, John Ireland caught garter snakes, which allowed themselves to be petted; the big bees investigated his head and never stung. The island was all dark forest and sunlit marsh, milder than the mainland and more clean. In March, when they came, the currants were flowering red in the sun. Last winter there had been no frost at all, they heard. Blue islands ringed the distance in every direction. The water smelled planetary; salt water from Arctic seas soaked beach stones. On the dazzling west shore Tom Sharp pitched canvas tarpaulins for housing. He fenced from the deer a garden to live on and a crop of timothy hay to sell. John Ireland, his brothers, Frank and Willy, and the twins, Viola and Vesta, lived outside, and the blue sea lighted their work and their play.

On his fourth morning on the island, John Ireland was collecting driftwood on the stony beach—a lithe, handsome boy in a round hat, whose frowning black eyebrows shielded his eyes from the light. He had walked around the sharp sand spit on the south point. Two bays met there, and two winds; they raised a line of waves that lay on the flat sea like a rope twisted of two strands. He watched terns fishing this line of waves, and gulls circling it crying.

Along the beach came a big boy whose neck slewed off to one side. He had narrow shoulders, a wide chest, and thick arms and legs. This was the first island boy John Ireland had seen. His open smile was sunny, and he met John Ireland's eyes without guile.

"You getting you some firewood?" They faced out towards the water, the big boy and the small one. John Ireland stared at the stranger's enormous shoes, black brogans the size of cordwood.

"I am," John Ireland said. He placed the wood on the cobbles and found his pockets. He just moved here, he said—his family came from Whatcom. Had the other boy ever been to Whatcom? He saw that the boy had long ears, like an old man. His limp hair curled behind his ears and down his neck.

He had been all over, he said. "Do you ... want to row out to Victoria with me tomorrow?" His voice was soft, forced.

John Ireland said he would like to awful much, but he had to help out at home. They just got here, and his father wanted to get a crop in right off. They were living over by—

"Say," said the boy, and a thrilled note in his voice surprised John Ireland, "have you got you a horse or ... anything?"

No, but they were fixing to buy some sheep when they could. His father, John Ireland said, dressed his own self in the harness and pulled the plow. "He says it's strictly easy here in the sand."

"Plowing ... sand." A rip in his gray union suit showed a dark flat nipple under his overalls.

John Ireland picked up his armload of driftwood. He said he had to be going, and asked the boy where he lived.

"Listen—" The eyes looked down glassy at John Ireland from deep in the flesh. He asked John Ireland if he had two bits for some honey from Victoria.

He did not have anything, John Ireland said, and added that it was pleasurable meeting him. He turned back the way he had come.

Just a dime, he said, clumping after. "Anybody's got a dime."

"I wish I did, but I don't have anything."

"Let's see."

"What?"

"Let's see those pockets."

"I told you—"

"Why would you want to cheat me out of one jar of honey, when you've probably been ... rolling in honey all winter and I've had none at all? Look here—"

And he fetched John Ireland a kick in the back. John Ireland turned, dumped the wood up at him, and took off. He heard the boy coming two loud paces over the stones, and felt him jump on his back. The two went down together, punching silently. John Ireland landed a good lick on the boy's big nose, but that was the only lick, for the boy seized a billet of wood, pinned him with a thick knee, and lit into him, drubbing with the wood. He heard the stones grinding by his ears, and heard the blows hit more than he felt them. There was sand and gravel in his mouth; he was fourteen, used to fighting his brothers. He rolled against the knee and unbalanced the boy. The boy rose fast and kicked him, first with one shoe, and then with the other. This was the serious part, for the kicks lifted and moved him by bits along the beach. John Ireland from his knees let fly a stone at the streaming, attentive face, and when that failed he tucked himself up, to his everlasting shame, till the boy left off kicking and his footfalls crashed away. He saw that the big boy had left him the driftwood. There was no shortage of driftwood.

"Jesus wept," said Viola when John Ireland came home sopping red from head cuts. He had broken two or three ribs—or eight or nine, it felt like. He skinned off his clothes then, and skinned off his clothes repeatedly over the next weeks, in order to walk into the water up to his neck and stand quietly till he shook, for the cold water was anodyne and analgesic, all they had.

The boy's mother called a meeting in the schoolroom about this fight. His own father, and the boy's mother, and Miss Arvilla Pulver, attended; so did Lee Shorey, a respected family man. They brought the boys together. By then John Ireland knew that the other boy's name was Beal Obenchain; he was twelve. John Ireland Sharp told his version. Beal Obenchain accused him in return so violently, with such heartfelt outrage, and named so many appalling provocations—the hurled load of firewood, the slung stones, when he was just offering friendship to a stranger—that the adults concluded that John Ireland was mostly in the wrong, and told both boys not to fight. After the meeting John Ireland walked into the water and stood. Six weeks later he was interested to note that the broken rib ends itched, in a hundred small looping, pulling, scratching motions deep inside him, for three days while the bones joined, precisely as if they were knitting together, as the expression had it.

There was work all spring and summer, and no school till the dead of winter. John Ireland borrowed mildewed books and read them. He stayed away from the big boy Beal Obenchain until one day Frank and Willy, Viola and Vesta, and all the island children were building a raft near his family's stretch of beach. He joined although Beal was there fitfully, giving orders or stalking away, and it went all right. Beal Obenchain had a wide, lippy smile that forgave the world. After that he joined every day, and it went blamed fine; they built a fleet of four rafts or five rafts, depending on whether a shakebolt counted as a raft, and poled the length of Coward Bay.

In September neighbors helped Tom Sharp and his wife knock up a cedar-log house; they chinked it with moss. From time to time Lummi Indian families paddled ashore and sold a salmon for twenty-five cents, or traded for hens' eggs. The Lummi children felt of the twins' thin hair. That winter the Sharp children attended school, where John Ireland distinguished himself as a scholar. Just before Easter a sloop sailed by on fire, decks and sails: it was carrying quarried lime from San Juan Island, and a deck leak wet the lime and it caught fire. By the time Tom Sharp got his skiff in the water the boat had sunk yellow and smoking, and he never found a soul. In April, Lee Shorey had the idea of raising Angora goats. A brother of his had bought Madsen Island to breed black cats for fur. Tom Sharp acquired sheep from Lee Shorey, painted two stripes on their ears with pokeberry juice, and turned them loose with everyone's sheep, on the north-side bluffs.

It was in May that the Sharp family met with an accident; they drowned, except for John Ireland. That drizzly morning, at about eight o'clock, big Axel Obenchain was splitting shakes to roof his barn. A kingfisher flew clattering down the beach. Axel Obenchain looked up and saw the red skiff adrift with the current in Helfgott Channel. He rowed out to it, in only a breeze, and found it empty of all but two wet shoats and a hair comb, and no explanation. John Ireland said later that they all were taking the shoats to sell to a man on Orcas Island. No one could swim, not even Frank. There was one set of oars in the oarlocks, and one set was missing.

John Ireland was collecting eggs in the marsh rye behind his house when Axel Obenchain in his green rowboat fetched up on the current with the empty skiff tied on. John Ireland saw, and met him at the waterline. His tangle of beard was wet.

"You' fotter?" he asked, and John Ireland told him, looking at the wild-eyed shoats. The shoats scraped and rattled their hooves on the skiff's sides. John Ireland lifted them out, and they ran to the mud flats. "You' mutter?"

"She went, too—they all went."

"You' sister? Brodder?" Axel Obenchain was a red-faced, red-bearded man; gold fuzz covered his arms and hands, and edged his red scalp thinly, catching the light. He stood beside his green rowboat, and water pooled over his shoes. It was still raining.

John Ireland held both hands on the skiff and studied the far water for heads. The dark dots he saw resolved into puffins, rigid as clowns. There was a crack of yellow light behind the distant islands; the water was gray and oily-looking, and the rain pitted it. His father purely hated, he remarked once, the look of rain falling in salt water. They all had wanted to go to Orcas Island. The buyer on Orcas raised tulip bulbs. His mother wondered, did he know what a couple of pigs could do to a flower bed? To bulbs in particular? She had tied up two black hens and carried them aboard by the feet, in case he changed his mind. Now the tide had not even covered the streak on the sand that the skiff cut when they slid it down to the water. They had eaten their breakfast mush together an hour ago. Viola had slanged Frank, and their mother said, "I want you calm!"

"All both?" Axel Obenchain said. He was a muscular, worn man, whose red eyes always looked weepy. "Mein Gott."

With Lee Shorey, and the herring fisherman named Clarence Millstone, and the boy, he launched the red skiff again and rowed searching Helfgott Channel and its shores on Orcas and Madrone. They found nothing, not even the oars. During the day the clouds broke up, and by sunset there were fifteen colors of clouds over the water and fifteen colors of sky between them. The men helped John Ireland drag the skiff above the tideline and settle it on logs. The islanders watched from their cabins; everyone knew. Clarence Millstone, a muttering, generous little man in a bearskin coat, came into the house with John Ireland, lighted the lamp for him, and left. The boy found a dried salmon wrapped in parchment on the table, and what he knew to be the last and only cheese on the island, and a Testament with pages stained red and yellow by pressed flowers, and two pies.

The world just disappeared from your side, John Ireland thought over the next months; the people you knew were above the surface one minute, and under it the next, as if they had burst through ice. They went down stiff and upright in their filled gum boots and soaked skirts; they stood dead on the bottom and swayed with the currents like fixed kelp, his mother and father and sisters and brothers standing in a row on the ocean floor.

Miss Arvilla Pulver was a broad-shouldered, curly-headed thinker, who had a great hooting laugh few people ever heard. She boarded on the Shoreys and supplied them and the schoolhouse with wood. Of her island pupils she required the broad and shallow curriculum set by the county, and a great deal more *ab extra*, for she hoped to send at least one island youth to college, whither a single teacher had sent her. While she was at Oberlin, studying New Testament and American history, her father, her mother, and her brother back in Pittsburgh died of typhoid fever. It came from the public reservoir. The city fathers, who possessed private wells, would not raise taxes to filter the common water, lest they inhibit industrial growth, so typhoid fever ran from the tap in the yard; her family drank it and died. It made her sit up. Over time she had come to believe and pray that an educated, humane generation might actually arise from every American hamlet, and work selflessly for the nation, to break the power of the Interests, meliorate living and working conditions, ban corruption, end exploitation, and redistribute wealth. This was her program, and she would begin here.

Of the island pupils, only John Ireland Sharp seemed capable of entering that aerial world of scholars, educators, and reformers wherein she herself had found a purpose, a livelihood, and a home. He was a dark sprite of a boy who gazed at her gravely while she spoke, and set the other boys to laughing with low-voiced comments she heard distinctly, and sometimes found droll herself. Once, while she tried to look stern, her great hooting laugh broke forth and startled them all; the littlest Shorey started to cry. John Ireland was needle sharp. He sailed through his studies, borrowed her Dickens and her Eliot, borrowed her Berkeley and her Rousseau, and her *Life* of Thomas Jefferson.

"It is Cicero you will need, my boy," she had told him over the woodpile, "and Caesar, Virgil, Livy, and Ovid, in the Latin, and later Homer and Plutarch, in the Greek." Her pale eyes shone. She was young, with the skin of a baby and the swift erect movements of the little ones in her ABC class. Could she daunt him? She could not. He began with a will, in the schoolroom after the others had left. He twisted his legs under the bench, grasped one handful of his black hair, and lost himself in the firm channels of grammar, his mouth open, his pencil strangled near its tip, while she rinsed the desks and swept the floor. By April he had begun translating Caesar's *Gallic Wars*, and he loved the game of it, making the gibbering old general make sense. Privately, Miss Arvilla Pulver thought of the book as Caesar's galling wars.

When the Sharp family drowned in May, John Ireland was fifteen, and by local men's reckoning not an orphan but a young man without family who could peck and scrape his way like everyone else. Clarence Millstone offered to work him for shares at the fishery. John Ireland, for his part, had no heart for anything.

It seemed to him that his submerged family listed north and gestured towards Lummi Island every day when the sea flooded in from the Strait of Juan de Fuca, and listed south and gestured towards Whidbey Island when it drained back out. They swayed like singers in a chorus under the pillars of the sea, enraptured in its vaults. Deep in his mind he followed them down and swayed to dirges with them there, for he had more taste for their company than he ever knew, and there was nothing to do up here on this dumb-show shore, in such a world, where people staked other people to the earth, and God pinned people under the sea among crabs. For a year or two he could scarcely bear to look at the surface of the water, hating its gold-leaf insubstantiality which looked from above like the tender sky it reflected, and looked from below, he imagined, like the lid of a coffin, which it was.

He supposed he wished to continue his schooling. He could, Arvilla Pulver knew, leap from there to college, and fly from college to the world. Arvilla Pulver knew further that she could not herself see John Ireland through all his college entrance requirements. The most she could do was prepare him to be prepared by Miss Jean Zumwatt at her sunny Oberlin Academy, where scholars could work off board and tuition in chores. She told him about Oberlin Academy; wisely, she did not tell him that Miss Jean Zumwatt prized and cherished orphans in particular, and kept for them a bureau full of shoes.

Also fervent on the subject of orphans was Martha Obenchain. She was a famously warm and biddable beauty, whose hourglass figure, masses of dry, straw-colored hair, and marked, serene features were demonstrably the fairest on all the islands, and arguably the fairest on the coast. Not only the men and boys of Madrone and Orcas, and businessmen from the mainland, but also Lummi and Skyhomish men from the reservation, and Tlingits and Kwakiutls from British Columbia, and quarry workers from San Juan Island, independently invented the happy habit of dropping by the Obenchain place to borrow or return a grubbing hoe, to peddle a fish or a hide, or to inquire about the news or the weather.

When a seagoing canoe beached on the stones, or when a neighbor came larruping from around back of the house, Martha Obenchain, peeling potatoes at a table in the sun, rose and put the kettle on, tickled pink. She wore high-necked dresses in every season. Her simplicity and innocence bespoke her virtue. It was part of her character to possess pies in

every season. She grew La Gloire roses and La France roses, the exacti-
tudes of whose culture formed the burden of her discourse; she fed
unfledged flickers and red finches on mealworms and gruel. When people
spoke to her she nodded, rapt and pleased. She was not sensible of her
wide, sharp smile's displaying her perfect teeth; she was not sensible of the
ethereal tissue of skin around her eyes, so white it looked translucent and
lighted from within. When she learned that the Sharps had drowned and
left John Ireland, she seemed to hear bands of music playing.

Martha was the wife of Axel Obenchain, whom men found difficult
and whom she adored. She was the mother of Beal Obenchain, who troubled her, and of Nan Obenchain, who inherited and even magnified her
radiant grace, and who in pigtails dressed sheep for the island, salted mutton, and delivered it on a wooden sled. Now Martha would be the mother
of John Ireland Sharp, too—the foster mother—for she and Axel resolved
to take him in. They could fix him a bed on the pantry table, and roll it
up by day when Martha canned; she would not mind a bit.

Arvilla Pulver agreed it would be for the best; Clarence Millstone
shrugged and offered to help the boy transfer his belongings—"shift his
itkus"; Lee and Eliza Shorey were relieved.

John Ireland Sharp pitched a fit. Martha and Arvilla had called on
him late one day to give him the happy news. Coming in the door, they
discovered blue mussel shells on the table, and deduced that he had been
feeding on mud-flat fodder fit for hogs. They saw his fine-featured face lit
wildly from behind. He had let the fire go out and was wrapped in a
bearskin reading the Police Gazette on the bed in his boots by a cedar
torch, and that settled it. He would not go, he said, and ordered them out.
He slatted the mussel shells to the floor, and raised cain. Even as the two
women pocketed the Police Gazette, even as they led him from his door by
lantern light that flung their shadows enormous and swaying down the
beach grass, he continued to say through his limp hands that he was fine
where he was.

Within a week a peg-leg old soldier named Billy Teece was living in
the Sharp house. Billy Teece had been a Confederate prisoner during the
war, ordered to fight Indians in Montana; now he was loose in the West.
He nailed horseshoes and barnacles festively to the log walls outside, and
burned Tom Sharp's bench for fuel. Soon he had tamed a seal pup with
herrings. John Ireland kept passing by the house; manfully he sought to
accustom himself to bottom facts. Over the summer he borrowed books of

travels and military history from Billy Teece, and petted his baby-faced seal, which lolled on the hearth. As summer lowered into fall, he sometimes shared the old soldier's pan of potatoes. He played a game of hot potato with the seal. It beat going home.

CHAPTER XII

In Axel Obenchain's log barn, John Ireland milked a brown cow. Her calf bawled outside, and she answered. He had led her alone into the dark barn where he could tie her; he had closed the wobbly calf outside the door. Now he could barely see. He listened hard between the cow's despairing calls and the calf's, trying to hear the hissing milk change pitch as the bucket filled. She was giving a lot of milk these days. He had removed his hat to secure his forehead against her right flank below her rib cage, where it dipped. He felt her warmth and smelled the sweet milk, the manure in the gutter, harness leather, and the heady, fermenting hay. When he finished he untied her and opened the door to let her scramble out, so the calf could strip her while he milked the others.

The Obenchain family owned three mixed-breed cows. The cows ate ferns and brush all winter, and supplemental flakes of hay. When they bogged in the marsh, Axel Obenchain hauled them out with a rope. Axel and John Ireland, and occasionally Beal, milked and poured. Martha and Nan scalded the pails, pans, strainers, and cans in the kitchen. Martha churned, her hair bursting from its pins, and molded butter playfully in tubs. She could make sweet butter from soured cream by washing it well. Axel rowed the butter, and all the cordwood the green rowboat could hold, to Roche Harbor on San Juan Island—a two-day row—and sold it all to the Roche Harbor Lime Company, which housed dozens of hungry workmen. The family did well at this business; Axel Obenchain had a way with animals, and the market was good.

"Isn't it striking?" Martha Obenchain said at supper, and handed round the pan of biscuit. She had sent off for a china lamp, which now blazed from the table's center like a bonfire and sent her lashes' shadows flickering around her soft eyes. "I can see your faces."

John Ireland glanced up; his black hair flared over his ears where his hatbrim crimped it. "Yes, ma'am," he said, for no one answered. His foster mother smiled with her characteristic and unflagging delight; her small white teeth glistened; her barely restrained masses of dry blond hair caught the lamplight and wagged with her motions. She filled her dress of lavender-checked outing flannel, its skirt gathered tight; a fringe of lace tricked out its high neck, sleeves, and hem. Beneath her dress she wore for a bustle an opened tomato can threaded on a string and tied around her waist; she wore flour-sack drawers, and looked like a million dollars.

Back and forth from the stove moved young Nan, graceful and listless. She leaned into the lamplight to pinch spilled salt and throw it over her left shoulder. A nimbus of glints shone around her golden head and moved when she moved, and her pigtails swayed. Sometimes at supper she knocked on wood with a knuckle or pointed a wedge of pie away from someone's heart.

Axel Obenchain had asked the blessing; when he tucked his head, his beard spread over his shirt. Now he sat, red-eyed and furred as a bear, and addressed a forked potato by biting off both ends. John Ireland at his elbow felt his foster father's brute size, and felt his thick, soothing sense of his own worth and the worth of others. He had slightly more use for children as a class than Tom Sharp had, though John Ireland longed for his father. Together by day, comfortably silent, Axel and John Ireland scythed, raked, tedded, and shocked rye and bluestem grass for hay. They spread manure from a wheelbarrow. They sharpened and greased their tools. They fought back the second growth with ax and brush hook, and burned it. They whipsawed lumber by hand and built a henhouse. Now, in the dead of winter, the hens were warm and still laying—laying "cackle-berries," as Martha Obenchain called eggs.

Still, Axel Obenchain seemed a remote wonder and a freak to the boy, as his grandfather had seemed during their trip up the Skagit—too experienced in unimaginable worlds, too magnified to grasp. John Ireland had missed the pioneers in their glory, and like the other boys who grew up hearing about them, he despaired of himself and of his puny and pampered generation, and hoped, but doubted, they could make it up to the world somehow. Martha talked about her husband tirelessly, even when he was nigh, and recommended his virtues to all her gentleman callers; she described him to his own children, and praised him especially to John Ireland Sharp, the passive expression on whose alert, dark features led people to tell him things. She told him stories he thought about when he worked by Axel's side.

Axel Obenchain arrived in Washington Territory from Hamburg when he was seventeen. His German-speaking family joined a wagon train from Council Bluffs, Iowa, and he signed on as a paid stockman with another family. His parents stopped in Oregon, but he kept going. He walked with the train's oxen all day, led them across rivers, bathed their eyes and feet, and found them grass. Martha judged that he had been an A-1 drover, surpassing all others; he was a big, red-faced youth who knew his duty.

Axel wanted to learn English; a German farmer in the train had advised him to learn all the English he could. In Olympia, Washington, an innkeeper directed him to a lumber camp up on the Skagit River. He contracted for a year's heavy labor replacing a trampled bullwhacker for the lumber camp. He knew that he would learn to speak to the hook-tender, the hand-skidder, and the men who worked the saws in the timber while he goaded his ox teams down the skid road. In the spring, throughout the summer, and all fall he worked through daylight; he chained, yoked, and led the pale oxen, which wore brass balls on the points of their horns. Except at meals—no one talked at meals—he talked to the men everywhere. His accent improved. Soon all the men could understand everything he said, and he could say most of what he wanted to say. When the mountain snows piled up, the camp moved in a body; the men transferred downriver to shanties on the Skagit delta flats.

On Axel Obenchain's first night down out of the mountains, he walked alone into the sloughside trading station they called a town. He found a saloon and stepped up in his calked boots to the bar. He was eighteen, a man bigger than any man in the saloon that night, and proud of his hardness. He asked for a whiskey.

The saloonkeeper asked him a question. He repeated his request for a whiskey. The saloonkeeper fingered his mustaches.

He asked for a beer. The saloonkeeper evidently could not understand him, and, mein Gott, he could certainly not understand the saloonkeeper. The saloonkeeper called other men to him, kindly, and they put to him shouted questions he could not answer. He gave his name and pointed to his chest. The men in the saloon asked more questions. Covered with confusion, Axel Obenchain left the saloon and walked back along the winter beach to his shanty. Only when the other men returned from their drinking did he determine something that—he ultimately told Martha, and she told John Ireland, laughing helplessly and rocking by the stove—he should have determined earlier: the loggers were Finns, and he had learned Finnish in the logging camp.

* * *

Now they were eating boiled venison Beal had shot, though he was not there. Beal had a spotted yellow dog, Bonaparte, which he trained to herd deer into the water. Deer swam smartly in the water—and gazed around calmly, balancing their antlers—but they were slow, and easy to hit; Beal shot them with a Kentucky rifle. When he dragged in a deer he weighted its spread legs with beach stones and driftwood to clean it. His mother boiled the meat in canning jars and stored it over John Ireland's pantry bed beside the jars of floating sow belly, beside the jars of pink salmon whose black skin detached and swayed when he crossed the floor, beside the pink rhubarb, the cow beef, and the swollen berries for pie.

Axel distrusted his son Beal, and thought him a shirker, but he reflected that his own father had thought him a shirker, too, so perhaps it was the way of the world. Five years before, on the other side of the island, Axel shot a big buck off a cliff, and was skinning it on the beach. Beal was small then, long-headed, and watching. Axel had opened up the deer and was taking out the intestine, when the deer woke up, and opened its rolling eyes. The boy picked up a loop of intestine and ran off with it down the beach, while the deer tried to rise and follow. It kicked at Axel; he struggled to hold it down, to avoid its hooves and rack of antlers, and to slit its throat. He saw the boy running down the beach, with the gut trailing after him like a streamer. It uncoiled slick from the deer's belly like rope paying out from a tub, while the deer tried to run after it. The belly emptied before Axel could get the animal quieted.

Of course, he told himself later, the boy was young then, but still, he had not liked it. He doubted his father had thought him cunning, as he began to think Beal cunning. He suspected him—on no real evidence—of extorting from Nan some, if not all, of her sheep earnings, which properly belonged to the family. Sometimes when he entered the house at odd hours, the talk in the room broke off, and either Martha or Nan, at work, looked agitated, while Beal, standing with his hat on, in a pale sweat, gave out a radiant smile and left.

Beal ate at odd hours. He was fourteen now, as tall as his father, rumpled of forehead and fitful. He had stopped going to school that winter. Miss Arvilla Pulver was glad to see him gone—he was, she told Clarence Millstone in private, "a case of bad behavior." She meant he was a coward who studied bullying; observation had already taught Miss Arvilla Pulver that most cowards did. Beal worked for Clarence Millstone, making beach fires on the tideline and netting the sparkling blue herring the fires drew. They cleaned the herring, smoked it, and packed it in barrels. He mended net; he shaved barrel staves; he rowed to Victoria for hoops. Catching fish, it turned out, took a hundred years. Beal persuaded his mother to let him spend most of his pay on lamp oil to read by, and he slept that winter in the barn.

John Ireland kept out of Beal's way. He milked in the barn when Beal was gone. They used separate paths through the woods, and when they met on the beach, which was the island's highway, one of them, by turns, moved back into the woods. In early summer Beal had tried secretively, smiling his winning, eager smile, to get John Ireland to help him build a dock. John Ireland refused, and walked deliberately within Axel's earshot. Beal got Nan to build his dock, and she was still working on it—her yellow pigtails tied back with a strip of muslin while she straightened nails and hauled driftwood lumber and logs—in November, when a storm on high tide carried its wrecked parts off. John Ireland was a grown man before it struck him that when they were boys on the island, Beal had possibly often been afraid of him, John Ireland.

CHAPTER XIII

After supper, John Ireland took a lantern outside. A freezing northeast wind cleared the sky. Out to sea, waves broke row on row, and their stripes of foam shone weakly in the starlight. Nan had in mind to replace her mutton sled's runners. She had asked John Ireland to help her, for she was plain mashed on the dark-eyed boy. He never noticed, then or later. Nan was thirteen . She had cached a plank in wild roses down the beach; now, shivering beside beach grass before the house, she scraped the barnacles from it with a stone. She watched John Ireland labor with red hands, trying to rip it along its length with a crosscut saw. He had pulled his round hat low against the wind, so she could not see his eyes, only the lamplit concentration in his curved mouth. He set the lumber pieces on edge and toenailed them to her bloodstained sled—a fir slab smoothed with sand.

"Go on in and get warm," John Ireland said to Nan. "We can sand the runners tomorrow." He handed her the lantern, and she took it into the house. Waves splashed glowing on the beach and rolled stones. Overhead the hard stars uttered their gibberish from horizon to horizon. How loose he seemed to himself, under the stars! The spaces between the stars were pores, out of which human meaning evaporated. John Ireland pocketed the nails, picked up the hammer and saw, and headed around the house to the barn.

The barn door was open a crack; a light from inside cut a yellow slash on the frozen dust and grass. From outside, John Ireland quietly looked through the door. There was Beal's bent back, and the new calf's tan hindquarters between his legs. He was straddling the calf and strong-arming its head in a twist. A candle on the floor threw the six-legged shadow on the barn logs. The calf's legs skidded and sought a purchase. Beal lifted its head and held its shoulders between his knees; he stepped and John Ireland ducked back. He looked again and saw Beal's hatted head bent down, his long ears half out, and the limp curls trailing over his dark jacket collar. He was wearing Axel's gum boots. The calf's eyes rolled and showed crescents of white. Beal held its lower jaw in his right hand and bore it around, and the calf's neck stretched so its muzzle faced first backwards, then spiraled on around towards the front. John Ireland watched in the shadow and urged himself to step forward, perhaps brandishing the hammer.

Abruptly Beal let it go and stepped off. The calf dropped on its forelegs, got to its feet, and hung its head; its fast breaths showed as vanishing puffs of vapor. Beal walked towards the wall behind which John Ireland stood, and John Ireland held his breath. Beal returned to the light carrying a crowbar, caught the skittering calf, wrapped a double length of jute baling twine loosely around its neck, and tied it. He placed the crowbar inside the loop and swiveled the crowbar end over end. He was astride the calf's ribs and the calf struggled. As the crowbar turned, loops built up on the baling twine neatly. At six or seven loops, the calf's head dropped as the Skagit Indian's head had dropped on its stake, like a weight in a bag. Its legs stilled and sagged. Beal lifted its head by the crowbar; his legs gripped its flanks again, and he continued to wind the crowbar.

At the moment when John Ireland judged that the twine must break, Beal stopped. He arrested the crowbar with one hand, raised his head and looked around. John Ireland ducked back. He ducked back into the wide starlight and crept down the path to the house, to the frosted back door which led to the pantry and his bed. He could return the tools to the barn tomorrow. He went to bed in his clothes and lay awake. An owl called from the fir forest. How could an owl think it was spring?

* * *

After several minutes, Beal in the barn lowered the calf's body to the ground and stepped over it. His eyes looked blurred and glassy, and his left shoulder slewed down. He began to unwind the crowbar but its ends hit the ground or the calf's hip. This calf had been nothing but trouble: too stubborn to throttle, and it even bit his thumb. He had had a bellyful of it. He cut the twine with a knife.

As the twine snapped he felt his own bonds loosen. The empty, extinguishing grief he had been carrying for no reason was lifting. It had been an airless demon that blew him into bits and hammered and scattered the bits. Sometimes it pinned him so he could not move; a few days before he had stood on the beach, a hollow boy still as a log in front of his own cabin, while it pounded him like a piling into the sand. Now he felt his own substance begin to fill its place. Whenever he noticed it was lifting, he knew it was as good as gone, and he rose as vast clouds rise on a fair afternoon.

Exhilarated, he tossed the dead calf over his shoulders, carried it to the green rowboat, and rowed it offshore, where he dumped it. The water was wildly rough; he took the troughs on his quarter, skidding down, and clawed up slopes feeling his lungs fill and his arms grow in power. He would live among the living, and not suffer.

The next morning Beal rose exultant and descended to the family breakfast table, where his excited mother asked one question too many, and required him to glare and silence her. John Ireland bolted his mush and left. Martha, distressed, apologized for intruding and talking too much; Nan apologized for bumping him with his bowl. His mood this morning was forgiving, and expansive, and they recognized it, so they called themselves to his attention so they could see the deep smile he ordinarily bestowed only outside the family.

Beal pushed up from the table. He had a free rein for his projects now, and his life before him, for Clarence Millstone, who never ceased taking advantage of him, had let him go in a temper, when Beal called him a "son of perdition." No matter. He had escaped again, and gloriously, with his life, when he had believed lately that only death could relieve him. One stubborn calf, in a world of calves? Did his accusers know how very much more he would sacrifice? Did they know how courageous he was, in fact, and how willfully in control, to muster out of his paralysis the vitality to save himself?

* * *

That spring John Ireland flailed peas in Axel Obenchain's barn. He weeded carrots and rhubarb, and hulled dried popcorn off the cob into a can. He finished the *Gallic Wars* and started on Cornelius Nepos. He took up botany with Billy Teece, and found the frail sweet cicely hidden along sheep paths; its ferny leaves precisely fulfilled their destined forms, and its stem grew square like a mint's. In the forest, pink bells appeared on the salal bushes, and white flowers bloomed on the dogwood and salmonberry. The varied thrush abruptly took up its song midstream, as though sunlight had poked it. The hummingbirds returned the day the butterflies emerged; frogs wailed in the marsh, and the summer constellations swung up out of the sea.

In men and women on Madrone Island, daylight developed cracks through which the northbound light streamed onto forgotten scenes. Tableaux in strong light, and strong shadow, arose on the smell of broken loam, and haunted the lengthening afternoons. Clarence Millstone, fetching a bleached doeskin to the Shoreys as a present for their new baby, recalled a friend who died of chill twenty years earlier, after swimming his swamped canoe ashore. Martha Obenchain, who smelled of mildew, ground fishbones for her roses with a rolling pin, and thought of Axel as she first saw him, pumping water with his hat off, right nobly, and washing his hands. Axel Obenchain remembered losing a team to thirst on the overland road, where one dying white ox, Belle, eyed him tenderly from the yellow ground, as if with understanding.

John Ireland, pale as a field mushroom, knelt to hill potatoes by the dooryard. He noted that two years had elapsed since he and his father had rowed the red skiff up to this silent island and settled the family in. Three and a half years ago, he and his father had journeyed up the Skagit River to survey the Skagit passes in the high Cascades. Kneeling this day in the sandy ground by the Obenchains' door, he tallied his losses soberly, and tamped the earth about the vine stems one by one. Ordinarily he thought little about himself, but now he recalled that on the Skagit River he had been a careless Whatcom schoolboy, who said, "It really grinds me," when he found the river water cold.

One fair day, every man and boy on the island, and Nan Obenchain, spread out and herded all the sheep from one end of the island to the other. They drove the foolish sheep through the grass openings and hill pastures to the narrow southern sand spit by the sea, where Beal and John Ireland had fought. Down on the sand and beach rye, the stiff lambs jumped as if the ground itself were tossing them or flicking them. There on the sand spit the women, gladdened from rowing, met the sheep penning with a picnic. The sky was calm and streaked high overhead, and the beach was dry and airy, unfamiliar. The sea smelled, and the wild rose that grew in the rye. They all drank hot tea under the circling terns that peered into the braided standing wave at the tip of the spit.

A blade crew had sailed from East Sound that morning; their sloop stood Indian-anchored offshore, a line from its bow hitched to a beach log. While the blade crew sheared wool, the islanders culled the lambs and bound the earlies to sell for three dollars a head. They medicated sheep's sore feet and marked their ears. John Ireland saw his family's sheep, painted with two stripes of poke juice, and he turned them over to the Obenchains for his keep, though Martha protested and wrapped him in an embrace from behind, and he stiffened.

CHAPTER XIV

1885, Whatcom

On the night of November 1, 1885, the Whatcom elementary school principal, John Ireland Sharp, stood indoors wringing his hands. He was twenty-six years old, a small, neat-headed, carelessly dressed man whose expression, ordinarily courteous and alert, was grim. Through his parlor window he saw blazing lights draw closer. He heard a wet slapping of feet and, as the lights approached, murmurs.

"Stay back," he said to his radiant wife, Pearl, who loved a parade, and who was finding the thought of a parade in the dark of night especially enchanting. Pearl was the former Pearl Rush, a striking black-haired beauty, whose parents founded the town of Whatcom. John Ireland and Pearl had been married for four years; their sons, Cyrus and Vincent, were upstairs, asleep. Peering into the dense, shifting shadows outside, John Ireland recognized top-heavy Jim McGusty, his colleague in the reformist People's Party. McGusty held a lantern at the head of the shambling crowd, and its flame illumined patches of his open, youthful face. McGusty worked at the sawmill, and he and John Ireland met twice a month at the Blue Moon Saloon to talk politics.

"John Ireland Sharp," McGusty called out. "John Ireland!" The crowd halted for a moment, turned towards the house, and lowered their coal-oil torches. "Aren't you with us?" John Ireland stood still in the parlor and said nothing.

The crowd turned and went on. The torchlight glazed the wet backs of greatcoats and jackets; the people looked like turtles. Over John Ireland's head, Pearl was looking for faces, as he was. The public-spirited minister was there, hunched against the drizzle; he was formerly the mayor of San Francisco. The town assessor was there, Judge Carby, and the county road commissioner, John Hathaway Myers, and his gimpy wife, with her shawl tied over her hat. These men, like most in the crowd, were new members of the Knights of Labor, who had joined, John Ireland suspected, for this occasion. The marchers were quiet. The mud on Lambert Street softened their tramping. After they passed, John Ireland could mark their passage up Lambert Street and down Elm by the wavering yellow light their torches cast up house walls.

John Ireland stood limp at the window long after Pearl had retired. He was so ghastly pale, the freckles on his forehead seemed to float above his skin. He was not a sagacious man, but rather a fastidious one, and he was feeling—feeling down to his carpet slippers—that socialism had failed. Last week members of his own People's Party, men and women to whom he had devoted his highest allegiance, called a mass meeting in Whatcom. There they determined to expel all Chinese people from town by November first. Two Chinese men owned laundries in Whatcom, and another twenty-five or so worked at clearing the forest. At the meeting, people resolved to drive from the region, town by town, these contraband Mongolian slaves, as the Whatcom Bugle Call identified them, who spread vice and disease, and degraded honest labor. There was another depression on. The Central Pacific had laid its track, and Chinese men washed up on the coast looking for work, like everyone else; they worked for cheap. "Politely," the paper said, the People's Party's local leaders called on the Chinese men and told them they should leave. They left. Now November first had come, the Chinese men had gone, and the town was holding a torchlight parade to celebrate. Congregational ministers had sought to prevent the expulsion, in vain. At the window, John Ireland scratched his chest, unwittingly, at the same spot over and over.

It was leaders of the People's Party, too, who called the Congress of Sinophobes. The Congress of Sinophobes, heralded and approved by all the papers, would have its first meeting two days hence, on November third, in Seattle. People in eight districts had elected men to the congress; Whatcom's representative was Jim McGusty. John Ireland was following everything in the papers, irresolute. Should he miss this meeting, as he had missed the town meeting?

As it happened, on that day Pearl seemed to need him at home. The Congress of Sinophobes elected the mayor of Tacoma as its head. The Chinese Exclusion Act forbade new immigration; the problem at hand was ridding the territory of those already here. The next day in Tacoma a mob, in the guise of battling the Interests, herded the "pigtailed" Chinese into boxcars and shipped them to Portland, Oregon. The Interests—the owners—had imported the tiny Chinese as cheap labor, the Sinophobes said. After the boxcars left with the Chinese, the crowd burned their houses.

John Ireland had supported the reform movement since his island boyhood. After college he had engaged as a schoolteacher in New York, on Manhattan's East Side. Here at last was the cindery thick of things, the incontrovertibly real world. Here a young educator could lead his pupils from wretchedness towards enlightenment by showing them the corruption and vice of the system that entrapped and victimized them. John Ireland was by then a short, full-grown man, languid in manner, delicately molded and dark in feature, and zealous to share the fruits of his own victory over despair. It was rough work. His scholars slept through school because they worked nights in steam factories and mills. Their tubercular mothers, appearing wild-eyed at the school, took occasional and surprisingly muscular swings at him on general principles. Their laboring fathers, whom he never met but saw in type, were angry or broken; they blunted their misery with whiskey, and talked of striking it, somehow, rich. When they lost their jobs to immigrants—who signed on at the docks for starvation wages before they knew the price of living—these men stood in breadlines. Many lived on sidewalks and warmed themselves at bonfires of trash. Then their children stopped coming to school; the children slept on hay barges on the East River. John Ireland saw them there, more than once: in each of the several hundred docked barges, the heads of sleeping children protruded from nests of hay shipped down the Hudson for the city's horses.

He wanted to teach his knife-carrying boys and sullen girls Cicero, as he had been taught Cicero as his ticket out of his world. How could he articulate to their families in the flophouses, or to the bony children themselves, that they needed Cicero in the long run—or at least literacy and simple reckoning—instead of the children's wages for medicine, plumbing, heat, meat, room, bed, funeral, burial plot, and gravestone now? His fellow teachers abandoned the struggle and quit to join the scramble for dollars.

"A man can make quite a strike importing cork," one colleague told him. Another, when he quit his teaching post to sell advertisements, crowed, "I can feel my money feathers start to grow!"

One afternoon at an auction he witnessed the owner of the Best shoe factory slap down $105,000 in cash and bonds for a chestnut racehorse. Earlier that same day his most promising and endearing pupil, a quick Sicilian boy who was a born scholar, told him manfully, shaking hands, that he was leaving school to work for five dollars a week in the Best shoe factory, where his parents and sisters also worked, so the family could eat. He wanted to for the sake of his sisters, the boy said with a significant look—apparently hoping John Ireland would understand what he grasped only later, that the family was trying to prevent or delay the sisters' falling perforce to prostitution.

During those days in New York, John Ireland followed the construction of the dazzling Vanderbilt house on Fifth Avenue, which cost three million dollars in Caen marble and Louis XV furnishings from a French palace. In the Hunt stables, the horses retired for the night dressed in linen embroidered with the Hunt family crest. The uptown swells paid two thousand dollars a day for suites on transatlantic steamers; sensitive travelers, the papers reported, brought their own cooks and physicians. The mother of one of his flophouse pupils was a professional pickpocket; another mother was a "thumper," who tried to feed her family by robbing rich men in hotel bedrooms.

Here in the Northwest after his marriage, here on the frontier where a family could still farm a claim, hunt, and live on clams, John Ireland continued to hear the sighing and lamentation of the cities. He penned jeremiads for the paper denouncing the Interests. He cheered socialist speakers in Seattle and Tacoma; he recruited Whatcom reformers and held Wednesday night meetings in his parlor on Lambert Street. He read Charles Fourier, called himself a Fourierist, and tried to entice first his wife and then his tall friend, Clare Fishburn, into founding with him a summertime phalanstery on Madrone Island. He wrote speeches for, and gave money to, any local politician who might help prevent, on this fresh and democratic coast, runaway capitalism, and the hellish exploitation and inequity he had seen in the East. Last spring John Ireland had contributed two months' salary to the populist cause of Mary Kenworthy. Mary Kenworthy was an inspired leader and a thoughtful and articulate thinker. She lived in Seattle, a widow; she called the rich "our dog-salmon aristocracy." John Ireland quarreled bitterly with Pearl over the money.

This winter, however—the winter of the torchlight parade and the Congress of Sinophobes—when John Ireland wandered off to hear Mary Kenworthy speak in Seattle, she no longer addressed the rights of man. Instead the slender, black-haired orator listed the wrongs of "Chinamen." She roused the crowd by calling all moderates on the Chinese question "lackeys of those thieves who stole our timber and coal lands." No one gainsaid her. When later Judge Burke, an Irishman, spoke out to urge the rule of constitutional law, people booed him in person, and the newspapers ridiculed him in print. When Methodist ministers spoke out to urge Christian charity, people ignored them. A new law forbade Chinese people's owning real property. John Ireland had written articles for the labor newspaper, the *Seattle Call*. Now this same newspaper called the Chinese "scurvy opium fiends" and "rat-eating," "chattering, round-mouthed lepers."

CHAPTER XV

1886, Seattle

Early Sunday morning, February 7, 1886, John Ireland walked to the Ocean Dock from a Seattle fleabag hotel. Fresh-faced Jim McGusty had tipped him off; he caught the last Seattle steamer on Saturday. He told himself he was curious to see what happened. Now the morning sky was low and gray, and it was raining lightly.

John Ireland saw, on the lampposts between the hotel and the dock, wet homemade signs. The signs called all Chinese men "John": "Go

Home, John," "Go, John," and "Right Now." While he was sauntering through the gray-and-black waterfront with his hands in his pockets, mobs of men were entering the shanties of three hundred and fifty Chinese men, and bearing the men away. John Ireland knew, or suspected strongly, that this was happening; he knew it for certain when he saw, blackening a distant waterfront street, the crowd.

The workers, dressed in dark jackets and coats, were herding the Chinese men, in blue or black tunics, down to the Ocean Dock, to ship them to San Francisco. The Chinese men walked softly in their white-soled shoes. Onlookers—men and women—collected near John Ireland, in front of a wooden warehouse. More onlookers, swinging sticks, followed the workers, who drove the Chinese. As the loose crowd approached the foot of Main Street, John Ireland was struck by its silence. Boots knocked on the plank street. When the crowd reached the dock, onlookers cheered, jeered, and tossed their caps. The Chinese men kept their heads down; people were beginning to strike them. Some wore pale coolie hats, flat at the top, which made targets.

The black steamship *Queen of the Pacific,* bound for San Francisco, was tied up at Ocean Dock. Its bulk blocked the dull light from sea and sky. When the gangplank creaked out and its wheels met the wood dock, the men in the crowd tried to press the Chinese men on board. The steamship's purser, a short man whose tight uniform showed the deep arch of his chest, stopped them. The captain stood above him at the ship's rail. A respectful delay revealed that only nine Chinese men had the requisite seven-dollar fare to San Francisco.

"Look in their money belts!" The men nearest John Ireland were restive. "They wear all their gold in money belts under their pajamas," a big logger in stagged trousers confided to John Ireland. "Only some of them," put in a clean-shaven expert. "The others squirrel it away under their floorboards."

Uniformed policemen, wearing wet silver stars, milled about, greeting their friends. Mayor Yesler came, and the sheriff. Soon everyone on the dock heard the fire bell ringing its alarm. The fire bell would bring from their comfortable breakfast tables the Home Guard—moderate Seattle men armed with rifles and shotguns, who had sworn to protect the Chinese men's constitutional rights. The moderates held that people should expel the Chinese by persuasion, not force. "Oh, look," said a toothless old man near John Ireland. He gestured, and John Ireland saw horses drawing onto the dock two open wagons heaped with the Chinese men's household goods. "They're doing this decent. That's the only way, I say."

The nine Chinese men paid their fares, walked up the gangplank, and disappeared through a companionway. Below, John Ireland shrank from a hat passed through the murmuring crowd. Suddenly Mary Kenworthy, slim in a black dress and jacket, jumped on a crate, gleeful, to shout up to "Captain Alexander, sir!" that the passed hat had produced six hundred dollars. John Ireland forgot, in the moment's press, that by expelling the Chinese workers, Mary Kenworthy was earnestly trying to relieve her neighbors' want. Her pale face shone before the black hull like Moses' on Sinai; her cultured voice carried, and the crowd hushed. She waved a piece of paper—a promissory note, she cried, guaranteeing the balance of the fares, fifteen hundred dollars.

The captain at the rail did not buy it. Through a bullhorn he said that only another eighty-five men could board, on the cash in the hat. "Damn your eyes," shouted up a man in the crowd. John Ireland could see the waffle-iron scar on his face from a logger's calked boots. The captain said the next steamer, the *Elder*, was due in six days. "Damn your eyes," the scarred fellow said again, conversationally. "I'll skin them alive," John Ireland heard. No smoke came from the *Queen of the Pacific*'s stack. Rain pocked the water. On the dock, the purser began separating the Chinese men slowly; John Ireland saw his delicate hands on their muscular shoulders. "We come up from Tacoma for this," a pale whelp told the big logger. "Every one of them devils as hisses, by Christ, better get on board and scoot off to sea damned quick."

In the confusion of men, John Ireland saw a rough Whatcom man named Ajax. He knew that the Semiahmoo cannery fired Joe Ajax every winter; he knew that the Ajax children shared one pair of shoes and took turns at his school, that the baby had died of whooping cough, the mother was sick on her feet. He greeted Joe Ajax, who glared; in a hand blue with cold, he was carrying a wet cowhide billy. John Ireland glimpsed Beal Obenchain, too, head above the crowd, his gaze animated, his dark lips pursed. Men were shoving the Chinese men, who drew together. Most wore queues and the loose, thin, collarless suits that everyone called pajamas.

Near John Ireland, one long-jawed man in a black tunic held up a blue cloth bundle to protect his head; a blow knocked the bundle from his hands. When he leaned to retrieve it from the dock, a woman's buttoned brown shoe appeared, stepped on his wrist, and held it. The crowd parted. With a limp, almost comical gesture of the fingers, the trapped hand signaled "Uncle." The shoe lifted, the arm withdrew. The shoe kicked the bundle away, while John Ireland watched, curious, and the crowd drew together. A bent fragment detached from the crowd; the blue-shawled figure of a young woman, intent, followed the bundle to kick it repeatedly and finally knocked it overboard into the chuck.

At the top of the gangplank, the steamer's purser solemnly toted up and took the men's fares from the hat. The line up the gangplank was a single file. John Ireland kept track of the long-jawed man on the dock who had lost his bundle. When that man eventually achieved the safety of the gangplank, John Ireland studied his black-tunic-clad, straight back, as if he might read some expression there.

Abruptly John Ireland backed off the dock and started down the waterfront towards the steamer for Whatcom. Someone had just struggled through the crowd—"I'm from Judge Greene's office"—to present Captain Alexander with a piece of paper, which made the captain halt proceedings entirely, and propelled John Ireland into leaving. If the paper was, as rumor had it, a writ of habeas corpus, then the captain would have to release the Chinese people from the ship. They would walk down the gangplank and into the mob.

At the same moment, rounding onto the dock, marched the Home Guard—a batch of richly dressed young lawyers and old clergymen. White-faced, they marched upright and out of step; they carried rifles and shotguns. John Ireland judged this as good a time as any to go home.

Nothing in his experience altered him more, not even his falling in love, for from boyhood he trusted his judgment, and he had given the movement his whole heart. "God help me," he said to himself on the Seattle dock, "I was wrong." By then he had concluded that socialism had not failed. He himself had failed, intellectually, by misjudging badly, for ten years, its champions here on earth. If the allegiance that his thinking produced was worthless, he had wasted his life. In the riot from which he made a timely and judicious exit on the dock that day—the riot that broke out when the Chinese men disembarked from the steamer—five people were wounded and a logger was killed.

Later six Sinophobes stood trial for conspiracy and the grand jury freed them. One of the Sinophobe leaders tried for conspiracy was George

Venable Smith, a sincere socialist thinker, who called his indictment for conspiracy "an attack upon free speech, upon the rights of labor, upon every man who earns his living not by speculation and plunder but by the sweat of his brow." Having rid the region of Chinese, George Venable Smith formed a high-minded cooperative colony on Puget Sound. The People's Party swept the next election. By then John Ireland Sharp was the principal of the new high school. He continued to study and reflect, but he had no hope for it, and the habit was sad as a hobby.

In the weeks after he witnessed the mob on the Seattle dock, as John Ireland toiled in his principal's office and walked to elementary classrooms, the memory of that one Chinese man's narrow back, in a row of black queues and straight backs on the gangplank, returned to his mind. The wet black cloth hung loosely from the man's shoulder blades, and it rose and fell visibly as he breathed. John Ireland realized that the rising and falling back reminded him of something, which he soon identified: the Viking blood eagle. He had read that the blood eagle was an artistic and favored torture of the Vikings. With an ax, the Viking split his victim's back; quickly, skillfully, he drew out the lungs on their bronchial branch and called his friends over to watch as, with the victim's final gasps, his bleeding lungs flapped, like the wings of an eagle.

As a moral thinker, John Ireland admitted the categories right and wrong only, and could not compass or endure complexity, misstep, or paradox. If the socialists were wrong about the Chinese, they were corrupt. He washed his hands of them—here was an act—and renounced all their pomps and works, and relinquished the movement to which he had devoted ten years. In effect he also removed himself from situations that might test his courage. He abandoned all social writers to their utopias and toy soldiers, and left himself nothing. Literature pained him, and science addressed nothing of moment. One day, a week after the scene on the Seattle dock, he found two unemployed Chinese men loose on the streets of Whatcom. They were brothers—one thickly built and one wiry. He hired them for his household, hid them, and ignored them. He did not inquire about their experiences, and he decidedly did not attempt to interest them in their rights.

He stayed home. He held no more reform meetings. Halfheartedly he began keeping notes on the weather, which big winds concocted here where the North Pacific met the mountains.

On the mainland of North America, the sole object for which he altered his routines was Mount Baker. For the sight of its remote glaciers and snows he sometimes hired a buggy and drove north from Whatcom and onto the Nooksack River plain. Many days the hazy sky hid the volcano's cone, and then John Ireland pleased himself by finding patches of glaciated white heights above the sky, higher than clouds. People had climbed to Mount Baker's summit now. Sometimes the crater smoked, and John Ireland thought of Pliny, who asphyxiated when he rushed to investigate the eruption of Mount Vesuvius. Pliny also reported that strong men, and brave men, possessed "hearts all hairy." As John Ireland's sons grew, he took them fishing on Sundays.

BOOK III

EUSTACE
AND MINTA

CHAPTER XVI

1874, Baltimore

Eleven years earlier, in the spring of 1874, Minta Randall, of Baltimore, Maryland, turned to say, "Thank you, Marsha," when that servant set before her a flat bowl of terrapin soup. The soup's vapor condensed on her spectacles; she saw the many ruddy faces in the dining room blurred. Curving silver, porcelain, and crystal gave back the candles' flames in gleams. At twenty-three, Minta had grown up to be lamentably short, mothers agreed, but regular of feature, and kind of heart, if unrealistic. Her head was square, and her limbs were round; her jawline sloped; her brown hair she had pinned into a bun. For this occasion she wore the same gown of blue brocaded silk that she had worn to every second dinner, cotillion, and ball all spring, for she had few gowns; the vanity of dress fittings wore at her spirits. In a few weeks she would have no use for new gowns. Minta tasted the soup and tried to catch her myopic mother's eye with a smile. Her sister, June, sixteen, spotted her from far down the table, gestured towards their fragile mother with a pickle fork, and rolled her enormous eyes.

On Minta's either side at the head of the long table sat two men whose presence she felt keenly. Her father, Senator Green Randall, was a stout, coiled man who was bald save for a crisp ring of black hair that circled his head. He was bending the full, welcoming force of his attention on Mrs. Honer, the red-nosed matron tricked out in rubies who would be Minta's mother-in-law. At Minta's right sat Eustace Honer himself, his stiff back unbending a bit with the wine, whom she would marry tomorrow. From his very sleeve and solemn cheek seemed to spring a torrent of awareness that threatened to topple her.

Eustace was the second of four Honer brothers; they had four older sisters. He was broad-shouldered and square-headed, fervid and quiet; he moved energetically, smiled rarely and widely. Minta knew him from childhood, when he learned poetry, dashed about on tall horses, flogged his resolute way through the Knapp School, and played fiercely at lacrosse—a game their friends the Penniman boys introduced into the United States. His family, who exported tobacco under the Honer name, was neither English nor Episcopalian, but they had lived in Baltimore since the Revolutionary War, and had sufficiently broken away from the music-loving, book-reading, theater-going German community to mingle with the higher, if emptier, English society, to ride to hounds, dine at the oldest clubs, and present their daughters at the Bachelors Cotillion. Minta fancied she would have loved him, for his particularly moving blend of qualities, if his family had been cannibals.

Minta had been drawn to him—as she put it to herself at first—for three years, since one June evening at croquet on her own lawn, when he had looked at her over his shoulder and she had felt herself tumbling forward into his eyes. He played croquet as if it were a noble and agreeable duty; he stayed on the lawn alone after his friends left for the night. From her chamber Minta heard wood strike wood. She looked down from her window: fireflies rose under the oaks, and beyond on the moonlit grass moved the sober figure of Eustace, broad and bent to his task. Now he sat at table subdued and patient; of course, she thought, a formal dinner afforded his enterprise no scope. She studied the reddish skin of his wrist, where his cuff creased it.

When Eustace finished his course at the University of Virginia three years ago, he mentioned at a hunt dinner that he proposed to mine diamonds in Johannesburg. He sought backing from bankers. He grew a faraway look and rode off alone after hunts. The following summer he told Senator Randall after church that he had newly resolved to establish a pearl trade in Papeete; he began to haunt the harbor and thump schooners. Within six months he confided to Minta, between quadrilles at a ball, that he had settled on inspecting the Gobi Desert for science. People lost interest in Eustace Honer, and when he spoke wistfully of teaching the Gospel to Apaches, they nodded, and when he proposed to farm on Puget Sound, they changed the subject.

Minta Randall alone, who loved Eustace, saw that his chief characteristic was steadfastness. It was unswerving devotion he had to give. He sought a consuming task.

Senator Randall sat back and conversed wholeheartedly with Mrs. Honer. His pale, soft features, and his pleased, warm expression, masked his mental alertness; he was making a catalogue and index to every speck of family information her conversation yielded, for that was his habit. Everything interested him, and the complexity of families' relations and fortunes was a marvel. As he watched the red tip of Mrs. Honer's handsome nose brighten while she talked, and as he remembered all she said, he was also sensible of—and he easily ignored it—his longing to quit his thirty-two guests in the dining room and seclude himself with Minta in the library.

It had been Minta, more than his own wife, Louisa, with whom for twenty years the senator thought he shared the deepest sympathies, and enjoyed the complete understanding of their mutual keen judgment. He found her beauty perfect when she was a child—her chin admirable, her lines graceful, her eyes noble and expressive—and when she matured into a short, thick-necked, myopic woman whom others considered plain, he persisted in seeing her beauty. He judged her a genius for attaining the routine level of accomplishments he would have expected of the dullest son; she learned her Latin and French, played the piano with ten fingers, read newspapers and formed warmhearted opinions of events. Above all she rode with him, trained with him, and hunted with him, the family's ambitious, springy horses, whose breeding she followed with intelligent interest. Her modesty capped her charms, for she never gave off trying to convince him that among her classmates, her own attainments were commonplace.

That she possessed any life apart from the occasional dinners and rides they took together, he did not believe, though rumors of her impulsiveness reached him. When she was six she notoriously gave her pony cart to the groom's children; when she was ten she harbored in her hotel room half the cats of Rome. One night when she was thirteen, she and the Gill boys hoisted the Poultneys' carriage to their barn roof; when she was sixteen, she cut her hair, sold it outside town to Negroes, and stuck the cash in the poorbox at Saint Paul's. Her father forgave her these peccadilloes and attributed them to his absences, for she was yet a child.

Later, at the Albemarle in London, at the hotel in Deauville, and even in the railway coach from Furka Pass to Lucerne, women of refinement noticed Minta's generous nature. They complimented her genuineness, her serenity, and her willingness to relieve want; they afforded her valuable introductions. Her beautiful, brown-eyed sister, June, although still unformed, nevertheless struck a more brilliant appearance, and the senator thought the European matrons most discerning to take up Minta in her stead. His wife, Louisa, pointed out, however, in their stateroom crossing back to Baltimore from one such sortie, that Minta's European champions were all in their eighties and nineties. Most were purblind, and all were relics of a churchy and morbid piety whose time had passed.

When Minta first took to walking out with Eustace Honer, Senator Randall beat his best saddle horse, Highway, and cut his eye; he stayed in empty Washington, ashamed, throughout that summer, while his family repaired to Narragansett Bay. Now, of course, he was reconciled to the wedding, if not, at heart, to the marriage. The women had long since taken over; the issue had contracted, rumor reached him, into whether or not Minta should wear her spectacles for the ceremony. Nevertheless he agreed silently with some of the talk which reached him at home and at the Maryland Club: that if Minta Randall at twenty-three judged Eustace Honer steadfast, then love, however delightful a state, was as usual blind, and softheartedness, however amiable a quality, was as usual stupid. Baltimore's wise people were so convinced of these hard truths, and so religiously faithful to these doctrines, that five years later, and ten years later, their censure and dismay having moved on to other objects, they did not admit as contrary evidence the abundant, living fact that Minta had been correct.

Minta had only tasted her soup; she did not eat the imported sole, redhead duck, and roast that followed. She did not know that the fragile skin on her forehead and cheeks shone like an oil lamp. The solidity and warmth of Eustace at her side soothed her. He was talking across the table, through a candelabrum, to the oldest of her Biddle uncles from Philadelphia, who wore a split beard. "...She was the duchess of Chichester's daughter," the uncle was saying, "and a noble beauty she was, too, with a throat white as snow. She stopped in—" The service interrupted him. Eustace turned his small head. For a moment, Minta's glowing glance met Eustace's burning one, and their knowing smiles meant plainly: Soon, we will gladly exchange all this for a farm.

Eustace had passed the previous summer roaming the West, as so many curious eastern men did, young or old. By steamer he journeyed in small stages from hotels in San Francisco along the coast to Victoria,

British Columbia. He visited two University of Virginia friends who had emigrated; he found one at his cattle ranch east of the Cascades, and one who at twenty-one was sole vice-president of a bank in the frontier town of Anacortes, on Peter Puget's Sound.

Eustace returned to Baltimore from this trip stunned. In the fall he rejoined their merry and roguish set. At a picnic on a thin bay beach, Minta saw him; she was alarmed and intrigued. The sun had yellowed his hair; he had played three-card monte with gamblers, her delighted sister June had reported, and drunk "blue ruin" on a passenger coach roof. Now, at the picnic with a dozen friends, he sat on a flowered cloth spread back where the woods met the sand. The servants were passing soft-shelled crabs on a platter, breaded and fried.

When Eustace found his tongue, he earnestly described what he had seen. His friend's brick bank, he said—gazing embarrassed out over the water—stood on a naked corner where two streams of mud, called streets, crossed. On the other hand, it was a bank. His ranch friend had a library full of books, a piano, twenty dusty horses, and a wife who left for the glossy comforts of Portland every winter; he lived in a log house and saw nobody but the scurviest pack of Indians imaginable. On the other hand, he shot bears. Both men were costumed oddly—one unfashionably, the other wildly—and both were wholly unchanged in character except for an exuberant air of freedom he had never before found in any man.

Eustace had fetched to the picnic several of the brochures the railroad porters disbursed; Minta and June looked through them. Their paragraphs rang out with the great destiny of the new regions in Washington Territory, on Puget Sound, the last frontier, where the good, old life could still be found, and, not incidentally, found to converge upon the railroads' and harbors' inevitable creation—from the straight forests and building cities—of the good, new money. June, who at fifteen knew a sham when she saw one, walked down to the water's edge.

"You could go," Eustace said, turning to his friend Edgar Gill. Edgar Gill was yellow-headed and freckled; his father was a surgeon, and he himself studied medicine desultorily. "Not me," he said. "I aim to make my mark here." He waved a stiff crab. He said that in thirty years he would be found at the Maryland Club, listening through an ear trumpet, and arguing the merits of Bonaparte. Minta rose to join her graceful sister by the water; June was younger than the rest, and might feel slighted.

Crossing the sand, she heard Eustace telling the world that out on the coast, the grass was green all winter; he heard it for a fact. Moreover, skies were clear "from April to October." Could anyone believe it?

When, over the following months, Minta Randall found that Eustace apparently reciprocated her profoundest and most secret feelings, she thought she had never lived before, or knew what life could hold, or what absolute power one heart could exert upon another. She perceived no trace, fossil, or echo of this wild sensation anywhere around her, and concluded that she and Eustace had invented it together, which would be, she thought, just like them.

It was Minta, in fact, who first proposed that they emigrate after their marriage, take up farming, and rear their children unspotted from the world. The two—both short and supple, Minta flushing behind her spectacles, Eustace delicate-featured and resolute—whispered and pressed their plan over many a long walk up the avenue of oaks that lined the entrance to her house. Their friends met their proposal with superstitious awe; they never doubted they would succeed, and gloriously. Their families, by contrast, doubted, mistrusted Eustace, counseled restraint, and tested in several fraught, late-night conversations the likelihood of extricating the pair from their plan and preventing the move. The Honer brothers and Minta's sister, in a show of concern, allied with their parents to inquire in a body, what did they know of farming?

Now, in the crowded dining hall, Senator Randall rose to propose the first toast. Chairs scraped the floor, and her family and friends sprang up about Minta. The servants watched from doorways; Minta was a favorite. She reddened; she caught her sister's amused, ironic eye.

The couple had answered their critics hotly by displaying pounds of information in agricultural books and pamphlets. They answered their own few misgivings with their faith in their own qualities: faith in their two courageous and enterprising spirits, in their willingness to endure hardships and to learn, in their love for each other, and, should these spiritual powers flag, in the hundred thousand dollars which combined they would bring to the venture.

CHAPTER XVII

1878–1884, Goshen

The Nooksack River was born of a drip in a cirque at the tongue of a glacier hung on a western rampart of Mount Shuksan. The drip froze into an icicle, which dropped into a small pool; a runnel from the pool threaded a high valley out of the cirque and through the mountains, adding seep to melt and swelling so fast that a mile from its source a man needed one-piece rubber waders and a stout stick to cross it. This was the Nooksack River. It ducked into the forest, chuted between foothills, and fell asleep on the Nooksack plain.

The plain spread from the foothills to Gooseberry Point, the Lummi reservation that bounded Bellingham Bay. The plain spread smoothly, without shadow, because the river had rolled over and over in its sleep, or dreamily swished its heavy tail, and flattened everywhere the land. Emigrants who knew farming looked for river silt under the fir forest, and found it; it made a likely loam lightened by sand. They cleared the woods with oxen to farm it, grazed cattle around the stumps, and planted peas.

A logjam on the river was perforce the head of navigation. The settlement radiated from there, so pioneers called the village "the jam," and said they were "farming the jam," until Mrs. Dovie Dorr named it Goshen for respectability. Its first settlers were squatting miners, cardplayers who cut a few trees to buy whiskey, and farmers and families from the plains states, who planted the bright bottomland clearings in timothy hay, strawberries, apples, and plums. The soil was rich and deep, farms prospered, and lilies grew by doors and fences. By 1873, the village of Goshen already had a school district and a school, a post office, and stern-wheel steamer service to the dock on the river. It had two sunny churches, several stores and houses made of lumber, a rooming house in the mud, where Conrad Grogan and the Sharps stayed on their journey down from the Skagit passes, some plantings of lindens, apples, and maples, and many flowers. It was to Goshen, twelve miles from Bellingham Bay, that many Whatcom settlers removed when the town of Whatcom bit, for the second time, the dust.

* * *

Felix Rush's sawmill flamed up in August, 1873. A crowd of Lummis looped themselves into a bucket brigade from the beach to save it, but it burned anyway. The mill was not insured, and Felix did not rebuild, for one month later, on Wall Street, Jay Cooke's railroad bonds failed, and financial panic depressed the country. The nation's whip cracked, and Bellingham Bay snapped; the precarious Pacific Northwest territories exaggerated each economic boom or bust. The price of lumber fell, and the price of land; only the coal mine's payroll kept Whatcom alive. A few Chinese mineworkers celebrated the new year in February by sending up skyrockets from the beach. When emigrants staggered into Whatcom from the overland trail, they found most of the town boarded up. In the fifteen years since the Fraser River gold rush, green algae had colonized the boarded windows, and so had mats of moss. That winter was so cold, snow lingered, and a cougar warmed itself nights on Ada Fishburn's shake roof near the chimney. She felt the walls tremble when the cougar jumped up, and in the mornings she and Clare saw its tracks in the snow.

A few years later, the coal mine closed; its San Francisco bank had busted in the panic, and its low-grade, sulfurous coal was always catching fire. The telegraph office closed. A storm wrecked the wharf. The brick warehouse was empty; the forest surged back into cleared lots. There were only five hundred people left on the bay during the panic, and only twenty families after the coal mine closed. They had no source of cash. For entertainment, Louetta Harshaw and Conrad Grogan started a literary society—the men debated the women—and the town built a new schoolhouse for its thirty-four scholars. Ada attended a costume ball in the schoolhouse as a Normandy Girl; Lura Rush came as Goddess of Night. Priscilla Judd trained two tiny, costumed girls to sing "When You and I Were Young" in British accents.

Despite these enticements, people bailed out of town, and Clare and Ada Fishburn were among them. They left in 1878, during the worst of the depression. Glee stayed in Whatcom to fish and court pop-eyed Grace in Seattle. The doctor left, and the baker, and the Sunday school superintendent whose son was in law school at Northwestern. Nine remaining families had children to send to school.

Ada Fishburn and her son Clare removed to Goshen; they had no money to go farther. Whatcom was dying, but Goshen flourished, and now outshone Whatcom in amenities, because good soil beats all, and if a man cannot grow rich, he can at least grow food.

In Goshen good land was cheap—only five or six dollars an acre improved, and a dollar an acre of forest. Ada reckoned, then, that her whole improved farm of 150 acres on the Nooksack cost the summer's worth of butter she sold to the gold miners twenty years before, and it made no sense, for you could raise a dozen or twenty milk cows on 150 acres—so people's notion of worth was worthless. Paper money was so suspect these days that the previous week a man who robbed a bank at gunpoint in Anacortes took only the gold in the vault and left the stacks of bundled bills behind, as not worth the bother. Ada and Clare walked their two hogs, two heifers, and a cow single file up the wilderness trail through the forest to Goshen. They sent their household goods by steamer; the freight charge about crippled them, but there was no wagon road, and the Nooksack Indians charged nearly the same freight rate for canoes.

When Ada and Clare Fishburn arrived in Goshen late in 1878, they found as neighbors Eustace Honer, his wife, Minta, and their boy. Eustace Honer had purchased 320 improved acres of the best bottomland in Whatcom County—in Goshen, where Humpback Creek met the Nook-sack—for $2,240 cash money. The Honers lived in the old log farmhouse while hired workmen built a ten-room frame house in the broad clearing by the river. The clearing was flat floodplain; from every point in the fields and yards, a person could see Mount Baker; the mountain looked unthinkably distant and high.

The workmen painted the new house white, plastered it inside, and sanded and varnished the floors. Minta chose flowered wallpapers in blue and rose. She bought mahogany furniture, marble-topped tables, a horse-hair sofa for each bedroom, and white draperies, all of which arrived on the steamer *Doris Burn*. Eustace planted imported lilacs around the porch and bought a pianoforte for the parlor. Minta hung family portraits on the walls, and her mother shipped her the old tall cased clock from Baltimore. She filled the crawl space and cellar with smoked venison hams and blackberry jam in jars. She hired her laundress's sister to tag after their son, Hugh, who was two, to keep him from falling in the river.

Eustace and Minta had lived in the old log farmhouse for eighteen months, and in the new frame house for two years, when Ada and Clare Fishburn arrived in Goshen. The two men met one day in the dark woods.

* * *

Eustace Honer and a Nooksack Indian man named Kulshan Jim were falling a fir. Honer was short-legged; his small, square skull made his broad shoulders seem ever broader. He parted his fine hair in the middle, like a saloon keeper, and the two sides of hair dropped in his face as he worked. He had on calked boots and his former best trousers, which he wore at his wedding. He applied himself to any task, and concentration animated his small features.

He and Kulshan Jim were working ten feet up the tree trunk; they stood at either end of a plank wedged in a notch. Four feet below them on the flared trunk was the pair of notches they had axed to stand on, in order to cut the higher notches to lay the board across, so they could stand on the board and saw the tree down. They had to saw six or eight feet up the trunk to get above its flare and pitch pockets. Sometimes they laid the plank across two springboards poked endwise in the trunk, but Eustace preferred to anchor the plank in a notch for stability.

The crosscut saw had replaced the ax in the timber. An ordinary crosscut saw was ten feet from handle to handle; Eustace and Kulshan Jim had to raise their voices to converse from one end of the saw to the other. Kulshan Jim was a lean young man of high birth who occupied a strong position in his family, and who had a respected wife and three children of his own. He worked barefoot and naked except for a thin woven waistband whose purpose Eustace never learned. Some Lummis had given him the name Kulshan Jim, after Komo Kulshan, Mount Baker. He drew the saw at waist height, over the axed undercut and through the fir's enormous side. Eustace leaned lightly as the saw moved, never pushing, and drew it back in his turn. The men knew this work; the saw's long grinds made rhythmical noise. Everyone called a crosscut saw a misery whip. They dragged the misery whip through the pitchy wood so the teeth bit. Muscles moved all over their two backs like salmon in creeks.

Out of the corner of his eye, Eustace saw a long dark shape in the slash. He stopped the saw. The man, who was Clare Fishburn, made his way around the trunks and branches in the clearing; he wore a smudged collarless shirt and a slouch hat. He was narrow as a pole, energetic at the shoulders, and crease-faced, hopeful-looking, and easy. When he reached the men on the tree he introduced himself and added carefully, it seemed to Eustace, and admiringly, that what they were doing was one good way to fall a big fir. Eustace looked into his upturned honest face.

What did he mean, one of the good ways? Was there any other way?

He and Kulshan Jim on the big board drew out the saw and hung it from the plank. Kulshan Jim jumped down to the ground, doused a rag in coal oil, and began deliberately rubbing the pitch off the saw. Eustace climbed down by a notch step and felt the broad earth through his legs. He looked at his yellow fingers as he parted them and forced them flat.

In four years of pioneering, Eustace had learned to ask questions. It was no shame for a man not to know everything in the world, as if from birth; everybody picked up things as he went along. He was twenty-eight years old, and it had surprised him, a little, that the other men in the emigrant coach seemed to respect him no less for his frank ignorance. They told him what they had heard about the Sound country: no grasshoppers, no prairie fires, no blizzards, no drought; and they told him things incidentally—like about damp hay's catching fire in the barn and about birthing a sideways calf—that gave him the fantods. Here in Goshen, Mr. Black Missou had set him up, and old Adolph Sharp, and the Veseys that ran the rooming house, and any number of Nooksacks.

"I wish I knew an easier way," Eustace said. "Do you?" He had heard of a man's sawing a fir alone, he told the new neighbor, by tying one saw handle to a tall sapling. The lone man on his springboard could pull his end through the trunk, and the bent sapling drew it back on the rebound. It sounded farfetched.

Clare took off his hat and scraped a handful of mosquitoes from his white forehead. He told Eustace how, if a man wanted to clear firs the lazy way and save his back, he could burn them down. It was a passel of fun, Clare said; there was not a thing in the world he enjoyed more than easing down a chair, maybe with a whiskey in his hand, and watching a tree fall of its own initiative and private enterprise. Clare's levity shocked Eustace, and attracted him.

The next morning Clare showed up early at the slicked-up Honer farmhouse. He carried an auger in his hand and a few sticks of wood under his arm. He took tea in the grand house and split a pie with Eustace. He met Eustace's short wife, Minta, whom he found both noble and agreeable, and who entertained a sturdy little boy, named Hugh, in her lap. When he first entered, the boy Hugh stood aside, as if at attention. Eustace's wife wore spectacles; their oval lenses, the size of a pair of eyes, were close-set on her broad face. She spoke so softly that she seemed to have no tongue with which to form consonants, and she looked straight at him. She agreed that Goshen, the gem of the Nooksack, was surpassing all expectations. Clare told Minta he just brought in two cougars, and collected the five-dollar bounty on each. She asked about Whatcom, and he told her.

Clare followed Eustace out to the timber. Eustace carried sulfur matches, a bellows, and a spade. They cleared some bracken fern and salal to bare soil, kindled a bonfire, and laid in it the dry sticks of vine maple Clare had fetched along. Eustace selected a big uncut fir only two feet away from the half-sawn one; this timber was so close, Eustace had to turn to pass his shoulders between the trunks. The trunks of firs and cedars tangled in the trunks of hemlock and spruce; they made a breastwork, a hedge high as heaven, like a thorn hedge an army grew to defend a town; downed trunks lay across downed trunks, and their branches, the size of trees, blocked the passage of wrens.

Clare drilled a tunnel low in the fir's trunk, a tunnel only a foot long; he used a one-and-one-half-inch drill bit. He stuck a stick in it. A foot above this hole, he bored another tunnel slantingly to meet it. When the stick twitched, he knew the tunnels met; he withdrew the stick and gave the auger a few more twists. Now, with a conspiratorial smile at Eustace, he poked the fire with the short spade and picked out a few yellow embers the size of thumbs. These were dense vine maple embers; they burned long and hot. Using sticks as tongs, he worked them down the top auger hole; the bottom hole, Eustace saw, acted as a draft. Eustace tipped back and looked up the long trunk, a view he generally avoided as discouraging. The trunk was 190 feet high, he reckoned; it grew straight as a mast for 90 or 100 feet before the lowest branch. It was purely worthless, all this tonnage of tree—the farmer's cross. There was four houses' worth of knot-free lumber in each tree, but buying milled lumber was cheaper—if you had more money than time—than getting the trunks to the mill.

Wet as it was, Clare said, the fir would burn. He thumped the bearded old trunk warmly, as if it had been a favorite horse's rump. The embers were almost two feet from the trunk's center, but they were in far enough to burn the tree. Did he want all these Douglas firs down? These six, say? Eustace did. They spent the morning poking embers into drilled trunks. In those same hours, Eustace and Kulshan Jim could not have finished sawing through the first trunk. While they worked, the men appraised each other; they weighed qualities, and sized strengths. Clare was nine inches taller than Eustace and one heap poorer, and he saw Eustace did not mark it. When Clare left, the first trunk was steaming like a potato.

* * *

All day Eustace kept an eye on the trees. He shot three merganser ducks, split cedar rails for fencing, and received a shipment of manure at the dock. By suppertime he saw steam and smoke seeping out of the fir trunks' bark everywhere and blowing back white, like hair or fur. He knew fire jumped treetops and burned out of reach, burned down trees instead of up, and the northwest wind was blowing. That night in bed he pitched about some, and Minta soothed him down, then worried herself when he slept. The next day the wind backed to the southwest, and it settled in to rain. It was the light rain he was used to out here, rain they all worked through every winter without noticing it—cool, blowing, drizzling rain that rarely broke. Deep inside, the fired trees were burning. Weak yellow flames curled low from their trunks.

The next day the trees started to fall, one after the other, and shook the earth so the house jumped. The house rose, he thought, like a loose clapper that slides up and bangs the bell at the fair when you hit the strike plate with a maul. The house rose, and everything in it rose, too—the cherry beds, tables, and carved chairs, the china bowls and silver spoons, the basin and buckets and brassbound trunks, the mirrors, portraits, and hunting scenes on the walls, the flour sack and bluing box and saw set and seed potatoes—they all jumped inside the house, and the house jumped, and everything settled back down just as it had been, mum. When the second tree started to fall, Eustace was digging a post hole. He heard the wild splitting and groan he had heard many times before, the sound of wood fibers tearing and breaking. He shouted "Tree!" and jumped to look. It sounded near, as though someone were ripping his brain, one thread at a time, out of his skull. The wood's shriek changed to cracking and crashing, loud as war or fire, when each tree sheared down neigboring trunks and stripped their boughs and bark.

In twenty-four hours, all the trees had fallen—about twenty-five tons each. Shreds of cast green lichens, like bits of beard, blew into the house, with twigs, bark, sawdust, and plain dust. Two trees dropped into the field and pounded trenches that Minta would notice the rest of her life. Eustace broke up a few fires that started in the woods and slash. The charred stumps kept burning. Over the next few weeks, if ever hard rain snuffed a stump, Eustace fired it up again. The fir roots were so pitchy that a man could burn them right in the ground.

Some of the downed trunks were taller than he could reach. They were the size of railroad trains in the woods. Standing in slash, he scaled all the timber, trimming boughs with an ax. Every month or so, he burned another downed fir trunk into sections: he drilled two deep auger holes and poked in embers every five feet for two hundred feet. When he had scaled and bucked all the timber, he dogged the logs with a maul and yarded them with chains on sleds. He hired a driver and two ox teams for four dollars a day, and with their strength sledded the bucked logs together at the edge of the field, to burn them.

The dense smell of burning fir, and of sharp, poignant burning cedar, was the smell of that land at that time; Eustace smelled no other air except when he went into Whatcom, where the sea's whole air surprised him. From the wharf he could see all the land smoking in every direction. Each mill burned sawdust and shavings; each house, shop, and saloon in village, reservation, and town kept a fire in the stove all summer, and in the stove and fireplace for the other ten months. Each farmer did what he could to burn slash and stumps from the forest that wasted the land and sprang out again when a man turned his back.

Over the next six years, steadfast Eustace labored at these border acres whenever time allowed, expanding his hop fields. He burned down firs, lopped trunks, bucked the logs, yarded and burned them. He wore through a pair of calked boots and four pairs of trousers a year. His plug hat kept his brown hair out of his eyes. He developed what he called "a weather skin," and wore shirtsleeves outside in any weather. His hands grew hard as antlers. The balls of his thumbs were thick as plums.

With Kulshan Jim or with Clare, he sawed down cedars eight and ten feet across and left stumps the size of houses to plow around, because as good as dry cedar was for kindling, it would not burn in the ground. He discovered a big fir he had to leave standing, which was twenty feet through the trunk. He got a photographer to take a picture of it instead, and Minta and Hugh stood in front of it for scale; Minta held the white-dressed baby, Bert, who moved his head.

He knocked out the alder saplings and rampant blackberries that followed his labors like dogs at his heels. Earnestly, frowning, he burned out the salal, bracken fern, fireweed, and Oregon grape by chopping their bases and returning. He broke up with an ax the dusty old wind-thrown trunks higher than his head, and burned out their green moss covering. He chopped down the hemlock saplings that grew in straight avenues from the downed logs. Each of these sprouted saplings ran two or three feet through the trunk—the size of what, back in Maryland, he used to call a tree.

In those six years, Eustace put his five best acres in hops, using Nooksack labor. He had set out to farm the land scientifically, and was now content to farm it at all. He spent almost all of their nest egg paying for labor. He cleared five more acres, ditched five, and fenced twenty. He built a cedar barn seventy-five feet high, a building larger than any other in the county, whose interior rooms were so ample that clouds formed under the roof. The farm yielded so much hay that this Pantheon of a barn was inadequate to store it. He could not easily sell the surplus; in Goshen everyone had hay, and the cost of freight was too high to ship it. He bought hens and henhouses, six dairy cows, a bull, and some yearling calves, three or four horses, and a pony and cart for the children. Back in Baltimore he had been a broad-backed young man who used to do some sailing. Now his limbs grew hard as pipes, and his blood vessels spread outside them like thick vines. His square forehead was white and his cheeks were dark and smooth-shaven; he frowned, trod the land as its master, and drew up a list of duties every morning.

Eustace and Clare worked together often, and hunted the hills and fished the river together, and smoked their pipes, resting their eyes on the wide river or the drowsing fields. Resolution burned in Eustace and made him grave and sincere; gaiety and hopefulness animated Clare, and blew him about. Clare's view that a man could enjoy this life eased Eustace's urgency to succeed, and moderated his mental habit of measuring himself, his material gains and losses, against the doubt and dread of his parents, and Minta's parents, in Baltimore, and, more urgently, of measuring his know-how and enterprise against those of the men who preceded him in the region—Clare Fishburn, Norval Tawes, Black Missou, and the late Adolph Sharp—men who had passed their infancies cutting cordwood and paddling canoes, and who, he imagined, discussed his skills and fortunes daily over dinner.

CHAPTER XVIII

1884–1885, Goshen

Eustace and Minta Honer rejoiced in the region's healthful climate; this was indeed the invigorating and glorious country the railway brochures claimed it was, for white settlers. Typhus and consumption were common in eastern cities and rare among settlers here. Here the poorest man had his own dwelling even in town, and salmon, deer, and berries were free and abundant; the poor man and the rich man drank together and worked together, peeling back the forest like a cover, and opening the soil to the sun. Drinking water was pure and plentiful, and the west wind replenished the air every hour from the tonic and inexhaustible atmospheres of the Pacific. The native men and women that the immigrants found were hardy survivors—to put the best face on it—or their parents were, of the typhoid epidemic brought by traders, which halved the tribes' people fifty years earlier. The ruddy children came ten to a household. Here malaria had never visited; here light rains drove greenness into the grass all winter and smoothed the red cheeks of the women; here hermits in their eighties and nineties flourished in the woods upright, like the old trees.

The difficulty and expense of reaching Puget Sound at all, from anywhere on the planet earth including Oregon, had drawn men and women hard as mules, whose arrival proved their endurance. Ada Fishburn told Minta Honer that she was there one night on the dock in Whatcom when Mr. H. I. Hoolihan, who owned the only bank in Whatcom, tripped on a sack of potatoes and fell from the deck of the steamer just outside the bay. Hoolihan swam a mile back to the dock through the freezing water wearing his clothes and hat, clasping a packet of papers in his teeth, and carrying a rolled umbrella in one hand. He was eighty-five years old, he told the crowd on the dock, and he had no intention of buying another umbrella.

These past six years, Ada Fishburn had found Goshen more to her liking than Whatcom. She held the ordinary view that agriculture hewed closer to God's plan for mankind than commerce ever could, though she could not say why, unless it was that the sight of people struggling without hope pleased Him, which would not surprise her. In Goshen, Ada Fishburn was poorer than ever. The Fishburns' preemption claim lay back from the Honers'; there the soil thinned and mixed with clay. Ada added panels to her dresses' waists, and sailed competently into her tasks—keeping speckled hens and two cows. When she smiled, her bow-shaped mouth seemed to split her face, and her black eyes gleamed. Her cheeks, once round, were flat as shingles. Outside, she still wore a flat-topped sunbonnet deep as a pail, which had shaded her from the sun on the plains, and here kept the rain off.

Ada Fishburn had married Norval Tawes, the Methodist minister, who wore a top hat over his bald head to court her in a canoe on the river, and made her feel like a girl again in Illinois.

Ada had felt blue without knowing it all these years since Rooney died in the well, and she knew it now. Norval possessed some sorry habits for a man of God—as if he were an ordinary man—but he had some sand in him, and he seemed easily pleased with her, so his big old hairless forehead colored up and he pointed his pointy face at her wherever she went. Though she would probably die on the dear man before he got her to the church, and cause unnecessary grief, still she would follow her heart and let herself love him for that virtuous, uncomplaining restraint men have—Rooney had it, too, and even her grown boys, a kind of nobility, valor, hitching up their britches and keeping on—and she would make him a home at his half-farmed place, the parsonage indistinguishable from a shed, which could use some touches, and she would pay him back for making her feel shot up like a Chinese firecracker, and show him the tenderness she wished she'd had the sense to pile on Rooney.

When they all lived in the Whatcom stockade long ago, the Lummi woman Margot told Ada one morning that according to the Lummis, old age was the proper time to fall in love. Old age was the proper time to suffer romances, and jealousy, and lose your head—old age, when you felt things more, and could spare the time to go dead nuts over a person, and understood how fine a thing it was. This was how the Lummis saw it. Margot was a young woman; she talked to Ada over the wash trough. Ada was about twenty-three at the time and reckoned that old people, never mind toothless old Lummi people, could not feel half of what she felt, about anything, on a dull day.

She would have liked to see Margot again and talk to her about Norval. Instead, one day picking berries she had talked to Minta Honer, who was thirty-four, and generous about things, but truth be told, that day in the berry bushes she looked a little doubtful, as if she found something not quite believable about any pair of people but her and Eustace, who had thought it all up between them.

That summer in the long evenings, when the days' sunlight seemed to catch in the trees like fog and hang over the farms, changing colors but never fading, people all up and down the banks heard Ada's thin laughter over the water, and they smiled at their tasks or in their beds, for Ada was fifty-three years old now, and seemed tickled half to death. Her son Clare was a man, and so was the other son, the fisherman back in Whatcom, and no one, least of all Ada, expected her to get married before her sons did, or ever.

CHAPTER XIX

1885, Goshen

It was the women who finally got the logjam cleared. The county government promised to clear it every year, so steamboats and rafted lumber could reach upstream to Burnett—the farm town above the jam—and so that logs from Burnett could travel downstream, and everyone in Goshen could get rich on the traffic. But the government never did do it, for the government needed first to build roads and had no money to do anything. By '85 there was another hard depression on, and the county could not tax squatters or homesteaders who did not yet own their claims.

In the quiet of a rainy April afternoon, Minta sat on a striped sofa with two children in her lap at once. Minta was still round-limbed, and tender in expression; her square face she habitually tilted to one side, as if listening for a child. She wore a wide-skirted dress of black linsey-woolsey tricked up with black satin edging and ribbon bows at the bodice and waist. Lulu, their incomprehensible two-year-old daughter, rubbed her upper lip over this satin, to feel its smoothness. Bert, who was six, twisted around, and she held them in her arms as she had when they were new.

Beside them on the sofa, their older son Hugh, nine, quietly kept an eye on them all. The two younger children, whom she had hoped to calm and rest, began playing king of the castle in her lap; they scaled her wide skirt and tried to sit, both at once, on her neck. She helped Lulu up, and they slid down her skirt as a slide, so the game changed; she leaned to pull them up again, over and over. There was even, Minta thought, room for more. When Lulu slipped, Hugh caught her and restored her to Minta's lap, without changing his solemn expression.

Hugh was a bighearted boy, square-headed like his father and mother; his brown hair was curly on top and cut close around his ears. He helped his parents all day, performed his own chores quietly, attended school for its three-month session, and kept bees. Now he seemed to judge that his mother had had enough; he seized an India-rubber ball from the rug, and earnestly tried to strike a tune from the piano with it. When Bert joined him at the piano stool, Hugh gathered him onto his lap and gave him the ball.

Minta and Hugh heard the footfalls on the porch that announced callers. Mrs. Dovie Dorr and Mrs. Sarah Missou came in, shed their umbrellas, took tea, and stated their business, which had been brewing all winter; they asked the Honers to subscribe to the work of clearing the jam. Clearing the jam would free navigation for forty miles, they said, and they were taking the bull by the horns, and raising the cash and labor from the people directly. Minta pledged support. After they left, she worried, quite correctly, that subscribing a lot of money would make Dovie Dorr dislike her more, and so also would subscribing a little money. Dovie Dorr had befriended Minta as a newcomer ten years before, until—as it appeared—she realized that Minta had money; then in her mind Minta ceased being a friendless stranger in a new country, and became an enemy who needed, if anything, to be taken down a peg. In the end the Honers ponied up three hundred dollars, and Eustace's labor, for the good of the community. Minta and her friend Ada Fishburn Tawes helped call on every house and shack in the town and the woods, and scratched up fifty dollars here and seventy-five dollars there, and eighty hours here and a hundred hours there, and venison and dried fish and letters of credit, to clear the jam.

To subscribe workers, Ada and Clare hired a shovel-nosed canoe beyond the jam to take them upstream to the tribal seat at the forks of the Nooksack. There they found the Nooksack *tyee*, the venerable Hump Talem—a splendid figure who had a reputation among the settlers for dignity and kindness. Hump Talem was wearing a bearskin cloak and a mink hat with a tail. Standing in the gravels where the rivers met, he was holding a hand bell and preparing to call his people to evening prayers. His hair under his mink hat was white, and he had a white tuft of beard on his chin.

Not many Nooksack people survived the typhoid epidemic of the fifties or the smallpox epidemic of 1870. Many of those who did survive lived here at the snowy forks of the Nooksack; they hunted elk in the mountains whose glaciers fed all three Nooksack forks. The government treated the Nooksack people as signatories of the 1855 Seattle treaty, which established reservations, but none had actually been present; the river was frozen then, and they could not use their canoes. Hump Talem declined to join the Lummis on the reservation, and despised the governor for his thoughtless assumption that his people would join them. The Lummis outnumbered the Nooksacks, spoke a foreign language, kept slaves, took multiple wives, and were Catholics, not sensible Methodists like most of the Nooksacks. Did the governor not know that the reservation was once their land, until the Lummis drove them upriver? Up at the forks, the Nooksacks hunted and, increasingly, logged. They did not want Boston settlers on their land. Down at Nooksack crossing, other Nooksacks could own land if they lived like the Bostons, furnished two recommendations from the Bostons, and farmed—another cockeyed deal, most thought, and men like Kulshan Jim and most of his family were not yet ready to take it.

Hump Talem promised Ada Tawes a dozen workers or more at a dollar a day. The Nooksacks no longer feared Northern raiders, and would be happy to have the jam cleared. Back at the village, Ada and Minta rounded up more workers. Local bachelors and hermits, those coal miners who fared poorly at farming, cardplayers and hand loggers and starveling, honest prospectors, signed on for the work full time at two dollars a day, and landowning family men like Drew Dorr, Clare and Eustace, Judge Tarte, Black Missou, Elmer Pike, and Welshy Bovard took either two dollars a day, or what they called Indian pay, or none, according to their needs and natures.

It took three months to clear the logjam on the Nooksack, and Eustace Honer drowned doing it. The jam was three quarters of a mile long—a city of trees and logs that avalanches broke upstream, or loggers falled, or storms threw, or old age. It had been there as long as anyone, including the Nooksack people, could remember. A forest straddled the river on top of the jam. Fifteen or twenty feet above the waterline, Douglas firs and silver firs with trunks four feet thick were growing a hundred feet high from soil trapped in the smashed mess of logs. Birds nested in the trees.

When Drew Dorr blew the ox horn in front of the Methodist church at eight every morning, work began on the jam. The men brought peaveys, axes, poles, and, later, dynamite. The white men stopped at home for lunch, while their wives carried out meals to the Nooksack men on the jam. Little Bert Honer thought the jam a plaything; he climbed the bare, pale logs and waved at the men below. High on the jam, the six-year-old boy looked like a mosquito alight on the wide logs, logs whose tips, like candles, the rising sun enflamed. He skylarked across the river from one bank to another and back. He wagged and jiggled those sticks that wagged and jiggled, and made whole sections of raft and live trees undulate, so the flycatchers and lone kingfishers rose and flew off. The men kept waving him down. It took all summer, eleven hours a day, six days a week, to pull the jam. The men sawed, lopped, pried, chained, and hauled. They were almost through when Eustace's accident happened midmorning.

Eustace died in the common way; he slipped when a tree shifted. He fell, and the current pinned him underwater, against the jam. Clare and his mother's husband, Norval Tawes, saw him go down, but they could not see or find where he fetched up.

Eustace's own oldest son Hugh saw him go down, too. Hugh was near-by, prying at a snag with a pole—a blockheaded slip of a boy. He caught from the corner of his eye his father's dark figure drop. He looked up in time to see his father's mild face, in profile, going down surprised behind a patch of grass like a muskrat. Clare and the other men all crowded to dig into that spot on the dam—maybe his head was out of water somewhere. Hugh had the idea of searching the bank downstream.

He was gone two hours. His wide, flat mouth and pale eyes masked all expression. He hoped his father had swum through or underneath the jam, popped up downstream, and would now appear walking back, wet and relieved, but this did not happen. He hoped when he got back to the work the men would have found his father, and would be drying him out, maybe splinting up a broken leg or arm, but this did not happen either. Hugh accompanied Clare Fishburn back down the road, along the curved carriage road, and up to the house, for it was up to him and Clare to tell his mother.

Minta was shelling peas on the porch with Lulu, it was such a fine day—"a God day," she called such days, when the blessings of beauty and peace pooled, low like sunlight, on lawns and fields.

"Are you all through already?" Minta asked when they showed up, but no, they were not through yet, Clare had to answer. Minta took one look at Hugh's frozen face and she saw it all, and thought, as a woman will think: "I have been expecting this right along, and here it is." Her heart gave a contraction she could feel in her fingertips, and a kind of piercing alarm began in her head like a siren. She held her homely head high when Clare said Eustace got drowned on the jam, though her breath went out of her, to make it easier for Clare to keep telling her what happened to Eustace, so she could imagine what ran through Eustace's mind, and in order to set an example for Hugh, Bert, and Lulu, for much would be required of them all.

At the same time, the men working the jam sawed through a trunk, and chopped through another, and worked them aside with tongs and poles, to reveal Eustace's body trapped just under the water; they saw his dark, clinging shirt, and his arms loose and flowing with the current, and his head down. He was in a cage or mesh of logs.

Freeing Eustace's body, so his family and the town would have something on hand to pray over and bury, seemed urgent and good to the men on the jam, and it gave them something to work at. In another two hours Kulshan Jim, two of his Nooksack cousins, Norval Tawes, and Judge Tarte cleared a ten-foot hole through the jam to the water above Eustace, but they could not lever the logs that trapped his body, or jimmy him free with hooks and poles. They worked cautiously, for the jam itself was so reduced it seemed ready to pull. Judge Tarte, who wore muttonchop whiskers and a stovepipe hat, repeatedly glanced upstream, to see if any trees were coming down that might ram them and scatter the jam. Norval Tawes repeatedly glanced downstream, to see if any logs were detaching; his close-set button eyes kept moving.

It was Norval Tawes, who supported his ministry with handlogging, who remarked something that gave them all pause. When they got the jam thin enough and weak, the current would bust it, or a charge of black powder would finish it. The logs trapping Eustace would float downstream. Eustace's body would likely sink somewhere, and they never would find it. They needed to attach some sort of float to his body, so they could catch it downstream at the bridge. Judge Tarte asked Kulshan Jim, who was axing limbs from an alder, if their band had any big floats for sealing; they did not. If the Nooksacks needed an impromptu mooring buoy down on the sound, they did what everyone did—they tied the weight with a long line to a log. There was no shortage of logs.

For want of another method, then, Norval Tawes, his big face pinched, climbed down into the hole, sadly fished Eustace Honer's two dead hands from the river, and tied them one by one, lashing them tight at the wrists, to a woody mass of silver fir roots. Then he walked away. A young man in a top hat, Charles Kilcup, walked after him.

Late that afternoon the long work was over, and the river was clear. The dozen men on the jam would not use blasting powder, lest it tear up Eustace. Instead they sawed through a cedar log near the far bank, a cedar that proved to be a linchpin, and the jam slowly swung open like a gate.

"She's pulling," Norval shouted out, and they all skittered off to the banks. The jam made a peninsula that swayed and toppled. Some parts of it crumbled and fell, and other parts floated and spread. Everyone watched, transfixed, the way people upstream watched the river's spring breakup, for the few minutes' upheaval that changed everything. Here snarls of straw and twigs loosened and floated in a mat. Soil clumps and green grasses sank. Logs detached, entered the water bobbing, and floated away, like muskrats sliding from banks without concern. Trees untangled and took the plunge, splashed, and raised waves the straw mats rode. Their enormous root systems netted straw as they floated downstream. The men saw, spinning into the water, the particular silver fir trunk that bore Eustace's tied body around and upside down on its tangled roots; it bumped downstream and disappeared around a bend. The men watched from the bank for an hour, excited and bereaved. Their minds began to turn to the tasks on their claims they had left undone all summer.

Downstream at the bridge, Charles Kilcup and Norval Tawes snagged and caught the silver fir that carried Eustace Honer's body like a streamer. There were many men on the banks near the bridge by then, hauling off logs to sell; some of the same men had been working on the jam that morning. They saw Kilcup and Tawes unwrap the lashings from Honer's wrists and detach him from the wood roots. They watched them fold his body into a wheelbarrow, give it a helpless, tidying pat, and cover it somewhat with Tawes's jacket. The sun was setting when the two set off up the newly planked road to Goshen, pushing the wheelbarrow.

CHAPTER XX

Hugh Honer's round, downtilted blue eyes, set deep in his blocky head, were so pale the Nooksacks called him White Eyes. His sober "Yes, ma'am" expression, and his dutiful, quiet habits, made adults judge him admirable but dull. In fact, he was a deep one, tormented by inexpressible tenderness, and subject to concealed and wordless flights of joy. At his father's funeral, when little Josie Dorr told him about tying his father's body to the log roots, he never minded. He was stunned then, and overpowered by the living grandeur of the two teams of horses. The horses drew his father's coffin in a wagon from the house, down to the road, and up to a grass patch between his own hop fields, where they would bury him. No child in the settlement had ever seen such an expensive sight as two matched teams of horses, but all had seen coffins.

Hugh stood with stiff Lulu and supple Bert at the graveside. The Nooksacks stood together with their preacher. Before the funeral, in mourning for his father, they had shrieked and pounded on boards. Then Hugh heard that in their lodges they prayed for his father, on their knees, with their heads to the wall; this moved all the settlers very much, and they talked about it. Now Charles Kilcup, the little fellow in the top hat, was talking to the crowd about Eustace Honer; he spoke in English and Chinook. His wife, Queen of the May, was there, and their children. Then Hump Talem delivered a eulogy; he addressed the grieving Nooksacks in their tongue, and Hugh looked at his thick, snow-white hair, his splendid carriage, the tuft of white beard on his tan chin. A southeast wind was blowing and rattling the berries on the vines. At last big-faced Norval Tawes read Scripture and prayed. "O Death, where is thy sting?" Norval Tawes called out, and his little black eyes glittered on Hugh. Hugh thought: "Just about everywhere, since you ask."

By the time Hugh saw his father slip into the jam, he had already seen many people in the process of dying, and many people dead.

It was Hugh himself who recently found Clarence Fanjoy dead of a carbuncle on his neck. Clarence Fanjoy was an old miner who came down out of the Fraser River gold fields and lived in the woods with his *klootch-man*—"daughter of a chief," he always said, as did every other such husband who ever drew breath. He pecked around fishing and prospecting and cutting cordwood for the *Doris Burn* for cash. The week before his father drowned in the jam, Hugh had passed Clarence Fanjoy's cabin on the miners' trail towards the mountains. The young yellow dog jumped on him, fussing. Hugh knew the new dog, knew Fanjoy's cabin, and knew the old welcoming sign over its door, written on brown wrapping paper with a lead bullet: THIS HOUSE OPEN TO ALL SQUARE MEN. OTHERS, BEWARE.

Hugh found a smokeless chimney, the cabin door open, Clarence Fanjoy dead on the bed, and his *klootchman* gone with the blankets. Rigor mortis had enlivened Clarence's attitude on the bed. His shoulders had raised and his head started forward, so he seemed stuck in the act of getting up or hooting out to ask for something. A streaky red sore was dry on his neck; it was this sore, according to Grandma Zella Hyle who came later, that killed him. The *klootchman* had evidently stuck Clarence barefoot into his suit and shifted him around to the foot of the bed so his head faced west. She had wrapped and tied his jaw shut with a white handkerchief, propped his rifle against the bed, and placed in his two hands a stiff buckskin bag of gold dust and nuggets—worth, it turned out, over three hundred dollars—so his friends could potlatch him out of this world.

In Clarence Fanjoy's cabin that morning, Hugh had all the time in the world. The cabin's open door framed a rectangle of dazzling brightness. Hugh felt the stillness of the sunny clearing as a power: the radiant, breath-holding silence seemed just short of dropping a blessing on the world. That was two weeks ago. He had stood at peace, joyful, alert. He heard a woodpecker calling in the woods—Tew!—a sweet sound, and the silence closed mysteriously around it. Goldenrod and blue asters stood motionless, among motionless grass blades, intricate and enchanted. The clearing was a deep hole in the woods, and the sun shone down on the cabin gratuitously, forgivingly, freely, as it shines summer noons on water down in a well. He fingered the dog's hot skull.

The fluids in Clarence Fanjoy's body pooled on the downside; their darkness showed through his skin, so his toes were white and empty, and his heels blue and flattened like bags where they met the mattress tick. The upside of his face was white and the downside blue and black where the skin bulged, thin as gut, over the handkerchief. Hugh touched the back of one dead hand; it was cold as a mirror. He laid his hand over it, as if to warm it, then withdrew.

He knew Clarence Fanjoy likely sinned every day of every year as every person sins, as Hugh himself sinned, forgetting his Maker or ignoring Him, and seeking his own salvation and rise in the world. He also knew from many memorized verses and many of Norval Tawes's sermons that ordinary, scruffy sinners were said to be redeemed in advance, and under God's care and keeping. God himself had gathered up Clarence Fanjoy, and loosed him with the mobs in heaven, where he could fly among stars if he wished, visit old neighbors, or look down in wonder—finding Washington Territory—right through the cabin roof at his shucked husk in its suit on the bed.

Hugh saw that the black logs in the fireplace were wet, and black water lay puddled under them, where the Nooksack woman had carefully doused the fire. The cabin floor was swept, and the kettle gleamed. A bundle of dry fern roots hung from a nail. Outside the stoop, on the grass, was a Nooksack bucket—cedar bent square and sewn with spruce roots tight around a square cedar bottom. It was half full of salmon broth for the dog.

Now the coffin lay across the grave hole on poles. The two matched teams stood by the road with their necks down. The morning air was wet, and it commenced to rain, so softly that the water drops Hugh saw on his shoes and the backs of his hands seemed to have formed on him like dew. His mother was behind him, veiled. Around them the hop vines, staked in heaps to their high sticks and stumps, looked like a taller, living crowd—waiting dark and still like everyone—a crowd gathered to hear the preacher and bury the box.

Hugh was almost ten. He and wriggling Bert and mystified Lulu, following their mother, stepped up to the hole one by one, and scooped a handful of mud from the tailings. They each dropped a clod on the box and turned towards the house.

CHAPTER XXI

Minta's family was due on the steamer this afternoon. They were coming from Baltimore by rail and steamer to comfort her, she thought, for Eustace had drowned a month ago, in August, 1885. When she heaped dirt on Eustace's coffin she had buried her heart, and was running on momentum, as a ship sails a gale on bare sticks. She would make a show for her mother and father and sister June, for she could produce fineness in the wilderness bare-handed, and fineness meant the "living will that shalt endure." It was a Tennyson poem which she knew, and her mother knew it, too, for it was a creed:

O living will that shalt endure
When all that seems shall suffer shock,
Rise in the spiritual rock,
Flow thro' our deeds and make them pure ...

With faith that comes of self-control.

"Rise in the spiritual rock," she exhorted herself mornings, "With faith that comes of self-control." It was worthless. In every corner of their big house she stumbled into Eustace's precisely shaped absence, and in the yard, the woods, the fields, garden, and barn. She carried herself carefully, like a scalding bowl—plain Minta, whose neck sloped straight from her linen collar, whose clear forehead and high brows stayed fixed. By herself and for herself, she tried to be splendid. Only secretly, as she tended the quarreling younger children and worked the ranch, did she whisper to herself deep in her mind, "I am dished." For where, exactly, had he gone, and the intensity of his ways?

The day was cold; by noon the north wind reddened Bert's hands. School ran most of the year now, and Hugh was there, so it was up to Minta to carry some workers' lunches to the hop fields herself. She gave Bert two pails full of bread and cane syrup wrapped in paper; she carried a jug of sweet tea and a fawn haunch. She would present the fawn haunch to Jenny Lind, her *tillicum*—as she flattered herself—who was Kulshan Jim's wife. She did not know that these friends privately deplored the way she butchered venison; she cut across the meat's grain, instead of separating the muscles the way they grew.

Every morning the Nooksacks appeared in perfect silence at dawn to pick hops at a dollar a day. Jenny Lind took Lulu with them, and turned her over to the care of the woman called Queen of the May. Lulu had turned three. She wore a black dress that fell in a wide triangle from its tight shoulders and sleeves, and black shoes that buttoned high over her ankles—which shoes she evidently worked off the minute she got to the hop fields, for Minta had never visited the fields so early she did not find Lulu barefoot. Lulu passed her days with Queen of the May and the Nooksack children in the fields. She seemed to thrive in the atmosphere of the Nooksacks' close family life. When she was awake at home she talked all the time earnestly, with a baby's pleased look, but she spoke only the tongue the Nooksacks spoke, and Minta could not comprehend a word of it.

Minta and Bert headed down the path behind the carriage house through the timber: two dark figures low in the forest aisle. Bert at six was a floppy, apparently boneless boy whose arms and legs seemed to be held on by his clothes. Once Minta and he had ridden into the village and back, and he never for one moment faced forward on his horse. He was riding ahead on Old Snap; he turned around to talk exuberantly to his mother and boast, or to hit at branches with his stick, and remained turned around every step of the way. He kept a lazy hand on the horse's rump, flopped like a sack, and seemed not to notice when his horse broke into a trot. He rode a horse the way other children sprawled on a carpet. Bert was safe on Peaches, the young mare no one else could control but Kulshan Jim. Minta saw a spiritual quality in Bert, a species of knightly hopefulness concealed under his black lashes, which other people could not see; to other adults he seemed inert as grain or dried peas loose in a poke, who seemed to shift from place to place by pouring himself. Now Minta walked beside him, slowly, in a ruffled dress of black outing flannel.

The forest was cold and windless; a maze of leafless lower twigs grayed the middle space like mist. Soon Minta could see the light of the fields ahead, where the last rank of trunks ended in brightness down to the ground, the way the forest in Maryland broke off tall when it hit the bay.

She had five acres of bottomland in hops. She and Eustace had bought good land, because they could afford to; the topsoil was two feet deep. All the farmers in the Nooksack and Skagit deltas converted to hop ranching if their soil drained and if they could afford to clear land, buy root cuttings, and hire Indian men to stake the vines. A prosperous Nooksack neighbor, Semiahmoo Joe, had built a drying kiln, and lent it out for shares. These long harvest evenings, Kulshan Jim raked Minta's berries—which were actually flowers sticky from aphid dew—back and forth over the heated drying kiln floor. Kulshan Jim was no longer lean. He was thoughtful, worried, wide-faced and short-nosed; he wore a plug hat, a blue shirt, and galluses. He packed the dried hops berries in 150-pound bags for the Milwaukee buyer.

The cold sun streaked the fields. Everywhere charred ten-foot fir stumps supported the hop vines and the stakes that raised them twenty feet off the ground. The leafy vines climbed two strings up each stump and massed high over the stumps' tops, so that from the forest's edge the fields looked to Minta like a tepee encampment on the plains. She found the dozens of natives spread widely. The men, wearing overalls or breechclouts, shirtless, stood on ladders and worked the tops of the vines. The women picked from the ground. Minta could see, above the forest, the distant smoke from the camp on the riverbank, where bands of tribal families from Canada, and from over the mountains, lived during the harvest. The Nooksack people lived in houses up the river.

Bert flopped over to join the youngest children, who were hiding inside the sticky, tented vines. All their bare or black-stockinged legs protruded. Minta could see Lulu crouched laughing under the leaves, and she pretended not to see her, for Lulu dearly loved to hide.

Here came Jenny Lind's mother-in-law, Mother Nooksack, of whom Minta had an abiding horror, making her wide way over to greet her. Minta never knew Mother Nooksack; she saw her only as a figure, and was unaware that she did. Mother Nooksack was an old woman, over fifty, whose forehead sloped back from her eyebrows to the sharp ledge of her skull, so her head looked to Minta like a cold chisel, with braids. Most of the old Nooksacks and Lummis, men and women over twenty-five, had flattened heads like hers; their mothers had lashed boards over their foreheads when they were infants in cradleboards, to mark them as distinguished in birth.

Minta had been surprised, when she and Eustace first settled here, by the Nooksacks' daily preoccupation with rank, class, and wealth. It was worse than Maryland. No lineal descendants of Lord Baltimore could preen themselves more on their names, or could pitch greater fits when their offspring threatened to marry beneath them, than the Nooksacks who lived at the river's crossing. Minta had been happy to leave, as she thought, all that vainglory in Baltimore, and was amused to find it reproduced here, in what she told Eustace was its "smoked and dried form," among her Nooksack neighbors, the guilelessness of whose potlatching ostentation and the frankness of whose blanket-seeking for status made of the similar but better concealed passions of the Maryland gentry a naked satire.

"Minta," the old woman said now, as Minta crossed the field. "*Kah mika chahko?*" When she smiled, her high cheeks almost covered her eyes, and her low outcrop of teeth appeared, worn to the gumline from chewing dried fish. She took the tea jug from Minta and held her hand delicately, to lead her to the others. The first time Minta had seen Mother Nooksack, she was carrying all the household goods piled five feet high on her back—woven mats, white goathair blankets, sacks—and was walking down the trail bent over so her back was flat as a wagon bed, for which it served. She walked with two canes, as all the women did when they carried loads. They moved between fishing camps, hunting camps, and their winter village at the crossing. Her son Kulshan Jim had waited by the canoes, grandly, with the men. Carrying her load, the old woman looked to Minta like a bagworm in a juniper; only small and miraculously motile parts of her emerged beneath her teetering burden. Tied to the back of the load that day, like the tail on a coonskin cap, was an alert baby in a cradleboard.

Minta laid the lunch pails on the lumpy grass, one for the men nearby and one for the women. Lulu burst from under her vines and came running; her round bare feet churned under her skirts like a paddle wheel. The Indian men and women lowered their sacks and followed. The old women, wearing cotton dresses or doeskin skirts, walked bent. Two old men, wearing breechclouts only, had erect spines, broad shoulders, and legs bent and crookedly bowed—twisted down to the bones, the settlers explained to each other, from kneeling in canoes. Many Nooksacks were still picturesque to Minta after all these years, and she knew few of their varied personal natures. The young men and women glided over the humped ground gracefully as sloops.

Minta's other friend approached—Queen of the May. She was trying to drive the children ahead of her like chickens by awkwardly flapping her apron. She was long-backed, long-necked, and long-skulled; she had only one arm, and her empty yellow calico sleeve flapped with her skirt. She always wore a Gainsborough hat, wide as a tray, festooned with glass cherries and silk roses. She bound her braids with green satin ribbons. Her husband, Charles Kilcup, was the lively miner who delivered the settlement's mail by carrying it inside his top hat, and who bobbed when he walked like a fish crow. He had helped with Eustace's body.

Queen of the May greeted Minta with her customary tight-lipped glare. She scowled at the children, hers and Jenny Lind's, who hung back.

Minta was fond of her. She called all the settlers, in English, "cockeyed," or "bally," although she lived by choice in Goshen, in a split-cedar house near town. She took her newborn babies up into the mountains alone for a week, to pray, and her with one arm. Her first husband had died in the smallpox epidemic, and she startled Minta once outside the church with a song in English she said described him:

He et the meat, he give me the bone,
He kicked me out, he sent me home.

Queen of the May wore a baby in a cradleboard strapped to her back. Hiding behind her yellow skirt were Ardeth, seven, and Howard, three, a diffident, handsome pair. Queen of the May had warned them never to look a stranger in the face, for the stranger might be a magician who could steal their spirits if their eyes met, and hide those spirits in the mountains, or throw them in the river—and what would they do then? Minta was no stranger, but they were wary around her still. The Nooksacks called her Pond Eyes, for her spectacles. They had called Eustace the Nooksack equivalent of Ants in His Pants, which phrase he recognized as his name, but never understood.

Jenny Lind's black-headed children, Aigal and Frankie, crowded with Ardeth and Howard behind Queen of the May. Like the Skagit children, the Nooksack children bathed in the river summer and winter, to learn to summon courage and withstand pain. They no longer submitted to morning whippings, for crises and Christianity—first Catholicism, then Methodism—had diluted the bands' traditional training. Now the four children began pulling at each other, and Queen of the May waved at them her empty calico sleeve. Her gaunt cheekbones cast deep shadows, for she lacked back teeth. When young Hugh took their lunches to the Nooksack workers in the fields, he always sat with Queen of the May; he liked her as much as his mother did, possibly for her good-natured impiety and gloomy views. It got almighty earnest around his house, and even his mother, who dished it out, seemed relieved to escape it.

Overhead some white puffed clouds sped, and threw their blue shadows up the leafy stumps where the hops grew, and threw the shadows down the stumps' other sides and into the woods fast as snakes. It was early September, and smelled of winter already.

* * *

Jenny Lind sat on a log in the dirt beside Minta, Mother Nooksack, and Queen of the May. Lulu rolled over to her while the women talked, stood behind her back, and wrapped a fond stranglehold about her neck. Jenny Lind was in her twenties. Her face was oval and mournful, her lips composed and determined. The wakeful expression on her wide-spaced, heavy-lidded black eyes, her elusive laughter, and her clear skin, marked only by a single pock on her forehead, made her notable among the settlers for her beauty—for her conforming to the lithographed Fair Indian Maiden—as she was notable among the Nooksacks for her industry. She worked at something—spinning or mending or grooming her children— even when she was sitting down, the Nooksacks said; it was the virtue they most prized, as the settlers most prized a woman who got her Monday washing on the line before breakfast. The settlers called her Jenny Lind for her habit of singing, in tones they found unearthly, as she walked. Jenny Lind considered Queen of the May, her own sister-in-law, undignified and unmannerly, and tried to keep her distance. Now she bent to reach a lunch pail and brought an amused Lulu with her over her back. She fingered the child's thin curls. Jenny Lind's own children, and Queen of the May's children, waited, bumping each other, for lunch.

Here came the shovel-headed woman they called Mother Legree, wearing high-buttoned shoes and a cape. She joined the women by sitting on the ground and offering a basket of black raspberries. With Mother Legree was her somnolent slave, a pliant, dish-faced Kanaka girl from the Sandwich Islands whom the Nooksacks had stolen as a child from traveling Haidas, who in turn had bought her off the steamer from San Francisco. Mother Legree kept her slave's hair shorn to her ears, and worked her little; she represented wealth and status in her person, not in her labor. Often Minta had observed Mother Legree bent double carrying blankets and mats on her back while her slave sauntered behind her bare-handed.

Because her family was coming, Minta saw the scene with fresh eyes, and wondered if her mother, father, and June could find aught to admire in her Indian friends—or in any of her friends, for that matter. Jenny Lind wore a silver dollar alongside her nose, which usage was out of fashion in Baltimore, and Queen of the May possessed only those four front teeth in her head—two up and two down—and carried a wolf paw around her neck on an oily thong. From her hat's brim a silk rose dripped over one eye. All the women wore grizzled calico dresses or sooty skin skirts they smoked over fires, rather than washed, to discourage lice—a practice the

Dorrs and the other first settlers had enthusiastically adopted. Minta had seen the Kanaka slave girl, just last week, remove her blouse entirely; Mother Legree made her put it back on.

What would her family notice? Goshen was a big town now, by local standards, and it had a Normal School. Yet in Goshen many white men used the most villainous profanity. One excellent neighbor, Conrad Coombs, regularly paid for stamps by handing the postmistress a dead fish. He was an orator, whose hobby was geometry and whose passion was literature; he kept his voice in practice by declaiming Shakespeare to his cows. Hugh's schoolmate Mina Reese carried a doll whose hair was a human scalp. When the doll wore out, she moved the scalp to a new doll, and her loving mother sewed it down tight, so she could comb it. Minta's mother was fine porcelain, and such things might grind her; her sister June was, as a child, ironic, and might sling out anything. During her family's visit, Minta thought, she would invite Drew and Dovie Dorr for tea, and hope Bert could sit straight at table like a human, or her father's heart would break. She had been fretting most about Lulu, who of course would learn to speak English presently, but she had not truly begun on it yet. Perhaps she could pretend Lulu was sick, and keep her too far away to talk to anyone.

In the hop field, the women talked about the weather: it was windy; it was unseasonably cold. Minta had not learned the Nooksacks' language; the Nooksacks had learned some English, and everyone knew Chinook. They talked about typhoid fever. Typhoid was flaring up in Goshen, and a trapper they knew, called "the Cowwoolley," died of it. They talked about the children; Jenny Lind's baby had a name that sounded to Minta like beach stones being shoveled; she tried to pronounce it, to everyone's unwearying amusement, even the baby's. The children carefully tried on her spectacles. Jenny Lind was reserved, and so was Minta; neither pried nor presumed, and though they fell into many misunderstandings at first, they carried on.

Queen of the May's baby was crying. Its name was Green; it had green eyes. She fetched him off her back and nursed him in his cradleboard. He still cried. His tears wet the soft moss in which he was swaddled. Queen of the May propped the cradleboard against a stump, dipped a cup in the water bucket, and dashed the water on the baby's face. He stopped crying and looked scandalized. She returned with the cradleboard and set it beside her; the baby gazed around. Queen of the May bore herself severely, gaunt-faced; she never smiled. Once when her hat blew out its pins and flew off, Minta saw a bald curved scar on her skull. Her son Howard, a naked black-eyed boy whose round head looked too heavy for his frail neck, dragged his outgrown willow cradleboard with him onto his mother's lap. Minta had never seen Howard without his old cradleboard in one hand. When he grew sleepy, he begged to be swaddled back into it. Minta heard his mother refuse him gently, in her language that popped and hissed.

After lunch, Minta and her son Bert walked home; Bert wriggled ahead in his black stockings and short pants, like a horsehair worm in a rain barrel, upright and flexing. Mother Nooksack walked to the field's edge with Minta, and seemed to be praising Bert to her, possibly insincerely.

From the road Minta could see that sandy patch of riverbank where yesterday Lulu and Bert had made horse prints—the prints were still there. It was a favorite pastime of theirs—Hugh had started it. They each banged a barn board till a knot fell out. With a knife, Hugh whittled the little knots into the shape of horseshoes. Then Lulu and Bert spent hours down on the riverbank, printing the inch-long hoofmarks along the sand in straying paths. Yesterday they had called their mother to see. "Why, look," Minta said, as if astonished. "A herd of little horses has been drinking here!" Lulu always laughed, her cheeks tight as ticks; she understood English, though she could not speak it, and loved the joke.

Setting the table with silent Hugh that afternoon for seven—her family might arrive at any time—Minta remembered how Mother Nooksack looked. Minta had watched her turn back at the edge of the fields. Old Mother Nooksack had rocked along the field between the towering hop vines; her sharp head plowed into the wind. She was carrying her bag, swollen with berries. Her back bent over; her gray braids nearly swept the ground.

When Eustace was living, he had deplored, as all the white men piously deplored, the wretched and degrading lot of native women. One morning he had broached with Kulshan Jim this delicate subject, so close to settlers' hearts. He told Minta about it that evening at supper, so that Hugh, who was so watchful and careful he was like a little old man, could hear.

Eustace had come to rely on Kulshan Jim as foreman. This day they were clearing a patch of the wet vegetation that surged up everywhere on cleared land—hazel and alder, and plaguey thickets of blackberry. The two men conversed in English and Chinook while they worked, and paused to load their pipes.

Kulshan Jim's wife, Jenny Lind, was a fine woman, Eustace began. Kulshan Jim's composed face revealed a flicker of pleasure. The Nooksack women were all fine women, he continued; Kulshan Jim frowned. A fine woman, like a fine racehorse, was a noble creature who throve on tender considerations. She embodied, upheld, and transmitted the virtues dearest to humankind, practiced the most civilized arts, and in her fragility and sympathy spread the delicate influence without which men's lives would be coarse. Why then did the Nooksack men use their women like mules? Here Eustace broke off, surprised, and tucked his hair under his hat, for he had not meant to say this so harshly.

Kulshan Jim's round face stiffened. He shifted his bare feet, scratched a rust spot from his brush hook, and confessed in a low voice that as his people saw it, the Bostons used their own fragile women very ill indeed, for did the Boston men not sometimes strike their *klootchmen*, as if these women had been warriors of the enemy?

Eustace had to acknowledge that this was known to occur, but not among the Bostons he knew. The two had stopped working. Kulshan Jim took off his plug hat and drew on his pipe. His sister, whom the whites called Queen of the May, he said, was married to the white miner and mailman Charles Kilcup. She confided to their mother that Welshy Bovard broke his own wife's nose with his fist and broke her ribs with a stick of cordwood; he basted her regularly on Saturday nights. Even Charles Kilcup had been known to knock Queen of the May around when the children got out of hand. Kulshan Jim had been studying the Bostons closely for the past ten years, and he still could not understand how rich men could so lose their dignity.

A Nooksack who struck a woman would be disgraced, he asserted with some vehemence; the woman would return, with her wealth, to her family; the man would have to quit the tribe. Such a thing had never happened among the Nooksacks. All the Nooksacks pitied the Boston women—pitied them! he said softly, and his short nose quivered—whose houses were long journeys apart, who worked alone, got hit, and died young.

Eustace, sitting on a wet log, had found no reply. If he were a woman, which would he prefer? It was true that Nooksack men treated white women with delicate consideration, seeming to share the veneration for female gentility that was the frontier's secular religion. When he hired a Nooksack shovel-nosed canoe to take Minta to Whatcom, the paddler, whoever he might be, helped her in and out of the canoe as if she had been infirm instead of youthful and vigorous, and made many tender inquiries as to her comfort on the mats spread for her on the canoe's bottom. She had grown so accustomed to the paddlers' skill on the river, and so trustful of their unfailing solicitude, that she had taken to using these trips for naps. Eustace was now forced to consider, as he told Minta and Hugh that evening at supper, that the Nooksacks' deference was in fact pity; the Nooksack men were compensating for the Boston men's moral failings. The woods were fairly flying with arrows of pity from all directions.

CHAPTER XXII

At the end of the day, Jenny Lind brought Lulu home asleep on her shoulder. Square-headed Hugh was standing on the porch, keeping an eye on things. Since his father's death, he had taken on the role of the man of the family. For Jenny Lind he held open the door into the parlor.

Jenny Lind passed Lulu with a caress to Minta, arms to arms, and the women's eyes met. The child's round wrists were brown from the sun and cold to the touch; her curls were whitened and stuck with leaves. Minta noticed the boy Aigal, who was gravely extending to her Lulu's small, creased shoes. Minta took the shoes and thanked him. They could hear Queen of the May's son Howard bang and scrape his cradleboard outside on the porch. Jenny Lind carried a mess of white goat hair in one hand, a strand of which she began to spin into yarn by rolling it under her hand against her hip.

Often Minta persuaded Jenny Lind and her children to stay to supper, but not this day. Minta thought she had befriended Jenny Lind—who had in fact, with Kulshan Jim, consciously befriended her and Eustace before he was *melamoosed* on the logjam. They saw the settlers as homeless people, destitute even of their families, who did not know how to behave.

Jenny Lind and Kulshan Jim were serious Christians, though Kulshan Jim was considering slying out to the winter spirit dances. They bore noble names and held themselves aloof from passion; the capacity for prayer, moral discernment, and self-denial ran deep in both. They recognized and forgave Minta's condescension, which they despised in others. Now Jenny Lind gathered the children and left for home at the crossing—the big cedar lodge where ten families lived. Last winter the men had nailed carved trimmed gables to the rough lodge to give it style. They copied the Bostons' fashion in architecture, as the Bostons copied easterners' fashions, copied from London.

The steamer was late. Hugh gave Bert and Lulu their supper, then lit into the dishes, standing sad-eyed at the sink with his hat on. Minta put Bert and Lulu to bed; she sat with them in their room upstairs. She listened at the window for the steamer whistle and heard the cicadas' sharp droning in the trees. She felt the fullness of time, its expectancy, and the unbreathing, sham beauty of the world. The sun had dropped behind the forest and cast its blue shade on the farmhouse clearing. The long northern twilight was beginning to pool on the clearing; it leached yellow from goldenrod, blued the asters, and blackened the woods.

Her supper had perked Lulu right up, and now she expressed all sorts of incomprehensible wishes to her mother, who tried to calm her for the nightly Scripture reading. Lulu was holding a fuzzy brown doll that Queen of the May had made for her from cattails. Hugh was preparing to kindle the first fire of the year in the fireplace downstairs. This had been Eustace's job, and Eustace always began in the fall by knocking out the old creosote with chains from the roof, for fir was pitchy. Hugh began conscientiously by splitting cedar and breaking up packing boxes.

Upstairs Bert lay perfectly flat in the bed, as if he had no body under the bedsheets, and fixed up at his mother's face his round eyes. Minta took off her spectacles. She located in the prophet Isaiah the passage she sought as apt—for she hoped her children might come to regard God as their father and find themselves ultimately not bereaved but enlarged. For her it was useless so far, but the children were suggestible.

"Comfort ye, comfort ye, my people, saith your God," she read.

"... He shall feed his flock like a shepherd; he shall gather the lambs with his arm, and carry them in his bosom, and shall gently lead those that are with young."

She glanced up, to see black-haired Lulu frowning at the ceiling. Mysterious Bert was looking at her eyes deeply as if he had never twitched a muscle in his life except to follow her eyes slowly with his. His eyes were so big they looked flat; Minta fancied the hidden parts, like two goose eggs, must occupy most of his skull. She reached out a hand to stroke his forehead; his deep gaze did not break when her hand crossed its path, nor did his expression change when she met his eyes for a moment. What was passing in his mind? This is the one, really, Minta thought, who cares for me in the same wild way I care for them all; my arms long for them even when they are in my arms. Once last spring she had felt the same bone-deep sensation for Lulu—that Lulu was overwhelmingly the dearest of her children—when Eustace was plowing, and she had gone out and found Lulu asleep in the furrow.

"Have ye not known? have ye not heard? hath it not been told you from the beginning? have ye not understood from the foundations of the earth?

"It is he that sitteth upon the circle of the earth, and the inhabitants thereof are as grasshoppers.... Yea, they shall not be planted; yea, they shall not be sown; yea, their stock shall not take root in the earth: and he shall also blow upon them, and they shall wither, and the whirlwind shall take them away as stubble."

This is growing grim, she was thinking, when the whistle sounded. She put on her spectacles. The *Doris Burn* was in at the Goshen dock; its steam whistle piped out a musical note that probably startled the cows clear to Mount Baker. Right at this moment her family, most of whom she had not seen in eleven years, would be standing on deck with their hands over their ears, excited, deafened by the whistle, and waiting to disembark. This was their seventh and last day on steamers north from San Francisco.

Bert and Lulu popped up and she poked them back down. She said she would be right back with their grandparents Randall and their aunt June, but if they should fall asleep, everyone would still be here in the morning. She hurried down the stairs smoothing her skirt—the wide, black-velvet-trimmed skirt of a black bombazine dress. She told Hugh to put Old Snap to the spring wagon.

Hugh had solemnly erected over the kindling in the fireplace a tower of orange split alder, as orderly as a tall log fort whose top was lost to view; he broke off a lucifer match to light it, carefully enclosed it with the screen, and followed his mother to the stable.

In another twenty minutes she and Hugh were at the dock, where they found the Randalls and their four trunks. The little *Doris Burn*—not more than forty feet on the waterline—with its stern wheel and green trim, was a familiar, glad sight. It was part of what they all called the mosquito fleet, whose ships were said to float on heavy dew. It was so underpowered it had to stop its engine to blow its whistle.

There was Minta's father, Senator Randall, who, despite his urban top hat and striped suit, had already charmed the steamer captain and was listening in the wheelhouse, rapt, to what he later described with relish as "one of the man's exceedingly damnable stories." There was Minta's myopic mother, Louisa, startlingly shortened and softened; the thin, cultured tones of her voice trembled under her trembling hatbrim, and she carried a white parasol. The shock to Minta was her sister, June, previously a slangy hoyden on a thoroughbred, who was now a petite woman of twenty-seven, dressed in a woman's bustled and tucked peach-colored linen suit and a flat hat piled with bent flowers and plumes. Her big eyes glittered with awareness, amusement, and forced compassion, and she was attempting to look as though she had mastered this wild land and her sister's position at a glance.

The light was quitting the village like a vapor dispersing; the river still held a frail, cold pallor as if water itself shone; the gravel bars banked it. Above the river the sky was a slash of blue where planets swam between the black forest walls.

In the next twenty minutes the group was walking beside the creaking spring wagon up the dim road through the forest towards the ranch. The visitors had exclaimed over all—they had seen Mount Baker from the river. Steaming into Bellingham Bay, they told Minta, they had seen several forest fires in Whatcom—red flames fed rising white smokes. Now they admired Hugh's slenderness, curled brown hair, short nose, and large eyes extravagantly, saying he looked like every Randall and Biddle. In fact, as Hugh knew, he looked like his father and the Honers. He smiled stiffly to hear the Randalls claim the very nose off his face, for he recognized the generosity behind it. The Randalls had, in short, conquered their self-consciousness with Minta, when they turned up the road to her place and saw, in the clearing, her house on fire.

The roof had already buckled on the north side of the house. Red fire rose from its hole and from every window. Gray smoke billowed over the clearing and blocked the last light. An upstairs window popped and blew out, as if the dense, pouring smoke had punched it. Pieces of burning eave and wall fell and showed fire inside in yellow sheets that roared. The many silhouetted figures in the distance came forward and met Minta crossing the lawn—tall Clare Fishburn, Kulshan Jim and Jenny Lind, Norval Tawes, and the new schoolmaster—and none of them had Bert or Lulu, nor was Bert or Lulu to be found among the other knotted figures standing as close to the house as they could and watching.

CHAPTER XXIII

Two and a half weeks later, in mid-September, 1885, Senator Green Randall, of Baltimore, Maryland, woke up in a strange farmhouse in Goshen, Washington Territory. The last time he had slept on a mattress tick, he recalled, was when he was a boy visiting his grandfather in Annapolis. There they used corncobs in a mattress; here it was straw. Now he was a grandfather visiting his grandchildren, two of whom had died in the fire two and a half weeks before. He would take his widowed daughter, Minta, and his surviving grandson, Hugh, back to Baltimore, and they could start life over again, for this life had failed. Senator Randall was billeted now on some of his daughter's neighbors, two men and a woman. His wife and their younger daughter, June, were staying across the river with a family named Dorr.

Before breakfast in the kitchen, his hostess, Ada Tawes, read from Scripture. Among the verses, she read: "Who stoppeth his ears at the cry of the poor, he also shall cry himself, but shall not be heard." The senator wondered why she read such a verse at such a time. She was bony and thin-shouldered; when she stood, her shoes poked out from her skirts at a wide interval, so she looked ready for anything. Her hairless husband, Norval Tawes, concocted and spoke a homemade prayer on the spot in that Methodist way, a prayer that spread before the gaze of God Minta's misfortunes, which moved the senator.

The pair was his age, pioneers as his grandparents had been a century ago in Maryland—muscled, quiet people who understood their lives and their place in history, and who prayed hard, fast, and often, like men at war. They lived the way people lived in the East a hundred years ago—in big families, in poverty bound to the agricultural year. Ada Tawes wrapped meat in canvas and hung it out every night, for they had no ice for iceboxes.

Senator Randall was short, big-footed, and bald save for the ring of black, curly hair that circled his scalp like a wreath. To everyone he met he turned the mighty beam of his full attention. Following a reception for three hundred Maryland merchants and bankers, each of the three hundred men returned to his office reflecting on the private, significant look with which the Senator had distinguished him. He spoke softly, and remembered with unfeigned interest every man, woman, and child, Negro or white, that he had met since he was ten years old, as well as most everything he had read or heard. On his deathbed he could have cited the cost of freight by land or water in 1885 for Whatcom County, Washington, which he learned on the *Doris Burn*; he could have analyzed that year's Chinese crisis in the cities on Puget Sound, which he heard about at this morning's breakfast, and quoted depressed local prices for acreage, town lots, wheat, apples, and hops.

After breakfast the woman's grown son, Clare Fishburn, long and straight as water from a spigot, accompanied him to Minta's farm. People here called her farm "a hop ranch," as if the berries were willful creatures you had to round up and brand.

Clare Fishburn shambled beside him along the cavernous forest road. He was so thin he seemed to the senator like half a man, and one who had done a bit of everything out here, like everyone else. He said he shaved spruce staves for barrels, until the market dried up. He joined a blade crew and sheared sheep. He raised seed. He gambled on the Lummi reservation with friends, he said, and invited the senator to join them. He used to bring the Lummi women calico from Victoria, until the English shopkeeper on the reservation asked him to quit. He had just completed a course at the Goshen Normal School, to qualify him to teach school.

The sun was rising beside Mount Baker, and glossing its ice. On the rough ground in the clearing, surrounded by hayfields, was a blot of black soil where Minta's house had burned. From the center of the black soil rose a twenty-foot heap of bubbly boards, broken glass, roofing, cast iron, and charcoal. Someone had fired the heap to reduce it, and it smoked and stank.

A white tent stood nearby on grass. It was an officer's tent from the war between the states. The long northern light streaked its trembling walls.

Senator Randall with Clare Fishburn walked around the tent to its doorway, and heard heavy motions from within, sounds of breathing and possibly struggling, but no voices. Nooksack women wearing nose rings and aprons stood outside in silence with somber, short-legged children. When they caught sight of the two men, one of these women—a tall one missing an arm, who wore a wide Gainsborough hat, and whose young cheeks caved in—set up a courteous shrieking and pounded her feet, till the others hushed her.

"Hello, Queen of the May," Clare Fishburn said; his creased face showed simple pleasure. "How is Ardeth? We heard she had a cold." Queen of the May, tall as she was, turned up her long face to answer Clare, and the silk roses on her hatbrim slopped over.

Senator Randall found the tent doorway blocked by the bodies of Indian men. He saw the backs of their heads, their straight black hair, long as women's hair, unbound; some were naked above the waist, and their dark backs were bumpy with what looked like mosquito bites. Senator Randall glanced back at Clare, whom he would apparently need as host in his daughter's tent. Clare edged between two men, exchanging greetings, and Senator Randall followed him around the pole and into the tent.

In the center of the tent, on the trampled grass, was a canvas cot. On this cot, on her back, lay Minta Honer, gazing slowly above her spectacles from side to side. Four Indian men leaned over her, two on either hand. They raised their arms above her. She was wearing the same bombazine mourning dress, now dirty, that she wore when Senator Randall caught sight of her leading a horse and spring wagon to the dock eighteen days ago, the night the house burned. Here she was barefoot. Senator Randall had never seen any white woman's bare feet but his wife's.

What hath God wrought? This was his daughter, broken in spirit and come to every grief. Her wedding, eleven years before, was still talked about in Baltimore, for its munificent appointments, for the splendor of its decorated lawn setting, and for the bold romance of the young couple's departure by train the next day for Peter Puget's Sound.

Green Randall began his life as an Annapolis youth of high degree, whose family looked down on Baltimore, which was then, in the thirties of his boyhood, the second-greatest city in the country. The city nevertheless drew him, and when he was eighteen he apprenticed himself to a genial Baltimore lawyer; presently he passed the bar's oral examination, declined to practice law, and was elected to the state senate. In Baltimore he attended Saint Paul's Church, dined daily and expansively at the Maryland Club with old men of old families, presented his two daughters at the Bachelors Cotillion, and rode to hounds in the Green Valley Hunt. His fair wife, Louisa Biddle, daughter of Philadelphia's Singleton Biddle, had possessed the dewy beauty, supple long lines, and exquisite wardrobe that excited and sustained admiration. She gained admittance into Baltimore society and was petted, respected, and praised, only after both she and the several ruling matrons had resolved, by abandoning it in affection and fatigue, the ticklish question of who was granting whom a favor: was it Baltimore who stooped to receive Philadelphia, or Philadelphia who descended to grace Baltimore?

In 1880, the Maryland state legislature elected Green Randall to the United States Senate; thenceforth he removed, with a congenial domestic staff and a knot of clerks, to Washington when that body was in session.

Now, standing in the crowded tent, among half-naked Indian men looking down at the supine form on the cot, Senator Randall knew that Minta possessed all his heart again, and probably always had. She did not start when her raised eyes met his, though she twisted to read his expression, which was, habitually, that of a man equal to any occasion—which he hitherto, after all, was.

One of the Indian people had a flattened head and a forehead wide as a coal shovel. His stiff white hair he parted in the middle and bound with a thong; his cracked, thick face barely budged as he began uttering a thin musical chant, which droned and slid and caused the hair at the back of the senator's neck to stir at the roots. This man laid his two hands on Minta's one hand and began kneading her fingertips. He was, himself, lacking a finger. So was Senator Randall. The broad, wrinkled Indian man across from him took Minta's other hand in his and rubbed the fingertips; together the men worked up her hands to her wrists in their black sleeves. The older man moaned his repetitive chant in a tender, insinuating voice. They worked squeezing up Minta's forearms, elbows, and, carefully, forcefully, her upper arms.

Senator Randall glanced up at Clare Fishburn, who showed no alarm. The other Indian people in the room, and the motionless two beside the cot, attended to the proceedings vigorously, and from time to time exclaimed something in apparent approval.

"What are they doing?" the senator finally asked Clare.

"They are ridding her of ghosts." Clare bent over to whisper. "Her ghosts. They will squeeze them out of her toes."

Minta lay inert, her eyes closed. The older men raised her arms above her head and began pressing her sides from the armpits. Avoiding her bosom, they rubbed down to her waist. The two younger men began pressing down her hips and lower limbs; the two older men stayed working behind them as a rear guard.

It was the young, terrible ghosts of Lulu and Bert they were driving away, and any remaining ghost of her husband, Eustace, so the grieving woman could live at all. The headman was an old Skagit medicine man brought in for the occasion. When Eustace drowned, a month earlier, these same native men, including the old Skagit medicine man, had entered her yard carrying cedar boughs, which they lighted with matches and slapped, smoking, against the outside walls of her house. This house-beating by fiery cedar boughs sent the ghost of Eustace away, and banished it to another village they had in mind.

A week later Kulshan Jim's kindhearted uncle had arrived on Minta's porch. He was the peaveyman for a logging company up the river. He carried a basket, which he placed on the kitchen table and filled with water. He rolled up his sleeves and plunged both arms into the basket up to their elbows. Then he wrestled down in the water with the ghost of Eustace. He struggled deep in the basket, and carried on, until red drops of blood appeared on the water. The blood drops floated and shifted. Then he had tea and pie with Minta and Hugh, and left.

Minta never knew that Queen of the May had secured this service for her. Queen of the May had talked her husband—Charles Kilcup—into donating five dollars of their scarce cash to hire the expert to wrestle Eustace's ghost for Minta. Her own first husband had died fifteen years before in the smallpox epidemic. She spoke ill of him always, but she remembered that he had cut her fish for her when she lost her arm, and minced it for her when she lost her back teeth, and she wondered sometimes if his ghost was not abroad to this day. The Nooksack families that Minta knew were, in short, generous neighbors; they had the practice of many deaths, and they knew that ghosts were particularly harsh in the presence of other ghosts.

It seemed to the senator that it was a cruel song the flat-headed Indian man was singing, and that he was singing it to defend with his strength the sum of the living against the world's cruelty, and this was so. The old Skagit medicine man was also, in fact, a paid professional. Privately he saw his own people, and their friends like Minta, as vulnerable to affliction, and he saw all other people, along with the offended spirits, as affliction's source.

By the time the lower pairs of hands reached Minta's toes, the upper pair had circled her ankles around her dress's velvet hem. The men bent and strained, and first one pair of hands, and then the other, drove the ghosts down through the tips of each foot's toes, and out.

They were finished. The flat-headed man looked directly at the senator, nodded, and quitted the tent without looking back. The others followed. Minta opened her eyes.

There were four more men in the tent with Senator Randall and Clare Fishburn. They were bare-chested; one wore a jaunty green Tyrolese hat. These four men knelt on the ground, one facing each of the four tent walls. They folded their hands against their chests, closed their eyes, lowered their heads, and apparently prayed.

"I gather the native religions are in a transitional phase?" Senator Randall remarked much later to Norval Tawes. The men were waiting on the porch for supper. The snows on Mount Baker reddened as the sky grew dark. The rusty rock peaks called the Sisters faded into the sky. Norval Tawes rolled his shoe-button eyes.

Most of the Nooksacks are Methodists, he said, "but my colleague has run afoul of their winter dancing. Now many are joining the Indian Shakers." Indian people up the Sound, he said—tilting back his top hat from his pointed face—had recently formed the Indian Shaker Church. They combined longhouse rites, especially dancing, with Christian ones they got from Shakers. They called the Holy Spirit "Santu Splay," from the French *Saint Esprit*.

Norval Tawes was happy, he said—there was something in the interested, cherishing gaze of the senator that brought forth the truth—happy that the natives here enjoyed any of the comforts of religion, any religion, for their numbers were declining, and their lot was hard. He knew God heard their prayers, and he hoped and expected to meet them in heaven, but he did not know why God pressed down on them so hardly on earth—on them or, begging your pardon, Senator, on the rest of us.

CHAPTER XXIV

These mornings, Minta rose from her cot in the tent the moment she awoke, lest her thoughts overpower her. An unendurably sentimental verse pounded with her pulse, and she had neither the will nor, especially, the taste, to resist it. Eustace had given her a Christina Rosetti volume for Christmas. She remembered:

Never on this side of the grave again,
   On this side of the river,
On this side of the garner of the grain,
   Never.

Kulshan Jim had been first to spot the fire. He entered the burning house at a run, and saw at the top of the stairs the body of Bert, past saving. He searched for others and found no one; the smoke drove him out. Shortly afterwards, Minta, Hugh, and the Baltimore family arrived from the dock with the spring wagon. Then, in the clearing lit by flames, Kulshan Jim saw thin Hugh break from his mother's side and try to flit into the house. He caught the brave boy and held his hot shoulders most of the night, at first to restrain him, and then to keep him company, for no one had a thought to spare for him.

The thick-waisted, wide-faced man, brokenhearted, and the curly-headed upright boy whom the Nooksacks called White Eyes, stood side by side in the dark while the house collapsed and flamed. The boy kept the man company as well, for Kulshan Jim was losing his hope and his memories, and he smelled death everywhere he went. First the wagon trains' cholera carried off most of his parents' generation; fifteen years later, the settlers' smallpox, which came late to the Nooksacks, took half the people left. Many in his family died. The Bostons took their land. They drove their remnant up the river. Many Nooksacks hated the Bostons.

Kulshan Jim had adjusted to this new, terrible life. He adjusted to Methodism, adjusted to working the soil, adjusted to the Honers and the bad smell of their unwashed bodies, adjusted to his uncles and cousins despising him for enslaving himself, they said, for bread, sugar, and bacon—and then he lost Eustace, Ants in His Pants, who was powerful even among the Bostons, as powerful as Hump Talem in his way, and who had been, every day, his *tillicum*. Now Eustace's own *tenas*—babies—were burning. Who, then, was protected from evil?

Last summer Kulshan Jim had cut his thigh with an ax; he woke one night and saw his own open wound glowing, yellow-green, in the dark. One of his cousins had recently seen a star fall from the sky into the sea and then rise again, burning, and resume its place in the firmament. Possibly the world was coming to its end. Kulshan Jim had shorn his ponytail years ago, and wore his thick hair parted in the middle and combed behind his ears. With his hair swept back, and the fire's noise, he looked windblown; his small-featured face shone harshly in the yellow light.

Later that night—and word of this came to Minta—Kulshan Jim and Norval Tawes entered the wreckage and found Lulu's body under her own bedsprings. She had been hiding, it seemed, from the fire. Norval Tawes had observed this before in house fires; foolish young children hide from fire, hoping it cannot find them.

It was this thought of Lulu, who died under her bed before she learned English after all, that Minta rose to banish, and other thoughts like it, of Lulu and Bert while they lived and, oddly, most keenly now of Eustace. Her own mother had lost three children in infancy; Ada Tawes had lost two that could talk. In the last weeks they had each offered to Minta, separately, this morsel of theology: that God swept up early into heaven those children who were too pure for this spotted world, whose goodness and beauty were of too fine a substance to sustain life here below, but served appropriately for the heavenly life of angels. Minta had not answered them. She seemed to lack air.

The visit of Minta's family had given Ada Fishburn Tawes a turn. She found trembling Louisa Randall useless, overdressed, and biggety, as she perfectly expected to. She had not, however, expected to find her so "awful soon." The Randalls, setting out from Baltimore, had caught the Union Pacific in Illinois, and crossed the country the long way, to see the desert, as a brief diversion. From Illinois to San Francisco, the trip took six days. The overland trip from Illinois had taken Ada six months, and cost her Charley when the wagon wheel ran over him in the rut, and cost Charley the living world, when he was not yet four. At Ogden, Utah, the Randall family had changed for a sightseeing excursion to Salt Lake City, to gawk at the Latter-day Saints, whose basically thrilling religion forbade them striped trousers and stovepipe hats. In Ada's own wagon train were two families bound for Sacramento, who were traveling three months out of their way just to miss the deadly Utah desert, and they lost, not one, but both men, anyway, husbands and fathers.

Louisa Randall, come to find out, had carried a glass vial of salt water from Chesapeake Bay. At the Whatcom dock she had infused it with cold water from Bellingham Bay, and so mingled Atlantic and Pacific waters, and clapped the breadth of the nation's destiny into a vial and corked it. Louisa Randall, her long head and hands trembling delicately, brought the vial from her purse to display to Ada, who, spraddle-legged in her kitchen, poured herself, possibly for the first time in her life, a little drink.

Clare Fishburn enjoyed the acquaintance of Senator Randall, for he liked surprises, and for surprises, Senator Randall held the belt. Clare had met many southern men, but never before a southern gentleman. Green Randall talked incessantly about women. He referred to women, he relished quoting them, he seemed proud to be under their influence: "My mama always told me, 'Trust the farmer....'" He openly embraced women's concerns. He had occasion to recall "my aunt Eliza Randall's cherry sideboard."

"My, what a lovely piece of stemware," he told Ada Tawes when she set out the household's sole specimen. Clare saw his mother halt in her tracks, the corner of her apron still raised in her hand, and plainly stare at the back of the man's head. The senator conversed more with Ada than with Norval. Clare wondered what the pioneer Chot Harshaw would make of the senator; once at the mine he heard Chot Harshaw tell his father, "I'd as soon watch a bag of fleas as a woman." The senator changed his clothes every day and fussed with them. He never soiled his dimpled hands. He called a house a "hoose." He referred to a certain horse back in Baltimore as "a dear creature." He spoke without emphasis and softly, pulling his words, as if his tongue were not a muscle but a petal.

For all this, Clare was sensible of the senator's force—in the power of his attention, the tension in his broad-boned frame, his curiosity, his modesty, his vitality, his very unashamedness. He was, finally, his own man— even here where his sort of man was less than nothing—and Clare recognized this in him as any man would anywhere, and respected it. He came to understand how a legislature could send Green Randall, perfumed as he was, to the U.S. Senate. He thought for the first time that a man could be any sort at all, if he could carry it off. Men would measure him, at bottom, not by his qualities, but by this one quality alone, the degree to which he carried it off. Clare further recognized, by a certain lift in Green Randall's shaggy eyebrow, that the senator was, to a lesser extent, surprised by Clare's own self-assurance. Here were two men who each assumed that the other was intrinsically nobody and who, upon recognizing the assumption in the other, revised their views. Clare, however, mistook courtesy for the respect it simulates, and did not know that the senator, upon greater acquaintance, still judged him a nobody.

Minta paced through the making of morning tea. Someone had set up a stove on the grass in the clearing. She boiled a kettle outside, while her sister June slept on the other cot in the tent. Her surviving child, Hugh, bedded on the grass inside the tent; he was always gone before breakfast.

A new house was going to rise in the clearing. Drew Dorr volunteered the lumber he had ordered for his own new house; the Dorr family could wait. He roused the men and mustered them in the clearing, and they were already working whenever Minta rose. They hauled milled lumber from her dock on sleds, using three yoke of oxen—later it would cost Minta six dollars per thousand board feet common lumber, and eight dollars per thousand board feet finished. They were importing redwood from California for the flooring. Clare Fishburn, getting a running start on the frills, carved intricate fretwork in painted planks with a band saw, to decorate the porches and eaves. Drew Dorr staked an outline with baling twine on the ground; the outline looked big and empty. He set Clare Fishburn, Hugh, and the Reese children to gathering chimney stones away from the water. Minta dimly knew that stout Drew Dorr, and Charles Kilcup, in his top hat, passed her, carrying things; they were starting to saw, and their saws made noise. For all she knew, they hauled lumber all night; none of it had substance to her, or impressed her senses or her mind.

Ada Tawes appeared every day at the graceful white tent, and so did Jenny Lind. Wearing a big blue bonnet tied under her chin, Ada carried lunches to the workers in the hop fields and to the men who were building the new house. Jenny Lind, in a gray cotton dress and green apron, took the buggy into Goshen, singing, and brought back dressed venison, ham, salt beef, and bread. With Mrs. Randall they served the family—on a sawhorse table—dinners and suppers of salad, potatoes, meats, parsnips, carrots, salmon, berries, and tea. Jenny Lind and Kulshan Jim had moved onto their own homestead. Kulshan Jim hired, supervised, and paid the hops pickers from Minta's purse. He also took charge of the ox teams and horses, and these days he usually wore a piece of harness leather looped on his belt to mend later. He cut and bound oats and barley to feed the stock. Jenny Lind no longer worked in the fields; she lived the pious and graceful life of a community leader whose parlor had lace curtains and marble-topped tables. Now for Minta she managed the garden, the cow, and the calves. She brought Hugh a suit of clothes from her brother. Hugh had shot up, and his trouser legs showed his shins, like a logger's.

"Thank you, ma'am," Hugh said. "These clothes are real nice." He held his head erect and stepped back. Ada Tawes learned that Hugh had not appeared at school in the weeks since the fire. No one knew where he went.

One evening, at the table outside the tent, Ada spoke to Minta. It was dark after supper; the rate of the days' shortening was picking up. Clare and June were down at the river, washing plates and pans. Jenny Lind and Queen of the May and their children had gone home.

Ada offered to brush Minta's hair for her. "No, cut it," Minta said. "Cut it up to my ears," but Ada would not. Ada's blue bonnet had a brim deep as eaves; her head from outside looked big as a baby's, and a glimpse of her wrinkled face down at the bottom of it was surprising. She stood in her rectangular way, her legs spread, and unpinned Minta's hair while Minta sat mute on the puncheon bench. Long ago, after Nettie died, Rooney had brushed Ada's hair for her, and she remembered the sensation, the brush's soft bristles around her face, and the handling, which lifted her hair at the roots. Her old hands were about as rough and bony as his had been, and it was enough.

"Minta," she said from the depths of her bonnet, "Hugh has not been going to school, and when he's here you don't see him, bless his heart, and with the help of God you must stir yourself. For you have a child still living." She brushed Minta's dull brown hair till it shone, and pinned it back up, high over her ears so her spectacles would not tangle. Minta gave no sign that she heard, but she heard.

CHAPTER XXV

That night, Minta borrowed a Bible from the Reeses and began again reading Scripture to Hugh, sitting on grass in the tent by his side. Hugh was so thin he barely bulged the blanket; his shorn curly hair showed the angles of his boxlike head. His gaze stayed tense on his mother's face. She read flatly, low. He looked at her and wondered what he could do. All he knew to do was what his father did: keep the tools sharp. When she finished, she closed the Bible, pinched the candle, and sat on the grass beside his blanket.

Hugh heard the night settle in and its thousand cicadas grind. His mother rose and left, ducking between the tent pole and the flap without touching either. The grass released its scent, and the sound of cicadas poured into the clearing like smoke. The pale tent wall luffed at the boy's side. He lay still as a stone, sorting himself out.

Hugh had seen his father slip surprised through the logjam; he saw his white body brought home to the porch folded up in a wheelbarrow. He had not seen Lulu and Bert actually die. He saw Lulu in her open coffin, for she had not been burned at all, but only smoked like a fish. Grandma Zella Hyle laid her out. Grandma Zella Hyle was a bald-headed woman with a mustache, who attended fatal illnesses, injuries, and deaths. She arranged Lulu's hands around a Testament. Hugh had last seen Bert at supper when the two boys were splitting a pie so big it mussed their ears and their mother had to wipe them. He had seen two neighbors, a boy and a woman, dying, and he had seen a good many people already gone over to the other side, lying white-faced in coffins with their hair brushed smooth, as his mother's was now.

Hugh had heard strangers ask women how many children they had. From now on, his mother, like the other women he heard, would include the dead ones, but distinguish. They said, "Eleven children, eight living"; "Eight children, four living." She would say, "Three children, one living." Mrs. Odette Mannchen had scratched her babies' names into the oak headboard she and her husband had hauled behind oxen in a wagon from Missouri. When a child died, she printed "GB" by the name—Gone Before.

Hugh himself, like all the region's children, reckoned on the kinds of thrift that life's tight conditions imposed, its high interest payments.

Accidents happened, and human bodies were thin-skinned parcels out of which the force of life leaked at a prick. Hugh had a new schoolteacher; the old one, Professor Samuel Hooten, died of gangrene in a leg he broke when a mule threw him. He had liked that mule; often people heard him coming, talking to the mule, before they saw him. Broken legs and arms were common enough, but if any bone poked through skin, another singular spirit departed this earth in a month or two, just from that bit of bone's catching the death in the air, which it was not used to, and carrying it back deep into the body.

All deaths were accidental, or none was, for disease was just as random an accident as injury, and all die. None died prematurely, for death battened on only the living, and all of those, at any age. "Wherever the body was, there would eagles gather." Women took fever and died from having babies, and babies died from puniness or the harshness of the air. Men died from trafficking in superior forces, like rivers and horses, bulls, steam saws, mill gears, quarried rock, or falling trees or rolling logs. Women died in rivers, too, and under trees and rockslides, and men took fevers, too, and fevers took men. Children lost their lives as other people did, as a consequence of their bodies' material fragility; hard things smashed them, like trees and the ground when horses threw them, or they fell; they drowned in water; they sickened, and earaches wormed into their brains or fever from measles burned them up or pneumonia eased them out overnight. It was all the same and predictable except in detail, whether a heart collapsed and seized in an old woman, or a runaway buggy crushed a growing boy: the people took the boy's death harder, for they longed to have him with them longer, and to see him grown and fruitful. They were not ready for him to die, but they knew for a fact that death was ready. Death was ready to take people, of any size, always, and so was the broad earth ready to receive them. A child's death was a heartbreak— but it was no outrage, no freak, nothing not in the contract, and not really early, just soon.

Hugh was lying on his back in his blankets in the tent. For a moment he covered his eyes with his hands; then he folded his arms over his chest, and his pale eyes stayed open and turned unseeing towards the blackness under the tent's peak. Hugh had seen his friend and neighbor die, the boy Jan Missou, killed by a falling tree. Jan Missou was an irritable boy his age who grew white hair on his head and on his brown arms and legs. That was two years ago.

They were going down the road. The fir tops were blowing high over-head. Hugh felt no wind at all down on the deep road the forest walled. Jan Missou had run ahead down the road, and Hugh and the boy's sister Ethel followed; they dallied, and dragged and waved sticks, and Hugh was surprised when a Douglas fir detached from the forest like a splinter and fell across the road on Jan Missou. A fir tree two hundred feet tall, and nine feet through the butt, had branches like another thirty trees growing out of its trunk; one of these branches bisected and punctured Jan, so that red bubbles were forming between his lips when Hugh got up to him, and staining his white hair, and he died.

Jan Missou had been a pert talker who would say anything. Once when he was sick on the first day of a cold, he took to bed and said grand-ly, "Don't get fond of me, Ma—it doesn't look like I'm going to make it." The family teased him for saying that, then and later, but a tree fell on him, after all, and they buried him under a sapling plum.

Hugh had not budged in his blankets. He could see past his feet the triangular doorway change shape as the breeze stirred the tent. His flat lips were compressed as if to keep inside him the many facts he had to inspect.

Mrs. Odette Mannchen, down the Nooksack, who used to give Hugh and Lulu and Bert dried apples, caught her homespun skirt on fire in the fireplace when she was stirring mush, and Hugh saw her dying on a pallet in the Mannchen house the next week. She could not bear the bedclothes on her; she lay flayed and swollen, open to the air, and flecks of black skin floated loose on her liquids like islands. While she was on fire she had run off into the river; her son peeled the dress from her and most of her skin came off with it. Hugh thought now that he himself could have prevented this, if he had kept closer watch.

Odette Mannchen's own husband had drowned the year before when his canoe tipped on a log in the river. Together they had lost two infant daughters to the putrid sore throat, a married daughter to childbed fever, and a son to being dragged by a horse. The Mannchens had worn a track between their claim and the shed where Grandma Zella Hyle lived by a ditch. Hugh heard later that Mrs. Mannchen had aimed to die standing on her two feet, and when she knew her time was come she struggled up from the pallet, vaguely waving off her remaining sons and Grandma Zella Hyle. She struggled up and stood on the floor wavering and out of her head—"deep inside herself where they go at the end," Grandma Zella Hyle reported—and died.

Now Hugh's own house had burned with Lulu and Bert in it; he and his mother were living in a raghouse. Through its doorway he could see the dense black line of the forest behind the clearing, and frail, lighted segments of cloud. He had heard Clare Fishburn tell his grandfather at supper about last winter's Whatcom fire, when merchants set up tents to keep going. The joke was: "How's business?" "Intense." His grandfather laughed, and Mr. Fishburn had laughed longer, the way he did, as if to prolong agreement that the thing was indeed comical, but Hugh did not get it. Now he tried it aloud, and got it. He heard his mother and his aunt approach the tent whispering; he turned his face to the wall, feigned sleep, and fell asleep.

When Minta rose the next morning to put the kettle on, she found June already outside and halfway up a pole ladder against the new house's empty frame. Looking small-waisted and resilient about the spine, June was handing to Clare Fishburn, alternately, nails from a sack in one hand and drinks of tea from a cup in the other. June looked half Clare's size, and ruddy about the face; she was wearing a white lace fichu at her throat and a lace apron, which seemed extreme for construction work. Clare could easily have set the nail sack and the teacup on the second-story sill beside him, but here he was receiving these goods from June with glances of the greatest enjoyment, and Minta took it in, standing by the hot stove, surprised.

CHAPTER XXVI

Minta, waiting outside between the tent and the new house for the kettle to boil, understood she had made a certain small mistake eleven years ago. Traces of it reached her here with her family's arrival and estranged her from them somewhat, in a way that puzzled her until she put the pieces together.

She had been "crazy fond," as Dovie Dorr said, of Eustace Honer every day for fourteen years, since he glanced at her playing croquet on their rolled Baltimore lawn—every day but one. That was the day before their wedding. She remembered it now, and wished she had earlier.

Minta was upending the contents of her chamber when June found her there. A chaos of petticoats, fresh flowers in vases, half-packed trunks, ironed ribbons on hangers, and new shoes cluttered the room. June was sixteen then, a rugged, sharp-tongued, extraordinarily striking child, filled with romantic longings. Minta was looking for the borrowed sapphire stickpin, in a frenzy. It was when she found it that she abruptly turned to young June and complained of Eustace.

"Do you not find him stiff?" she said. "Perhaps fanatical in his habits?" She jumped to the edge of her bed. Her brown hair was unbrushed; it hung down her cheeks like a hag's. Her eyes were bright behind her oval spectacles, and her skin was pale. The outburst continued; Minta twisted her ring.

"Do you know who I find myself thinking of? Can you guess?"

It was Edgar Gill she dreamed of, she burst out, Edgar Gill she pined for. He was the blond, freckled, lively fellow of their set who studied medicine desultorily and who, when they were children, had seemed to play at favoring Minta—and to whom in fact Minta had not given one thought until that moment. She impulsively sang his praises and added with an actual sob that she hoped they would be married in heaven. June had lowered her enormous eyelids; her high brows rose, and, miraculously, she said nothing.

Minta never remembered Edgar Gill again. She loved Eustace, loved the smell of his neck and the mute depth of his feeling, loved his upright bearing at all his tasks, his unwearying courage, his unexpected delight in their children, and the demanding esteem in which he held her even when she was steamy, drenched, and exasperated, stirring clothes with soap in a trough with a stick when their laundress died. Another man with the same qualities she would not have loved, for only Eustace was precisely himself, driven and brave, with his square small head, red knuckles, and the particular pressure of his arms. She had loved him as wholly as a wife can love her husband, in full knowledge of every complex fault and every simple dearness, in the privacy of their own tenderness, in the public life of the settlement, and in the daily consultations and consuming labors their life required. In those last few years before he drowned, their hop ranch had at last started paying; their house was ample and comfortable, and their children were angels, every one.

About what had they ever quarreled? Only the ranch. Of course, the ranch was their life, top to bottom.

In the flood two years ago, half their stock drowned, and most of their neighbors lost everything. Their neighbors eked and scratched bottom; they did not. Eustace purchased new stock for himself, and for the Fishburns, Reeses, and Missous, and started his numbing labors again. Minta saw Eustace spending himself to make the ranch pay, and ignoring his family sometimes to make the ranch pay, and for what reason? They must have over a thousand dollars still in the bank, or if they did not, they could sell idle land.

Once a traveling drummer came by with a mechanical stump-puller; he would pull stumps for twenty-five dollars a stump. Forest land sold for a dollar an acre. For the money it cost to pull a stump, they could buy twenty-five acres of forest for Eustace to ruin himself falling and bucking in order to get it down to stumps that would kill him and Kulshan Jim both—or that cost twenty-five dollars apiece to pull. It drove her purely wild. Minta pounced on the illogic and emotionalism of Eustace. Why on earth turn forest into hops berries, over a period of many agonizing years, and turn hops berries into cash, over many more agonizing years, when they could wire for cash in a week? They could wire their bank, or either of their fathers, for cash. It was madness to spend life for money, when clearly wisdom counsels spending money for life. Why should sentiment and mulishness crowd out all reason?

Eustace, he made plain, saw Minta balking him in his one enterprise, the single purpose on which they two had agreed to leave their childhood homes, emigrate to this wilderness, and stake their lives. How could she question or block anything necessary to that end? Had she never understood all along? Once he ended the discussion by slamming his hat over his face in bed.

They had quarreled about this single, solitary sore point: their life. The quarrel made its presence felt, in varying degrees, four or five times a day for eleven years, and it was nothing, nothing at all. She knew at the time—she now fancied—that it was nothing. She knew it indeed on those still lost mornings when she felt her blessings so overpoweringly that she dropped to her knees by her bed and tried to thank the Lord in earnest for those blessings, so He would perhaps be moved—charmed?—into preserving them. From her prayers of thanksgiving she rose uncertain, for she suspected herself of superstition more than gratitude, and wondered if she felt her blessings so much as her fears. Although she held that God gives blessings, she could recall no evidence—in Scripture, sermon, or history—that He preserves them, thanked or not.

June, unfortunately, told—this is what Minta was concluding as she stood by the kettle. After the wedding June told their mother, who told their father; here in Washington—and Minta did not know this—she had already told Clare Fishburn, too, who did not believe her: that all along Minta had been performing a duty to Eustace, for she loved another, Edgar Gill. Her family's letters to Minta these past eleven years, from Baltimore to the West, had borne a current of pity. Minta had attributed this odd note to their understandable ignorance of her life, their mistaking material privation for spiritual misery, and labor for pain. Her mother had visited her only once, and had not seemed to take in much of anything, beyond the deplorable state of the region's two roads.

Minta's many happy letters home her family never believed; she protested too much. Instead Green and Louisa Randall believed that, as she had confessed outright to June, she loved Edgar Gill—for people ever prefer to believe those they love pitiable.

Consequently, when Eustace drowned on the jam and Minta teetered, her mother, father, and sister in Baltimore said to each other privately, It is for the best. She could now bring her children home, and in due course marry Edgar Gill, who had not married. Her parents and sister had set out on the Union Pacific Railroad to see the country, to comfort Minta, and to fetch her home.

Mrs. Green Randall crossed the continent framing the words she would say to her daughter. After the fire and the children's funeral she judged that circumstances made the saying of them both more painful and more urgent. Yesterday she had said them.

Minta was walking her mother to the Dorrs' after supper, wearing her same dingy bombazine and a flat felt hat, and barely speaking. It was raining lightly. Mrs. Randall wore a navy straw hat on whose broad brim a stuffed velvet bluebird sat, its dry toes sewn in black thread to the straw. Her corset, beneath her beaded, braided, scalloped, and flounced dress, cinched her so tightly it almost severed her, and she said she preferred walking to sitting in a buggy. The women out here wore their corsets loose, Dovie Dorr told her, because they worked all day. "Like slaves," Louisa thought; whatever the local custom, she would not let herself go.

The tall fir trunks ranged close by the road, and their boughs mingled far overhead and shed darkness down. Mrs. Randall had seen little of the country, for she was nearsighted and forswore spectacles; she received the ghostly impression of vertical black walls cut by bright patches of yellow and green.

A fearful note in her mother's familiar Philadelphia tone alerted Minta, and she peered away, as if interested, into the fretted dimness of the forest. Her mother spoke with her quivering chin lowered, looking away, as Minta was looking away on the other side. She said in a trembling voice that perhaps God was working out His mysterious purpose. In Eustace's tragic death. For back in Baltimore—did she know?—Edgar Gill had never married. Her mother neither looked up nor uttered another word, and Minta walked dumbstruck to the Dorrs' and home, while she tried to guess her mother's imaginings, sought to remember Edgar Gill in Baltimore, and felt her solitude like a pit.

This morning, at the sight of roundheaded June stretching over the ladder to hand nails and tea up to Clare, Minta recalled telling June, right before the wedding, something about Edgar Gill. What had possessed her?

Well, June was just a child then. Here she was grown, and smiling or laughing, from the evidence of her raised cheek, into the face of Minta's own familiar friend Clare—a man of the country, tactless and lighthearted and, not incidentally, ready to marry. Their father would forbid the match, and make a clatter, suffer, and acquiesce. Their mother would rise to it, bewildered and generous, as she had to Minta's own marriage to Eustace. How good it would be to have June here! Minta poured herself tea, and began slicing salt meat from the ice chest to boil and fry. She felt the first, brief rousing of life in her, for she had been fond of June then, when she was a fast-talking sister romping through life beside her, and might grow fond of her again now, while she was an ardent, alert woman who had something to smile about.

June Randall had made her debut in the month of June at home on the lawn between gardens. She wore, among other things, a headdress cunningly rigged with dozens of gauze spheres, in each of which shone, at nature's own fitting intervals, a firefly. That she was Minta's sister was evident from her fragile, excitable skin, which the fireflies illumined in green as the evening wore on, revealing her cheeks' delicacy, and doing nothing for their color. Both sisters were short. June's jaw was finely modeled, where Minta's sloped; June's head was spherical and Minta's thick and almost cubical; June's dark eyes struck around sharply, where Minta's were softened by reading. June roused, flashed, directed, and pitched fits, while Minta helped, learned New Testament verses, and trained horses to jump hedges. June could easily see that her own restless vigor and self-consciousness maddened the people around her; they had no way of knowing that her nature maddened her, too.

Their parents enrolled the two in separate private schools. They occupied their pew at Saint Paul's, attended grand opera in their box in the opera house's tier, and bore fittings on Charles Street. Members of their set "snapped jokes," rode their horses, raced boats, and got up excursions, as well as danced "the valse" at debutante parties and hunt balls. The young men flowed in and out of houses in Baltimore and its districts, and in Newport, Rhode Island; they moved in a body as whimsically and restlessly as sandpipers. The girls' mothers gave off complaining that no one knew where they might alight to dine, and simply ordered extra places set every night.

Minta and June shone in this, the world that knew them, but neither believed it was the only world. They had lived in hotels in London and in Deauville; they had heard talk of favorable matches between American girls and Spaniards, even. The older sister read novels; she could see books well, because they were close. June attended to the conversation of men, and thereby enlarged herself. Their own parents inadvertently planted in them a certain skepticism, for although their mother and father had catechized each of the girls from birth to grasp the creeds of Baltimore society, and to worship at its altars, their parents had equally and respectively urged upon them that the society of Annapolis, Maryland, or it may be of Philadelphia, Pennsylvania, was a more genteel, grander, older, and more particular society, both more correct and more gay: so that each girl, separately and privately, concluded that if within her own roof two authorities pressed such convincing counterclaims, the business rightly had no end.

Each girl furthermore observed that both the daughters and sons of Baltimore families in the Green Spring Valley and in rural Guilford—the vivacious offspring of the clans Garrett, Frick, Jacobs, Gill, Pennington, White, Poultney, Keyser, and Brown—often and disconcertingly married outside Baltimore society, married people no one knew, and nothing happened. When it came to the sticking point of marriage, the most powerful of mothers yielded with unexpected grace. A neighbor child who was upbraided and shamed at ten, for conversing with an unsuitable peer, was seen by the astonished sisters to be feted, dressed, and kissed, for marrying one. Of course, it was just such grace that made the mothers, and the society they upheld, powerful—it was society's single virtue—but the girls had not yet understood this, nor would they ever, where they were going.

CHAPTER XXVII

Later that morning, Senator Randall arrived at Minta's wide clearing alone. Overhead in the great, bracing sky, white clouds in shreds moved under gray clouds, and a light drizzle fell. This high, precarious latitude, and its snowy peaks visible from everywhere on the farm, and its heavy timber and blue light, overwhelmed Green Randall. The plants by the roadside bore white smooth berries, or pink hairy ones, or thorned leaves or glossy ones, and looked, among the ferns and moss, like trial plants of the beginning world. It was mid-September in Baltimore and in Washington, too, and there, he knew, summer lingered in the soft trees, and time held its breath. Here in this extravagant country, here on this buckling edge of the world, he was sensible already of the days' shortening, and the winter darkness bearing down.

He could feel the planet spinning like a bolo, ever faster, and flung into the darkness bearing him on it against his will. A man could, and did, accustom himself to change, but he could never yield to the acceleration in the rate of change. How had it come to be 1885 already, and how had he come to be fifty-six years old, when he was years behind in his understanding? Was he so near his own death? Every evening Ada Tawes lit the lamp earlier, as the sun fled south like a red-tailed hawk.

Advancing up the buggy road, the senator saw Minta's chickens step out into their yard cool as gamblers. He saw her barn, the size of which still staggered him; it was about as big as the White House. Then he saw commotion between the barn and the burnt house site: it was Hugh, soberly riding a yellow, hay-bellied, muddy-legged horse. He used a blanket for a saddle. A rope around the nose served for halter and reins. Hugh wore overalls and a red undershirt. He was permitting the creature to run over the hummocky ground; he hugged its ribs with his knees.

The senator found Minta splitting wood with a tomahawk, as he saw it. She slung billets into the stove on the grass with the same sure pokes their Irish biddies used at home. Her mastery of this arcana bewildered him.

She had showed them her hop fields, so graceful now when the climbing vines shaded the fields like garden trellises. He noted her acquaintance with the grimy, unearthly Indians swarming over her land, who
smelled of rancid fish oil, and whose old women and men had deformed
heads. He saw the short-legged, flat-faced men, in whom the black eye of
savagery and degradation could easily be detected; they met him quietly as
an equal and seemed to mock him with their adopted practice of shaking
hands. The Nooksacks' gentle voices confused him, for the senator was
accustomed to gauging a speaker's social standing by his voice; instead of
the harsh tones he expected, he heard the caressing lilt of Scottish lords.
He met the people he thought of as the brown squaws, including his
daughter's familiars—Jenny Lind, whose nostril was visibly pierced, and
outlandish rose-hatted Queen of the May, whose three half-breed children
spoke Nooksack, English, and Chinook. These barefoot children were
named Kilcup; there was a girl, and boys named Howard and Green. The
senator briefly wondered if his own fame had reached these parts, that a
part-time miner named Kilcup, who married an Indian, should name a
boy Green.

He was powerless to alter any of it. When young Hugh came home
from school, black soil tinted his shirt and skin as if he had been dipped,
and fir needles tipped from his hat. It would be good to soften and sterilize
his grandson's world, to put some meat on his skeleton, show him cities,
industries, and institutions, and fit him for his role and duties. For now,
the boy was death-stung. The senator imagined Hugh's clear young soul,
like a peeled peach, on which death's lashes had laid stripes. He must heal
up. He knew the boy would inherit a legacy from him, and what little
might be left of Minta's and Eustace's legacies, and their ranch. When
Minta moved with her son back to Baltimore the senator himself—or, if it
came to that, Edgar Gill—could instruct him by precept and example.

Minta seated herself beside him on the adzed log stoop outside the
tent, the stoop people kicked to knock clods from their shoes. Would he
take tea when the kettle boiled again? Together they watched Hugh working the fiery little yellow horse. June said the mare's name was Peaches,
and she was a cowboy horse only Kulshan Jim and Bert could ride. She
stared off, and the senator saw that Peaches now was resenting Hugh's
notion of slowing to a walk, and was all over the yard with her mon-
keyshines. Hugh circled her and held her still, to render her receptive to
any glimmering of philosophy that might enlarge her mind.

Senator Randall was full of hope. He would bring Minta home to Baltimore, her and Hugh, and restore the family. He would take her riding, the two of them off alone in the fields and woods, along the trail behind Guilford in back of the marsh where she used to watch the big blue herons set their wings to land in their roosting tree. When she looked up at the herons, he used to watch her long braid slide down her back.

"Minta, dear," Senator Randall said, "come back with us now. Your mother needs you."

Minta was digging at the log with a butter knife. Its gray wood looked soft as flannel. She stopped. She saw her father's intelligent eyes, and the wavy circlet of stiff black hair under his hatbrim. Never on this side of the grave again, she thought, for at this moment flat-eyed Bert alone interested her, who was dead, while Hugh rode his horse.

When her father spoke, his voice was satiny and sweet. Minta had met a sheep shearer once whose musical tones reminded her of her father's, and then a muleskinner and a dairy farmer—men who worked with animals, they all sounded like Marylanders.

"Let Drew Dorr build the new house. It will wait while you decide what to do with it. Just for now, until you get your bearings, you should be at home in your own place."

He saw Minta turn on him. "I am at home," Minta said. She set her shoulders at him, and met his eye above her spectacles. "This is my own place." Her voice had some grit in it. On the log stoop, she was proud as any woman in her parlor. Her skirt dragged directly in the dirt. She was stubborn now, unnerved, and not in her rightful mind. She covered her face with her stubby hands and turned away; he looked at the back of her head, her brown coiled hair, her hairpins pushing out. His very dear! The senator wished, as he had wished for a week, that he himself could have burned in the fire instead of the children. If he lived to be a hundred, and Minta was seventy-eight, he would struggle to shield her.

Only the passage of time would clear her mind so she recognized her own interests; he could wait. In the meantime she chose to live in a wet tent in a field among savages. She grew hops for beer—beer!—the selling of which decent women everywhere in America opposed with their whole wills.

The boy Hugh was growing up feckless and uncultured as these settlers' sons and half-breeds; he did not yet dwell in the United States. He lacked even the local skills, and could not make a fire without burning the house down, though no one would reproach him with it. He would end up insignificant and flighty as Clare Fishburn, whose sole asset and pride seemed to consist in what the senator saw as his chief liability and shame, his living out here at all. If you asked this wild weed about his own people, he could not give his grandmother's maiden name; it took him all day to come up with his mother's. Now Louisa reported that June was growing visibly foolish over this unlikely wretch, the particulars of whose remote prospects the senator declined to learn. When June made her debut at the Bachelors Cotillion in Baltimore, his colleague Senator John Sherman from Ohio had been present; he complimented Green Randall on the perfection of his daughter's back, which allowed her to wear a dress cut down to her waist. Senator Randall had been prepared, theoretically, to give his daughters away—but not to throw them away.

He laid his hand on Minta's lifeless shoulder for a second, then stood. Hugh, thin in his overalls, was leading Peaches to a paddock. He tied her to the rail and scratched the mud from her hooves with a stick. On the horizon, Mount Baker was hidden. The drizzle continued; the white clouds still sped under the dark clouds, and the black tree boughs at the forest edge wagged. Out here wind blew when it rained; at home, when the rain came the wind stopped.

The senator disbursed his rich energy with inborn frugality. Like every winner, he folded often and early. When he saw that his presence in the Territory of Washington could not hasten, but only delay, his daughter's recovery, his mind turned to the many legislative and local matters his long journey had left pending, among them his scheduled meeting with Cardinal Gibbons and Bishop Paret.

CHAPTER XXVIII

Senator Randall saddled up Old Snap and rode into town that morning to secure immediate passage home on the *Doris Burn* and the Northern Pacific Railroad. Soon he would see modern cities again: tall office buildings, and incandescent advertising signs, and paved streets crowded with cushioned carriages, buses, streetcars, and hackney cabs. At home in Maryland he would see rolled lawns, oil paintings, rich interiors, and trained servants; he would enjoy telephones, running hot water, gas lights, incandescent lights, furnace heat, and the company of stylish men and women. Mrs. Simon Cameron and Mrs. Cabot Lodge led society; their sensibilities were refined. Neither they, nor any men or women of his and Louisa's acquaintance, ever spoke of dollars, or discussed sharp business practices. Instead, like those well-born Europeans in whose capitals they passed the seasons, they expressed admiration for, and discrimination among, certain types of neck, brow, limbs, and personal carriage.

Old Snap, whom he rode into Goshen, had a rough trot. On the clay road, where it was dry, the horse sounded like a cavalry charge. The senator passed a crowd of redheaded children chasing chickens in a stumpy clearing by a peeling cabin. In Washington, D.C., the issues awaiting attention this session were civil service reform, tariff reform, and veterans' pensions—all attempts to damage the natural and remunerative alliance of business leaders and lawmakers. Out here the issues had the pitched, overbright quality of the land. The recent treaty with the Indian people at the head of Puget Sound required them to cede title to their lands and— to the senator's delight—free their slaves. Norval Tawes and Drew Dorr told the senator they worried because the Haida Indians' Queen Katherine had died; she had kept the Haidas comparatively peaceful, so the American coastal tribes had been safe. The biggest local question was how, and how soon, right-thinking men could drive the "Celestials," as they called the Chinese, out of the territory, to free up paying jobs. Yesterday's newspaper reported—the senator saw it with his own eyes—that a Chinese aristocrat had been caught turning his manservant into a pig. This rich man, who had a taste for experiment, had flayed his servant in sections, a bit every few months, and grafted the fresh skin of pigs onto him, until over years he had become a pig. The newspaper reported this soberly as hard news, along with boisterous reports of a second gold find at Ruby Creek. It would be good to be home.

Holding his reins gracefully, his stirrups so high he looked to be squatting on his saddle, the senator posted into town, lifting his wide hips up and down lightly, and posted back. He carried steamer schedules and rail schedules, so many he had been required to buy a sort of purse.

That evening, at the sawhorse table on the dirt, the family agreed that Louisa Randall, and only Louisa Randall, would return to Maryland with the senator. The women were wearing waisted jackets, and the men pulled their hats low against the sunset breeze. June would remain on this coast until Christmas, despite her father's urging—to keep Minta company, and to help her sell the crop and furnish the new house, they said, as if these wholesome projects would mend her spirits in a twinkling.

While they talked and night fell, they heard shots. The cicadas hushed. Hugh rose tense to attention. The shots seemed to originate north of town, where the upper creek came in. The senator, and the ubiquitous Clare Fishburn, recognized both the dull explosions of shotguns and the crack of rifles. An owl glided out of the forest and crossed the clearing, and a flicker sounded an alarm. The shooting continued, and Louisa looked at Minta across the table.

Then crossing the clearing from the buggy road path appeared little Angus Reese, Hugh's friend, who was hatless and breathless. He was red-headed like all the Reeses, and sharp as a tack. He trotted up to the table, looked around at the company, and paused to fool with the candle, saying his family had candles now, too, business was so good. Once they even had coffee. Angus was ten, still in short pants, and his black stockings sagged around his shapeless ankles. The senator saw that his pants and shirt were of homespun linsey-woolsey. The senator had not seen homespun since he himself was a boy.

The shooting, Angus said, was for Queen of the May. She was taken ill; the Nooksacks from the village at the crossing had paddled down to Kilcups' and were firing guns to frighten away spirits. A fever had her, the measles, maybe, or lung fever. Grandma Zella Hyle was there with her, and the Skagit doctor—"And it looks awful bad." Both Minta and Clare rose to go with Hugh to Kilcups' in town, but her mother restrained Minta with a hand, and she subsided, and gave Hugh a look that bade him stay. Clare left with little Angus for Kilcups', and everyone saw June look after his long-geared figure.

The next morning, Hugh led Old Snap with the spring wagon to Dorrs' and Taweses' to fetch his grandparents' trunks. The senator in his traveling suit, Louisa in a curved hat and carrying her quivering parasol, and Minta, June, and Hugh accompanied the wagon silently through the forest to the town dock, the way they had come.

Queen of the May had died during the night. Minta would go to her house as soon as she saw her family off. Now, walking the dirt road, they all heard through the forest the sound of distant singing. It was the Nooksacks in the village. They were singing "Shall We Gather at the River." As they drew opposite Reeses' clearing they could hear that the Nooksacks were singing in their own tongue. No one said a word, and no one ever forgot the sound, so mournful it was through the hazy forest and over the fields, and so frail the hope it offered, in so harsh a world.

June never returned for Christmas. She stayed in Goshen, where Clare Fishburn courted her. In April they undertook a sailing tour of the islands on a borrowed schooner, in the company of four other young men and women, with Glee Fishburn and Grace, who had married, as chaperones. In May she journeyed home to Baltimore to continue her part of the courtship by letters—hers mockingly impertinent and sentimental by turns—and in April two years later she met Clare there. He stood tall and tremulous with a gladstone in his hand, between the two gardens on the lawn decorated with paper lanterns for their wedding. When Minta and Eustace had first proposed emigrating to Puget Sound, June had never heard of such a place. Now she would marry Clare, her particular chosen, without whom she felt incapable of living her life, although he had never heard of Chesapeake Bay.

BOOK IV

OBENCHAIN
AND CLARE

CHAPTER XXIX

1891, Whatcom

Three years later, big Beal Obenchain stood on the mud flat of Bellingham Bay, north of Puget Sound, on the northwest coast of the new state of Washington.

It was ten o'clock on a cold March night. Obenchain wore a high-crowned derby hat; he held a knife, a lantern, and a coil of rope in one hand and, as he put it to himself, a Chinaman in the other. He and a nimble miner were bearing the Chinese man north across the mud flat towards the shore where the old wharf lit down. The tide was out. Overhead the sky was dark; no one would see them.

Beal Obenchain did not know the miner. He had found him half an hour before at a campfire far to the south down the beach, a clean-shaven youngster in a slouch hat and white shirt, with a white rosette in his jacket buttonhole. The miner said he was from Wyoming. He scrambled to keep up with Obenchain. Obenchain did not know the ugly Chinaman either, though he might be a local one. He spoke English. Obenchain had found him five minutes earlier; he was hurrying north up the beach towards town. He had a frail triangular jaw, which Obenchain had punched lightly, once on each side, to hush him. He did not want to knock him out.

Obenchain had chosen to tell the Chinaman his purpose, and he did so now: it was to "lash you to a … wharf piling and leave you to drown when the tide … comes in six hours … hence." It was an old stunt of Oliver Cromwell's, he said, which had not, so far as he knew, been tried in this region. "It's a stunt?" said the miner. The Chinaman broke away, and Obenchain snatched him back in two steps, by catching his queue. They walked around sharp firs that stuck out from the crumbling bluff, and reached the dim row of pilings, where the cobbles made noise underfoot.

"Bastard," the Chinaman said distinctly. In the darkness Obenchain could make out his wide, careless mouth, and teeth short as a child's. The Chinaman kicked the miner over. Obenchain swiped down to knock the Chinaman's face. Obenchain was tall and stout, thirty-one years old. His long head seemed to flow directly into his neck, for thick muscles covered a small jaw. The Chinaman began to utter something about the big crabs of which he had an apparently superstitious dread; the crabs would roll in with the tide. The little "Celestial" was fortunate, Obenchain thought, to have a role in his scheme, though he did not realize it. Obenchain would take as his own this surprisingly willful life spirit.

There was a salty onshore wind. From the blackness to the west Obenchain could hear distant seas breaking lightly on the mud flat. Tomorrow night the townspeople of Whatcom would be carousing on the beach till dawn, Obenchain knew, but tonight no one was abroad. The slouch-hatted miner held the Chinaman by the thick root of his queue, while Obenchain undressed him in pure darkness.

Obenchain's delicate fingers mastered the cotton frog closures of the Chinaman's black tunic easily.

"Why do they all wear these pajamas?" the Wyoming miner asked. He was shivering in the cold. Obenchain did not answer. Rather than kneel to unfasten the lowest frogs, Obenchain ripped the cotton tunic away. He removed from its interior a handkerchief, which he pocketed. With his two hands he felt of the Chinaman's trembling torso, which was scarcely greater in breadth than one of Obenchain's own thighs. Against the pale skin hung a dark bundle. Obenchain cut the cord that bound the bundle around the Chinaman's neck. The man kicked, and loosed a blasphemous oath, which the wind took. Consequently Obenchain, sighing, cut a sleeve off the cotton tunic, rolled it, and stuffed it in the man's mouth. He ran a doubled rope between the man's sprung jaws. He bound his hands high behind his back with the same rope, trimmed short, so that if the Chinaman pitched his head, he would pain his arms, and vice versa. He told the miner to heft the bound man; he stripped him of his trousers and his weightless slippers. The slippers' thick white soles alone were visible when he passed them to the miner. The miner took the slippers daintily in two fingers. "I've had enough," he said, and walked off to the north with his head down against the wind, as if he had suddenly taken a notion to try Alaska. Obenchain glanced after the miner and let him go.

The beach sloped; overhead the abandoned wharf seemed to swoop into the sky. Walking the Chinaman by the rope, Obenchain found a straight piling the tide would cover. With a knee he urged him up the rocks at the piling's base, and received a kick for his pains. He knifed a purple starfish, which was in the way, and pried it from the piling in sections. He lashed the Chinaman to the piling with rope; he took over twenty turns, tied half hitches, buried the rope's end. Then he lighted the lantern and held it to the Chinaman, who, above the rock pile, hung at the height of Obenchain on the cobbles below. Those hands bound high behind his back interfered with the snugness of the lashings, and made the body's top half seem awkwardly to pitch forward. Obenchain was damned if he was going to do it all over again; he had gone to enough trouble. The rope gag distorted the fellow's physiognomy considerably. The man's forehead was short, his nose wide. His rolling eyes struck out viciously, Obenchain thought, at parts of his own person. If he found one trace of reproach in the man's expression, he would knife him now. He no longer wished him well, but only ill, and every ill, for his experimental interest was giving way to hatred; these things happen.

There on the stones under the wharf, Obenchain opened the draw-string of the bundle he had cut from the Chinaman's neck. He withdrew a cold porcelain figurine, which proved to be a tiger, posed springing, with something in its mouth. He held the tiger up, with the lantern, before he pocketed it.

"Lord, let me know my end," he said to the Chinaman's face, "and the number of my ... days, so that I may know how short my life is." He rolled the Chinaman's clothes and tucked them under his arm.

As a final gesture, on the mud flat just halfway between the Chinaman and the low-tide water, Obenchain left the lighted lantern, so the Chinaman could study the water for the first three hours as it rose, until it tipped the lantern and washed it out. After that, he would perforce imagine the water, until it touched his feet. Then he could feel the water, and measure its rise against his skin. The flood tide would peak, at over eight feet, between three and four in the morning. Obenchain departed, and no one from the town saw anything.

The least singular aspect of the Chinaman's death for Obenchain was its possible consequence on the temporal plane. Obenchain knew that he was not afraid of the town. He was an intellectual, and the townspeople were laborers or sharpers. They were laborers or sharpers with pretensions, who never left the life of sensation but only refined its objects: when they had a little land, or a ten-year-old name, they switched in their boots from beer to sherry, and got them a Lummi Indian to cut their wood. Respectable people were those who avoided outcry. Obenchain was more than respectable; he was a natural aristocrat, self-made, whose high skull scraped the sky.

CHAPTER XXX

In the town of Whatcom the next morning, Clare Fishburn was working alone in his office, early. He was a strikingly tall man, forty-one years old. He was "all feathered out," as he put it to his wife, June, that morning, "in his glad rags": he wore a stiff standing collar and a tan linen suit and vest that already looked wrinkled. That morning he had threaded a gold-plated watch chain through his vest buttonhole. He had trouble with his necktie, which either compressed his standing collar too tightly and skewed it, or circled it too loosely and slid aside. He was ordinarily careless of appearance, but today he must represent his city—represent even his country—to distinguished visitors from just over the border in Canada. His bony face was freshly barbered. "You look just like the other big bugs," June had said at home that morning; she had a number of vivid terms for Whatcom's leading citizens. She looked at him fondly. They had been married and living in Whatcom for three years.

Bent at his downtown office desk, his knees at his elbows, Clare wrote a careful column of words and phrases on a single sheet of foolscap. He studied the list and stood. He was so thin he looked in the tan suit like a piece of new doweling or a hops stake. He had forgotten, when he came indoors, to take off his yellow plaid bicycle cap.

He took a map from a stack, unrolled it on the table, and secured its corners with inkpots. There were no frills to the map, not even a legend, but only a black grid of squares the surveyor had inked on top of the brown, irregular coastline of Bellingham Bay. The grid of squares was getting messy. Different sections, marked in different shades of black ink, angled off in every direction.

These were stirring times in Whatcom, and the map showed the changes. During the twelve years that Clare lived up the river in Goshen, his old hometown grew. Far-flung regions that Clare used to know as forest or farmlands were now solidly "downtown." Whatcom businessmen were building houses on numbered streets where he used to shoot ducks. Now Whatcom was ballooning. Its coming magnificence was plain to any man.

Jim Hill planned to end his Great Northern Railway on Bellingham Bay; the Great Northern had already bought up the local line. Jim Hill would build his transcontinental terminus on the south side of Whatcom, whose future was assured. Jim Hill planned to dock his Pacific fleet in Whatcom's harbor. The Orient trade would do for Whatcom what European trade did for New York. The New York newspapers, and *Harper's Monthly*, too, ran articles about the coming Great Northern Railway terminus on Bellingham Bay. Its prospects for wealth and splendor were limitless.

Daily the steamer from Seattle discharged a swarm of enterprising men in bowler hats, who would get in on the ground floor and ride to the skies. Clare was among the locals who looked over the newcomers on the docks. When the tide was low, the steamer anchored offshore; a big Lummi Indian stood out in the bay, threw each man and his bag over his shoulder, and carried him across the mud flat for a dollar.

"Eager newcomers," the Whatcom *Bugle Call* called these men. "Suckers," Clare's distinguished senior partners called them. "Crooks," his cynical friend John Ireland Sharp called them. June called them "plungers," and found their presence stimulating, she said—their crowding the streets in black claw-hammer overcoats, and speaking in northeast accents. Clare understood them to be men of vision. How they could help the common man, if only that man had a little capital! If, by whatever means, the poor farmer, or the college boy, or the landless immigrant, could lay up a few hundred, or a thousand, dearly beloved dollars, he could multiply it like the loaves and fishes without turning a hand, and then multiply the multiplied, world without end, amen—such were these magnificently inflationary times, such was this miracle of a country.

Naturally, under the circumstances, choice bits of the south side of Whatcom, in the form of inked squares, were changing hands. Clare Fishburn was the junior partner in the land company that bought the land last year, and was selling it this year. His land company was the biggest, but there were many others. Recently a physician came to Whatcom to practice medicine. Before he had been in town a week, he decided to become a real estate agent instead.

Clare's immediate neighbor at home, a redheaded, one-armed reprobate named Street St. Mary, had mentioned that morning that he would like to play a part, however humble, in the coming glory of the town. He had pieced and patted together $300 cash money, which he kept in a coffeepot. Clare dearly loved the "hard-boiled old owl," as he thought of him, and resolved to find him a likely lot, a hummer. Today was a holiday, but Clare was working. He wanted to secure a lot before Monday's steamer discharged another swarm of buyers. Street St. Mary and his $300 should get in early. Clare had already resolved that he would guarantee his friend's investment out of his own pocket, if the town's fortunes soured and hard times returned.

Taking a hand lens, Clare examined the waterfront. The grid of squares extended four blocks into the blank blue waters of Bellingham Bay, where schooners floated at high tide. "The more salmon for everybody," Clare had said when the company first platted the mud flats: "A man who builds on the mud flat could just stick a frying pan out of the window, and the salmon will jump in." The partner J. J. O'Shippy had given him a murderous glance. Clare had contributed only his wife's legacy of $35,000 to the company. The company brought altogether $250,000 in capital to improve the town of Whatcom. Clare's senior partners, who had long breathed the grave air that clung to such sums, found levity inappropriate.

Here on the map was a mud-flat lot, eighty feet by eighty feet. It listed for $6,000. Street St. Mary could secure it for—Clare paused to figure, and check the figure—for $420. He could build on pilings, or on sawdust from the mill; better yet, he could sit tight and continue as Clare's garrulous neighbor, and his young daughter's friend, while the lot's price swelled. The sum of $420, alas, exceeded the grasp of Street St. Mary's coffeepot. Searching the map, Clare moved farther from the terminus site. He moved the hand lens up and down; his long neck moved up and down like a heron's. The other partners relegated such detailed tasks to hired agents; the partners dealt with railroad owners and dined with eastern bankers. Clare Fishburn, however, enjoyed helping his friends. He enjoyed reading maps. He loved Whatcom, where he had grown to manhood, and he felt that the spreading grid of inked lines vindicated the hardships of the settlement's founders, men like his father, Rooney, and Felix Rush, and Chot Harshaw—which hardships, he would try not to mention to the partners, he had also mightily enjoyed.

He unrolled another map and smoothed it over the first. He knew the town by heart, but he felt obliged to check. At intervals he straightened his back and stood. When he stood, it was plain that he was what June once proudly called "a scissor-built man"—his legs were long and straight like scissor blades, and his shoulders narrow. He moved to the row of filing cabinets under the second-story window, and bent again to search the files and remove papers, which he studied in the window's airy light. More than an hour passed. He found a lot that listed for $5,000 and could be had for $300 down; it was quite a daisy lot, he said to himself—three blocks from the terminus site, abutting the proposed opera house. It was an agreeable site for a bank, a restaurant, or a hotel.

He found another lot at that price on the trolley line. This site now lay at some remove from the commercial center, but the trolley line was bringing business. At his desk he wrote detailed descriptions of these lots; he would read them to Street St. Mary later. After another hour he had four business lots close to the terminus, a possible fifth in the older part of town, near Carloon's store and the Birdswell Hotel, and a big clifftop piece back of beyond. He was pretty sure that the big clifftop piece, when cleared, would overlook the water and the San Juan Islands; he would walk up there tomorrow, Sunday, and make certain. He could take the whole family and call it an outing. His mother had scarcely been out all spring.

He pocketed his list, discovered he was already wearing his bicycle cap, and headed downstairs. His gray terrier, which had accompanied him to the office, woke and followed, scrabbling down the stairs and into the street. Clare held the brass door for the dog. Overhead the morning mist was clearing in a faint northeast wind. It was a fine day for a celebration— a fair freak of a day, since spring weather was usually even more dismal than fall weather, only better lighted. He would meet his family down at the depot. He saw men and women hurrying down the sidewalk in that direction. His bicycle, a black racer, was leaning against the stone office building. He mounted—splendid and gawky in his tall collar and tan suit—and headed across town. His high-bridged nose jutted out as far as the bill of his yellow plaid cap. His eyes were large and deeply hollowed, and his brown eyebrows were unruly. He waved at his friends on the raised sidewalks. The stiff-haired dog followed, barking.

The town of Whatcom had declared a holiday, for that day the first overland train to enter Whatcom was coming in from Canada. Leaders from the two nations would make speeches, and bands would play. Whatcom people had been slicking up their town for weeks, in order to present it in the best possible light to the Canadian Pacific Railway. The Canadian Pacific Railway had its western terminus in Vancouver, British Columbia, Canada, which city was only 45 miles distant. The Canadian railway would need a terminus somewhere in this country, and that might as well be Whatcom. Although such a terminus would never be more than the end of a spur line, and could never rival the Great Northern terminus in impact, its presence here would confirm Whatcom's importance, and the town was eager to get it. The partners in the Bellingham Bay Improvement Company, including Clare, were among the guests invited to dine at a banquet at the Birdswell Hotel following the ceremonies; they would bend elbows with the visiting brass from Canada, and perhaps twist their arms as well.

Clare rode his bicycle across the town, admiring the fresh red, white, and blue bunting and flags with which people had decorated office windows and lampposts. He felt himself as immortal as the nation whose destiny, as he put it to himself, he shared. No grass grew under his feet.

In the past two years, six states had joined the union—where would it end? The state of Washington, only two years old, was bigger than all New England. Whatcom County spread from the glaciated North Cascades to Puget Sound, the Strait of Juan de Fuca, and the Strait of Georgia. The nation itself was fit to jump out of its skin with energy, or pop into the sky; Clare knew it, and felt its might as his own. Steam engines simply exploded, on the nation's seas, on its lakes and rivers, and in its mills from shore to shore, as if from bursting power. Railways raced over the tremendous mountains, poked into towns, and bore their products to markets in São Paulo and Singapore; telegraph cables and electric lines linked local farmers to Wall Street, pumped water uphill, and lighted cows in barns.

England was still the first among nations, but America was snapping at her heels. How grand it would be, and how fitting, when this raw-handed and enterprising frontier country would rise to world supremacy! Already America surpassed England in steel production. America was catching up in coal production. Crowned heads of Europe deferred, as Clare understood it, to American businessmen. The finger of destiny was undeniably dipping westward and crossing the Atlantic to the new world's east coast—thence perhaps to traverse the continent, as well, and land right here.

The Canadian steam locomotive, pulling two coaches loaded with dignitaries, was on its way to Whatcom this very minute. It was Whatcom's first transcontinental railway train—the first "overland" train, as Clare said to himself—but it would not be the last. It would arrive in half an hour, at noon. Clare knew all about the memorable welcome Whatcom had planned. As the train pulled into the depot, it would pass under "an arch of living water." Volunteers from two fire companies would form the water arch high in the air, using their new, high-powered hoses. Then the bands would play, officials would make speeches, parents would urge babies to remember this day for the rest of their lives, and all the men would get drunk. This morning while Clare had worked alone in his office, he had been aware that a good half of his townsmen were skipping breakfast to get a running start on the celebration.

Clare loved this place, his place, and he loved his time—what a time! He loved his wife, June, his daughter, Mabel, the long-handled pioneers up the river, the neighbors in town, the Lummis, the music, the mountains, the light on the water, the present. His way traversed ten level blocks on dirt streets across the business district, where stores and office buildings ran three stories high. They were all wired for incandescent lamplight; they bulged with thriving enterprises. Today they flew a thousand flags.

He turned down the hill at Holly Street towards the bay, and discovered that he could not slow the bicycle. The brake fittings must have rusted over the winter; he had no brakes. It was with especial excitement, then, that he dodged families walking down the steep hill. He lifted his long legs from the pedals, steered with all his wits, and turned off, careening, by the depot, where an enormous crowd lined the rails.

To slow himself down, he tried to circle in a warehouse lot full of hitched buggies and wagons. At last he spotted a sawdust pile and stopped himself by driving into it. The sawdust pile "threw him something wonderful," he said later. He pitched over the handlebars neatly—flying just as if a horse had thrown him, he recalled in the air—and landed in the sawdust on his shoulder. The dog caught up with him there. When he was a boy and some horse threw him over its neck to land on his shoulder, often that same horse nosed and nudged at him, on the ground, with just the sort of solicitude the dog was tendering him now. From the dog, he found it touching. When Clare stood, it was a simple matter to find his yellow plaid cap, shake the sawdust from his hair, and brush his face and suit. He inspected his bicycle and found it undamaged; its new pneumatic detachable tires, imported from Ireland, had not detached. He left the bicycle in the sawdust and turned to the crowd.

The tracks ran down the middle of Railroad Avenue. People stood eight and nine rows deep on both sides of the street, as far as Clare could see—men wearing black overcoats and bowler hats, and women wearing blue or green felt hats and red-, yellow-, or brown-jacketed dresses. Thousands of people were there, from all over the region, and Clare had neglected to make some provision for finding June. June was short. So was his daughter Mabel, who was two, and so was Ada, his mother. Fortunately, right by the warehouse, a fellow was selling vulcanized toy balloons. Clare watched him blow them up and tie them to sticks. He saw the tan balloons dotting the crowd sparsely. Mabel would surely have one; he could start finding his family by looking under each balloon.

Under one tan balloon he found his friend John Ireland Sharp. Distractedly, he was carrying his red-faced son Horace, two, who was holding the balloon's stick in one hand, and crying. Pearl Sharp, resplendent in a fur-trimmed astrakhan coat and wide silk hat, towered over her small-proportioned husband. She was holding an older son at each hand. She beamed from one black-stockinged boy to the other, and made faces to soothe their youngest. Clare had taught science and manual training in the high school for two years before he quit a year ago to work full time in the land office; John Ireland, as principal, had been his boss and friend. John Ireland seemed not to hear the child crying directly into his ear.

It was John Ireland who told Clare the news: that the body of Lee Chin, the Sharps' own household employee, had been discovered this morning lashed to a piling under the disused old wharf and drowned. A fisherman had found the body on this morning's ebbing tide. "That is," John Ireland said, "he noticed Lee Chin's head and shoulders out of water under the wharf." The fisherman had rowed over to investigate. When they hauled the body up, it was naked. There were no wounds or bruises on it, but crabs had been at it. Telling this, John Ireland's ordinarily composed face, fine-cut and lightly freckled, looked jarred and askew, and his black eyes gazed up blankly at Clare.

Clare knew Lee Chin; he was one of two Chinese brothers who worked for the Sharps. Clare had often seen him, the small brother, nimble in a cloth cap, tending flowers in the Sharps' yard, burning brush, and accompanying the two youngest Sharp sons on walks to the steamer dock, or wrestling with them on the beach; he had a narrow head and a loose-mouthed way of laughing, which showed his small teeth.

"Who did it?"

"No one knows," Pearl put in, and abruptly began to fall to pieces. Searching inside her coat for a handkerchief, however, she sniffed, rallied nobly, and remarked that it would not do to display the whole family in tears. She used the handkerchief to wipe Horace's nose, and took him in her arms.

Single men and families were still arriving; a green landau came through the crowd, pulled by a twitching team of matched bays, whose ears were back. People made room, bumping Clare and the Sharps along the street. The dog crawled between Clare's legs. Pearl Sharp turned to admire the landau's oval glass window. Her black hair was swept up and under her hat's brim. Then she peered over heads down the tracks looking for the train. The Canadian dignitaries on the train, and their moneyed backers from London, would be accompanied by their wives—important women who were coming along for the pleasure of the outing, and who would be displaying the most up-to-the-minute East Coast and London fashions in the trim of hats and the drapery of bustles. Pearl was one among many Whatcom women who would study this elaborate clothing in glimpses, to garner ideas with which to instruct their own dressmakers.

Lee Chin was a merry, easygoing man, John Ireland said. He raised his voice above the crowd, and Clare bent to hear him. Like Clare, John Ireland wore no overcoat but only a suit, and a miserable, rusty silk topper that Pearl must have forced upon him.

Lee Chin had many friends, John Ireland told Clare. He enjoyed gambling, and traveled once a week to gambling spots in Seattle. So far as John Ireland knew, he staked small sums and paid his debts. John Ireland said that Lee Chin was the only Chinese man he knew who had a wife in this country. His wife had not liked the gambling. She was at home now, with the dead man's older brother, Johnny Lee. They were preparing the body for shipment to Sacramento; the two of them had, quite delicately, kicked the Sharps out of the house.

Clare expressed his sympathy to the family, shook hands with John Ireland, and set off awkwardly through the crowd. He felt sawdust inside his collar and shoes. It was fir sawdust, damp with pitch. He ran his finger around the inside of his collar and felt some of it sift down under his shirt.

Minta Honer, his sister-in-law, was starting across the tracks to greet him. She held her pale head high, apparently trying to keep him in sight through her spectacles. Her wide red hat and her green coat's attached cape made her look very short indeed; this shortness, with the vigor of her steps, and her open, myopic, sympathetic expression, made her seem an otherworldly creature, like a gnome set in the woodlands to sweeten life on earth for mortals. In fact, her mind was racing and forming lists of duties to perform on the ranch when she returned.

Clare met Minta and brought her on his arm to his side of the street, where the Whatcom volunteer hose company had arrayed its equipment. Minta's face was heavily formed, and her limbs were possibly thick, but her physique was trim, and her gloved hand on Clare's arm was so light he thought she had let go. She looked back over her shoulder at the crowd she had left. There, among the throngs of men, Clare glimpsed boys in short pants and black stockings, and young girls in dresses and coats down to their knees, and black stockings. Clare saw a brass cornet flash. Then he saw, where the crowd parted for the hose, Minta's slender son, Hugh, who in his fifteen years had seen so many people die. Hugh, in his dark shirtsleeves, was manning a section of flat hose for the opposing fire company, and looking sober and prepared.

Minta had not seen June, she said, but she would help him search. She added that Kulshan Jim was back in Goshen today, supervising the setting of the hop vines; she and her Goshen bunch would drive the buggy back right after the celebration, and could not linger to visit in town. She leaned to pat the terrier.

"What's this all over the dog?" she asked.

"Sawdust."

While she brushed at the dog, Clare looked ahead and saw Beal Obenchain. His head, like Clare's own head, stuck above the crowd, at the height of the balloons. He was wearing his high-crowned derby, tilted back boyishly; his hair curled under it, behind his long ears. Clare saw the good-natured expression on his wide mouth. He turned away. Clare knew Obenchain from the high school manual training class. He no longer knew everyone in town—there were ten thousand people living on Bellingham Bay, most of them newcomers attracted by the boom—but he knew almost every grown man who had lived here a few winters. As he and Minta moved northward up the street, they passed among strangers and greeted their friends.

Under a tan balloon they found young Mabel, and June carrying her. Clare's mother, Ada, was there, wearing a yellow sunbonnet, as if the busy streets of Whatcom had been an Illinois cornfield. Ada, in her impatience, was striking the street with her cane; the cane bounced up, and she caught it and struck with it again. Ada and Minta fell to embracing. In the past two years, since Ada had moved from Goshen to Whatcom to live with Clare and June, these two fond women, of different generations and differing backgrounds, regretted seeing less of each other.

Mabel extended her limp arms to her father, and Clare seized her up. She was a dough-faced, indolent child of two; she was wearing a large, flat beret. June straightened the back of Mabel's plaid coat. His own June was, Clare thought, the best-looking woman in town—her large features were delicately formed, her skin was radiant, and her trim figure was supple and finely dressed. She raised her enormous eyes to Clare.

"What's that all over you?"

"Sawdust."

A thrill ran through the crowd on both sides of the tracks, and voices moved up in pitch. The Whatcom volunteer hose was getting ready to show its worth. Whatcom County men and women were proud of the water pressure their hose companies could command. Wooden buildings burned down regularly, and powerful jets of water could, if not save those buildings, at least protect their towns—which also, heretofore, had burned down regularly. Clare saw his slow-moving brother, Glee, in shirt-sleeves and necktie, take a place at the unrolled hose. Jay Tamoree, in his forage cap, held the big brass nozzle; Glee was two or three men behind him. They were both members of the Whatcom hose. Its motto was "Get into the building." Both the Whatcom hose and the Goshen hose, across the tracks, had purchased expensive new equipment to deliver water under such great pressure that it could shoot a three-inch jet of water over a city block of three-story buildings.

The Sons of Veterans band, in uniform, struck up a frenzied march. Across the tracks, a cornet band in uniform began playing the same march at almost the same time. Here came the Whatcom water. Half a dozen men arrived to help Tamoree control the nozzle. They sent, to glad cries, a stream of water high over the tracks. But where was Goshen's half of the arch of living water?

Across the street, the Goshen men, whose fire company had won a prize for "fleetness of foot," were scrambling to locate and open the cocks that started the flow. The Whatcom crowd pressing around Clare and his family began to laugh, for Whatcom and Goshen had been rivals for pre-eminence in the region for many years, and Whatcom had won; now those farmers from Goshen could not even find their own ...

Consequently the Whatcom hose twitted the Goshen hose, playfully, by directing the stream at them. A few women on the other side got wet. Clare saw Drew Dorr shake his fist. The Goshen hose got its water on, and fired it directly across at the Whatcom hose. The stream knocked a few firemen over, and some spectators, like June, who were too close to the action. Two dozen Whatcom men took the places of the fallen and, outraged—"Can't you take a joke?" Clare heard Tamoree holler—shot the water with the utmost deliberation at the Goshen hose company, and began mowing them down, man by man. Someone shouted, "We're knocking them stem-winding!" The Goshen hose retaliated and scattered the shrieking crowd. The water pressure was truly impressive; wabbling jets from the two opposing hoses shot directly at each other across the tracks, and the spray splashed high in the air and made a river on the streets. Along came the train.

The Carpenters Union band was playing now. The train kept coming; the young engineer sounded the whistle. Clare and his family, breathless with laughter, were running back. Over his shoulder Clare saw that both hose companies were ignoring the train. Hugh Honer was shepherding some children away from the uproar. The train steamed right into the opposing jets of water, which broke all the windows on both sides of the two first-class coaches, knocked off ten or so top hats, and drenched all the men in their Prince Albert coats, and all the ladies, and all their hats.

Three hours later, Clare returned home on his bicycle from the Birdswell Hotel banquet. The banquet had been a fraught occasion, and Clare had made a powerful effort not to catch the eye of anyone who might, as he put it to June later, "bust out laughing," for any further amusement on the part of Whatcom's citizens could only hurt Whatcom's interests, which, Clare had to concede, coincided with his own. It was only now, riding his bicycle home, that he noticed that the water had soaked through his tan suit and wet the sawdust under his shirt and inside his trousers, and halted its natural downward drift.

Clare wondered if America in general, and Whatcom in particular, was altogether ready for glory. He banished the thought as ignoble, but it persisted. The mayor of Whatcom, speaking from a doused decorated podium, had been abject in his apologies. The mayor of Goshen could be said to have groveled. Mr. Lee McAleer, Whatcom's soft-spoken city treasurer, had produced from his person a truly impressive abundance of silk handkerchiefs, which he gave to the offended ladies to blot themselves. Nevertheless, two Canadian Railway vice-presidents were so incensed that they refused to deliver their speeches. When the soaked mayor of Vancouver appeared at the podium, grimacing, with his suit and shirt visibly stuck to him, the crowd hooted.

Things had gotten worse. On one side of the podium, a flagstaff flew the United States flag, and on the other, the flag of Canada. While the Mayor of Vancouver was speaking, a burly local patriot, the logger Iron Mike, apparently noticed that, from his vantage, the Canadian flag—Union Jack with maple leaves—appeared to be flying a bit higher than the Stars and Stripes. This would not do, so with a few close friends he seized the halyard and began lowering the Canadian flag just a touch, to even it out. One of these roisterers apparently got "bedoozled," the mayor of Whatcom explained at the banquet to an uncomprehending railway magnate from London—so "bedoozled" that it was only in attempting to raise the Canadian flag yet higher that he accidentally lowered it to the ground, where a number of strangers, possibly Mexicans, trampled it underfoot. This insult, perpetrated before six thousand spectators, had stopped all speeches, caused state senator Tom Downing to cover his face with his hands, and precipitated a hasty exit of all principals to the Birdswell Hotel.

Clare rode through deserted streets; the celebration had moved down to the beach. Perhaps—after he changed his clothes—he would see how it was coming. Street St. Mary would be there on the beach, in his buckskin trousers; he could offer him a choice of copper-bottomed deals. He could see for himself the piling where someone had found Lee Chin's body lashed and drowned in the tide. He could hear what people were saying.

CHAPTER XXXI

December, 1892, Whatcom

One year and nine months later, Beal Obenchain stood again in the mud of Bellingham Bay. He bounced on his big boot toes, stepped aside, and watched the saltwater mud fill his boot-toe dents. The tide was going out; it was a neap tide, which barely moistened the mud flats. From these mud flats, in the frequent depressions and panics that racked the Puget Sound towns, people scratched up inferior clams—horse clams, bent-nose and jack clams. The town's children waded here in summer evenings' high tides. It was the children who, the previous summer, found the top of the head of a Hindoo who jumped or was pushed from the Great Northern Railway trestle that spanned the bay in a wide curve. Digging revealed that beneath the Hindoo's head was the rest of him; he had fallen into mud so soft his feet drove into it, and it buried him upright. Things that people dropped from the trestle tended to accumulate on the mud flats, or wash up on the beach: so also did lost octopus traps, scuttled boats, and broken boom logs on a westerly.

There was an old shark carcass on the beach; Obenchain had passed it on his way to the open flats. The carcass represented a shark that had once been eighteen feet long; the living creature fouled in Glee Fishburn's gill net and drowned. Glee Fishburn had displayed the shark on the town wharf till the carcass exploded and stank; then he towed it out to sea and cut it loose. An autumn flood tide dragged it back shoreward and lodged it, disintegrating and crawling with crabs, against the trestle pilings. The crabs were yellow Dungeness crabs; they ate the flesh in their clattering fashion, by squatting over it and lowering what looked like arms from their mouths and passing bites directly into what looked like stomachs. At last Glee Fishburn responsibly enclosed the shark's remains in his ruined net and towed it south to the mud flat; he beached his boat on the flood tide and manhauled the mess up the beach. There, on round stones under a sandstone cliff, the shark had solidified, barely bothered by shade-chilled flies. The sun and the freeze dried and blackened it; rain ran down it; the northerly wind turned it to stone.

Glee's torn net rotted at once, and his manila line became a ridge of shreds, but the black shark carcass under the cliff ceased changing. It looked like a creosoted log, or a lava tube, or a vein of coal, or a gutter pipe. It was one of many obstructions on the upper beach that a man had to crawl over or walk wetly around. The others were all dead Douglas firs, whose spiked trunks jutted out from the crumbled cliffside and pointed seaward like artillery.

It was December. It was December all day and dark as the center of earth. Solid cloud pressed over the land and water like a granite slab. For three weeks, no one from the town had seen Mount Baker or any mountain in the east, or the moon overhead, or the sun. This morning the sun had in fact appeared fuzzily on the far side of a fog, but then the granite clouds had sealed the sky again. By noon, no one could see even the western islands. Walking on the mud below the beach, Beal Obenchain could barely make out the old wharf and its bent pilings, where twenty-one months before he had tied the Chinaman at low tide. He could barely make out the trestle behind the old wharf; he saw the dark bulge where the trestle flew out from the woods on the cliff, and the dark streak of its curved flight over the bay. A figure was moving along the trestle's walkway, out to sea. It was raining a little, and stopping a little, as it did all winter, as if the sky were a cold cave ceiling that dripped.

It was four-thirty, after sunset. The colorless light came from nowhere and dimmed, and the blue dark, like a purse seine, was drawing close. Beal Obenchain stood in the center of an ever-decreasing circle. He chewed a salty strand of bull kelp and spat the bits on the mud. He could still see, halfway out of the bay where the current ran, a dozen drenched cormorants, motionless in silhouette, riding a tide-caught log, but he could no longer see the raft of black brant sucking eelgrass under the trestle. He could see humped eelgrass in the mud by the water, and he could see black pools and channels of standing water everywhere splitting the flats. The shining darkness of the water carved the dull darkness of the mud into lobes.

There were gaudy patches of oil film visible at his feet. Whenever something died beneath the surface, its decay released a film of iridescent oils, blue and yellow, on the mud. Near one of these oil slicks, Obenchain found a lady's comb. A thought had taken deep root in his mind. Everywhere he walked, he saw big wormholes in the mud. There were bloodworms under there, bloodworms as fragile as egg yolks. If a man touched one while he was digging, it broke and spilled cold blood into the hole. There were lugworms under there, too; they always stretched and never broke.

Now Obenchain awoke from his thoughts and discovered his pants leg was soaked; a horse clam had squirted a load of water on him. He quit the mud then, and moved to the black eelgrass humps, where he trod on hidden skeleton shrimps, sea urchins, and snails. The rain picked up. The mud flat stank of cold live mud, fish parts, and fog. He was a stout man, but he was getting cold.

Obenchain had no ties on earth. He had rowed into Whatcom from Madrone when he was sixteen; he rowed up and down the tides for two days and a night. He sold his boat to a childless couple he found back of the beach, who boarded him free while he went to school. He held the fawning couple in contempt; he read Goethe in the shed. When he was seventeen he built himself a room in a cedar stump near the railroad right-of-way in the woods south of town. He raided fish traps for cash, or worked clearing trees; he ran a small undercover trade between the nearby city of Victoria, British Columbia, and points south. He adopted, fed, and petted mice; paid no taxes; rolled blanket stiffs he found alone by the tracks or in the hobo jungle on Chuckanut Ridge; one winter he cultivated the best women in town as an audience and a source of books. Bored, he invented games with dice and with cards; he bet on bad weather; he whistled; he made a spectacle of himself near the tracks when the passenger coach passed. He sent for translations of recent books from France. He baked light bread, cinnamon rolls, and berry pies.

He had come to the mud flat to think. He had killed a man near here almost two years ago, and was just deciding not to kill another.

Obenchain could no longer make out the high trestle, or the dull waterline. He recrossed the mud flat in a drenching dark and gained the beach, where stones ground loudly underfoot. Now he knew what he would do.

He would repair to his stump and draw from a bucket the name of the man he would not kill. The way in which he had resolved not to kill him was by threatening to kill him and doing nothing. Obenchain would let the victim live as best he could inside the radius of his power, in the knowledge that he was at any moment to die.

You simply tell a man, any man, that you are going to kill him. Then—assuming he believes you enough to watch his every step but not quite enough to run away or kill you first—then you take pains not to kill him and instead watch what he does, stuck alive on your bayonet and flailing. From your unregarded hermitage in the woods a strand of force would invisibly enter the town like a fishline; you could hook up Lee McAleer, the sharp city treasurer, who was making a killing in real estate, or the mayor, or any banker who floated loans and rode the boom like a cormorant. Killing the Chinaman had afforded less interest and spectacle than Obenchain hoped it would. He should have drawn it out some. When you kill a man directly, on no matter how gradual a tide, you do not, he discovered, actually take his life. You merely hasten his life's close and conclude it; you do not take it. His life force is not added to yours, nor do his guardian spirits flock to you; these forces perish, and nobody profits by them. You take as yours, bluntly, only his carcass if you want it, which is of no value or intrigue to any save to hungry crabs and his wife, if he has a wife.

If, however, you make a man believe that you will arrange for his dying at any moment, then you can, in effect, possess his life. It was as easy as eating striped candy. For how could that man perform the least or the greatest act with his whole heart? You would give him, like bondsmen, self-consciousness and uncertainty, and they would deliver him unto you where you sat. How could such a man eat a plate of food or lie with his wife or take two steps in a row without thinking the very thoughts you bade him think? You would own this man without your lifting a finger. You would pipe, and he would dance.

He passed the dripping shark carcass and distinguished, among the multiple textures of blackness, the dull path through trees up the sandstone cliff. The mud flat held more light than the land; the forest blotted it out. When he gained the clifftop, Obenchain walked south, seeing nothing, and felt with his feet for the tracks.

CHAPTER XXXII

A candle stuck in a turnip lighted the interior of Obenchain's stump. He sat, big and muscular as a walrus, on a thin cherry chair at a thin cherry table. He opened newspapers from a pile by the stove, and wrote deliriously on a pad. He was broad-backed, with delicate hands. His shoes were the

size of stove logs. Until recently he had to have his shoes and elkhide
boots and rubberized gum boots made for him in Victoria. He wore an old-
fashioned high-crowned derby hat, indoors and out, and a black coat
dense with grease, soil, and mold. His black pants were stiff as chimneys.
The pants absorbed clam juice, charcoal, dogfish oil, dishwater, potato
water, machine grease, and mud. A fine sand thickened the saltwater mud
from the pants' knees to their cuffs; the salt water never fully dried.

Obenchain's cedar stump was hollow at the butt, and two or three feet
thick in the walls—a ready house. It measured twelve feet across and ten
feet high, higher than most shacks. Obenchain knew two gold miners
who overwintered in a cedar stump on the Skagit River. He knew a farmer
near the Lummi Indian reservation who used an eighteen-foot-wide hollow stump as a four-story barn. On the lowest level the farmer stabled an
ox team; on the second level he stored grain; on the third level he piled
hay in bales for winter; on the highest level his chickens roosted and laid.

Yellow light from the candle on the table showed black charcoal
patches marring the house's walls, where Obenchain's many successive
fires had widened the room. He had built fir and bark fires on it, like a
Lummi who hollows out a cedar canoe. Between the charcoal patches, the
stump walls were red, and smooth and wavy in grain, for Obenchain had
split planks. He hated idleness and despised work; when work was
inevitable, and no one else would do it for him, he raged and stewed for a
week, then sailed into it cheerily, all will and vigor.

To split off planks, he hunkered first above the stump. At seventeen
years old he had been already monstrous in size upon his house, like some
heavy flying thing that had caught there. Then he stood within the stump
and hammered paired wedges down the plank's length. The cedar split so
evenly that the natives here—the Nooksacks and Lummis and Skagit—
had always lived in plank houses. Obenchain lived in a tree stump.

He paid a Lummi man two dollars cash to split and adz a puncheon
floor. The adz marks rippled the wood evenly, as light air rippled Puget
Sound, so when Obenchain crossed the floor he seemed to walk on water.
When he read in his bedding, his yellow candlelight picked out the adzed
ridges. They made a receding path of flecks, such as the setting sun throws
over the sea. He roofed the stump with shakes. He chiseled, sawed, and
burned out a door eight feet tall, so he need never stoop, and tacked canvas over the doorway. After the first winter he replaced the canvas with a
slab door hinged with harness straps to a fir casing. This door enraged him

still every time he looked at it, because it had cost so much trouble and humiliation to build. By the door, a stack of three packing cases held, in descending order, mildewed books, mostly philosophy; a deep cast-iron vat in which lay a single-action Smith & Wesson .44; and a tangle of hip boots, calked boots, and shoes.

Above the packing crates, as if for decoration, stood the springing orange porcelain tiger he had found tied around the Chinaman's neck; the disk in the tiger's mouth was an oversized coin. Nailed to the crate beside it, a lettered paper read: "Do the thing and you will have the power.—R. W. Emerson." Soot from lamp oil, candle tallow, and creosote coated everything in the house.

Obenchain wrote quickly down the pad to its bottom, tore off the page, and wrote again. He stopped, tilted back the cherry chair, opened a newspaper, straightened his hat, and wrote again. About 4,500 adult men lived on Bellingham Bay, and almost that many men passed through for a week or a year and moved on—miners, adventurers with capital, drifters with no capital, loose railway workers, loggers, eastern college boys seeking quick fortunes, farmers seeking cheap land. Obenchain wanted a settled Whatcom man, to keep an eye on. He had lived in Whatcom for fifteen years, since he was sixteen. Mentally he swept the town, street by street and house by house, for names. He opened the Whatcom *Bugle Call* and cannibalized its obituaries for survivors, and the rest of the paper for businessmen and politicians. Settled men were few and prized; they won elected and appointed offices before they had dried behind the ears.

Obenchain tore off a final page from his list and stood. From the table the candle flame outlined his shoulders and long head. When something agitated his mind, the bore of his vision narrowed. His heart pounded and his shoulders tilted. He skidded a bit now on a potato on the floor.

Outside in the woods, he emptied a cedar bucket on his house's dead roots by the streak of light from the door. A chilled frog the size of Obenchain's thumbnail poured out with the rainwater; he picked it up, breathed on it to warm it, and tossed it lightly out into the black forest, where its landing made no sound.

Obenchain's whistling made a faint, lively buzz. Inside, he sat on the cherry chair, tore his pages, and dropped the strips into the bucket between his knees. When he finished and stirred the strips, they clung to the bucket's wet sides. Now he raised his head and twisted it, like a saint in an ecstasy or a man whose foot is being amputated; his hand filled the bucket. His whistling stopped. His heavy arm stirred. His fingers scraped paper strips and gathered them into a clump, from which, delicately and with a pause, he peeled one.

"Clare Fishburn." He held it by the candle: Fishburn. Clare Fishburn was a thoughtless, passionate, ordinary man. As such, he would do nicely. He wore high collars, and occupied a high position. He was a partner in the land company that bought up and developed the south side of town. In his elongated, wide-mouthed person he resembled Abraham Lincoln, Obenchain thought, without the character. Lincoln wore a top hat; the other partners in the land company wore bowlers or fedoras; Clare Fishburn wore a short-billed bicycle cap, like a boy. He made much of his distinction—which Obenchain happened to share—as one of the few persons in the state of Washington who had been born there. Obenchain had known him before he bought into the land company, back when he was a schoolteacher. He taught laboratory sciences and mechanical arts to high school children. He was Glee Fishburn's brother.

Obenchain saw Clare Fishburn bent over a drafting board, or feeding a plank, semiconsciously and without respect, to a steam-powered ripsaw. He saw him self-important at the dock, wearing his plaid bicycle cap and a linen suit, carrying a briefcase; he greeted swells just off the Seattle steamer, and waved his thin arm to show them the height and breadth of Whatcom. He was the only man in town whose height Obenchain knew, for they were apparently the same height—six feet, three inches. Although he possessed a sort of nervous force, he was a foolish man of common clay, who derived his sentimental convictions from others: a sort of stretched boy, who laughed in the Birdswell Hotel bar so his long nose quivered, and talked about "pleasure" as though everyone agreed that pleasure was the first-rate thing. He held himself loosely, insensible to how a man of stature should walk.

Obenchain despised Clare Fishburn no more than he despised the others; they all lived by whim, they all lacked the very concept of will. They dressed in the latest agony of fashion: they wore red ties, or striped pants. It could have been J. J. O'Shippy, Ole Polson, or Lee McAleer; it could have been Wilbur Carloon, or Ascher Dan. He feared none of them, and consequently he admired none of them. Every man sought to be feared, and to attack first as the best defense, and these men all failed, where he succeeded. None of them knew it. The overblown esteem in which a thoughtless fellow like Fishburn held himself blinded him to his true condition—his failure, his puniness, and his cowardice. He thought he owned his life. He thought he owned his piece of the world. Obenchain's purely mental exercise would reveal to Fishburn, inescapably, the spectacle of himself as a whipped and trembling dog, one of more than one billion whipped dogs who trotted about the planet on business, naked and plug-ignorant.

Obenchain held the damp strip of paper open. Life is mind, he thought, and mind, in some spectral way, operates in words. In his very breath was power. He would tell a man his life was in his hands and, miraculously, his life would be in his hands. He would own Clare Fishburn insofar as Clare Fishburn believed him; he would own him as God owns people and sticks thoughts in their minds, to the degree of their belief.

What, pray, would become of Fishburn's former life? To what category of being belongs a dead life whose body lives on? When Obenchain knew Fishburn years ago in the high school basement shop and laboratory, he had a sharp-tongued wife, a dead-end job, a house on a hill, and a head full of nothing. His bosom pal was John Ireland Sharp, the high school principal, whom Beal knew very well from their boyhood on Madrone.

Should somebody hold a funeral for this dead life, for this man who had been free to fancy, however falsely, that he was free? Fishburn's body would live long after Fishburn's own life was effectively over. In telling him he was to die, in threatening to kill him, Obenchain would commit, tonight, the antithesis of murder. It was antimurder, he thought; it was conception, the conception of a tall slave, or the birth of a new man created by a word. He imagined that in many long years' time, when the body called Clare Fishburn should die of natural causes, he, Obenchain, would attend the funeral apparently as a townsman, but in fact as the real father of an only son.

Obenchain saw himself as a stranded mystic, who alone understood his experiments on the minds of men. He was a man of science, a man who had access to metagnostical structures, a man of methods contrived in purity, who knew secrets. He was in fact, even raising his arms, even smiling from ear to ear, even chewing his potatoes with salt like any man, a broad-shouldered genie in a bottle. His power coiled in his drawn-up knees; he was mighty because he was bound. He buckled himself down with constraints like steel harness, and grew strong resisting. Worldly wisdom was cheap and common. His mind recognized, nevertheless, that if the Powers That Be were to deny him their forces, and people tried to trap him, he could always use his mastery of the powers that are. If the sluggish and greedy laborers of the town should stir against him, he was smart enough to keep the sheriff flattered by losing at chess—and if that failed, he was loose enough to move on.

He should eat something. He struck a fire in the stove. He would call on Clare Fishburn after supper. He stooped before the stove door and fed the fire sticks, then fir bark. His broad forehead glistened. He stooped before the stove door, and his mind raced; his movements were smooth and controlled. He moved the bucket out of his way.

CHAPTER XXXIII

That night, Clare Fishburn, with a spoon in one hand and a daughter in the other, ate apple pudding. He was leaning in and out of the lamplight; he was telling a story in the dining room, between the kitchen and the parlor, and waving his spoon. He wore a fine wool suit, faintly striped, and new shoes. His nose was long, his forehead was long, and his jaw was long. His hair was so disheveled, and his frame was so tall and shambly, that even sitting he resembled the stick doll that dances on a slat. His lively motions kept the effect constant; he shifted his legs, jerked his arms, swiveled his neck.

"... He rode the goat. It was almighty fine. It was really killing." The night before, the Sons of Pioneers held their annual initiation. He had been home late; now he described it to his wife, June. June was still an ironic, passionate woman whose soft massed hair and round head, small size, changeable skin, and vibrant voice made her appear fragile.

The lodge met in the old Whatcom schoolhouse—a little room lined with benches. Peering out through a window, Clare had seen the firelit, elegant figure of Lee McAleer, the town treasurer. McAleer bent to heat a branding iron in the coals of a bonfire outside. Some men led in Wilbur Carloon, blindfolded. Wilbur Carloon would ride the goat—that is, he would join the Sons of Pioneers upon completion of its singular rite. Wilbur Carloon, who had come from Kansas to open a department store, was a short, solemn fellow whose yellowish hair made strange coils beneath his fedora. The blindfold covered his eyes; the ordinarily concentrated expression of his wide mouth was slack.

"Carloon took it like a man," Clare told June. "McAleer made a mighty show of fortifying him for the ordeal out of his flask. We all fortified ourselves. We bent him over a barrel and"—Clare's long, animated face reddened a bit and he hurried on—"lowered his trousers. I brought in the branding iron for him to smell. He could hear me go out the door for it, and come back in. I put it up to his face—it was glowing—and he held himself real still. He could smell that hot iron, and feel it on his face; so could I."

June knew all this. They did it every year.

"Lee McAleer slipped out when I did, and got the cold iron. He'd kept it in the icehouse all day, and he carried it over in a bucket of ice. He dried it off real quick, I lowered the hot one, and he ..."

June listened, smiling, without looking at Clare; instead, against her will, she followed his apple-pudding spoon as it wagged over the blue tablecloth, as it wagged over Mabel's fair head and good dress, and over Clare's own shirtfront.

"... laid the cold one on him." Clare applied the spoon to the air, and the pudding spilled; it was nothing, just the floor. "Carloon jumped a mile. Two miles. And we all burst out, of course. You should have seen him. He ... his"—a pause, and his deep, amused glance met his wife's—"squeezed together, and he jumped a mile, and didn't let out a peep." Clare himself, he recalled, at his own initiation, had screamed blue murder.

"It was killing," he concluded, "but not so fine as last year." Clare hoisted his shoulders and dropped them; they were thin as dowels inside his striped suit jacket.

Last year someone had tipped off the initiate, Tom Tyler, a Californian the Whatcom land boom attracted, who was already a city councilman. The boys initiated Tom Tyler in the same schoolhouse. They held up to him the hot branding iron to smell, and laid on him the chilled one. When the cold iron touched his skin, he whirled around and drew a revolver and shot out, and the Sons of Pioneers all dove for the windows. Clare threw himself under a bench—he thought he was, as he said, "fried gent, and no breakfast forever." Two men sailed out the door; two men smashed through glass windows and landed outside; and two men stuck in one window, trying to get out at the same time. There was a drawing of it in the *Bugle Call*—the two men stuck in the window—for the town appreciated the story. Tyler had loaded his cartridges with cotton-wadding blanks. He fooled the whole lodge and frightened the boys, when they were supposed to be fooling and frightening him. He had stood before the barrel in the empty room, a bulky, mustachioed man, holding his revolver and laughing his teeth out. He was, by all accounts, a first-rate sort.

Old Ada Tawes was clearing the table. She was no taller standing than Clare sitting. On top of her head was a small white roll of hair, the size of a corn dodger. Now age had pulled down her bow-shaped mouth and round face, taken half her teeth, and thinned the brows on her clear forehead, so her expressive eyes looked even bigger and blacker than they had when she was young, when they blazed out from a bonnet deep as a bucket.

Ada looked baked. If there were any more initiations to tell, she said, Clare would spill not only the pudding but the child as well. Mabel slid lower on Clare's lap. She was an India-rubbery-looking person even when awake. Her moist child's face shifted from one half-formed expression to another; even while she climbed things, even while she marched boisterously about the house, she retained a limp sleepy look. She had thin, reddish hair and skin pale as putty; her round limbs looked jointless and unmuscled. She was a jot shy of four years old—born on Christmas. If she heard her father's exalted voice at all, it was through a bright fog of sleep.

On the back porch the door banged, and banged again: Ada was throwing salmon scraps to the dog, the dog that had been crying pitiably since sunset, as though it had not yet in the length of its life so much as seen a morsel of food, yet knew, with its dying breath, that there was such a thing, inexplicably denied to it of all creatures alone.

Something else happened, Clare told June. She cocked her round head, at the crown of which her brown hair lay loosely coiled. He unfurled a long arm to turn up the wick of the lamp in the center of the table; light rose in the room.

"They elected me treasurer," he said. He met June's intelligent gaze. Her fine, high brows outlined the rim of bone under which her eyes were deep as wells. He loved to know her opinion of things. There was not a bill in the House of Representatives or a flowering bulb in the garden of which he did not consider his wife's probable opinion before he framed his own, if any. This day he had solemnly promised himself three or four separate times to withhold this new prospect until he determined what he himself made of it. There she was, however, looking at him in the precise and welcoming way she had, and although he remembered his promises to himself, he blurted it out with relief.

"... Which is no account in itself," but the first treasurer was Ank Larsen, and he was state senator in Olympia now, and he wanted to retire. Before him the Pioneers' treasurer was Lee McAleer, and now he was the treasurer of Whatcom. Clare gave Mabel a squeeze and uncrossed his long legs. He could have stopped there, but he did not stop; he kept his voice neutral.

"... And McAleer and Tom Tyler walked me home afterwards and asked me to consider running for public office in '94." He recalled McAleer's modest voice, the way his rich clothes hung on his thin frame, his hesitancy, which marked respect.

June's expression took on a touch of primness.

It was a long way away, it was another two years, Clare added, swinging one foot a little and studying its shadow on the floor. It would be a great honor.

"What office? The state legislature?" With widening eyes. "Congress?" Since June's father had been first a state legislator and then a United States senator from Maryland, she held views.

Nothing national, he told her. It was just talk, anyway. Maybe the state legislature, say. For the People's Party, which was all the cry—for freeing silver and kicking the bums out. The People's Party had almost carried Whatcom last month in the presidential race.

He waited for her remark, which came.

"Hurrah, boys," she said.

June's voice was soft and ironic; it could generally kill a man, if she did not cancel it out.

They were running late. Clare himself had begun fixing the pudding long after dark. He had peeled the newspapers from the apples in their carton in the cellar and chopped them—red and white Kings, green and white Gravensteins—into a yellow bowl. He shunted the stove's heat into its oven, where eventually the king salmon steak baked, and five brown potatoes baked, and the dark pudding frothed down the sides of the yellow bowl. Now it was after eleven, and Grandmother Ada was shuffling her feet. He and June were starting to stare, and small Mabel was asleep, her loose mouth tidily shut. His must be a slatted sort of lap, Clare thought, but Mabel had a way of softening to fit any occasion, as though she had no bones. The skin on her hands was hot; her hair gave off a sour steam as she slept.

Clare scraped hardened brown sugar and butter from the yellow bowl's side; he offered it to June—who smiled her radiant smile, shaking her head—and ate it himself. He had meant to pick up some sherry; he wished they had a boat. They could get a rowboat, at least, for Mabel. They could get a bicycle for June, and he and June could ride out together next spring. Tomorrow he would surprise her with an electric sewing machine.

Honor had come to him, and distinction, in a modest way, as it had come to the expanding town. It was only last year that he put up June's $35,000 legacy and joined the Bellingham Bay Improvement Company. Now his share was worth over $100,000. The company ran ahead of the Great Northern railroad, buying low and selling high. It was simple and solid, and they were, as J. J. O'Shippy said, "purely coining money." Men saluted Clare in the street, and sought his advice and influence. He had served as county clerk, as city assessor. Every day more eastern capitalizers drew into town and plunked down cash. Every year Whatcom platted more building lots, chopped more roads into the forest, flung out wharves. The way business was swelling and his investments boiling up, he fancied getting a horse and carriage—a high-seated victoria, and a certain beautiful, freckled mare with a high, long action, which J. J. O'Shippy might sell. They could build a carriage house by the cowshed. He would enclose the front porch, extend another porch beyond it over the imported lilacs, and root more lilacs farther out. He and June would add to the family. They could pick up a beachfront parcel in the islands this summer, hurry to roll up a cabin, build a rowboat or buy a sloop, and tour the islands, maybe keep bees.

June carried stacked dessert plates to the kitchen. She wore a pinch-waisted dress of pearl gray, ribboned in dark rows, and a white dimity apron. Grandmother Ada soused the dishes. Clare sat alone. His vest hung open. His high starched collar, of the sort that pressed into most men's jaws, extended only halfway up his long neck. His brown hair he disdained, ever, to comb, for his mother had combed it too painfully when he was a boy, and he was no dandy. Every morning he parted his hair with his fingers and pressed it down. By day he drew on and slipped off his bicycle cap a hundred times, and by evening, as now, his stiff curling hair rose in every direction, and added two more inches to his already exaggerated height.

In another eight years he and June would own this house. They could own it now, but the capital was doing more good on the loose. Their money was no longer tied solely to real estate; recently he had sold shares in his company worth fifteen thousands, and tucked them in a spread of three solid things—bank certificates, the gas company, and national railroads—for which prudence he was now grateful. He was becoming a man of substance.

Eight years ago, when he was a man of thirty-four living in Goshen, his real life had not, in his present view, yet begun. His life was formless and scattered, a series of stabs at a life. He enrolled only halfheartedly at the Goshen Normal School, and qualified himself as a schoolteacher in science. He met June the following September; he was building Minta's house. June roused and flashed wonderfully easy, and the skin on her face colored up; she spoke so softly, in such quaint accents, a man could hardly hear her, and so sharply he could be sorry he tried. Her physique was scaled down. Her stranger's dark glance included him in some particular joke, the details of which he had been eager to learn. He quailed before her fearsomely firm opinions about some things, and stepped forward to solve her childlike perplexity about others. She possessed five or six accomplishments, more than any woman he ever saw.

Then he had got started: he came home to Whatcom married to June Randall, who was, as he put it to himself, "quite the finest thing he had struck." He signed on at the new high school as professor of sciences and of manual training. He bought the Golden Street house on a twelve-year mortgage loan, and fathered Mabel.

When he married, Clare set his net, and it held. Good things accumulated; their life grew and spread. Languid Mabel arrived, and a son who did not live. He and June had added a front porch to the house, and a cowshed; they had dug a garden, to which they added a new row every year. Chance had added to them an aggrieved terrier and a bobtail cat. When his stepfather, Norval Tawes, died, his mother came; she and June ran the house. They bought an organ for the parlor, on which June knocked out ballads and hymns so fiercely her hair came down and her face flushed up. He planted a row of poplars. In the shop he fashioned cherry frames for two watercolor prints of Niagara Falls; June hung the pictures in the kitchen. He refinished the chairs; he made windfall-apple cider; he painted the house blue. Every spring he vowed to quit teaching school, and every summer he missed his pupils and searched for them on the streets. Every month June reminded him to pay the mortgage. He resolved to quit teaching one spring when J. J. O'Shippy told him, at the Birdswell Hotel bar, that Senator Green Randall's $35,000 legacy to June was sufficient to qualify Clare as partner in the improvement company. He gave John Ireland notice then, for the following fall.

Everything was his idea of a good time. He would do any favor for anyone who asked. He greeted his friends on the street by saying, "Are you abreast of what's afoot?" He never answered letters. Once he walked fifteen miles to save half a bit on twenty pounds of potatoes. He never deliberately told a lie, and he rarely happened to keep a promise. He told people he hated schedules, appointments, finances—anything fussy or detailed. It was fine to have a drink, and almighty fine to have a family, and damned fine to have it rain the day he said he would fix the roof. Now he could be city treasurer like Lee McAleer, and race yachts; he could be a legislator in Olympia, even governor, and do some good, and celebrate. If he ran for office as a People's Party candidate, O'Shippy and the other partners would not like it; they supported the gold standard, like most easterners who had capital. Well, they wanted a local boy to join the company, and they got one.

Clare blazed with health and abounded in the goodwill of men. He was what Tom Tyler called a crackerjack, and all possibility. He lived at gale force; he moved between activities at railway speed; he had to. Everybody did. He sought deeds and found tasks. He was a giant in joy, speeding and thoughtless, suggestible, a bountiful child. He whistled in bed every morning and fell asleep every night after tea. His wife laughed at his jokes; his mother waited on him; his red-haired daughter rode on his shoulders, and bounced her heels in his heart.

Sitting alone, Clare could see, reflected in the dark window across the table, the yellow gas lamp floating and globular like a planet or star. Beneath it, and also floating over the outside dark, were reflections from the kitchen window behind him—which contained again, golden, the gas lamp, and his wife's round head in motion, and Mabel near and spread pale along the darkness, and a cluster of vaporous teacups on the table, and a cold bottle of milk.

CHAPTER XXXIV

When Clare's caller came, June was finishing up in the kitchen. Old Ada was in her upstairs room, probably reading her Bible after seeing Mabel to bed. Clare was alone at the table; on paper he was reckoning sums. He heard the doorbell and walked through the parlor to answer it, surprised, thinking: it must be midnight.

The big man, whom Clare recognized, ducked under the doorway to enter. He pushed into the parlor, blinked in the lamplight, and stopped abruptly in the middle of the room. The dark parlor furniture shrank; did Clare himself so occupy a room? Under his curved hatbrim, Obenchain's soft eyes looked muddy about the skin. Clare had no idea what Obenchain would do.

He offered him some tea. "I'm sorry we're plumb out of sherry." As Clare spoke he shooed the yellow cat from the fringed sofa and picked up a doll, a painted doll, which had been standing on a flowered cushion. Clare started to seat himself to put his guest at ease, but rose again, uncertain, and stepped forward. He had seen a long-barreled revolver tucked in Obenchain's pants.

"What do you want?"

Obenchain told him. He said, looking sideways at Clare and then idly at the tops of the lace parlor curtains, "I am going to kill you ... as it happens." Both men stood in the decorated parlor, their arms tense at their sides—Obenchain coiled in his loose stained clothes, and Clare attentive in his wrinkled suit. Obenchain pressed his jaws together. Clare held himself still.

"I am going to kill you, shortly ... for my own reasons ... with which you need not concern yourself." His voice, between characteristic pauses, was a pressured baritone; it filled the small, still room the way the brocade-draped organ's noise filled it when June pumped it and played, panting, and her shoes knocked on the pedals and the whining notes swelled. Concern yourself, Clare thought.

Obenchain's white forehead rumpled. "You might look at it this way: you have not much longer to live." When he lifted his head, Clare saw that his eyes, set close in the brownish skin, were glassy; they caught the lamplight and reflected it in gleams. Clare had never been truly fond of the fellow.

"What are you saying, man?"

"I have considered it a part of ... justice, to impart this knowledge to you."

He was earnest, frightened, and arrogant; he rarely looked at Clare. The men were standing within a foot of each other. Clare wondered if Obenchain always packed a revolver. He heard June climbing the back stairs.

I was going to mend this doll's head, he thought. He understood that Obenchain did not expect him to speak or respond in any way; his role was to listen until the speech wore itself out. "The topic of justice," Obenchain said, "has long ... interested me."

Obenchain raised his thin hands upwards, to the height of his shoulders. "Your life, Mr.... Fishburn, is in my hands." His lips spread, and he looked, Clare thought, right tickled with himself. Obenchain read too much; everyone knew that.

Clare tried to concentrate on what the man was saying; he wanted to learn his place in this scheme. He could not, however, follow it. "... always by your side," he was saying, "waking and sleeping, early and late." His dark lips were askew, and his voice was urgent.

"It need not, of course, have been you, but it . . . was you, delivered up to me this evening. You"—his voice surged and fell, his high-crowned derby bobbed—"whose life I hereby ... take." Clare could see only that Obenchain believed himself. He was uttering a creed. Clare hoped to get him out of the house—mighty carefully—so he could think, or sleep on it. How long had it been since he had faced someone his own height? Obenchain was burly and wide—twice the man Clare was. His agitated face seemed to loom above him closely, as if the moon had inched up on the earth, and people who noticed it nearer on the horizon looked away, embarrassed.

Obenchain broke off. He held himself in control. Was this the young man Clare knew from the high school, Beal Obenchain, who finished his work early—he made his birdhouse, cookie cutter, bookshelf, doorbell—and read books in a corner, licking his fingertips? Now, with his head cocked back, he was examining Clare as if he were an unusual binding on a book. He flashed his wide smile and confided, "I picked your name at random from a ... cedar bucket." Clare wondered what June would say. Would he tell her? The weather would be clearing any day now; it would be a shame, if Obenchain killed him, to miss a fine northeaster, when he had waited so long without grousing for a clear day. What would the sheriff say? He had seen Obenchain and the sheriff together in the Blue Moon Saloon, playing chess. Perhaps the new doctor could declare him unfit, and send him away. A weariness overcame Clare, and intolerance, and a wish to sleep by his wife in their bed.

"You will excuse me now," he said. "I was just going upstairs." Clare prepared to turn his back on him and start mounting the stairs. If Obenchain drew his revolver he would hear it, and kick back with full force.

Obenchain, however, was leaving. He had never taken off his hat. He found the door and was ducking out, and saying cordially, "Forgive the lateness of the occasion. One must strike while ..." Clare closed the door. He heard Obenchain's heavy tread descend the steps.

Clare had been so young, ever since he could remember—so young, and so full of ideas.

CHAPTER XXXV

Clare extinguished the dining room lamp and the parlor lamp; he smelled the heavy coal oil. He found a doll in his hand. He replaced it on the sofa. He fetched a log from the back porch and pushed it into the stove.

Obenchain sounded as if he meant to kill him that very night, or on Christmas, or the next day. What about the sewing machine? Ada knew where he had hidden it in the cowshed. Who would tell Street St. Mary when the market for his lot was peaking?

As soon as he blew out the parlor lamp, the yellow cat cried at the door. Clare opened the door to let her out. He looked into the night.

Obenchain was still there. He was standing still as a boulder in the mud lot below the house, barely visible in silhouette against the distant water. He was facing the house, a wrathful shouldered hump beneath an old-fashioned, high-crowned derby. Clare did not know if Obenchain could see him; the house was dark.

"Go away," Clare called out. "Go home. Go away!"

Clare lay in bed under the tall, cold window. His long, sharp feet poked the blankets up; his long, sharp nose poked into the air. When June asked what Obenchain had said, he answered that he only wanted to use his old steam lathe. When June asked who he was shouting at, Clare said it was a stray cat hissing at their cat. These were just about the first cold-blooded lies he ever told her. Now she was asleep. Clare knew Obenchain had no reason to wish him dead. Lunatic Obenchain liked reasons; he had a bucketful of reasons for everything he did, which he would explain to anyone who could understand them.

Obenchain understood his own reasons, however, and Obenchain believed himself. He was unpredictable, he was perhaps drunk, or having a spell of nervous excitement, or cold-out crazy; he was perhaps acting on someone else's orders—but for all that, he was not kidding; he was earnest. Clare had seen the man's meager eyebrows draw together in a bulge under his hatbrim, from the effort of explaining; he saw the incongruous, imploring smile. Clare's life had become important to Obenchain. And so, even while he lay in bed that first night, Clare began the process of believing him. Who was he not to believe Obenchain, when Obenchain believed himself? People do what they believe they will do. If a man believes he will fall a certain tree, Clare thought, then he will probably fall that tree, and he will not if he does not. If a man believes that your death fits his plans, however obscure, then your death fits his plans, however obscure, and he is the one with the gun. Clare could try to kill him first, or he could take his family and leave, or he could try to get him locked up. For how long? What would Obenchain do? When?

In the high school shop, Obenchain would do almighty anything. Once he shouted suddenly, addressing the class. He knew what power turned the big saws; he knew the limits of cold chisels, the ontology of gases, the secrets of numbers on the rule. The sweat on his white forehead shone in the basement windows' light. People swindled him, he confided to Clare, whispering; they tried to take advantage of his honesty. His mind was quick, and his hands were sure. One-fifth of Clare's students failed manual training; Obenchain excelled, and led the class. Sometimes he wandered away, wounded, when Clare was talking to him. He loomed over the schoolboys, head and shoulders. He funked his first term of algebra after a week; he could not stick it. Clare found him once in the hall standing still, with his jaws open like a sea lion's and his lips stretched down like the lips on a cedar mask.

Obenchain mastered his nervous weakness, Clare knew, more every year. His vehemence took on the force of coherence, the force of a large and balanced battery of ideas aimed at a single point. He possessed skills. Once at the livery stable Clare had seen him pinch the eyelid of a skittery horse, to hold it still for haltering; he seemed to have the eyelid by his fingernails. The tormenting trick worked; the horse held its very breath. Obenchain was erratic, but his wrath and distrust were steady. Most people were afraid of him. Respectable families multiplied in the town, and the south-side roughs and criminals—hoboes and cardsharks, old buffalo hunters, train robbers, bounty hunters, deserters, and murderers—had diminished in numbers and notice, while ordinary hermits abounded.

People said that Obenchain could read Greek. They said he was a genius, who would make the town famous. They said a falling tree had cracked his head when he was a boy on the island, and one of its branches jabbed into his brain. They said he ate cloudberries, which are poisonous; they said he ate soap. They said he swam in the bay at night, trailing eelgrass, and lay stark naked on the rocks like a seal. They said he had a hand in tying the Sharps' Chinese employee Lee Chin under the old wharf at low tide. People said every sort of thing.

Clare was looking at the window beside the bed; it revealed nothing and reflected nothing, for the sky and the house were dark. June, he wanted to think—June with her deep-arched eyes, and limp Mabel, and his straddle-legged mother, carrying on in the house without him, as if he were late forever, and they were holding dinner. For a moment he saw June and Mabel stiff and blurred and bewildered. He could not, however, keep them in mind. If he died now, his life would have been a brief, passing thing like a hard shower. If he died later, having done more, it would be no different.

Now, as streamers of colored fog began to advance on the black clearness of Clare's thoughts, he found he could not recollect why he had been so all-fired busy, all these years, congratulating himself, like everyone else; no wonder people were so astonished to die. Every night, Mabel centered herself on her feather-bed to sleep and never extended a finger or toe, for she believed herself to be surrounded by sharks and black death. She was right. She was surrounded by sharks and black death. He used to know that, too, when he was a boy, but it had slipped his mind.

CHAPTER XXXVI

Four notched cornerposts of Douglas fir almost forty feet high extended through both stories of the Fishburns' house on Golden Street, from the ground to the eaves. Because of these long cornerposts, when the wind blew, the house swayed like a grass. Golden Street crested the ridge of a hill overlooking Bellingham Bay; it took the full force of the southwest wind that stormed all winter. When a gale was blowing, or more—when it blew seventy knots, or eighty, and waves broke off and wharves broke up—then houses blew down, but not theirs.

Ada's was the attic bedroom, and she liked riding storms while she slept. Tonight was dead calm; from the bitch light by the bedside window rose an even flame. She still called it a bitch light, although it was a tallow candle. In her day, they had no wicking to make candles, so they melted bear grease or fish oil in a tin pan and lighted a twisted strip of rag in it, and it was always a devilish mess, even before the children slatted it over—a bitch light. Ada laid a hot brick wrapped in a towel on her feather-bed, climbed in, worked the brick down to the bottom, pinched out the bitch light, and drew up her blankets.

Now she was wide awake. Her husband Rooney belonged to the Pioneer Association. So did her second husband, Norval Tawes. Members were those men who arrived before 1855, the year of the Indian War. The Pioneers let Rooney join because he was on the overland road in '55, making his way here, which almost counted, and there were not enough old-timers left by the late seventies to make a good club—not that they had all died, but they had quit the settlement, "absquatulated," when the coal mine closed and the town folded. Her family stayed through the hard times—it cost too much to leave the region. They moved out to the country. In Goshen her son Clare joined the Brotherhood of Owls. So did her other son, Glee, and Norval, her husband; they all joined the Brotherhood of Owls.

With her eyes opened wide in the bed, Ada repeated to herself: "'For we are strangers before thee, and sojourners, as were all our fathers: our days on the earth are as a shadow, and there is none abiding.'" She did not say this to herself now because she was old and thinking of dying. In fact, she said it less often than she had in her twenties and thirties, when she thought every week she would probably die, as every week those around her died; for now it was clear that she was the one abiding, and abiding. It felt like the longer she stayed here, the more she was a stranger. She did not know these new people she saw everywhere. They seemed overconfident.

The town she mastered had vanished; the prettiest girl in the settlement, Ethelda Olney, whose glory seemed eternal, had passed over to the other side twenty years ago, without a tooth in her head. The governor of the territory had gone to glory before her, and all his eager soldiers; the wiggly little boys she used to know were dead of old age. There was almost nobody left to die that she ever knew or cared to know. Even all the good horses were dead. The gravedigger's spade turned more earth than a plow. She would look up from wringing a chicken's neck as fast as she could, and there would be God Almighty wringing a person's neck slowly, as if He had no sense, and didn't know the difference, and hadn't saved us people like He said, in his mercy.

She buried two strong husbands, each of whom falled trees, nailed things shut and chopped things open, hauled things, built things, shot things, and handed her jars down from high shelves; and she buried one boy and one girl, each of whom jumped up from the table, skinned over the woodpile, hopped on the floor, and lighted out the door. She had felt old to herself the whole time, and yet she was the one left out in the weather—what Felix Rush used to call "topsides." The two husbands and the two children were so vital their clothes seemed to quiver, and so lively she never got a good look at any one of them. They had each of them gone before her, and lay still, one by one, and she hoped to see them again, for she missed them every day of her life, and she hoped to hold them in her arms, even, if that wouldn't cause trouble between the men.

She had her sons Clare and Glee now, and they were fine men, but frankly, she had seen better. This had nothing to do with her feeling for them—she felt for Clare and Glee as much as she felt for anyone living or dead—but the times had gotten inside them in some ways as they aged, and made them both ordinary. Which they were not meant to be; no one is. No child on earth was ever meant to be ordinary, and you can see it in them, and they know it, too, but then the times get to them, and they wear out their brains learning what folks expect, and spend their strength trying to rise over those same folks.

New people came along and filled in for the dead. New people swarmed out of the wagon trains and into the forest, and she had seen them come; new people poured down the steamers' planks and onto the wharf; new people jumped off the railway cars and onto the platform; new people slid down from their mothers' bellies and into a pair of hands. When at first in the settlement they all had nothing, Ada alone possessed a pair of scissors and a ball of string, and so she used to rouse to calls in the night, to bring her pair of scissors and string to somebody's cabin, and aid the growth of the territory's population. She was good at catching babies, and good at many things, but she wondered what it all was for.

She knew her way around—around a cook stove, around the long steels she sewed in waists, around men and boys and girls of every propensity—but her mastery convinced her less than it had. The concerns of June and Clare captured and mesmerized the household, and swept it up, but to Ada Gleason Fishburn Tawes their excitement over Whatcom's fortunes looked shortsighted, and the wildly rising prices, in dollars, of acres or corner lots left her cold. Yesterday she heard Clare tell someone he was "in the deal business." It was a vanity tossed to and fro of them that seek death. Everybody had a good roof, and the cougars and bears were gone; the town had incandescent lights, planked streets, and a railroad. Harmonizing with these improvements, in a spirit of thanksgiving to the Creator, was proper and good. Every jot and tittle beyond that, every chasing after distinction and a backlog of money, was chaff and blowing wind; the dazzle of it blinded people, and the clamor of it deafened them. They were helpless, scared, and pretty near cultured, so they tightened the houses and raised cities as bulwarks, as suits of armor over suits of mail, to shield them from the pointy glance of heaven. On the scales they are lighter than a breath, all of them together. It was the same in Washington and in New York, she felt, and London. It was all the Brotherhood of Owls.

Mabel, her granddaughter—Mabel she understood. Of all God's works, little girls were the superior article: broadest in sympathy, deepest in wisdom, and purest in impulse.

Before supper that night, Mabel had played on the floor, twisting her doll. Her back was erect, and her dark red pigtails hung straight to her waist. Her head turned around, mad with joy, on a neck not much bigger than a finger. When she laughed her milk teeth showed, and a mocking awareness shone inside her eyes so Ada did not know where on her face to look that would not break her own heart or perplex her. Children were like that, a miracle every minute, which people liked to ignore. She, Ada, had a daughter just that clear of brow once, just that coltish, and priggish, and tender to the core.

That child, Nettie, had died of earache; her initials, N.G.F., Ada wore printed on a slip of cloth and braided into a hair ring a Lummi Indian woman named Margot gave her when they buried her. Hearing a helpless child cry for an earache that was entering her brain was not even the worst of it. Charley was the worst of it, who went into the rut. She knew how to bear her sorrows and go on—not that anyone who lived has any other choice—and she offered up her burdens to Jesus on the cross, who was supposed to bear all our sorrows for us once and for all. But He had troubles of His own, and it did not seem right to do, nor did it help a whole lot, or even any.

Tonight in her attic bedroom Ada had worn her way through Psalm 119, a wearisome Scripture that irked her every time she read this verse: "It is good for me that I have been afflicted; that I might learn thy statutes." She still could not get a hold on it. What statutes did she, Ada, need to learn that bad? Back in Illinois they had a neighbor who held his children's hands in a fire to impress lessons upon them. No one mistook that man for God, though he taught the same way. What statutes did Nettie need to learn, that her whimpering with the earache was good for her? Or Charley? The statute about loving God? The statute about loving your neighbor? That each of these neighbors was as precious to God, and should be to her, as her Nettie was, as her Charley? Then let Him eat neighbors. It was too much to ask.

Ada felt the house tremble a bit, as it did when the front door closed. She seemed to perk up nights like a screech owl, Ada thought, though she dragged around all day. As soon as she hit the pillow, pictures formed in her mind of the yellow overland road and the hushed gray beach where the feather-bed lay rolled on barrels, when bare Chowitzit appeared floating on the water still as a duck.

They had wandered in the desert like the Israelites, her and Rooney and all their train, and prayed God would see them through. The big world scared them all; it was, Rooney said, "hell's own baking sheet." She could not open her eyes upon the red hills without a speck of soil on them except what would grow sagebrush, or upon the blinding flats, or up into the dry, hard sky, without estimating from hour to hour how long she could last here alone. Rooney made those same calculations, deep in his mind; she knew because she asked him, one night in the wagon before Charley died.

The oxen used to vomit. When there was no water, Rooney fed them bread. Ada and little Clare washed the oxen's eyes with drinking water cupped in their hands, and rinsed the oxen's pink tongues for them in their mouths, to get the alkali dust off so the beasts could endure to go on. Rooney poured warm bacon grease down the oxen's throats, to save them from the alkali poisoning. But the oxen died just the same, some of them, died of thirst or eating goldenrod or not eating anything or having mortally sore feet. Half the stock in their train died, or the Sioux ran them off. People died, too, mostly the men; they drowned at crossings, they contracted the deadly chill and passed in a few hours from life to death, or they just gave out. A bride died of measles with her baby; two brave farmers died diverting a buffalo stampede, and saved the train. Crossing the Deschutes River in Oregon, two men tried to swim their own horses across, rather than pay Indian fellows fifty cents a head to swim them, but they drowned.

On Sundays they stopped when they could, and appointed one of the men preacher for that week, and while he preached and read the Bible to them, they kept on working. They had to wash clothes, cook beans for the week, shoe the animals, and fix what broke, and they hoped God understood that they had to do these things straight through, so they could cross the mountains before it snowed. Every single Sunday the preacher picked them out something to read about the Israelites' crossing the desert. God told them not to touch the mountain, in Sinai, or he would break forth against them. They did not touch the mountain, but it seemed like He broke forth against them anyway, as He broke forth against her in sight of the mountains, and she hadn't touched a thing, either.

The Israelites had been captives in Egypt, and God led them through the desert as a pillar of cloud by day, and a pillar of fire by night, which their train could have used, either or both. And where were those Israelites now? Where were the great kingdoms they feared? Ada reflected in her high bedroom. They had been captives in Babylon, and you never heard a thing about Babylon anymore; they had been captives in Egypt, and Egypt, so far as she knew, was now just barely hanging on. The Roman Empire was the biggest thing the world had seen, and Roman soldiers in Jerusalem crucified Christ, and now there was no Roman Empire after all, and no Holy Roman Empire either, which she heard of in a blab school on the plains. All this time the broadest-minded among the Israelites worried about the nation of Israel, and the city of Jerusalem, or Philistia, or Rome, which were small things, after all, and changing ones. Worldly power and wealth moved on from them to London, and would move on again.

All of those people in the Bible thought they were alive, and sought urgently what they sought, and willed what they willed, and feared what they feared, and every one of them is dead as a tent peg. Their precise love for each other and their knowledge died with them, and those are the people God spoke to, by the brook Kidron and out of the burning bush and on the Mount of Olives. They never thought of London; London never once entered their minds. They are all completely dead, Ada thought, and dead are their children and their grandchildren and all those rolling rows of generations between them and us who got born, grew old, and died; they turned up and around like teeth on a hay rake, and then down, and we are the front row now.

Tomorrow was Christmas. Maybe out in the shed right now the cow was trying to talk to the sewing machine. Rooney used to give her a ladle for Christmas, or a tub. Ada moved her feet off the brick and rolled to her side. She had a head for adventure when she was a merry girl. She had smelled the branding iron, and it was cold. Then she felt it, and it was hot, and she was burnt.

CHAPTER XXXVII

January, 1893, Whatcom

Every day was a day in which Clare expected to die. When he awoke at first light on Sunday, January 6, he regarded his sleeping wife gravely. Her head lay lightly on the mattress and smoothly, flush, as a clam rests in its shell. There was a perfection and composure in her pale, round face: her long eyelids fitted over her eyes precisely; her lashes spread in a radiating arc over her cheeks.

June's face was home to his eyes. He had looked at it so often, for so many years, that he half believed it was his own face, as near to him as his own thoughts, which he saw expressed in her vivid skin and eyes. The reflected light from human skin was the most moving sight Clare knew, because knowing people—his parents, and Mabel, and June—was, he was coming to believe, his deepest experience, and he had never known anyone without seeing this light. He admired the supple and irrigated quality of June's skin; it took a shine to the coming day. Light masses shone on her cheek and brow, and passed subtly to shadow in the soft, expressive hollow over her eyes.

He had taken out a life insurance policy. The bottom fact was, however, that June would marry again, at once. Men from all over the world were pelting into town, and there were no women. At Conrad Grogan's funeral, two men exchanged blows over which of them would walk the widow home—and Maud Grogan was homelier than a hedge fence. The new doctor told Clare that in every saloon, and in the Birdswell Hotel bar, men asked him, casual like, who was sick. June was young. Any man would admire her animated, miniature beauty; she could turn her round eyes to anyone she chose. Who?

Lee McAleer, the town treasurer, who wore a fawn-colored suit? McAleer was building the many-turreted mansion up the street. June liked the look of the water from that lot, she said, and she learned what was in every crate carried to the site—stained-glass windows, a white grand piano, a carved, curving banister, an electric stove. On the other hand, she called the new minister, Broadbent King, a crackerjack. Further, she liked the lively little mortgage agent, George Bacon, as Clare himself did—he traveled to New York twice a year and carried a fund of stories. She said once that she used to favor short men. Or would she return to Baltimore and marry a sweet-talking pansy in a pink coat? Perhaps, Clare thought with a pang, she had been eager to remarry from the first.

June had been blunt last night, and surprised him. She proposed to bake bad salmon into a pie for Obenchain. Her sense of intrigue was highly developed. He forbade it—he had watched a dog die from eating bad salmon—and she went on the prod; it was her life, too, she said, and she wanted to be able to do something about it. Now she was sleeping. A strong southwesterly wind rattled the window and meddled with the cottonwood and the lilac bush outside. He heard the cow moo and went out back to her.

The wind was blowing, and somewhere the sun was rising, but nothing budged the layer of clouds. They lived in a lidded pot. There was nothing inside the pot but the gray grit of the sand, the damp wood houses, the mud streets, and the freezing sea. There were no heavenly bodies at all, and there was no sky, only the world's tight lid. It hid the mountaintops, and snagged in the hillsides' scratching firs. Clare's forehead felt the cow's warm side. He had no complaints.

At the breakfast table, Clare watched his mother carrying dishes to the sink. Her dark skirt was shiny at the seat; her tiny white bun looked like a pincushion. Clare could no longer remember how she looked when she was young. She used to fly at her work, laughing at herself. Suds covered her smooth arms when she wrung dark water from shirts. She had possessed that ironic self-effacement that comes to the young mothers of sons. She was at her best the butt of teasing, the sentimental favorite. She was perforce a corking good sport, who preened herself on her sons' joint capacity to sail into scrapes, cut shines, and produce mad antics and cracked limbs in novel combinations. She used to laugh, protest, and hush, grieved, for it was no use, no one minded her. Pearl Sharp was the same way now; she snapped jokes at herself before her boys did.

Were the fathers of daughters similarly fixed? Did the hero who conquered his bride become a handyman who never learned the language, the dearest object of daughters' jokes as the merry life of the household swirled past him trailing ribbons? As the only man of the house, Clare wondered. Would he live long enough to father a boy he would never meet?

His mother was cheerful in the mornings, as though the day might offer her something. When had he seen her standing without a pot or hatchet in her hand, or sitting without a lapful of mending or unshelled peas? She was old now, shrinking perceptibly. Her scalp showed, yellow, through her hair; she panted and paled. Above her black eyes two soft ridges, pricked with a few thick hairs, showed where her eyebrows used to grow. Sometimes she thumped her bodice with her knuckles, the way she poked a dying fire, inquiringly; she winced when she walked. At night she stroked the dog by her chair with a cane.

Ada believed, Clare assumed, that people left here for somewhere else. She would be happy to leave plates. She studied her Bible and books in her room, and carried loaves and milk to shanties on the beach—where the people were, she said, "homeless as poker chips." She liked to argue Scripture, yet he had known her to do it only once in her life. She was still muscular, too, and able. She could split shakes from a bolt with a ten-penny nail. It was a trick everyone had seen. Once she hefted two calves a mile up to Judds'. Now she carried dishes back and forth, being of some use, and thinking God knows what. He had not done right by her, and now there was nothing he could do.

Now he would die first; he would go and prepare a place for her, if there were places to be had. If there were tables to be had, he would set a table for her, and bid her sit and eat. But there were no tables yonder, and no plates, and not a speck to eat. It was hard to picture a place without some sort of plates.

He looked at his own plate. He had eaten his two strips of meat and porridge and was not dead yet. A few days ago he had decided not to think any further about being poisoned at home. Obenchain had talked about killing Clare specifically, as though pinpointing him alone from among all the throngs of the living demanded a precision that attracted him. He would not want to risk killing someone else in the family by mis-take. Or would he? Would he take them all by some neighbor's doctored pie? Or would he poison their water? Obenchain might do anything. But of thinking of poison there was no end. He would eat boldly, and hope yet more boldly. Everything tasted good.

Now June caught his eye; her round face was tremulous, inquiring. Inquiring about what? About poison, he realized; she was looking for him to choke and turn black.

He had told June last night about Obenchain's threat. Now she was seeing things this new way, with death in the pot. This was no fun; he briefly regretted telling her. For amusement he surrounded his throat with both hands, grimaced, gagged, and dropped his head on the table.

Daddy?

Mabel, wandering by her chair in a blue sailor dress and black stock-ings, had been wrapping a stuffed woodpecker in string. She variously amputated, bisected, and strangled it, idly, while addressing it in the most tender terms. For her sake, Clare pulled himself together. June gave him a murderous look. She was right; it was not funny. He knew his all-conquering good humor wore at her, but it was his nature; it was too late to change. He touched his wife's hand, but she rose just then and slipped away to the kitchen. Was he too soft for her? He followed her, uncertain, and laid his hand over the bulky bow at the small of her back. He told her that he had watched her sleeping that morning. She turned to him, confused, and bit her lips.

There was a wagging patch of light on the wall above the sink; the bushes outside the dining room wagged, too. The planet wagged on; the man who planted those bushes was dead. And time, for Clare, had sprung a leak.

For he was on his way, it seemed; he was a man already exited. To these familiar people in the kitchen, Clare thought, all of time was a secure globe in which they floated protected from one end of things to the other. June stacked the clean dishes and hung the towel by the stove. Grandmother threw the bones out back to the woeful terrier, and started mixing dough for pies. Mabel sat on the kitchen floor in the peculiar way she liked to sit, with her back straight and her legs askew, as though they were broken or popped at the hip. Her limp red braid was loosening down her neck. She was sewing a flannel dress on the stuffed woodpecker.

"Quit your fooling," she said to the woodpecker. "You make my tail ache."

Clare could see the dark at the edge of the plain. He felt a hole in the wall behind him; things rushed out that hole. He was running low on air. Yesterday, talking with John Ireland in front of the high school, he had imagined and seen the long horizon of bay water and beach begin to tilt and upend. On the low side a gap appeared, and water and houses and schools and all the world's contents slid into the gap and blew away.

Possibly everyone now dead considered his own death as a freak accident, a mistake. Some bad luck caused it. Every enterprising man jack of them, and every sunlit vigorous woman and child, too, who had seemed so alive and pleased, was cold as a meat hook, and new chattering people trampled their bones unregarding, and rubbed their hands together and got to work improving their prospects till their own feet slipped and they went under themselves like Eustace Honer, protesting. Clare no longer felt any flat and bounded horizon encircling him at a distance. Every place was a tilting edge. "And I will wipe Jerusalem as a man wipeth a dish, wiping it, and turning it upside down." Healthy as a daisy, borne up on the affection and esteem of townsmen, colleagues, and friends, central to his family and himself, he had been spreading his activity and contribution into worldly things in their multiplicity, which now slid away disintegrating like shooting stars and left him directionless in the tumult of his own death. Time was a hook in his mouth. Time was reeling him in jawfirst; it was reeling him in, headlong and breathless, to a shore he had not known was there.

Twelve days had passed since Obenchain had told Clare he was going to kill him. Everywhere Clare went he saw him. Five days ago it was Obenchain in the crowded street at dusk, his lower lip hanging. Last week at the new post office he became aware of Obenchain when, from the corner of his eye, he saw one pale forehead as high as his own above the other heads, as if the two men were lighthouses. He saw Obenchain smiling in Grace Fishburn's store, wearing his hat over one ear; saw him from his second-floor office window, pacing the center of the street agitated, like a bear on a chain; saw him once more looming alert and limp in the vacant lot below the house, cast in silhouette on the bay.

Yesterday when he and June were replenishing the woodpile, Clare had glanced up to see Obenchain just disappearing down the back alley. The alley ran behind the cowshed and a tangle of blackberry bushes. Clare had leaned on his maul and peered hard through the thorns to learn if the ungainly, wrinkled form had kept moving or stopped. He could not tell; he could not decide if he had seen a dark piece of a man moving, or if he was now seeing a man holding still, or a patch of gloom and no man at all. He had stood and studied and pondered, until he began to see, not Obenchain, but his own self as a man with a revolver behind blackberry thorns might see him: a target as isolated and still as some poor stiff before a firing squad. Would he then fall handily in his own yard by the garden with his wife at his side?

June was carrying two alder rounds to the chopping block; she had not noticed anything. Small beads of drizzle like birdshot made a halo around her hair. Clare felt immense in his own yard and stripped, like a barked tree. He was trembling in a desert, and neither blackberry thorns nor buildings hid him from the limitless, empty fire of the sun. Could it be that he, who had been a fearless boy, was a cowardly man? His mouth had gone dry. "He hath digged a pit for my soul." He quit the yard then, tucked tail like a dog, ducked back into the house without a word, and sat idle, clapping his hands repeatedly over his bony knees, away from the windows.

CHAPTER XXXVIII

Now something crashed. Clare woke in the kitchen to see Mabel fly out of the pantry, crying. She had dropped something. June and Mabel had been carrying armloads of jars past him, he realized; had he been in their way? Mabel had just dropped a loaded tray of plum preserves. He saw every glass jar smashed on the pantry floor. Now she had run away. This alarmingly bright and self-sure little Mabel, of whom Clare usually lived in some awe, was crying too hard to help clean up her mess. Clare considered Mabel a human marvel, and her accomplishments miraculous. She ordinarily hung out over the stairs to make an entrance, wagging her stockinged legs in their ruffled skirt like a pendulum. She lettered her name, opened umbrellas, and erupted forth to give precisely articulated opinions on household matters, which startled Clare as much as if the cat had spoken. She possessed a queer, manly chuckle, which arose from her smooth depths at apparent random. If anyone asked her, "How are you?" she replied, looking away, in a stolid, thrillingly low voice, "Good."

He found her crying on the parlor sofa, twisted in her blue sailor dress. She was four years old, too old and too big to pick up. Clare picked her up.

He picked her up and bore her from station to station around the parlor. Its dark wallpaper repeated a ribboned bouquet of pale flowers, over and over. Absurdly he pointed Mabel's face towards each window in turn, as though she were an infant still and might see some bright sight over his shoulder to distract her. He pointed her at the organ, its lacy carved front, its many ivory-ringed plugs. She cried wetly on his neck; he smelled her familiar, sour hair. What had he done with his life? He had been arranging things and putting things to rights, so he could get started.

Beyond the window's lace curtain the cottonwood tree in the yard seemed real enough, and the sky's gray light seemed handmade for the moment's heat like any fire. This was, however, a year among years, and him dying early. The whole illumined, moving scene would play on in his absence, would continue to tumble into the future extending the swath of the lighted and known, moving as a planet moves with its clouds attached, its waves all breaking at once on its thousand shores, and its people walking willfully to market or to home, followed by dogs. He had thought he was younger, and had more time.

* * *

He carried Mabel outside to the porch, and toted her around as he did formerly, when the porch was new, and so was Mabel. When had she grown so big and heavy? She kept slipping inside her sateen bloomers and her dress; he hoisted her up. She hushed her crying. Now, Clare knew, she held herself still so Clare would not notice her and set her down. He noticed her, but he wanted to carry her on the porch a while longer.

The Chinese people required their offspring at least to pretend to honor their ancestors, to speak of them respectfully and carry steamed rice to their graves. It was not the American way. He would be one ancestor of Mabel's grandchildren, at best three strangers away. They would be careless, wretched, ignorant great-grandchildren, badly behaved, who would swing on swings in the bright sunlight of those future days without a care in their cruel, cussed hearts, and who would never have heard mentioned one Clare Fishburn of Whatcom, Washington, who was once a prominent figure in a local way, and considered, by some, to have possessed promise, vigor, and enterprise, who might even have attained high office.... Was this not silly? Clare had to stop. Or who, he concluded to himself, at any rate loved his life with all his strength. He looked down the hill, across the vacant lot where Obenchain had stood. The wind blew from the southwest. Pieces of Mabel's hair wrapped against his face. She hid her sleeves in his coat. Cloud parts were leaving the sky. Sea ducks were leaving the water. The morning high tides of winter were gone. Night after night, Orion dived unseen to the west behind the clouds and died young. The wood stems of the lilac bush by the door were banging together. Those blunt stems would be gone soon, broken into lilacs.

Clare set Mabel down; she idled into the house, limply, to dress for church. He felt the blood returning deep in his arms. Before going inside, he looked out. The sea was yellow and swollen. Snow had vanished from the foothill ridgetops. He could feel the planet spinning ever faster, and bearing him into the darkness with it, flung. These were the only days. "The harvest is past," Clare thought, "the summer is ended, and we are not saved."

There was not time enough to honor all he wanted to honor; it was difficult even to see it. The seasons pitched and heaved a man from rail to rail, from weather side to lee side and back, and a lunatic hogged the helm. Shall these bones remember?

CHAPTER XXXIX

When Clare had told June last night, they were alone in the parlor, late. He had fallen asleep and wakened to see June picking up Mabel's toys with her head cocked like a robin's, looking at him.

He told her right then—she started, for he spoke as soon as his eyes opened—that he had not long to live, that he would die one of these days or nights soon, that he knew because Beal Obenchain had told him the night before Christmas that he was going to kill him, and she was not to worry because nothing could be done. Now, June never worried, because she never believed that "nothing could be done." Something could always be done; that is what people were for.

She sat down, and it sank in. Her black-sleeved arms rested on the best parlor chair's brocade arms, and her head alternately bent and rose as she thought of things. She was thirty-four to Clare's forty-two, fair-skinned and brown-haired, restless. Her oval eyes were set in deep arches under high brows. Now her tender expression firmed and her brow lowered. What did Beal Obenchain have against him? Nothing; it was just some notion he had seized. It sank in some more.

She could, June had said in her soft Maryland voice, shoot Beal Obenchain. It would be easy. He lived alone in the woods by the tracks, where any vagrant, any swindler or gambler or ruined miner or drunken logger, could shoot him for any reason. No one would find him for days—maybe even till Almighty crack—and no one would ever suspect Clare Fishburn, never mind June Fishburn. Why would these ordinary, quiet townspeople want to murder someone?

"Why indeed?" Clare said. He was leaning forward on his chair, clasping his hands together, his arms on his high knees. Obenchain was "not all-the-way normal." What if he was just blowing off steam? "Why should anyone go murder a poor lonely bugger who raved?" Clare knew that Obenchain was not just "bloviating," that Obenchain was truly a bad hat and would do him in.

Clare did not, however, intend to murder, and said so. Capital threats are not capital crimes; you do not shoot a man unless he is actually in the process of harming you or your family; you do not cold-bloodedly kill a man under any circumstances, and you by golly do not let your wife do it. It kind of goes against a former teacher's grain to shoot a student. Funny how bloodthirsty women can get. When he was a boy, some men down on the Skagit had lynched an Indian man—"tried him before Judge Lynch," they called it—and come to find out, their little old wives had egged them and goaded them into it. One man got so irritated watching the Skagit's legs twitch he took off directly from the scene, and his family never clapped eyes on him again. Presumably the Indian fellow was even more irritated.

Of course, he had thought of oiling his duck-hunting shotgun. He did get himself a sidearm, a double-action Colt Lightning. He thought of corralling his friends George Bacon and big Tom Tyler to stand guard or fight. With a Bowie knife, a fighter could rip open a man up close before either one of them could draw a revolver, and he could throw a knife faster than Obenchain could raise and aim a gun—if he were a knife fighter, instead of a partner in a land company. He had passed a few fine years as a boy throwing a Bowie knife at tree trunks and hay bales, and he knew enough about it to know it would take another few years to get his skill back. He had thought of everything, and here was June thinking of it all again.

"Don't go near the water. Don't go out alone." Her round head turned towards him, and away, and back. "... And we must move." This wrought her up further.

"We can move to Portland and tell no one where we are going. We can sell this house for cash—it must be worth thousands now. You take the train tomorrow, and your mother and I will follow with Mabel when we have everything packed."

"... And when do we come back?" Clare saw that June was pink and heated. Her skin was always a thin membrane; she changed colors faster than a cloud. Her face seemed everywhere as liquid and live as her eyes. She subsided, looking down at her lap, but her cheeks still glowed.

"And when do we come back?" He asked more softly again, and June thought it through and fired up, "Anytime we're ready for you to die, we just hop a train. Just say when."

He reminded her that his livelihood was here. Was his voice shaking? He wanted to set a brave example for his young, small wife, who had been reared delicately among women. He kept forgetting that she noticed when he tried to set an example, and flared.

Steadily he brought out, "I have no preferment in Portland, and no position, and know of no proposition." Clare talked this way when the thought of her powerful family in Baltimore shamed him. He refrained from mentioning his new post as the treasurer of the Sons of Pioneers, and his possible candidacy for the legislature.

"You can't be a partner in the improvement company if you're dead." June sounded awful contemptuous, as though he thought he could. "Besides," she added—she lowered her voice to a resonant bass, to startle and reconcile him, a trick he knew, which usually worked anyway— "besides, we have no need of further prospects." She could be pompous, too. "Our gains have advanced these past few years. You said so yourself. We can live the rest of our lives without your making a stir in anything, and still have a portion to settle on Mabel and any other children."

"I fancy making a stir in something," Clare said. "I've dropped anchor where I can do it, and I'm not going to let an old pupil of mine drag me off it."

The matter of his not working at all merited no response; he could barely endure Sundays. Secretly Clare thought June would be better off here in Whatcom, in this familiar, cluttered house, when he was gone. There were many distinguished and warmhearted families now in Whatcom, right up the hill, and June and Ada knew them, and their well-educated offspring, better than Clare did; June had a flock of friends here on the block, and she had Pearl Sharp a mile away. His brother Glee and Grace were just a few blocks away, with their children, and June's sister Minta was nearby in Goshen. Portland, Oregon, had always sounded to Clare like a harum-scarum sort of menagerie. Twenty years ago Portland used to boast that it had forty millionaires; Conrad Grogan used to add, "—who eat in the kitchen." Having never lived in any big city, Clare had a horror of them all, and supposed their citizens must live perpetually as lost, footsore, cleaned out, and lonesome as he was when he visited.

He poured himself cold tea. The parlor's high windows were glossy and black, and the lamp's light streaked them at random in gold. June had draped a fringed scarf over a picture frame's corner and heaped blue glass grapes there, as if women commonly stored grapes on the picture frames. He broke out in a fresh start, "Then do we live in Portland as nobodies, hoping every minute he never finds us, or wondering every minute if he actually meant to kill me at all? That's sorry living. Or do we hope he decides to murder someone else? Who?"

Clare regretted this latter tack, for arguments from universal morality tended to pass June right by when she was roused; you bet your boodle she hoped Obenchain would murder someone else, anyone else, and she would gladly help him pick.

He was waiting for June to coil down. It would take her several days, he thought, to study their possibilities as he had studied them, and get to the bottom facts—several days to conclude that nothing could, reasonably and honorably, be done.

Now this morning, standing chilled by the sink, Clare saw from her set frown that June had been brooding already, and wanted to chew over things some more. It was hard to see her expression when she bent her head, because her full length reached only to his middle ribs; he saw the untidy curved parting of her brown hair. June put out her hand as if to take his arm, and he allowed her to lead him back outside on the windy porch.

"My dear," she said, "look. You know the sheriff, don't you? He could assign a deputy or two to protect you. This is a law-abiding, civilized little town." Clare winced. She always called Whatcom "little." It was not Baltimore, that he knew; it was in fact a darn sight more civilized, as far as he could make out from magazine stories about that city's blood tubs, bludgets, and drummers, but June had grown up there in a kind of castle, without taking much in.

The two leaned on the cold porch rail, facing out. They could see beneath them the lower hill with its bare houses, the growing business district, and the dull sea spreading beyond it under thick skies. The railroad trestle curved across the bay in a pencil line from south to north, and three straight wharves met it. In the harbor two steamers rode at anchor, and the *Doris Burn* was tied at the main wharf. Warehouses and coal bunkers stood on or near every wharf, and new lines of driven piles trailed into the water. A breakwater enclosed a wharf of coal barges and the dozen or so schooners and sloops that worked all winter. This was his town, and in his way Clare had helped build it, as he had helped break its wilderness as a boy. Out on the sea, near and far, were blue, forested islands, and the big ones bulged with mountains. Clare and June looked out, and their eyes roamed the islands unseeing, while they discussed protection under the law.

The rule of law thinned and petered out south of town, they knew. Loners lived there, some of them vicious—horse thieves, it may be, or swindlers, old buffalo hunters who indulged in every vice, bank sneaks and bilks. Down at Deception Pass, prisoners worked the rock quarry; they lived in convict camps at Oyster Creek ravine. Some of those boys would shoot anything that glittered. In the mill towns, police rounded up vagrants into chain gangs, who did the city's work; no one remarked on a murder a month. On Chuckanut Ridge, south of town, two masked men robbed trains. An old Indian fighter shot a three-card monte dealer in the hobo jungle, for cheating. The "True Love" bandit had come through; on a railroad bridge he shot two blanket stiffs with his characteristic split bullets. He had the letters TRUE LOVE tattooed on the backs of his fingers of both hands, one capital letter to a finger; he killed a man with a bed slat, escaped from prison and kept killing, thrilling the populace, including Clare, who had only half hoped that sort of stimulation was past.

Clare's enjoyment of some of these old stories derailed the talk, and irked June. He turned and bent again over the porch rail to watch her, his long features lifted up. Did he ever tell her about Bad Jim? He was an Indian man who pushed a settler off a cliff. When the sheriff came for him he played dumb, and asked the sheriff to show him the scene of the crime. The dim-witted sheriff took him up to the cliff, and Bad Jim pushed him off. Did she know about the mutton poachers? Out on the islands, people were stealing sheep. A policeman caught two men on a hidden beach salting mutton, and he made them row back to town with the evidence in the rowboat. They rowed all night, and when they got to the dock, the policeman jumped off with the painter. The poachers took a look at each other, pushed off, and rowed away.

Mabel came out and twirled dully, like a hanged man, in her new Sunday dress—white ruffled and yoked dimity trimmed in red braid and bows—which Clare told her was "the ant's ankles." Pleased, she perked up, plucked at her black sateen bloomers, and said she was going down the street to display her glory to her cousin Nesta. Soft-faced Mabel had the whiskey voice of an old sot. Her grandmother Ada had fixed her braid, turned it under, and tied it with a wide satin bow into a Cadogan knot; Ada had pinned a stiff straw hat flat on Mabel's head, blacked her little shoes—and she did look an angel. Clare watched her flit down the steps, her black-stockinged legs apparently boneless. He stopped talking and watched, noting everything. Into the silence June said she was cold, so they moved into the parlor. There the high plastered ceiling, tall windows, and polished floor exaggerated their words. Clare sat folded on the sofa, and June paced.

Well, she said, Obenchain did live south of town in that stimulating country, but they lived in town, where letting your cow run loose was the likely crime; recently the sheriff ran in the mayor for it. People in town would make a complete row if Obenchain killed Clare, and scarcely any row if Clare killed Obenchain. Clare was an established man. Last summer an established man named Wilt Mint shot the brains out of a drunk no one knew, for making a remark about his half-Indian daughter, and the jury ruled the death accidental. Last year the Whatcom *Bugle Call* reported a wanderer found south of town, headless, on the rocks below the quarry; hunters found another newcomer shot through the heart in his cabin. Neither crime was solved.

June had a point. Clare had the impression—largely from John Ireland's bitter comments—that the law deplored, but tolerated, murders of strangers and itinerants, along with Chinese people, Mexicans, and the odd Hindoo. Obenchain was a loner, and Clare the sort of stable citizen the law prized. Obenchain, however, was no stranger. He had lived on the bay for fifteen years, and people knew him by sight. A few years back, south of town, some men set out to lynch Jay Tamoree's youngest brother for braining his wife with a billy—but they gave off when one of them recalled them to their moral senses by remarking that "it was a shame to hang a man who has been so long in the country."

Clare wondered aloud—what if he had pitched a knife into Obenchain's heart on the street at dusk, or in the post office? He might get off on self-defense. In the state of Washington the winner of an ordinary fight or brawl, whose opponent was dead, could claim self-defense and walk away, whereas in Canada the killer had to show he tried first to run away. Clare was sufficiently known and respectable, and Obenchain was sufficiently mysterious and disreputable, that witnesses might perjure themselves for him, but he wanted no part of that.

June, for her part, thought it their brightest hope next to moving—that he should send Obenchain to his reward, without witnesses. If Obenchain killed first, he would leave town or hang for it, but Clare would be dead. If Clare got the jump on Obenchain, he might go to prison, but he would get out alive, in time, and they could go on. She preferred any degree of disgrace—she said ardently, her voice rising and hoarse—to losing him. Clare was surprised by her vehemence; she truly wanted to save his bacon. He was touched. This was a wealthy woman. She set him to thinking as much as Obenchain had.

CHAPTER XL

That afternoon after church, the women bundled off to a bake sale with Mabel and her cousin Nesta. The previous year a similar sale raised eleven dollars for the new library, and they had high hopes for this one, as well. Mabel wanted to take the dog and the stuffed woodpecker and make a party of it; then she balked at putting on her coat, which she felt was, like all her clothing, too short. Clare heard June reminding her that when she was twelve, and not a day before, she could wear long skirts.

When in time the house grew silent, Clare put on his wool gabardine vest, jacket, and hat, and embarked on a walk. Devil take Obenchain; "May the old Satan absorb him," their neighbor Street St. Mary would say. Clare would go out alone, by the water; he hated knowing he had been cowering lately, and slinking around corners. He turned off Golden Street and headed downhill.

In the past twelve days he had watched his own increasing detachment. Throughout his life before Obenchain's threat, he awakened some mornings and perceived that things were easy and pleasant, and some mornings, by contrast, he fancied that things were fixed and dreary, and these moods reversed from hour to hour, wherever they started. Now things seemed, for the first time, simply big, all day. He had begun to view his own Golden Street—its well-loved fresh houses, its three lilac bushes, Lee McAleer's gabled mansion a-building—altered into an abstraction and revealed as a piffling accident, as a certain street in a certain town. Whatcom was a town among thousands of towns—the town in which most of his haphazard life had elapsed. His time, furthermore, was a time among times. This bright year, this new 1893 with its shifting winds and great, specific clouds, this raw-edged winter with its stiff mud and gray seas—this was one year.

He had begun to wonder where, in this series of accidents, the accidental part left off. Could he as readily have been an actor, or a lawyer, as a partner in a land company, when he felt himself so profoundly to be a partner in a land company? Would his friends admire some other sort of fellow just as well? Was he to June only a man among many men? Worse, was she to him only one of many women he might have married? Might he just as readily be living on some other street, in some grievous town in Wisconsin he had never heard of, with some other woman—a woman he did not know? It was a terrible thought. He did not like strange women.

Clare was walking downhill on a dirt street through the town's residential south side. He passed many clearing fires; some entertained the cold children who poked and stirred them, and all barely singed the piles of wet slash they were meant to burn.

A few days ago he had seen a magazine photograph of uncovered skeletons. An Indian man and woman—"A Brave and His Squaw," the article said—had been unearthed by a farmer's plow near Kingston, New York, where they had lain "embracing in death" for an unknown number of years. Clare saw two human heads and some bones stuck in clay. The skulls looked, like all human skulls, identical, phrenological, medical, and like no one he had ever met—not even like the dead Lummi man buried in a canoe and hung from a tree, whose dried face howled. These skulls possessed no faces. They had no noses, no skin or hair or tongues, and clay blocked their eyes. The former people were as flat as scars on a clay pot; they were a stratum between soils thinner than groundwater. Their clavicle bones and ribs spread on the same level as their teeth. Below their first few ribs the skeletons scattered; the people seemed to have lost interest. The pair had only one pelvis between them, no spine, and no legs or feet save a few bright bones ringing them at random, as though moving water had stirred their grave. There was clay in their ears, clay in their eyes, clay in their mouths. They did not look unearthed. They looked earthed.

No wonder you're cold, he thought. There was a story he and June knew about two drunken Irishmen. The first drunken Irishman sifted into a cemetery one night; he tripped on a heap of dirt and fell into a freshly dug grave. From the bottom of the grave he moaned, "I'm so cold, I'm so cold." Another drunken Irishman, also at large in the cemetery, stumbled to the edge of the grave and peeped in. He heard, "I'm so cold, I'm so cold!"

"No wonder you're cold," the second drunk said amicably. "You kicked your dirt off." When Mabel was an infant in her cradle, June had replaced her covers many times a day, and many times advised her, No wonder you're cold; you kicked your dirt off. The woodland Indian husband and wife had kicked their dirt off, had kicked their flesh off by accident, and carelessly frozen to death.

Clare had held the magazine open on his knees and looked at the photograph a long time. What did this dying mean about the two who had lived? Had they known they were going to die? Had they seen themselves as they really were, as temporary partners on some swift passage, like traveling strangers who band to ford a stream together, or to winch wagons over a mountain pass, and who part and scatter? Were all marriages made in the shadow of death, and were they as such mere conveniences? Was his to June? Likely that bony pair had not seen their marriage as made in heaven and continued there. Probably they had not thought about it at all, any more than he had. But what should they have done? What other life was possible than a life made trivial by death?

A fresh, stiffening wind blew up between buildings. A dull sheet of water—stretching from here to Japan—gleamed behind the precipice of the town. The colorless sea and the colorless sky were batting the dead light back and forth.

What Clare really wanted to know was this: Would he ever see June again? Mabel? Would he ever see John Ireland again, whose sad thoughtfulness and passive, striking face occupied a deep portion of his heart? Would he ever see anyone again?

It was a novel, uncomfortable question, linked in his mind with the shed church he attended as a boy and with his mother's floppy Bible, whose assigned chapters he had memorized and recited with his shoes on, in his gingham suit. He knew that forty years ago in the West they used to say, "Ain't no law west of Saint Louis, and no God west of Fort Smith." But now God had been planted in the West for two generations—God, women, and railroad trains. Towns welcomed churches for their civilizing influence and noble architecture. Their preachers raised more questions than they answered, as Clare took it. Chief Seattle had heard much about a common heavenly father who had come down to earth to live among people and save them. He remarked, "We never saw him," and men repeated this, chuckling, in the hotel bar. Clare approved plain talk. Would he ever see John Ireland again, dead Eustace again, or June again? Would there be something they could do together, like old times? No. He should call on everyone he knew, to say good-bye—all those people whose time and location on earth accompanied his, whom he had come to care for.

His father had died many years ago in a freak accident, they called it; he had not seen a hair of him since. Death had opened wide its mouth and consumed his father from end to end as a cat eats a mouse. He had been forty-two then, as Clare was forty-two now, but pioneer years must have been queerly longer, because his father was stale and dug in by then, and Clare was just getting going. From time to time he dreamed of his father standing mute in his overalls in a family-filled log cabin. Everyone welcomed him, saying, "Rooney! We all thought you were dead." Clare himself gazed at the old skeesicks, overcome with affection and shyness. Gradually he always understood that, in fact, the man was dead. He had no will, no love, and no way to express his embarrassment for the overexcited living. He was an apparition the family's hopes could not sustain; his form faded as their faith failed, and where he had stood was only the sooty log wall. These past days as the winter mired in its darkness, he dreamed this dream again, and others like it.

Now his way overlooked the eighty decent, cleared acres of Happy Valley, where the Irish lived—the "Terrestrials," as the railroad bosses called them, for they were the labor alternative to the Chinese men, whom everybody called the "Celestials." Street St. Mary recently sold a building lot down there by the creek, including what he called his "Hungarian rights," by which he meant riparian rights. In Happy Valley was one block where Negroes lived; some were pioneer settlers who had moved up from Oregon as early as '43, when the Oregon colonial legislature banned Negroes from the colony. Here all was peace and amity, of course, for his town of Whatcom afforded a fair shake for all true men— the more the merrier, and he strictly hated to leave. He liked it here, and—forgetting the foreboding sorrow that tightened down on him every fall, forgetting his grief, his despising his life during all the colored October days when winter darkness accelerated into the afternoons—he thought he always had.

Downtown was quiet and windy; it was Sunday afternoon. Clare passed the new furniture store, the new branch post office, the dreary new grammar school, the printing office, the dry goods store, the new stone courthouse, the department store which had a roller-skating rink on the second floor, the Catholic church, and the big green-lumber Birdswell Hotel, with balconies and porches. Three years earlier these city blocks had been lots full of smoldering slash. Now there were steel streetcar tracks set in planked streets; one of his former students conducted the green streetcar, and rang a tinkling brass bell. On the streetcar's side a Lummi artist had painted a mountain, and a farm at its base.

This afternoon he ran into slim Wilbur Carloon and his stout wife, Dolly, who climbed down from the elevated plank sidewalk to inspect a wagon loaded with Chuckanut stone. Wilbur Carloon's hair, visible under his small fedora, was yellowish and coiled. He had dark, heavy-lidded eyes. He wore a short black coat, a brown vest, and a green-striped collarless shirt fastened with a brass stud. The Carloons had a passel of children at home, including a boy whose eyesight was bad. Wilbur Carloon worked day and night at his department store, and Dolly helped Ada settle in the poorest newcomers down at the tar-papered tents on Fiddler's Green. They had been newcomers themselves, and everything they had went into the store.

The Carloons greeted Clare—"Professor Fishburn." He asked them, "Are you abreast of what's afoot?" Still afoot, it turned out, were repercussions of the Canadian Pacific Railway celebration, which had gone down in history as "the great water fight." Whatcom's guests from Canada and Great Britain were so incensed at their soaking, and at the trampling of the Canadian flag, that they were discussing the insult in the Chancellery in London, in the Foreign Office in Ottawa, and in the U.S. Department of State. Why had the Whatcom police force failed to control, identify, or apprehend the perpetrators? Well, because, Wilbur Carloon now told Clare, international investigation had revealed that the Whatcom police force included, harbored, and to some extent comprised the perpetrators. After many ticklish discussions, the diplomats dropped the matter. The Canadian Pacific Railway, of course, took its U.S. terminus elsewhere. Dolly Carloon was laughing. "George! But it was fun," said Clare.

He stood down on the street with the Carloons. They pointed out the skeletons of buildings going up—the new bank, the many new real estate offices, another hotel, another warehouse, new offices for the coal company. Was the town building too much? Dolly said it was not building enough, and families lived in tents, but the mills couldn't keep up with demand, could they?—and her big face broke easily into a sympathetic smile. She was wearing a vast army overcoat, and brogans. It was Sunday, but they could hear the ripsaws in the south-side lumber mill.

Clare walked on with the Carloons; they moved up to the sidewalk and tried to stay out of the wind. Clare had seen them haul into town two years before with their wagon loaded with merchandise they could not sell on the droughted plains. A sign on the wagon's side said: "In God we trusted, in Kansas we busted." Now Dolly was wearing the hat she wore that day and always, a black felt hat peaked like a roof. They wound between coal wagons and drays loaded with lumber and pipe. Dolly asked, had Clare heard about this new fellow Albo Keppleman? He came up from California a week ago and mentioned he might start a brick business. Already he had orders for one million brick.

Clare felt a clatter on the plank sidewalk and looked up to see Arthur Pleasants making his way towards the Birdswell Hotel. Arthur Pleasants was a vigorous, disdainful, thick-necked man from New Bedford, Massachusetts. He was in his forties, and he had no legs. He was pushing himself along the sidewalk on a wheeled platform softened by a yellow pillow, which platform he propelled and steered by wielding two canes like canoe poles. He was wearing a frock coat with satin lapels; its split tails spread neatly behind him on the platform, so he looked like a nesting swallow. He pushed past Clare and the Carloons without a glance; behind his knotted, angry face, Clare thought, he was probably adding and multiplying sums.

"What a cheering sight," Wilbur Carloon remarked. Dolly said, "I'll say," and Clare nodded.

Arthur Pleasants had been a familiar figure in town for two years, an outside investor who excited gossip, for he was known to move across the West from town to town, and to dip down, like a water witch's forked wand, wherever a fortune was to be made. The sight of him was a sure omen that this was the place. He had landed in town a full year before the New York papers wrote up the Whatcom boom; he had bought up three hillsides and three warehouses a full year before *Harper's Monthly* had published James J. Hill's intention to end his Great Northern Railway on Bellingham Bay.

Wilbur Carloon jammed his fedora down against the wind; it pushed out his red ears. "Did you see the headline in the *Bugle Call* last week? 'Tell the Emperor of China to Send His Merchants!'"

Clare had seen it. "Those boys better ought to pipe down," he said.

The night the newspaper came out, John Ireland had appeared—his finely cut face wet, and drops balled on his overcoat—at Clare's own parlor door after supper. He brandished the *Bugle Call* and waxed irate: "This is the same newspaper ...!" He ended by despairing, groaning through his hands, "This is the same newspaper." The same newspaper, he meant, that urged the expulsion of all Celestials, seven years ago. On matters pertain-

ing to Chinese people, John Ireland was, in Clare's view, touchy as all
billy hell. Clare had skimmed the column beneath the headline. It
rehearsed the old song, intended apparently for tinhorns just off the boat:
that Whatcom was the jumping-off place for the Orient, the wealth of
whose trade would jingle in local pockets.

Ada had been leaning by the parlor lamp that night, sewing steels in
the seams of a waist. Without even raising her head, she remarked, as she
usually did when this topic boiled up, that she had seen it all before. She
had seen it not once but twice: "in '72, when the Northern Pacific did not
come, and last year, when the Canadian Pacific did not come." But she
had not seen this before, Clare said; he addressed the thinning white hair
on the top of her head. "Local folks drummed up those other booms. They
spread rumors. They wanted it to happen, and they were the only ones
who believed it would. This time, it's in the New York papers."

Now, downtown, Clare reiterated that he had seen the headline. He
took his leave of Wilbur Carloon and Dolly. He shook hands with both,
bobbing over their hats, then turned westward and down to the water.

He stepped into silence; light widened around him. On the other
hand, he thought, could this din rattle eternity? Was there some work he
should turn his hand to now, in his remaining time?

At the edge of town Clare passed the gasworks and the generating
plant, from which black wires bounded out on poles. The plank road
turned back to dirt and ran flat, crossing some local railroad tracks. Restless white clouds blew and stretched under the leaden cloud cover. Often
the cloud cover seemed to be lifting, but Clare was not fooled. At best a
crack might appear over the horizon, sometime next week or next month,
down which the red sun would fall burning for ten minutes in midafter-
noon before darkness resumed.

He came to the shore. Before him in both directions, white and yellow driftwood logs repeated the shoreline's curve above tideline. Basalt
and graywacke cobbles made the upper beach; bays of wet sand interrupted it. Wind kicked up whitecaps in the incoming current offshore. The
breaking waves were only a foot or so high, green and oily-looking, for
Puget Sound and the Strait of Juan de Fuca were surfless inland seas, a
crack in the continent where the Pacific poured in and calmed.

CHAPTER XLI

Clare walked south by the beach. The sky was dimming already, subtly, as though someone were slowly lowering the wick of a lamp. Far offshore, gulls were crying into the southwest wind over a herring ball in the water, and diving into it, and rising blown with more cries, while the dark water churned as if the sea's floor had broken beneath it and let loose.

He had enjoyed many friends, made himself important first to Whatcom High School and then to the Bellingham Bay Improvement Company. He had fathered an extraordinary little girl, taught boys and girls to weigh gases, taught boys to build birdhouses, and sold lots. Why had he possessed such an unwarranted confidence in himself? His shoes ground on the stones. Before him, where Obenchain lived, the rising bluff supported deep forest—dripping timber that extended, with few holes, to Humboldt, California.

He could see a bird's tracks below the tideline, where the line of black and red gravel gave way to sandy mud. The tracks appeared out of nowhere, as if God had formed a creature and set it down. Three toe claws poked holes in the mud, and a wide web connected them. The bird had walked, manlike, along the shore with a steady, firm tread. Clare followed the line of tracks, his neck forward.

The webbed tracks looked witless, as if the bird lacked a head. Abruptly now, the tracks stopped—with the two feet pushed deep at the claws. The tracks ended for no reason, and the sandy mud in their path was blank; the bird had flown up. Clare turned and saw that his own passage had made blunt tracks, too, in the gravel; he was trailing himself, and his tracks ended under his shoes.

He was, in his entirety, a spool of footprints, starting north of here in the settlement beach cabin where he learned to pull himself up on his mother's black skirt. His trail vanished and resumed as he walked and rode through his days and years; he lived twelve years in Goshen and moved back to Whatcom, walked to and from the high school and office. Now on this beach his track went winding behind him like a peel, as though time were a knife peeling him like an apple and would continue through him till he was gone. His tracks, his lifetime tracks, would end abruptly, also—but he would have gone not up, like a bird into the sky, but down, into the ground.

"I shall go to the gates of the grave," Clare thought. It was a passage from Isaiah, in which dying King Hezekiah turned his face to the wall. "I shall go to the gates of the grave: I am deprived of the residue of my years. I said, I shall not see the Lord, even the Lord, in the land of the living: I shall behold man no more with the inhabitants of the world."

A man would not know which step was his last, to pay heed to it. Where on the face of the earth would his footprints be fresh when the trapper tracked him down? The boys would have to carry his body along its last few routes.

He needed to learn how to die. He had learned everything else as it came along—how to read, drive a team, scythe a field and winnow grain, fall a tree, miter a corner, how to use and fix a lathe and a steam saw, demonstrate electromagnetism, set purlins for a roof, cut pipe to plumb a sink, machine an axle bearing, price a section, and sell a lot—and he excelled at what he learned, and now he had to learn this next thing, to release it all. Was it not important? How does a man learn to die when the experts are mum?

Old Conrad Grogan, the surveyor, nearly died, was all but dead, and came back to life and stood up still thin and erect—his black mustaches combed over his lip, his yellow hair in thin strands, potbellied, competent—and lived another six years. To Clare it looked like Conrad Grogan threw himself into those years: he started the debating society, married a hard-favored widow down on Whidbey Island, brought her back, whacked up a treehouse for her grandchildren, built himself a little sailing dory painted red, and strode the streets of the town right lively, his face creased and shining. Then he took to bed screaming for a few days, and panted for a few days, turned purple, and died. Clare did not know if Conrad Grogan died well, either the first time or the last, or what it took when a man had only general warning, or if he could work himself around to where something was required which he could then produce on the spot, such as, for example, courage—which would not loosen the tight situation, but would please him and cap all he had learned. He imagined June's voice adding, "Hurrah, boys."

Chunks of tan foam spume blew over the beach stones; when one chunk tumbled into another, their stiff suds stuck together, and they trembled.

Clare had not seen much sunshine lately. The needle on John Ireland's aneroid lay pinned to the left, as if the wind held it down. The mercury in John Ireland's thermometer stayed in the forties day and night. Clare had seen colored engravings in the weeklies, and read stories, which suggested to him that winters, in other places, were both colder and sunnier. Before Obenchain's midnight call, he had taken to walking out at night—after living by lamplight many hours before retiring—stepping out in the drizzling alley and searching overhead for any small coincidental series of gaps in the many layers of cloud that might open upon a star—for he remembered, of course, that there were stars.

The tide was coming in, and Clare moved up off the gravel. He climbed over the black shark carcass that Glee had dragged in—an enormous, irregular rind. He rounded the pitted sandstone ledges of the headland, sea ledges awash and sharp with barnacles, and crossed a beach, stepping on massed logs that storm waves stranded. The logs' old dried roots stuck up higher than his head, tall as he was. It would be melancholy to break a leg coming back in the dark of night. He presented a good target now, raised against the pale sea and walking straight on logs five feet down from the brush cover. He glanced into the dense woods, but had to look back at once to mind his footing.

He was finding—now, in his forties—adult life unexpectedly meaningful and grave; the path was widening and deepening before him. Tragedy is a possibility only for adults; so is heroism. When he studied in the Normal School in Goshen, he was already in his thirties, and he transformed himself into an Englishman, which elevated him in his own eyes. He affected a long walking staff and a jacket cut loose in the Norfolk style; he called his young colleagues "chappy" and said, "Oh, I say." It was the best he could do from there. He was sincere, and read English history and jurisprudence, Carlyle, Dickens, whom everyone read, and especially William Wordsworth, whose lyrics stirred him in a way he could not describe. He followed horse racing, and investigated several family coats of arms; to some guests on his mother's porch on the Nooksack he offered cream sherry. There had been a girl who liked him that way; he gave it up when he gave up the girl.

Was he still so insubstantial, a man without existence except as a posing figure reflected in others' eyes? When Lee McAleer and Tom Tyler walked him home from the Pioneers' meeting, and mentioned to him a possible candidacy for the People's Party, why was he so much set up and almighty swelled about it, when he was no better a man than he had been that same morning?

He had consumed his life, meaning to get started; he had played false and, perfectly pleased, bought into a scam. He followed the news; he floated like a sea duck with the crowd. The momentum of activity lulled him. The *Bugle Call* and the *Post-Intelligencer* endorsed it as real, this sheer witless motion and change. The minister, the biggest men in town, the most pious women, and everyone he knew except his mother endorsed it as real; they followed the news. He had gone along. He had burrowed into the whirling scheme of things; he had hitched himself to the high school men and the real estate partners, to the growing town and the immortal nation and its sensations, events, and shared opinions. He had lost the fight with vainglory, and the fight with ignorance, for what he now guessed must be the usual reason: he had not known there was a fight on.

When he read English history eight years ago, the excitement of its principals astounded him. Leaders waxed overwrought about nothing—about events that did not come to pass, or that did, and settled in, like tree trunks that fell and made a ruckus for a moment but were soon webbed over by moss. Their resounding speeches had sounded tinny and arrogant to thirty-four-year-old Clare, dead as those men were, and so mistaken in matters of moment. William Pitt and Lord Palmerston were stilled and powerless, and so were their opponents, and they had been powerless then in their periwigs, and fancied otherwise, and confused London Town with the Milky Way. Oh, they could easily degrade and worsen the condition of other men, they had that power, but only with fantastical exertion could they remedy or ameliorate it. They could not alter their own peeled nakedness, and were supremely unexcited now.

Clare walked bent, his long neck down and his chin up. He could still see, on the freezing water, the dark dumb ducks floating in rafts that tipped and rode swells. The overpowering, slushy sky was closing down. He should go back, he knew, but he went on, and his thighs itched and tingled as they always did when he walked in the cold. He made for a stretch of sand ahead. When he reached it he stopped and drove his hands into his pockets. Torn seaweed littered the sand, and wet fir cones, bottles, and twigs.

Naturally society cherished itself alone; it prized what everyone agreed was precious, despised what everyone agreed was despicable, and ignored what no one mentioned—all to its own enhancement, and with the loud view that these bubbles and vapors were eternal and universal. If

June had stressed to Mabel that she was going to die, would she have learned to eat with a fork? Society's loyal members, having sacrificed their only lives to its caprices, hastened to entrap the next generation into agreement, so their follies would not have been vain and they could all go down together, blind and well turned out. The company, the club, and the party had offered him a position like bait, and he bit. He had embedded himself in the company like a man bricked into a wall, and whirled with the building's maps, files, and desks, senselessly, as the planet spun and death pooled on the cold basement floors. Who could blame him?—when people have always lived so. Now, however, he saw the city lifted away, and the bricks and files vaporized; he saw the preenings of men laid low, and the comforts of family scattered. He was free and loosed on the black beach.

Clare sat on a log, shaved strands of a plug into his palm, ground them to powder using his knife handle as a pestle, and loaded and lighted his pipe. "As a lion, so will he break all my bones ..." Having felt his freedom, must he now die? Conversely, could he endure this freedom, when it burned in his stomach and smoked in his throat?

In the match's flare he could see a swollen line of sand grains trailing over the hard beach in scallops. The back swash of the last high tide dropped sand grains there. It was in the summer of '83 that Krakatoa exploded. Clare was in his fruit-grafting enthusiasm then, and did not remark the famously sublime sunsets the ash caused around the world, because sunsets here were routinely sublime. He did notice what the newspapers proclaimed in the following months: that the explosion caused one wave to travel the sea, wash over Java and Sumatra, and drown thirty-six thousand people. Those thirty-six thousand people reproached him, as he read the paper and sipped his tea on the puncheon porch, for he was a good democrat, and believed that any man was as good as any other, roughly.

He had asked his mother if she thought God punished those thirty-six thousand people for living wrong, and visibly shocked her. She replied that they were all going to die anyway, which shocked him, and she added that it was time he got married, which he knew.

His eye sought the line of forest on the headland, but its black silhouette was lost in the black sky, as if the sky had abolished it. To the south he could see no fires from Finn Beach. Out over the water, in three directions, distance sputtered out. The wind had fallen; the tide made a small approaching noise like gibberish.

The dark was now thick, flannel. Its blackness had texture and depth, like that of a charcoaled page, in which dark clouds billowed.

Here, in all the world, there shone only his own light—his red burning tobacco, and the glowing dottle beneath it, and the black unburnt bits above. There was no other light, human or inhuman, up or down the beach, or out on the invisible islands, or back in the woods, or anywhere on earth or in heaven, except the chill and fantastical sheen on the sea, whose cause was unfathomable. Before him extended the visible universe: an unstable, thick darkness almost met the silver line of the sea. A long crack had opened between the thick darkness and the water. The crack, half the apparent height of a man, gave out upon a thin darkness, black without substance or stars. He looked out upon the thin darkness, and seemed to hear the souls of the dead whir and slip in its deep fastness. They wanted back. Their bodies in the graveyard on the cliff could not see to steer their sleeping course, their sleeping heels in the air.

It was nearing five o'clock now. When Clare stood, his shoes on the beach rolled stones. He smelled the chill on the rising water. Inside his gabardine jacket, under his vest and collarless shirt, and inside his long-legged underwear, his flesh was losing its heat. By the time he rounded again the headland towards the town, his fingers felt to one another like pipe lengths. He wanted back, too. Obenchain's stump stood on the cliff between him and the town; he had gone too far. He heard his own footsteps. He inhaled and exhaled tensely, as if he might topple; he seemed to taste mineral darkness on his tongue, or ash, like the moon. It was too late to walk on logs; he felt with his feet for the narrowing beach. Ahead, a dim light smudged the cloud cover over the town, as its dwellings and streetlights cast up into the muffling blackness their lamps. He was not yet home.

He came up on Pearl Street by the town wharf. There he saw, in the frail light of the warehouse lamp, an orange sea star wrapped round the wharf piling. It was a starfish with many thick, short arms. It looked like a swollen medallion the size of a dinner tray, and alive. Clare had seen a sea star's thorny hole of a mouth; the mouth was at its thick center, on the underside, on the piling. Oystermen knifed starfish on sight, for a starfish humped its suckers around an oyster, forced open its shell with its contracting arms, vomited its stomach out of its own mouth, inside out, insinuated it between the oyster's parted shells, and dissolved and digested the oyster's soft parts directly. Now, as Clare passed, the black tide was wetting the beast, and it detached itself, one orange edge at a time. Its crusty nubs moved thickly. Their tubes loosened their grip on the piling, and the animal dropped into the water.

"Thus saith the Lord," Clare thought, climbing past the town to Golden Street, "Set thine house in order; for thou shalt die, and not live."

CHAPTER XLII

The next day, January 7, at noon, Beal Obenchain rose from his blankets on the floor of his stump and put on his high-crowned felt derby. The coiled hair on his chest and back had grown through the fibers of his union suit; it happened every winter. He fried Danish bacon for breakfast, and spent the day's dim light propped on the blankets, reading a Russian novel about choleric men who lived on cucumbers.

Obenchain for many years had been tormented by a life he found unendurable. He could not stomach the company of people, whose blithe words and glances showed they presumed he shared their life and views. In the company of women he shut out their excited voices and observed their jaws flap and their lips extrude and open like fishes'. He resented the hotel clerk, the trolley conductor, a peaveyman in a logging outfit, and even a solid citizen like Glee Fishburn, for addressing him as their fellow, as if they owned the keys to his nature. Only in solitude could he rid the air of their confident, possessive noises. On the other hand, he could not bear solitude. After a few days alone, he heard the silence grow hollow under the trees and over the water, and a suffocating rage rose in him. He flailed like a drowning man looking for other heads on the water.

Before sunset he pulled on his stiff pants, jacket, and mildewed boots, and called on Glee Fishburn. Glee supplied Obenchain with dogfish sharks, whose oil he rendered and sold to loggers. Glee and his wife, Grace, lived above the general store she kept on the town's booming south side.

Enormously agitated, Obenchain barely stirred himself to rear back onto his legs and walk to the town. His broad, flaccid face was composed and still; his legs seemed scarcely to move. He tramped cinders along the railroad right-of-way and mashed over the forest trail through grape holly, bracken fern, and wet salal. He was like the Skagits' fearsome, noisy spirit which lived in swamps, wore moss on its head, and walked knocking down trees or making fire seem to flicker up their trunks. He emerged wet in the raw town near the store, where the trolley tracks, set between planks, looped back.

Through the store's plate-glass window, between its gaudy painted letters, he could see that the black-haired girl was standing in the store—Glee's oldest daughter Vinnie, whose name Obenchain did not know. She was pinned at the counter, listening to Street St. Mary, the redheaded, one-handed old claim jumper, who was buying and selling land all over the county. Street St. Mary was Clare Fishburn's immediate neighbor on Golden Street, and Obenchain had already considered using him in some way to pique or scare Fishburn if he relaxed. Maybe Clare had already started mistrusting this foolish man; it would be interesting to watch for.

The girl caught sight of him and waved in her wholesome, mindless way, and Obenchain had to humble himself by ducking through the door—which rang a cursed bell—approaching the counter through the aisle crowded with barrels, tables, and bins, and asking her if her father was in.

He was still on the water, Vinnie said, and should be back soon. Because Glee was fishing, oblivious, Obenchain was being turned away by this chit of a girl in public; he stood crooked and wholly still, betrayed. He overpowered his chagrin—which he recognized as possibly extreme—by fixing his attention forcibly down on the fresh-faced offspring behind the counter, Glee Fishburn's spawn. Had the girl seen her uncle Clare Fishburn—was he acting queersome? He wished to know, but he also willed never to chat, so he stood torn, and did not ask.

The only other person in the store was Pearl Sharp, John Ireland's handsome wife, whom Obenchain knew; she was standing close to a display of hatpins. A dark silk scarf, tied in a bow under her chin, held her wide-brimmed, plumed hat. Was she staring at him? She would not expect him to address her here, and he did not.

The store's white bobtail cat cried to be let out. Vinnie crossed to the door and held it open. The bell rang again; the cat stood in the open door. "Why won't the cat go?" Vinnie asked Obenchain.

"He's showing his power over you. He's rubbing your nose in it." Obenchain was leaving. "It's the law of the universe."

He left; his trouser leg brushed the cat's head, and he gave Street St. Mary a wide smile. He stepped off the plank sidewalk and into the street, and shouldered his way between two ox teams, four yokes apiece, which were pulling wagons of Nooksack lumber to a building site. He passed wagons, buggies, and drays, passed delivery vans painted with framed battle scenes on their sides, passed construction crews carrying hod, planks, and quarried stone, and turned down to the beach.

When the door shut behind Obenchain, Street St. Mary turned. He wore, with an air, buckskin leggings and a stained collarless shirt. There were wormy brown strands in the whites of his eyes. His thin red hair he plastered in a scallop over his head, from one red ear to the other. Through the plate-glass window he watched Obenchain move down the street. Obenchain carried his bulk delicately; his ungainly head in its black hat he turned and tilted deliberately, from side to side, like an amateur actor. He had seemed strictly normal today. Street St. Mary had seen him at the livery stable when, as the saying went, "he might have sat for a picture of Up Against It"; then he looked coolly crazy, like he'd climb your frame if you wished him good morning. Street St. Mary was a stubby man, who had lost his right hand in a misunderstanding. He had stayed out of Obenchain's way since the day he saw him lift up a pinwheeling horse and face it the way he wanted it before he set it down.

"That Beal Obenchain's a queer outfit," he remarked to young Vinnie. "Queer as Dick's hatband, and always has been, poor devil."

"He's a right acute man, I'd say, and nice as pie half the time. How old would you reckon he is?" Vinnie Fishburn herself was sixteen. Her aunt June Fishburn used to say that Vinnie would grow into her big-boned beauty and leave; she had already grown into it, and she had no intention of leaving.

"Beats me. How old is a log? He looks to be about suffering through his middle twenties."

Pearl Sharp spoke up from deep in the aisles: "He's almost thirty-two." Vinnie and Street St. Mary looked over at Pearl Sharp and waited for her to add something, such as how she knew, but she looked down unconcernedly at a box of bluing. An astrakhan coat, with attached cape and fur collar, encased her tall, noble figure.

"He is a lazy fellow," Vinnie said to Street St. Mary, "and a moody one, but I don't know as he's done any wickedness on this earth." Laziness was a hobby of Street St. Mary's, and he admired it. He had often heard his father back in Maine perk up when a man called another lazy: "Mark," he would say. "That one they call lazy, he will be a great poet"—for he had known it to occur. Now the baby in the corner woke and fussed; Vinnie picked him up and kissed his bald scalp absently. Her dark bangs came halfway down her forehead and left an inch of pale brow above her vivid face like the matting on a picture.

Street St. Mary pressed on the counter. "People say Obenchain worked for Pig-Iron Kelly. I heard it myself from Johnny Lee." Johnny Lee was the Sharps' Chinese houseboy, St. Mary suddenly remembered, and he wondered if Pearl Sharp, now with her back turned, had heard him; he never could watch his tongue. The scalloped strand of red hair fell across his face; quickly he picked up the end from his shoulder, lifted his hat, looped the strand over his head, and clapped the hat down to hold it so that some hair showed under the brim, all the way across his forehead.

"Who is Pig-Iron Kelly?"

That was only a while ago, St. Mary thought—actually about eight years, if you tote them up; this bright-eyed creature Vinnie would have been too small to take notice.

Pig-Iron Kelly, he said, as if reluctantly, started out smuggling whiskey across the Canadian border from Victoria. He went down the strait, by night. He had a sloop painted black. Street St. Mary waved his one freckled hand.

"If the customs man came across the water to check on him, Kelly dropped the whiskey kegs overboard on lines, and pulled them up later."

"That's not so bad," Vinnie said. The better-beloved half of the town used to smuggle whiskey, from the men's stories.

"... Then he started smuggling Chinamen in the same way. The profits were rather large as to figures"—St. Mary raised his invisible eyebrows—"but the fines were worse if they catched him."

He told the rest of it. This was one very dear girl, with whom St. Mary often conversed.

Pig-Iron Kelly, as Street St. Mary told it, loaded five or six Chinamen and stood them on the deck of his boat when it was illegal to be a China-man at all, let alone possess a number of them. He sailed out from Victoria and hove to in the dark and lonely waters around the islands. Then he and his helper—maybe Obenchain—tied pig-iron weights around the Chinamen's necks, and roped their hands together, and sailed on. Kelly kept a bright lookout for the customs man, who wore away years of his life trying to catch him at it. The customs man found him and boarded him sometimes, but he could never turn up any evidence: for when the cus-toms cutter appeared, Kelly threw the evidence overboard, just like the whiskey. Only with the Chinamen, it was no use retrieving it, of course. He heaved them over the side, he did, and that was an end to it.

"But there were plenty more Chinamen back in Victoria, just honing to work in the canneries," St. Mary concluded. He liked a certain friski-ness to affairs. Vinnie's dark, round eyes stared off to somewhere far behind him. What if her father, fishing, turned up a drowned batch of pig-tailed Chinese men, all roped together, in his net?

"Look alive there, Sis," St. Mary said, and the girl came to. He was a tenderhearted man, and he considered Vinnie Fishburn to be a perfect daisy.

It was last spring he had proposed to this striking, milky-skinned girl, with her splendid physique and her hardworking ways. He proposed, in fact, to most everyone, for he longed for a wife to pet and expend the excess of his good nature upon. Two years ago he advertised for a wife in the Oil City, Pennsylvania, newspaper, and also in the national magazine *Heart and Hand*. Three months later, no one had answered his advertise-ments but a fourteen-year-old humorist in Wilkinsburg, Pennsylvania, who signed herself "Avenue St. Joseph."

The day that letter came, Street St. Mary found himself some good friends in the Blue Moon Saloon downtown, and he must have lost his way home in the dark. The next morning he woke to find Clare Fishburn pulling him to his feet and looking blamed cheerful.

"Thank you, boy," he had said into Clare's shirtfront. He was lightly frosted. They were in the Fishburn garden where the bulbs were coming up.

While he brushed the frost crystals from his clothes, St. Mary received, in a vivid flash, insight into the cause of his predicament. He explained to Clare, outraged, "My pipe knocked me over. I got knocked clean over by my pipe." He never smoked a pipe again.

Vinnie Fishburn had turned him down nice as pie, and looked

touched, even, when he made his best offer—"I promise I'll do all the churning!"—and made him feel like he might have hoped to plan a home for her, if he had been thirty or forty years younger. He still liked to shoot the breeze with her, and balloon it some about his rising fortunes. Today he had told her about his newest sensation, a real estate deal that came up smiling, and made him a winning worth thousands. She welcomed him in the store, without encouraging hopes. He was getting to be a connoisseur of proposal rejections, and Vinnie made hers right handsomely.

After Street St. Mary left the store, Pearl Sharp stepped forward with her purchases. She tilted over the counter. What did Vinnie think of Street St. Mary's good fortune? Pearl's color was up, red on her cheeks; the sphere of her black hair glowed behind her high collar, and she seemed giddy with excitement, as if Fishburn's store had been a crowded ballroom. Her silvery astrakhan coat had fur buttons, which she left open.

She knew Vinnie admired her: hers was the first family of the town, her husband was the high school principal, and she herself was charming and well turned out, which attributes she polished, for although she did not herself prize them, they were all she possessed. In fact, she brought to the least occasions a fervidity and an ardor that stimulated people; the tips of her shoes seemed to dance beneath her skirts. "That woman's a peach," Vinnie had heard her father remark carelessly in front of her mother. Her mother had held her peace.

Pearl Sharp smiled and met the girl's luminous gaze. Vinnie was a lovely specimen, an asset to the town, no matter if her great-aunt had run a brothel. She suspected Vinnie of possessing character: she led her high school class in scholarship, worked eight hours a day in her mother's store after school, minded her brothers and sisters right down to the baby, and shifted the cooking and the wash.

"Could I hold the baby?"

"What?" Vinnie started, then passed the baby, who never noticed. Vinnie wondered if she herself was getting slow. At night she flogged at the store's account books, then her schoolbooks. She and her mother turned off the gaslight at two or three every morning and lighted it again at six. Vinnie did not rest but those few hours. Her mother stood in the store while Vinnie was in school, and slept when she came home and took over.

Pearl fussed over the dazed baby, handed him back, and paid for two glass-beaded hatpins. She dropped the paper of hatpins into her reticule, which hissed against her skirt of silk georgette. A Lummi acquaintance of hers came in—the historian Edna Smith, wearing a blue straw hat and a dark overcoat—and they exchanged greetings. It was stimulating to get out and about on these short winter afternoons. She left the store with a wave.

When Pearl Sharp stepped into the street the light was reddening behind the clouds. The bricks on the new bank across the street glowed. Workmen crawled all over it, and their boot soles looked aflame. This building would be all sorts of fine. It was going to be a branch of a bank in San Francisco. Street St. Mary, who sold the empty lot, had seen his outlay swell by a factor of five in a year. He had told Vinnie in the store. He was able to sell the lot for three thousand dollars, although he had spent only three hundred dollars for it; he sold his equity, just his equity, for fifteen hundred. He was buying more lots. Another fellow came in from Cambridge, Idaho, put two hundred down on a lot, and sold his equity a month later for eighteen hundred dollars. He lived in a tent on the beach, eating potatoes boiled in seawater; he played pinochle all month, and left. Pearl was eager to inform her husband about equity, for it meant that they needed only hundreds, not thousands, to ride the boom.

CHAPTER XLIII

The sun had set, and John Ireland Sharp was reading in his parlor library, when he heard his wife's clicking tread on the porch. On the library shelf above his desk was the flat cougar skull he had brought back from his boyhood trip up the Skagit; he lugged it around wherever he moved, for no reason. It had been eight years since the Congress of Sinophobes proposed and finished its work. In those years he had matured into a small, neatly made man, lax of back and limb, whose dark, carven features were distinctive and alert. His magazine's pages brightened for a moment when Pearl opened the door. He heard her whirl into the kitchen and confer with Johnny Lee, probably asking if the boys were home yet. He could not hear the man's soft replies. At the foot of the stairs she paused, undoubtedly hanging her astrakhan coat and hat.

Her high voice unexpectedly called, "John Ireland, are you home, dear?"

"*Ad sum,*" he answered, and she appeared at his library door, slender and flexible-looking at the waist in her trim, steel-seamed basque and voluminous silk skirt. He folded back his magazine. Pearl stood in the doorway; her cheeks and lips were red from the uphill walk from town. She wore a white lace tie at her throat.

"Do you know Street St. Mary"—she burst in—"who lives next to Fishburns on Golden?" John Ireland nodded, amused. "Well, it seems Mr. Street St. Mary ponied up three hundred dollars and it swelled up to fifteen hundred dollars, because of equity—have you got a piece of paper?"

She was standing by John Ireland's desk. Taking paper and pencil, she drew quick pie graphs for him, which illustrated her breathless explanation of the principle of equity. Things stimulated her nerves and drove all else from her mind, so her brown eyes flashed and she lost herself; conversely, sometimes she paled, fretted, tugged at her clothes, and covered her small face. Now she put the pencil down firmly and smiled over her shoulder at her husband. Her thick hair smelled of the dampness outside—the dark mud flat and fir sawdust and smoke smell of the town—and her eyes roved his impassive face.

Further, did he know about Lee McAleer, the town treasurer? He sold one lot three times in one day, and made a thousand dollars, just like that. Now he was hiring Chinese men to haul sawdust from the Nooksack mills to the mud flats, to make new land to sell.

John Ireland nodded his head. People were hiring Chinese men now. Eight years ago Lee McAleer and his ilk were pounding them into boxcars. John Ireland's air of limp resignation made him seem older than his years. His dark brows met over his nose; light freckles dusted the skin around his black eyes and his cheekbones. Every evening he exchanged his principal's boiled shirt and three-piece suit for overalls, a modest habit that formerly drove Pearl wild, till she gave off bucking it. He sifted about barefoot in the house, or he wore what even his sons considered a blasphemous and spindling pair of carpet slippers, the sight of which made his wife bilious.

He knew Lee McAleer, indeed: he knew him for a slim, courteous scoundrel like Alcibiades, for an agreeable blatherskate who wore linen suits and yellow calf shoes, and who assumed every man lived by the same natural law—get all you can, and keep all you get. He knew and liked Street St. Mary as a goodhearted old claim jumper and rip-roarer who could not read a contract. It did not surprise him that these might be the sort of men his wife admired, for nothing surprised him. With a shrug, he turned back to his article, then looked up again, smiling politely, and scratched through his shirt under his overall strap.

From beside him at his desk, Pearl studied her husband's dark, keen face. For a bright man, he was by nature languid to the point of droopiness, though he did not miss a thing that interested him. Apparently, riding the boom on cheap equity held no more interest for John Ireland now than riding the boom on moneylending had last year—although if they had started out with only a few hundred dollars at thirty percent when she first proposed it, they would now have, well, messes of money. That way, however, was not in John Ireland's character. His indifference to his own fate complemented her ambition; formerly, it charmed her. He had heaved himself from a remote island homestead to commencement exercises at Oberlin College before he was twenty, obtained a post as school principal at twenty-two, and then evidently lost his enterprise; he met the world as an old man who had flagged, or stopped. She would try to light a fire under him again at dinner, and over the next few weeks, but he was punk wood. They had been married for twelve years. He was not a bad sort. Pearl gathered up her reticule and started upstairs.

She turned back to call, "Beal came into the store."

From his study came John Ireland's deep voice. "How did he appear? Did he greet you?"

"He never looked towards me. He asked after Glee Fishburn. He seemed touchy as a boil, but basically all right; he spoke with the admirable Vinnie."

Pearl's was the first white family to settle on Bellingham Bay, and the first in prominence among the few who stayed. Her father was Felix Rush, who owned the sawmill on which the settlement depended, and her mother, Lura Rush, fed every immigrant man that wandered into the region, embraced with tears Ada Fishburn and every white woman who came in new after her, enumerated to them Bellingham Bay's advantages and prospects, loaned them furniture, and gave them seeds. The education in morals this couple impressed, with hazel switches, upon their rowdy sons, they neglected to mention at all to their daughter, who seemed charming and complete as God made her. Shakily, Pearl taught school for three months in the summer; the tall Fishburn boys tied hairs around flies, and set the flies fighting in midair. She quit when a real teacher came; she said she did not want to "teach ignorant children."

By marrying handsome John Ireland Sharp, the new principal, who could talk earnestly about Demosthenes as though he lived next door, Pearl fulfilled her family's destiny to lead the town in culture. He was, as one of her brothers said, "educated to a feather edge." His socialist fervor she alternately admired and ignored. She respected learning, and considered hers to be the most tasteful and educated family in a wilderness of rowdies and wolves. She was no rowdy herself, nor yet quite a wolf, but a harum-scarum creature, fervid and giddy, who befriended strangers. She crocheted dresser scarves for her friends and knitted mittens for their children; she raised funds for the library, sang one of the lead female roles in annual operetta productions, and headed the board of the Benevolent Society. When the U.S. Navy coaled up its northern Pacific fleet in Bellingham Bay, it was Pearl Sharp who planned the balls in the Birdswell Hotel where society entertained the naval officers—not, as in her parents' broad-handed day, both officers and men. She decorated her own big house in an Oriental mode, with dark touches of Egypt.

The sea at the town's feet, with its shipping and fishing, did not concern her, nor the forested islands she could see from the windows upstairs, nor the lone, plunging mountains at the town's back. Tremendous forces animated these splendid prospects, and the tough truths they taught coarsened men. Her sons when they were six knew more about their world than she ever would, just as her brothers had: her sons could read tidal currents, recite steamer and rail schedules and crews for the whole county and enumerate their cargoes; they could split shakes, catch and gut fish, saddle and ride horses, row, sail, and find trails to the reservation and Lake Whatcom; they could name and shoot ducks on the wing. As the older boys grew, they discussed with their father the execution by electrodes of a prisoner in New York, the philanthropies of Andrew Carnegie, the motives of Jim Hill, and the movement of William Jennings Bryan to free silver. These were things for men and boys, Pearl Sharp would have judged if she had reflected on the matter, and on this error she settled into the complacent ignorance of some women of her station, such as it was, who wondered why men disrespected them.

Everything inside her house's walls held her ardent interest, and she excelled there. She lived indoors like a quartermaster, and supplied the troops; she played Authors tirelessly with her boys on the floor, decorated with brocades and sculpted wallpapers, studied in fascinated alarm magazine accounts of the extravagances of millionaires, and read catalogues. She was vain in her whims, goodhearted, indulged and indulging. She considered herself a socialist and a reformer. Loving and marrying John Ireland Sharp, she had hoped to possess for herself, in time, a share of his depth—which, however, it turned out, was not offering shares.

Pearl opened her reticule on the bed upstairs and brought out merchandise bit by bit. She examined each article by incandescent lamplight, behind curtained windows. In addition to the glass-beaded hatpins for which she paid at Fishburn's, she had picked up a few more things for the harmless refreshment of it. There was a pair of black kid gloves, a sterling-silver teaspoon, and a handful of postcard art reproductions from Florence; there was a blue Staffordshire-ware pot of toothpaste, a pair of black sateen bloomers for a little girl, a white coiled egret feather, and a package of clarinet reeds. The pot of toothpaste had been a challenge, for by then her bag was almost full. She had her eye on a box camera behind the counter. Smuggling it from the store would be a project she would postpone for a year or more, having learned that the pleasure drained from things once she got them home. Where would she hide the bloomers? The clarinet reeds she would store openly with a dozen identical packages in a canister in the cellar marked "reeds"—Johnny Lee had never commented. Maybe one of her boys would take up the clarinet.

Downstairs in his library, John Ireland Sharp rubbed his eyes and moved the china lamp. Pearl had a bee in her bonnet this time. Every few months, her ordinary shopping trips downtown wrought on her nerves, and he knew why. Once a year, in the spring, Grace Fishburn called on him at his office in the high school. She sat before his desk, her wool-braided basque tight, her long chin forward. She had freshly poufed up her yellow bangs into a snarl, behind which usually perched a stiff little blue straw hat shaped like a bowler. She was as calm as he was, and inquired about his sons with interest. Then, with dignity, she produced a brown-inked accounting of his wife's unpaid shopping trips. He always noticed Grace's index fingers—red and rough down one side, from breaking string. His fingers used to get that way, too, and infected, from carrying dead seals by their eye sockets.

He settled on Grace Fishburn with a check. He placed the check in her hand—he never liked to see people drop money down for another person to pick up. Then he praised those of her children whom he knew, inquired about the younger ones, and conversed about the state of business. "Biz is very fair," Grace had allowed last spring, and the phrase stuck in his mind. Of one of her boys, she reported last spring, "Aw, Archie's broke his dad-snatched arm." The two had been meeting as colleagues over this matter once a year for eight years, and they were at ease with each other, and shared mutual and sympathetic regret for it.

After Grace Fishburn left, the principal always looked over the list: so many clarinet reeds again—why clarinet reeds?—a half-dozen spinning reels, a paper of pins, a silk necktie, spats. Half of the entries were in the pointed hand of the oldest Fishburn child, the talented Vinnie. Vinnie was leading her class and would probably deliver the valedictory oration. He knew that Grace Fishburn tried to set aside a few dollars every month to send Vinnie to the university in Seattle. He did not know that Vinnie herself forbore eating lunch in order to save for the same secret purpose.

Now John Ireland marked his place in his magazine carefully with a flattened twig of fir. He turned, with a familiar gesture, to regard a drawing nailed to the wall beside his library desk. Why not abandon hope here in Whatcom, retire to Madrone Island, and live out his days on a stone beach, watching the sun wheel?

It was the island that he loved, if he could be said to love at all; his life on the mainland he bore as a duty. The ink drawing showed a dark series of scratchy, poignant clouds, whose broken masses were the picture's subject. A frail line far below them divided the sea from the sky; a layer of lapped lines indicated islands on the horizon. The picture satisfied him only by evoking its occasion: he had sat on an island beach log, his bare feet in the cool gray sand, and studied the irradiating northern light. The light glowed in colors from the center of each cloud and fired its filaments down the spectrum towards the blue; the light rendered his pen's precision absurd, but it gladdened the man and filled his lungs. The water had been slick that day, and marbled with calm. The skies were piled and complex. He looked at the picture often, to remind himself that the insubstantial vastness still and always obtained over the island and was ringing its colored changes unobserved, and to submit his ordinary concerns to its wide glance. Why not clarinet reeds, really—what was the harm in it?

He spent a few weeks on Madrone every summer still. His oldest boys,

Cyrus and Vincent, favored it more when they were small. His wife was not drawn to the island solitudes at all. The queer cormorants, crying gulls, and mournful old-squaw ducks oppressed Pearl's spirits and agitated her nerves. Her corset stays rusted. Of the many accomplishments at which she shone, none was available there. Her warmth lacked objects; she visibly lost luster as her dresses dulled in wood smoke, and she moped.

John Ireland blew out the lamp and waited, motionless in the dark, for his wife's treble call to supper.

CHAPTER XLIV

When John Ireland Sharp returned from the East to Bellingham Bay to head one of its elementary schools, he was a bookish, unaffected man, zealous for reform. He met Pearl Rush at a theater dinner following a production of *A Midsummer Night's Dream*, in which she appeared as a majestic and radiant, if high-pitched, Titania. Living in Whatcom after living in New York, New York, had jolted John Ireland's habitual studiousness and made him sit up and take notice; he noticed Pearl Rush. She was thirty years old; she had turned down a hundred suitors. He was twenty-two years old, too young to think of marrying, but he lost his head. Pearl was the first and only girl he courted, and she stormed his heart, in the company of the scented forgotten land and its skies.

The uncanny differentness of her gender staggered him: her fragile collarbones raised the fine cloth of her bodices, and veins threaded her white wrists where her cuffs slipped. Her coiled hair was an alien, entrancing substance, of which he thought her insensible; her smooth feet were nimble magic, her eyes ... It was all as the books said. He had never before noticed a woman, it astonished him to discover—let alone inspected one—and he recognized this bewitchment for love as the poets knew it. After a few months' acquaintance, he began to feel her absence from his side as amputation behind his breastbone, which constricted his breathing so he heaved at the air and sighed without catching his breath until she returned. The only cure for this condition was marriage, and so he discovered how marriages were made, as poultices.

The notion that he, in his otherworldliness, could win the heart of a creature so handsome and finely wrought astounded him, but he began to believe perforce that he had won it, from every evidence. His existence was stirring him more profoundly then than it ever had. The revolution and invigoration of his deepest fibers he knew to be a gift of the universe; no merit of his earned this awakening from the sleep of his life, this parting of the skies that admitted the *mysterium tremendum* to illumine and rattle all things. John Ireland Sharp was grateful and honored to know for the first time the blizzarding might of the universe, and to perceive its moving him from without, as the moon moves the seas without their contrivance or consent, as the unmoved sun spins its orbs.

So moved, he had wed Pearl Rush at the Methodist church. She wore red and yellow roses in her hair like Titania, and he looked up at her beauty, alarmed. They built a six-bedroom house on Lambert Street. As he now saw it, they accustomed themselves to each other's company at first by a surfeit of it, until they had dinned it into their heads that this unslakable happiness was permitted. He taught her Heraclitus' fragment lxxii: "It is a delight of souls to become moist." He found Pearl superior in capability and intelligence to other women. She was exceptional—a marvel of womanhood, the other members of which seemed so shallow when he met them on the street.

The appearance in short order of their infant son, Cyrus, prolonged the upheaval in each, but altered their separate senses of it. Pearl, who in twelve months had rarely removed her vivid glance from John Ireland, in the space of weeks fell wholly under the infant's spell. The infant's was essentially the first new face that came along, John Ireland noted grimly. To him its odd person, inner and outer, lacked all recognizable qualities.

From the mussed scene of this new couple's enchantment, which scattered its props into almost every corner of the house that had so recently been the stage for his empty and breathless suitor's longing, John Ireland Sharp withdrew. He withdrew to his library, making, in effect, a respectful and conceding bow from the waist, and there he remained every free hour until bedtime, for the duration of the marriage. There he read, if the truth be known, the socialist newspapers, to kill time, and the socialist and other weeklies and monthlies to which he subscribed. He settled down into a new relation with his prize. He wished her well. He sympathized with his wife's later, theatrical pleas for his full attention, for he loved her in a mild way, and he was happy to honor her always and to notice her from time to time—but for the rest, it subsided, as an earthquake subsides after rearranging the landscape.

He got back to work. His chief work, as he saw it, was to propel and enhance the socialist movement to wrest power from the Interests. Deep in his mind he searched for the thread of his personal thinking, which he had mislaid when he courted his bride. He found the thread where he left it—on social classes in America, and the ever-fainter possibility of justice in their relations—and picked it up, relieved. His duties as principal, first in the elementary and then in the secondary school, engaged and distract-ed him, although he found himself less empowered to direct curriculum and hire teachers, and more obliged to supply, maintain, promote, and defend the respective institutions, and to furnish detailed accounts of their material transactions, than he hoped. In his own mind, he was a social thinker; he became an educator to earn a living.

He traveled often to Seattle and Tacoma to hear socialist speeches; he came home on the overnight steamer *Kathy Anderson*, and entered his library, thoughtful, loose-backed, alert. Another infant, Vincent, came weakly into the world, and made little Cyrus appear comparatively inter-esting and appealing. After a pause, another boy was born, whom they named Rush, and finally Horace. John Ireland was the proud head of a growing family, and happy, if somewhat haunted; he bivouacked benignly in a corner of the house.

Eight years ago, as the winter darkness drove up into the afternoons and the ceaseless rains began, he "lost his faith," as he put it to himself, in socialism, when the socialists led the drive to expel the Chinese people from the region. At that time John Ireland had composed in his mind a forceful letter to the *Bugle Call* and the Seattle *Post-Intelligencer*. "We can only view with alarm …," the letter began. He wrote it and never sent it.

During the dregs of that winter, John Ireland gave up on himself. He was not fit for this world. Like Obenchain, he preferred seeing to being seen; when Pearl told him he was handsome—she still said things like that—he regretted not having gone into the hermit game. He had erred. He had disappointed his wife; he had squandered his ableness; the highest ground he had reached was confusion. Classical authors no longer inter-ested him, for where they were shrewd, he knew it all wearily, and where they were stirring, he regretted their innocence. He loosed his fingers from every effort. For all this, his townsmen deferred to the dignity of his titled position, called him "Professor," and beseeched him to address them on every topic. Their misplaced esteem grieved and oppressed him as per-sistently as did the multiple personal failures their esteem so vividly recalled. He observed that other men enjoyed at least the solace of fellow feeling, from which communion they excluded him by way of honor—honor to education itself, which alas he symbolized to the town, will he, nill he. But John Ireland did not linger on this analysis.

When in these past few years he found himself seeking the company of gulls and fish crows, young children, and the tolerant trees, he knew he did so not only for their indifference to his person, and their welcome unselfconsciousness in his presence, but also because he admired their own purities and solitudes under the thrashing skies—the birds' stepping into corpses, the pretty children's watchfulness, the humility and rigor of the trees.

Horace, four, appeared at the library door in silhouette, except for his ears, which glowed red. He halted by the sliding piles of old newspapers and weeklies on the floor.

"It's time for dinner," he said, and it was.

John Ireland rose and touched his son's shoulder; he regarded the boy's slender neck, and thought of Hippocrates: "A child is blended of moist, warm elements.... A man, when his growth is over, is dry and cold."

Together the two moved into the dining room, where Johnny Lee, sturdy and pigtailed, with his nightly supercilious glance at John Ireland's overalls, was serving a brace of ducks.

CHAPTER XLV

Glee Fishburn stood in his single-ended dory, held his oars out of the water, and looked across the bay towards the town. He saw the black curving railroad trestle nearby, the wharves that met it over the sheeny water, and the dark hills of the land where the uncut forest edged the sky. His eyes ran over the scraped hillsides where the colorless town rose. He saw the sweeping Birdswell Hotel, the big stone banks, Carloon's department store, the three-story office buildings, the depot, stores, and warehouses. He knew that men were raising more hotels and banks and every kind of building. No noise of hammers or saws reached him out in the strait. Above the town, houses and turreted mansions punctuated the plats to the edge of the clearing, where forest met mud. Smoke from slash fires and stoves lay low. It was dusk. Things looked *skookum* in Whatcom, and nothing was amiss there or here on the water.

The wide spectacle of the sea and sky moved Glee. The still, graying sky revealed the water for the colorless, lighted, enchanted stuff it was. To the west, featherweight islands with blue mountains on them floated hushed on what looked like air or fallen sky, and it was this same ethereal vapor that his dory plied. The dory's every detail of splintered gunwale, net, mast step, and cleat looked uncannily sharp. Mist or pallor whited out the horizon. Glee drifted detached like a soul among planetary islands in space. A line of black logs trailed from his boat like the tail of a kite; it was his gill-net corkline, which seemed to dot the sky like geese.

Glee Fishburn—long-legged, potbellied, and slope-shouldered—was almost forty. He was a hidden, smelly man, who carried himself with the dignity and gravity of his freedom and skill. He pulled free fish out of the sea, and he was his own man. In his boat and onshore, he rarely sat; instead he stood alert, careful as an expert, and kept an eye on things.

He was fishing the winter Chinook salmon, which he called kings. A sockeye salmon weighed six pounds, a pink five pounds, a coho eight pounds, a chum eleven pounds, and a king salmon twenty-five pounds, or eighty pounds, or a hundred and twenty. The Indian people called it *tyee*, a big man, a chief, just as the whites did—a king.

Storms had kept Glee off the water for a week. Last night he rowed out at dusk, when the water calmed, and he had now fished a night and a day. His forehead was pale and curved; his wide-set brown eyes were calm; his long, thin nose was red at the tip and wet. He had twenty king salmon and about that many big dogfish, loose in the bow. Some days and nights he caught fifty kings and twenty dogfish, and some days and nights he caught two hundred dogfish and thirty kings. It was the same in the summer, when he used a smaller-mesh net for sockeye, and caught more dogfish sharks.

Last night his oars had stirred the green phosphorus in the water, and he saw his wake glow behind his path. Each pull on the oars pushed a globe of green light behind it underwater; each stroke brightened a slash across the glowing path, so his dory's passage marked the sea with tread. He had rowed eighty feet down the corkline—the length of the hanging net—and seen a yellow glow down in the water, near or far, for each salmon the net gilled. He could count the dogfish underwater, too, by the more beautiful glowing snarl of their violence. In the black of last night, his net splashed lights in the boat when he hauled it; the invisible water smeared yellow lights across his hip boots like stars. More stars splashed up the boat's sides; sparks pooled in spiral galaxies on deck. When he picked the net the lights crushed to glowing powder across his gloves and died.

He would pick his last set and go in. Hand over hand he pulled the wet net over the stern. A big red jellyfish tumbled onto his belly, and pieces of it fell down his hip boots. He wore gloves, but bits of it stung him anyway. He dropped the net to throw the jellyfish's thick body, the size of a platter, over the side; he chased its transparent fragments on the deck and slid them up the side and over the gunwale. He kept piling the net in a heap. Every few armfuls of net on this haul showed a gilled salmon or a dogfish. The long salmon caught themselves tidily, head-on; they were too wide to go forward, and their gill covers prevented retreat. They glistened with life, dark and spotted, tough-skinned, like the land's trees. Their black lips worked stiffly, and Glee could see their black, conical tongues. Their circular eyes never flinched. He worried them out of the net and heaved them forward with both hands. A very big king salmon was five feet long; Glee caught a few of those every year—each the size of his wife, Grace.

The rubbery dogfish had to move to live. Caught dogfish tangled the net, and bit through it, and caused mourning, discomfort, and grief. Working down through many snarled layers to untangle a dogfish took Glee ten minutes a dogfish. Now, picking a three-foot dogfish out of an eight-foot snarl, Glee moved cautiously. The live shark thrashed in his hands and tried to bite. Its body was nauseatingly soft and boneless; its low-slung shark jaws snapped their rows of sharp teeth. It had a long pink spine on its top fin that was poisonous. This spine easily punctured any glove Glee could reasonably wear, poked into the meat of his hand, and stung it like snakebite. Spine wounds cost Glee three weeks out of the summer season, when his hand was too sore to work.

Glee took time for a spot of cruelty. When he freed the many layers of net from the dogfish's spine, teeth, and tail, he held it in his hand and twisted its spiny top fin until it tore loose. Then he jerked the fin down the fish's back, so it ripped a long strip of skin with it, and threw the creature, trailing its fin behind it on a bleeding leash of its own skin, forward.

He was keeping dogfish for Beal Obenchain. When he was not keeping dogfish for Obenchain, he still tore the fin off in the same way, and threw the fish back into the water, to teach it a lesson.

Glee gave the dogfish to Obenchain for free, although the going rate was two dollars a hundred pounds. Glee knew he was one of many good-natured people who did things for Beal. Beal's will was strong, and he was not above playing for sympathy. Glee liked his world smooth and pleasant, as most people did, so he went along with him. Beal Obenchain rendered the dogfish's liver oil and sold it in tobacco cans to loggers for a dollar a gallon. The loggers used it to grease skids; Glee had done it himself when he was a boy. He had run along the skid road—the peeled logs that made a track to drag logs over—and slushed grease on the skids. If the skid logs were greasy enough and frowed smooth, three or four bull teams could move a turn of logs across them in a chained line, out of the forest to the bay or the river, where they floated to the mill. For small operations it was simpler to lay a skid road than railroad track. Like all human things, it kind of worked, on a good day. Like all frontier things, its mechanism, its parts, and their sources were laid bare, despookified, so that few thought of glorifying man and his creeping works under heaven.

It was dark when the dory's bows slid rattling over beach stones, and stopped. Beal Obenchain stood stiff on the shore. Glee stepped out, full of deep, inarticulate feeling, and turned, slope-shouldered, to look once more at the western sky, where the clouds' burnt radiance edged the dark. On the water he partook intimately of both the sunrise and the sunset, and he hated to quit the fantastical party by going ashore. He stamped his feet. He removed his gloves and shook hands with Obenchain gravely, formally, as he shook hands with everyone, like a Lummi man, unbeholden in his dignity. Obenchain's cold hand was long and thin.

Obenchain admired Glee's firm, spread stance and hard arms, and he pitied and contemned him, for he considered his wife a shrew.

Obenchain saw the dark enormous kings heaped in the dory, and the bloody dogfish beside them. In a great sockeye run, men stacked salmon on the beach like cordwood. They drove horses into the rivers up to their shoulders to drag the full nets from the water. The fish in the nets gleamed, half dark, half light, and curving. For the fish the glutted cannery scows would pay a nickel apiece, or nothing. Fishermen were always caught coming or going, like the gilled salmon: either there were no fish, or the price was down. Grace Fishburn would try to peddle these king salmon, gutted and salted in barrels; she kept three or four barrels around the counter at her store, and talked them up. Obenchain knew she wanted more; she grew up with nothing, and stayed small, while Seattle and now Whatcom rose high around her. It was not his problem. It was his problem, however, that Glee seemed to have brought him only about twenty dogfish. Maybe Glee was cheating him by keeping some back for himself, or maybe he was so lazy he let them slip out of the net. People were always going back on their promises to him; he was used to it.

Later that night, in the privacy of their rooms over the store, Grace swept a few fish scales like silver dollars from the floor while Glee, standing, honed his knife. Men were making money on top of money these days, and Grace Fishburn heard it all at the store. Dollar flew to dollar and stuck. Deadbeats and gamblers were rich, and swells and high rollers were rich, and so were careful men; they bought and built and expanded. Grace took notice and, from time to time, commented.

Last summer was bad for sockeye; the runs failed. Glee had nothing to sell to the cannery at Semiahmoo. The people there are nincompoops anyway, he had told his wife, "the Semiahmoo nincompoops."

Grace leaned the broom on the stove and clasped her husband. She hung with both arms around Glee's high waist, whimpering, and asked, "Do you love me?" There had been a lot of this lately, Glee thought. First the sockeye runs failed through the summer. Suppliers' prices soared all fall and merchandise got scarce, because of the boom. Then, as the winter's dark began drawing around the day from both sides like a purse seine, Grace had taken to hanging on him when he was home.

Grace clothed her alert, substantial person simply. Her brown eyes darted; her smooth, hard face caught the light. By day she manned the store's counter and ordered everything from a hundred suppliers; by night she took inventories and kept accounts in floppy ledgers. Widows ran businesses in Whatcom, and divorced women ran businesses, but not other married women. She seemed independent, but she clung like kelp to an oar, and grew distraught. Did Glee love her? Did her children love her, admire her? All six children kept moving, lest she fasten on them. In fact, Glee had had, sadly, a bellyful of her. Eighteen years ago he sailed the length of the Sound to court her in Mother Damnable's kitchen; now he sailed away every possible day. He plain despised her; he endured her; he reviled her; he deplored her. He only somewhat admired her. He had grown up without sisters, and he considered a competent woman a living treasure, which was just as well. Now he had been on his feet for most of two days, working. He kept his gear mended and his tools sharp. Not many men fished all winter. What else could he do?

"Truly love me?"

"Not much," Glee said, for he liked to speak clearly. He looked at her brow, at the familiar widow's peak from which her curled pouf of hair rose like a breaking sea. The notion crossed his mind, briefly, for the first time in his life, to give her a bang on the nose, to settle her down.

CHAPTER XLVI

Still later that night, Obenchain stood on the beach far below the bluff south of town where he lived. There was no moon, no stars, but only the yellow light from his fire, which flicked up his jaws and caught his hands moving in the dark. Visible in the black depths beyond Obenchain's fire, at an uncertain distance and height that might have meant land or sea, dotted pricks of light burned at random, and winked unevenly, like stars. These marked the hobo jungle down the beach. Immeasurably farther beyond them, more fire holes and lantern holes pitted the darkness. These specks represented Finn Beach, where loggers helled away the winter in driftwood shanties they leased for a dollar a year. Obenchain's fire made a red rip in the near darkness. Darkness invaded his figure lighted in streaks, and cut off overhead the billows of illumined smoke, and surrounded and snuffed the sparks that rose and vanished.

He moved into the darkness, humming, and returned to the fire with something like a pail in his hands. He upended it, and its contents dropped into a vat. Darkness enclosed his flickering figure as two palms shelter a candle's flame, and inside its lighted arch his arm moved a stick in the vat.

He had Clare Fishburn where he wanted him. Coming back from Glee's dory this evening, Obenchain had caught sight of Clare Fishburn on Water Street, and Clare saw him. The gas lamps had switched on; everyone on the street had looked up, and Clare's fast glance met Obenchain's eyes over a dozen heads. The man started like a hooked fish; his thin shoulders jerked and rose. Obenchain stopped walking and watched. Clare ducked into the pharmacy, where Obenchain lost him for a minute until he saw his gawky form edging beside the corner window. Slowly, Fishburn turned his head as if to peer from the window sideways. Was this the action of a free American? Obenchain stood alert on the plank sidewalk while men passed below him; his eyes fixed on the pharmacy window. The back of Fishburn's head rotated in the other direction, and the bony side of his cheek appeared, his eyebrow raised. Obenchain's wet lips formed the words he knew filled Clare Fishburn's mind like a voice: "Where is he? Where is he?"

Clare was his baby; he was gone beaver.

Obenchain stirred the curling livers. The muddy-smelling smoke and vapor rose up his trunk as it would rise up a chimney, and followed him when he moved around the vat to avoid it. He stepped back into the darkness and reappeared holding three pale fragments of wood. He bent and fed these to the fire tenderly, and a silent spray of yellow sparks lifted. The wood itself began to burn green and pink, for it was driftwood, and the salts in it shed colored gas. Grains of sand glowed and burned out.

Later the fire was a pile of embers. The bulking figure bent to lift glowing sticks from its edge, and tossed them one by one towards the sea—the sea whose shine they made suddenly visible a second before they hissed and blinked out. Like star shells shot into the night at Sebastopol, the burning sticks illumined fitfully the rim of the try vat, now cooling in the tide. The man picked up the try vat's bail and quit the beach.

In the flat forest at the top of the cliff, Obenchain drew near his house; his feet felt the path. He kept late hours to expand in the night, when no one laid claims on his thoughts. All day he had longed for the darkness and its energy. He was a cultist of energy. Capturing the mind of Clare Fishburn was an act conceived in energy and performed in energy, Obenchain thought, and the experiment's success produced more energy, which boiled in his own veins. Other men in great joy felt buoyant and winged. Obenchain, having channeled the universe's flow of power to himself, felt blessedly weighty and substantial: too thick to dissolve, too anchored to drift, too heavy to float, too cemented to break to bits. The heavy trunks around him seemed to usher him home. His own broad cedar stump swelled out of the forest floor; he stepped through the wet ferns that grew at its base. He pulled open the door and felt for the matches. Raising his head, he spoke:

> Gilead is mine, and Manasseh is mine,
> Ephraim is my helmet, and Judah my sceptre.
> Moab is my washbasin;
> on Edom I throw down my sandal to claim it;
> and over Philistia will I shout in triumph.

His voice was breathy, carefully controlled, and quiet. He felt hope surge through his arms and legs; his lungs filled. He lighted the candle, and his face appeared—his long and thin nose, his small eyes, almost hidden by the soft, brownish skin around them, his straining mouth.

> I will sing unto the Lord, for he hath triumphed gloriously:
> the horse and his rider hath he thrown into the sea.

He lowered his head and stared at the rippling adz marks on his puncheon floor. His voice continued, muted and rhythmical. "... The depths have covered them: they sank into the bottom as a stone.... Who is like thee, glorious in holiness, fearful in praises, doing wonders?"

BOOK V

SPRING

CHAPTER XLVII

March, 1893, Wyoming

Howard Kilcup, eleven years old, and his brother, Green, eight, were thrilled to pieces. The Pullman conductor, Mr. Tommy Cahoon, would take off his cap for them. They had been badgering him all morning, and now, when every boy and girl on the train clogged the aisle, he was doing it: he showed them where he had been scalped. The top of his head looked like glossy wax or frozen rags, red and yellow; the bright puckers and slicks started above his eyebrows and ears and extended halfway down the back of his head, above a fringe of hair. The Sioux had scalped him years ago, when he was fishing in a creek near Cheyenne, Wyoming—right here. The train had just pulled out of Cheyenne.

"The painted savage took his scalping knife," the conductor said, "and run it clear around my head"—his hand jiggled, demonstrating—"took ahold of my hair, set his big old foot against my chest, and pulled with both hands. My scalp come clean off," he told them, "with a sucking sound I can hear in my mind to this day, and the Indian keeled over backwards."

One hard-bitted little girl asked, dropping a curtsy, "Could I feel of it, please?" and Howard Kilcup shuddered for her lack of manners. Mr. Cahoon said, "No, Missy, it is my highly personal scalp, that the good Lord healed, and not even my dear wife touches it." So saying, the stout man put his braided cap on again, and commenced slicing a soft apple, which he divided among the children.

Howard and Green made their way between first-class cars to their own.

"Mama! Mama!" Green came calling, and his older brother told him to wait till they got there. They were wearing white shirts with broad Peter Pan collars, which extended over their tweed jackets' lapels. Green's suit had knickers; Howard's had long pants. Both wore round wool hats.

They could move between shaking cars as smoothly as the conductor could; they were old hands.

"Mama! he showed us his scalp where they scalped him! Oh, Jerusalem!"

Minta raised her square head in its flat black hat. She wore a black worsted dress, both dusty and greasy; ivory combs held her hair. June had been reading beside her, at the glaring window. June's pale linen duster, though sooty, seemed perfectly pressed, and so did the blue suit of slubbed silk it protected. The boys' older sister, Ardeth, was reading in a seat across the aisle.

Green's long face was all animation, and his voice piped over the rattling wheels. "It didn't look like skin at all—it's the bossest thing I ever saw—you must ask him to show it to you, you must."

"I don't expect I will," Minta said, and Green's face fell. He had green eyes and straight, dark, rusty-looking hair like his brother's; he parted it just off center and wetted it all day with a comb at the fountain to train the sides back under his hat. Minta patted his hand. Howard told her, and his aunt June, what they had learned, that the Sioux had scalped Tommy Cahoon when he was fishing a creek right near here, in Cheyenne, and the top of his head came off with a sucking noise he could hear in his mind to this day, and it had healed over and was a sight. And the Indian keeled over backwards.

Howard was a black-eyed, long-jawed boy who wore clear spectacles for no reason. He was shorter than his younger brother, and considerably, as he saw it, more manly and restrained. He had barely slept on the train either way, to Baltimore or from it, for boys frisked about down the length of the cars all day, and men gambled and bloviated all night, and he hated to miss any of it. A bandit had robbed another train last week and taken forty thousand dollars cash and jewelry from passengers, and this could happen, too, at any minute, and he would save the day in a number of ways, while his foster brother, Hugh, looked on and remembered every detail to tell Kulshan Jim.

A crowd of children came trooping through their car towards the rear, and Howard and Green joined them; the door closed behind them. Ardeth unpinned her stiff straw hat to pat her roached-back, glossy hair, gave her mother a long-suffering look, and bent again to her sooty book, *The Miserable Ones*. Ardeth was fifteen. On the trip to Baltimore, Ardeth had been known to sit in a separate car all day and pretend daintily to the other passengers that the rowdy boys were strangers.

June turned to Minta and remarked, "Those two are almighty pious about scalping Indians, don't you think? It could have been their relatives, after all."

Minta colored up and held herself still. "The Nooksacks?" she said sharply. "Our own relatives are more likely to have scalped people than the Nooksacks." June could not let go this matter of the children's Nooksack blood. Yesterday she had reminded Minta that, for all her expenditures, the three would "probably go back to their own people." She thought of them as a unit, like a litter; it was wearing thin on Minta, who had hoped this long trip would manifest to June the truth, that she had four children, of whom she was burstingly proud.

"Of course, you are right," June said softly, inclining her round head. "You have done so much for those children; I hope they are grateful." She added with her high brows raised in innocence, "I wonder whether it was our Biddle relatives in Philadelphia, or our Randall relatives in Annapolis, who indulged in the greater number of scalpings." After a glance through the window, she returned to her book, a society novel by Augusta J. Evans.

She simply could not restrain herself, Minta reflected. It was impressive, how people's natures persisted from childhood directly on through to the grave, in every circumstance. Grateful! Did June ensure that her own Mabel was grateful? Did June know the extent to which these three children in particular, and their Nooksack relatives in general, had saved Minta's life? June had met Queen of the May, the children's mother, only in passing, however, in the weeks following the fire. June had not known or depended on native neighbors as she had. June had not known the Nooksack *tyee* Hump Talem, who presided with dignity over the forks of the Nooksack wearing a mink hat and a bearskin cloak, or the beloved chief Skookum George, another powerful-framed man, who had died. June had married and moved straight to Whatcom, a town with office buildings of brick and stone, and trolley cars, and everything else. The fourteen years' difference in their circumstances as brides might have been a century.

June had been present the spring morning seven years ago, when Charles Kilcup called on Minta and asked her to take the children. She and Hugh had moved from the tent into the new house—the fine new empty house Clare Fishburn had built, which had fanlights over the doors and carved fretwork on the eaves and high porches. June was staying with them, ostensibly to keep Minta company, and not incidentally to enjoy the novel and cheering friendship of Clare Fishburn. Charles Kilcup had come in just after breakfast. He wore a creamy primrose in his buttonhole, as many former miners did. He removed his silk stovepipe hat, and searched in it for the envelope addressed to both Minta and June.

"From your mother in Baltimore," Charles Kilcup said. He glanced twice at June, as most men did, for her face, with its wide, deep-lidded eyes, dazzled and she dressed her neat figure tightly. Kilcup himself was slim and strong; like the fellow in the local song, he had "tunneled, hydraulicked, and cradled." Minta had seen him amuse his children by picking up an empty sugar barrel in his teeth and tossing it over his head. He had been white-haired since he was twenty-five. He was known to have a brother who, with his wife, was minister to the Modoc Indians on the lava beds up the Sound; they lived on bread made from ground waterlily seeds, and all their children had died.

He had come on a sorrowful business, he said, and took a bench seat at the table. He was not getting on since his wife had died—he called her "Cora," which was news to Minta, who had never heard her called anything but Queen of the May—and his children needed a mother's care. He would move on to Alaska Territory to do some placer mining, he said, and held Minta's gaze evenly—if she would take the children to rear. They were good children, as she knew, whose heads had never been flattened; "Ardeth is seven and does the work of a grown woman—" and the miner's eyes then filled with tears, which spilled down his smooth cheeks.

"Of course," Minta said quickly, "I would be honored to rear your children, or keep them till you send for them. They are fine children I have long admired—" and here Minta, too, grew tearful above her spectacles, and her voice cracked.

Isn't there something I should be reading? June thought. She rose to stoke the stove. She herself would never have children; they everlastingly died after you got fixed on them, and led you into bottomless waters where you lost control. If some abandoned urge came upon her later, she would raise chinchillas.

Kilcup seemed to ignore his tears. He had been a bugle-and-taps boy in the Confederate Army.

He was stone broke, he said to Minta, but he would give her the rights to his claim for the children's keep. It was a good hundred and twenty acres with improvements, worth about two thousand dollars, and another thousand dollars in fir timber. "I don't figure to come back."

Minta had no need of his land, or his cedar board-and-batten house, and she said so; he should sell it now for a grubstake, though she could not understand how anyone could bear to leave Goshen. She herself would provide for the children and in every way treat them as her own. In fact, privately she could scarcely wait to hold Green, one, on her lap and let him play with her face, as all her children had; she wondered, did he like laps? She would soon know.

Charles Kilcup said he would sleep on it. He returned the next morning in a torrent of rain and proposed he sell the claim on the open market through an agent. He would split the proceeds with Minta, who could use it as she wished. She had no need of it, she said, misliking the turn this had taken, but Kilcup insisted. The three scrubbed children were there with him, Green crawling and dragging his own willow cradleboard on the floor. Ardeth and Howard were dripping and listening by the stove, and Hugh was keeping an eye on them all and listening, too, so she assented to ease the man's heart and shorten the talk. She wiped her spectacles on a corner of her apron. She would educate the children as far as they wished; she would read to them, start Ardeth with her own flower bed this spring, and they all could take picnics to Birch Bay.

So it had happened, more or less. They took picnics to Birch Bay. Charles Kilcup never returned, or sent word. Howard and her surviving son, Hugh, shared a chamber, and so did Ardeth and Green. On the walls they hung a framed tintype of their father and mother sitting stiffly with Ardeth, who was then a blurred baby. They missed their parents something terrible. They trusted Minta and soon began to love her in their several ways.

Kulshan Jim was their dead mother's brother; he and Jenny Lind took the children to visit their cousins, and dispensed sober advice to them— "Have forgiveness for people. Hold sacred all creation. Be industrious, for you will be working all your life." Ardeth, Howard, and later Green received this advice severally, standing still and alert, their arms pressed to their sides—which receptive posture was itself the first teaching. Several years ago Minta learned that Jenny Lind and Kulshan Jim had talked with Kilcup about rearing the children themselves—for they loved them wholeheartedly, and knew they could give them a tender home—but concluded that Minta needed them more. One morning in those early months, Minta was carrying a water bucket across the yard when she felt its weight lift. It was Ardeth, who had crept alongside. She was wearing a stiff little blue straw hat, curved at the brim like a bowler, and she was pushing up on the bucket with both arms.

Ardeth, Howard, and Green never obscured the memory of Bert and Lulu in Minta's mind, nor replaced them in her heart; instead the new three gradually assumed vivid places beside the two's shadowy and wailing figures, as if a heart had been a banquet table infinitely expansible. She and Ardeth, in particular, enjoyed a sweet, confiding intimacy that comforted both. Contributing to Minta's contentment was her vain conviction that, while she herself resembled her parents, Green and Louisa Randall, in no particulars, and had fully formed herself, Hugh and her foster children were the work and product of her hands; they resembled her in every particular, and in unison they reproduced her entire.

Hugh rarely let the boys out of his sight those early years. He teased Ardeth, who, as she grew, was proud of her daily baking. When company came to supper he would raise his plate to his pale eyes and turn it around slowly. "What might this be?" he asked, and Ardeth would answer, "Pie." "How do you spell it?" Ardeth did not really mind when Hugh staged this deplorable act in front of Jenny Lind and Kulshan Jim, or in front of Clare Fishburn and Ada Tawes, who well knew how the family carried on at home, but she was disgusted when he pulled it before the schoolteacher, a sorrowful young man of noble demeanor and delicate breeding.

Howard grew and got his clear spectacles and a brass cornet. Although he was only eleven, he joined the Goshen band and played at balls, at railroad celebrations, and at the Fourth of July. Recently he had grown interested in the Indian Shaker Church; he watched the winter spirit dances, and was welcomed. Green grew more, and rode fast horses out of sight of the house. Howard worked under Kulshan Jim every free hour, and Hugh did, too, when he was home from the university in Seattle. The younger children were all passed forward in school every year, and life was going handsomely for them now, but Minta knew that if they left the region they would encounter hardships, for they would be half-breeds in the eyes of the world, and nothing else, till Kingdom come.

Through the dusty coach window beyond her sister, Minta saw bare earth, red and brown; dark sage dotted the ground thinly on south slopes,

and more thickly on north slopes and down dry ravines. Pronghorn ante-
lope in groups of five or six turned their slim heads to peer at the train as
it passed. What these creatures ate or drank, Minta could not picture.
God made harsh lands and flowering lands. Riding the Union Pacific from
Kansas City, the travelers had boosted up the long rise of the plains
towards the Rockies. They followed the Platte across bare Nebraska,
traced the North Platte into Wyoming, and were now crossing the Great
Divide Basin under a white March sky.

After supper, the mountains appeared low in the distance like an
ocean swell: the Wind Rivers, white with snow. The rushing sage and creosote and saltbush pulled at the mountains, but they drew no closer.
Minta considered the Rockies inferior to the Cascades and dull, for they
lacked form, height, and glaciers. The volcanic cones she loved—Mount
Baker and Mount Rainier—had enormous forests at their skirts, and
waterfalls that drained the meadows above the forests, and precipitous
snowfields and glaciers that rose above the clouds. Still, she kept her eyes
on the gray Wyoming mountains now. The mountains were imperturbable,
frank in their cruelty, and they meant she was nearing home.

CHAPTER XLVIII

Minta and June were returning from their father's funeral. Green Randall
had retired from office five years ago, after serving two terms in Washington. The country was going to the devil, in his view, and every kind of
agitator stirred every kind of mob. For many years he had feared economic
chaos. Consequently he had given their inheritances to his daughters
early, on their marriages. He spent his days at the Maryland Club, listening to shriveled men in frock coats, whom he had once held in awe, argue
over whose family home it was that held the very ball, in 1803, at which
Napoleon Bonaparte's brother Jerome fell in love with local belle Betsy
Patterson when her gold chain tangled in his uniform.

One morning a month ago, while his valet was dressing him, the senator interrupted with a wave the ongoing story of the valet's personal
woes, to which he had given the full force of his attention every morning
for five years. The valet froze, amazed.

The senator said, as if winning a point, "I know that my redeemer liveth." His face turned flaming red, his scalp above his black circlet of bushy curls also turned flaming red, and he dropped and died, while the valet was still holding out his yellow coat.

Minta knew she had disappointed her father by not moving back after Eustace's death and the fire. He seemed to think he had loaned her to Eustace Honer like cash that would revert to its owner at the estate's settlement. He never dreamed that farming was her chosen work. He possibly imagined she would have joined him if she loved him, for parents ever measure their children's devotion by their propinquity—she owned she did it herself with Hugh and Ardeth, though she knew better. She had never told her father, and she idly wondered if he had learned, that the white tent in which she lived with June and Hugh after the fire in fact belonged to Union officers during the war; they used it as field headquarters in Virginia.

Crossing the breadth of the country eastward, Minta had worried about her mother, as her mother had worried about her on the same tracks eight years before. She found Louisa Randall trembling in her mourning silks, and well. She never mentioned Edgar Gill. Minta saw that she had been living for thirteen years, when she was home from London and Venice, almost solely in the congenial company of Marsha Washington, their former slave; the two played elaborate games of cribbage at a corner of the dining room table.

The arrival of so many guests for the funeral, and so many relatives shortly thereafter, evidently stimulated the household. Their mother and Marsha Washington cut blossoming cherry branches, magnolia branches, and wisteria vines to perfume the rooms and halls. Louisa Randall displayed only the vaguest interest in Ardeth, Howard, and Green Kilcup, reserving her myopic gaze for Hugh. The first evening she had asked Minta, "Do ... their people? ... use ... forks?"

"Only on strangers," June had put in, then.

Their father's papers included an eight-year correspondence, ending at the senator's death, with one Nelson Truax, officer of a shipping company in Portland, Oregon. The two men had apparently passed blue stories and political views across the country for those eight years; they exchanged family news, and offered greetings and fond regards. Only Minta recognized the name. Nelson Truax had been captain of the steamer *Doris Burn* in the eighties and had transported the Randalls up and down the Nooksack—a voyage of a few hours—on their visit to Goshen eight years before.

On the journey east Minta had told the children that by custom, children were mute and sessile on trains, and looked from windows, learning their country. After the first few hours, this did not work. Everyone's favorite recreation was rushing out at stations to see the emigrant coaches. New settlers were streaming into the West; they traveled with all their goods and livestock. Minta stood on shaking legs and saw hundreds of crates of red hens; she saw coughing boys crouched on cinders next to the rails, milking cows. Immigrants to Goshen in the past fifteen years were mostly Norwegians, who had lived and become Americans in the harsh Dakotas, and who said, "By dumb!" Norwegians liked Puget Sound, saying its beauty resembled Norway's Romsdalsfjord. Swedes came. The Swedes and Norwegians did not mingle, or even, that first generation, get along, and they recoiled when people confounded them. Still, no one, not even an enemy, ever mocked an immigrant's speech.

When Minta first arrived in Goshen, nineteen years ago, she and Eustace found wild creatures—a hermit orator who preached at his cows, a lady-loving smuggler who spoke three Indian languages, a housemaid who lived in a tepee on donated crackers. Now the settlers came in families, and they already held views on maintaining appearances. They noticed and marked deviations. In the past few years in Goshen and upstream in Burnett, new settlers had, overwhelmingly, arrived from Holland. Minta found it grand to watch the clearings expand and the town grow graceful. The Dutch built gambrel roofs on their barns; they introduced sleek Holstein cows. Jenny Lind reported, laughing quietly, that her new Dutch neighbors, when they had scrubbed down the house, the children, and the stock, started scrubbing at the trees. Here in Wyoming there were no trees, and there might never be much settlement, if the soil Minta saw from the train was any indication.

Minta favored farming. At home she paced the land, no taller than a lily patch, choosing which parcels to clear, ditch, plant, and fence. She put in plums and apricots; she abandoned alfalfa, for the climate was too wet; she extended the hop plantings northward, planted plums in the Kilcup fields, bought calves, smoked pork, sold cheese, and hired men and women. It was prudent, she learned in the first years, not to grow more wheat and oats than her stock needed for the winter, for freight prices were so high it was cheaper not to have it than to try to sell it over the mountains. In the past few years she simplified still more by buying her hay from neighbors, so she could concentrate on hops.

Farming stimulated her, but maintenance irked her; she scalded the milk pans, mended fence with Kulshan Jim, painted the enormous barn and the porch, saw the horses groomed, the carriage and buggy wheels repaired, the hop poles cut, the plums pruned. She sometimes reflected that factory workers, for all their reported miseries, at least had to maintain only the floors of their apartments, or it may be of their hovels, and their clothes. At home when the weather dried, she would need to replace the barn roof; the sun had cracked the shakes. She needed to replace the carriage house roof as well, for its shakes had gone mossy in the shade; she had poked a penknife right through shakes and boards. In June and July, when her neighbors were engaged in the great work of haying and were competing with her for workers, she would be manuring and weeding hop vines. Had there been enough rain at home to set the new hops' roots? But not so much they rotted or washed out?

It was a melancholy fact that the other hop ranchers on the coast avoided Minta. They turned their backs to her; they distrusted her, and counted her out. At issue was prohibition, and the fair sex to which Minta belonged. Hop growers opposed prohibition, naturally, and so they opposed women's suffrage by logic, and opposed Minta Honer by extension. The region's hop ranches were yielding sixteen hundred pounds an acre—three times the yield of New York and English soils—and a pound of good berries fetched a dollar last fall, though it cost only ten cents to produce. Minta employed eight men most of the year, sixteen men to tie vines in the spring, and scores of families during the harvest. If women voted, and prohibition succeeded, and no one ever grew hops again, what—she wondered—would befall all these people? On the other hand, why should not women vote, who had opened up the country shoulder-to-shoulder with the men? Minta had voted in '84, when Washington became the first territory to enfranchise women, and in '86. She served on the election board and sat on both petit and grand juries. In '87 the Territorial Supreme Court declared women's voting illegal, and rescinded it.

"Mama," said Ardeth from across the aisle, "look here at the cowboys," and she did. Dusty figures were riding fence in the middle distance, wearing tall hats; their short horses stepped around tumbleweeds. Minta moved over to sit by Ardeth, who took her hand.

June looked at the cowboys, too. "They're no bigger than elves," she said, "take away their high heels and hats." June was missing Clare, whom she now recalled as seven or eight feet tall.

From the window June noticed a black storm raised behind the oblivious cowboys and over the empty prairie. The storm spotted only one small arc of the horizon, like a thumb smudge on the lip of a bowl. Far away, lightning flashed inside the cloud's vaults and illumined its tiers. Below the cloud trailed a wisp of darkness like a mourning veil. She had seen such a storm from a passenger coach eight years ago, when she journeyed to visit Minta with her parents after Eustace drowned. Her father had told her that the fragile veil of darkness, no bigger than a flock over the hills, was a violent storm of rain. It was hard to believe. She saw bare miles of red and white mineral slopes, then and now, which sagebrush speckled; she saw blindingly bright skies in every direction, on which the still, curved storm floated like a hawk.

It altered her views, that storm eight years ago. Beneath that little smudge of a storm cloud, she imagined, all violence harassed the people, if there were any people. If there were any people, they were at that moment running for shelter and safety as if theirs had been a real storm such as she, June, knew from experience in Baltimore, Maryland, where houses collapsed and barns blazed and carriages blew up into trees. June was a sensible creature, and she had reflected, gazing from her Pullman seat, that very possibly, their supremely real Baltimore, Maryland, storms looked like this from offshore.

"... Look at that little smudge on the horizon there, over the land," one squinting bay crabber might say to another as they spread their net in blue water. "It's a little squall setting there in the west"—and all the while the Randalls' elm trees were firing out of the ground in a line like artillery shells, and their roof was ripping off and smashing on the mums.

Her sister, Minta, believed in heaven, and June did not. She began to wonder then how people who believed in heaven could endure living, for the sight of a storm so far away, as it must ever appear from heaven, and the picturing of the people below it, for whom the storm was real, presented as chilling a view as astronomy did, and made a girl, however finely fashioned, doubt her importance. The sight of that dot of a storm had softened her up for the suit of Clare Fishburn, though he never knew it. Freshly jolted by her trip, she could regard him both as a rawboned pioneer, who lived three mountain ranges and two deserts away from Baltimore, and also as a livehearted creature, who stirred among the living of her generation, and who bestrode the spherical world under its weathers just as she did, for a while.

When she met Clare at her sister's farm in Goshen, she started to love him for the same reasons men liked him: for his skipping ways and for his broad and undiscriminating enthusiasm for all things equally: for a piece of organ music or a plate of corned beef, for snow or no snow, for whatever he was doing at any moment, for planing a plank or drawing the fiddle bow at a dance or shaving his face. He looked like a tall boy burnt out from playing—haggard and sweet-faced, thin, quick to laugh, and quick to forget. Now town life had roused in him a half-baked pomp, which could get worse.

If Clare had been killed, how would she know? Mr. Tommy Cahoon would walk down the aisle with a telegram for her. June caught her breath every time the conductor's wide uniform jacket appeared in the door; she looked at his hands, while the other passengers undertook quick studies of his head. Perhaps he would tuck the telegram in his jacket and take it out at the last minute. She leaned her round forehead on the window and tried to pray, which only vivified her own helplessness. If Clare lived, the state legislature would get him. Lee McAleer, the smooth Whatcom treasurer, did not ordinarily propose ideas for the benefit of others; there must be a catch to his wanting Clare to run.

She shifted in her chair. She herself could have designed a far better rail route, if anyone asked. The West, as she saw it, did not look nearly so grand as the pictures people brought back. This first-class coach, called a Pullman Palace, was dirty as a hen roost, and its reclining chairs multiplied the varieties of discomfort.

She was finding her sister's company oppressively noble. Minta lacked modern qualities. She resembled the pious matrons of her grandmothers' generation, only they were old dears, really, and in fashion in their day, as Minta was not in hers. Minta was hard to corrupt, sincere, and no more entertaining than a pan of dishwater. She showed Ardeth more marks of affection than she showed her own sister. If Minta had not lost her husband in the river and two children in the fire, she might have become one of those mighty country women who sailed into things laughing, who stuck hogs and wrung necks and swatted children, all the while telling rough stories over her shoulder. June reflected, however, that Minta had never been that clobbering, swaggering, amusing sort. She would have enjoyed her more if she had been.

June was missing Mabel, too. She had ideas for training Minta's children, which she barely forbore introducing. As their express coach skirted the Wasatch Range and bowled down into the Snake River Plains in Idaho, June tried to read to Green, who, as it happened, had never favored laps. He preferred opening and closing windows. Every time he opened a window, ash and cinders blew in. She bribed him with horehound drops and tried to recall how Mabel's hair smelled—something sour—when every morning she fixed it with a black bow wider than her head.

CHAPTER XLIX

Hugh Honer sat with the men in the smoker. He was seventeen—curly-headed like his father, thin, with a wooden, wide mouth and alert light eyes. When he saw the bare mountains his thoughts fell again into their old track: would he have opportunity, in Whatcom, to stop at the store? Many times?

He longed to see Vinnie Fishburn, who worked in Fishburn's, her mother's store. It was the nobility of Vinnie's brow he told himself he admired—the way her black bangs curved halfway down her forehead and framed an arc of clear skin above her eyes—and maybe it was. Only a month ago, when the two were botanizing along the abandoned tramway south of town, he had stepped close to Vinnie, near a big trunk. She held still and trembling like a foal, this big-boned, ordinarily forthright girl, and he raised his hand slowly to her face and swept his palm under her bangs to brush them back. Then, holding his breath, he inspected for science her forehead in the fullness of its curve. Since then he had rehearsed this moment so often that he could no longer recall it in its richness, but only the thin version he told himself. He wondered at which repetition he wore away its power—the fifth? the eighteenth?

His family would stay with the Clare Fishburns in Whatcom for several days. He could see Vinnie in church that Sunday, which was Easter, but he hoped for more. He personally could tend her sister Nesta, a complete menagerie of a child, and her other sister and countless little brothers, so Vinnie could get beforehand in her schoolwork. She might well remark a difference in him, for now he had seen the country—"the breadth of the land," he would tell her.

He had seen open coal pits, steam mills, iron bridges, blast-furnace chimneys, and barges bearing sand for making glass. Tall buildings had not impressed him, for he had heard much about them, and found them mere buildings, extended up. He heard, too, about wealth in the East, but not, however, about poverty—the children with chilblains on their faces who roved the waterfronts in gangs, the sockless men lined up for handouts, ash-faced women and girls who worked the districts. Outside the coal-dusty terminal in Baltimore he saw Whistling Cicero, a wandering Negro who carried a tin kettle.

"Watch this," someone said, and put a penny in the kettle. Whistling Cicero smacked his lips and spelled "Constantinople," emitting, between each letter, a shrill whistle that turned heads a block away. People laughed. Hugh kept his eye on the man's unflinching, pigtailed daughter, who looked to be ten or eleven—the age his sister Lulu would be. The sight of that hard-eyed girl wearing a shawl tied over a dress too small to button was something he would describe to Vinnie, who shared, he thought, his vision of their future. "That sight marked me," he thought he might say.

In Illinois, he had marveled at the fertility of farms, where winter grain grew thick as fur. In Maryland he studied his grandmother's green, rolled lawns. He rode his grandmother's tall horses. Each was so slim and smooth, he felt as if he were riding a dragonfly. His grandmother's coach-man's livery—green and gold—matched her four-in-hand coach, and also her phaeton. He himself had more than once stepped into the springy carriage body, perched on the upholstered seat, and ridden suspended and racing down Baltimore's paved streets. In the thick of traffic downtown, his own glossy, matched trotters joined the others smoothly as salmon join salmon underwater. At every intersection he braced for a collision, but none came. He had underrated city people.

This trip had set him back a term at the university in Seattle, where he was studying general sciences, but it had given him a heady look at Johns Hopkins University, where he hoped eventually to study medicine, while living with his grandmother. The dean at Johns Hopkins, who knew his grandfather, told him that Baltimore children had the highest death rate in the country. Hugh assumed carriages killed them. Now he would help out at home until next term began; he could likely catch the train into town from time to time for dances and church picnics.

In front of Hugh in the smoker sat a long-legged, red-eyed young fellow who had the overdrawn look of an Eastern college boy. He had a piece of sticking plaster on the edge of one of his ears, where apparently a barber nicked him. The college boy folded his newspaper and addressed his neighbor, who wore a bowler hat and muttonchop whiskers like an old-timer.

"Tell me," the college boy said in a quavering voice, "has a young man a better opportunity to secure wealth and preferment in the West than in the East?" This stylish speech impressed Hugh.

The old-timer rubbed his pitted nose. He said something Hugh did not hear. He said he personally knew of a waterfall in Oregon that was a good proposition. He said there was a good proposition in Port Townsend, and there were excellent propositions along the Great Northern route, where Jim Hill had granted the towns a clear thing. Pretty work!

"I have thought myself," the college boy said, "that opportunity in the East was used up. The cities are unhealthy and ridden with vice. But the East has the capital." The car's swaying and bumping made a hash of his elocution.

"... I myself have been said to possess the needful application. Do you find me capable of making a good impression? In any case," he finished lamely, "I hope to be making a stir soon in something. What do you think of the proposition at Humboldt Bay?"

"Oh, that is a washout,"—a shake of the muttonchop whiskers. "Dead in the shell. Some say business is falling off everywhere. Now, Idlewild! There's a likely town. And Florence—"

In the aisle, standing by the porcelain cuspidor, a long-necked salesman, wearing spats and a silk eye patch, boasted to the businessmen behind Hugh. He had single-handedly bested whole railway trains of immigrant farmers. In one instance he sold one immigrant a hayrake for five dollars, he said. Sold the same fellow ten rolls of baling twine, a gold pan, and a fireproof safe. Sold him tools to build a barn.

He tilted his blond head towards the heavens at the thought, then leaned into his audience, lurching with the train, and extended an arm to the back of Hugh's seat.

"... And he's bound straight for hardpan desert."

He straightened up and smiled. "Hardpan desert. There's no soil, there's no rain, not a tree, and the blamefool bugger fancies building him a barn to hold all his hay! Where do these beef-witted people come from, I ask you, who go at things so bald-headed?" He drew up a knee, to strike a match against the seat of his pants; he lighted a cigar. "And the little piffly wife makes the children shake my hand and say thank you."

This same outfit had told the whole smoker yesterday, "Them mugwumps are not strictly by nature what you would call ... men," and it looked to Hugh like the college boy made a note of it.

Hugh had been taking it all in for a month: McKinley's gold standard, which most city men on the train favored—"I'm a gold bug, myself"—and Bryan's movement to free silver, which most westerners and all farmers on the train favored, as did almost every man in Goshen and Whatcom back home. Coining silver sounded right to Hugh, too. Westerners proposed it to ease the poor, they said, and eastern bankers reviled it. Hugh took in the train's other sensational topic, this summer's Chicago Fair. There a man could see tall buildings of twenty and more stories—supported by steel frames and served by hydraulic elevators—and there all the up-and-coming women in the world apparently hoped to make each other's acquaintance. Hugh heard it on every line of track to Chicago and from it, and even from the immigrants:

"I promise to take you, honey, sweetheart mine own, and no mistake—when I make my killing, when I strike it rich, when I hit pay dirt, make a winning, have the dooteoomus, and can roll, highball, boil, fly ..."

The prosperous Norwegians on the train played panguingue, starting after dinner. Hugh hoped someone would start a game of cooncan, so he could learn what it was. On the coach he rode east, two ranchers from Arizona played cooncan clean to Chicago. One of them won from the other two thousand oranges, five gallons of wine, seventeen buckskins, and two hundred heifers, and they wrote it down. He had missed this famous event, night after night, by sitting back with a book after he settled his little brothers down. Hugh knew to watch out for the "pink cuffs"—the cardsharks that rode the rails and fleeced sheep at three-card monte. They all wore pink shirts, he had heard—so perhaps they were not strictly needle sharp, after all.

That night, while the steam pipes clanked in the smoker and the salesman with the eye patch rubbed a hole in the grimy window to see the stars, Hugh fell to talking with the red-eyed college boy. His name was Arthur Flockheart; he was a hopeful, pompous, dreaming youth from Cleveland, bound to Portland to visit his grandmother. A barber had indeed nicked his ear; while he and Hugh talked, he scratched off the sticking plaster, and the nick bled a bit. He wore a reasonably white shirt and collar, a blue neckerchief knotted at the ends, and a jacket too short for his wrists. He crossed and uncrossed his long legs, and banged his knees together.

Hugh listened to him soberly for an hour before he spoke to ask, "Do you happen to know about a game called cooncan?" Arthur did not. He owned he enjoyed a game of pinochle with his Phi Gamma Delta brothers. And his saintly grandmother, who was said to be failing now, had taught him to play three-card monte for two bits, which was first-rate fun for a little boy, but it palled. How do you play? With a monte deck.

Two hours later, Hugh's luck had started to sour, and his column of silver winnings was down to a line of three coins, when Tommy Cahoon passed into the smoker with a yellow telegraph envelope in his hand. Tommy Cahoon stopped at the table by Hugh. Hugh Honer? He passed the envelope across the table, with a respectful nod, and moved on. Hugh could see the pink streak below the conductor's cap all around the back of his head.

"Excuse me," he said to Arthur, who was looking soulful. He rose and made his way forward to the space by the door. Could something have happened to Vinnie? Would her father, Glee, think to notify him? They would not know where he was. Could Kulshan Jim have telegraphed—did the barn burn up with the stock? He slit the yellow envelope carefully with his pocketknife. Inside he found no telegram but only a small white card. It bore the engraved seal of the Union Pacific Railroad and read, in engraved type: "Beware. You are in the hands of a professional gambler."

CHAPTER L

That night, alone, crossing the bunchgrass wastes of Idaho, June pulled from her bag a framed pen-and-ink portrait of Clare as a young boy. He had posed standing outside by a chair in a short suit, with his shoes touching; he held his hat cradled on a bent arm. Someone, presumably Ada, had slicked his thick hair down. He was seven or eight years old, unconscious and hopeful, with an infant's undamaged mouth, a pleased sense of his own preciousness, and deeply shadowed eyes. What a fine man he would become, this vague, blunt boy! The artist had moved his quill pen fluently; the line of rust-colored ink split in two where his strokes came down fast. The moment was past; the paper had browned, the boy had vanished, and the artist, too. June knew that chair, though; it was in Ada's room now.

June had been unnerved and vexed all week, all month. She had left home for Baltimore in a swivet. Had Mabel by now witnessed Obenchain's shooting Clare? She ought not to have left. Her father would never have known or missed her, departed as he was. If Obenchain took after Clare, Mabel and old Ada would have no one to run to except Street St. Mary, whose drunkenness, like any white man's drunkenness, Clare and the men found comic, and June and the women found tragic.

Her father had looked radiant in his casket, Marsha Washington told her; twenty or thirty years had fled from his face, and his hands, crossed over his suit, looked "ready to pick up the reins of a horse." Why the semblance of life comforted people, June could not fathom. She could not bear to imagine lifeless Clare looking as if he might at any moment open his eyes and speak to her. She could not bear to imagine Clare laid out in a long, thin coffin on the dining room table, which she would have to move into the parlor: Clare stiff as a railroad tie, his crinkled eyes closed with coins, his jaw slack, his boisterous bones stilled in a blue suit. Yet this was precisely how she imagined him.

Now she searched the few ink lines of the portrait's head for a sign of the man her Clare would become. She found instead a familiar phrenological structure—the narrow skull, high ears, and flat forehead—and an unfamiliar uncertainty in the expression, as if the boy were himself looking for the man. It was June who was searching, and imagining the vagueness, so the boy looked lost. He seemed, wonderfully, to need her comfort for his half-bright, unfeeling troubles, and to need her knowledge of him to bring him forth.

Minta once suggested to her that nothing moves a woman so deeply as the boyhood of the man she loves. June had heard Clare's stories, ordinary as they were, striking as they seemed. She imagined the boy Clare in all his nascent nobility and susceptibility, wholly unknowing—as the artist dipped his pen before the old log house by the bay—that this moment would catch not him, but her, as long as she lasted. She wanted him boy and man, both ways. In the early days of their marriage she had learned the scars on his knees and hands: "I jumped from the roof," he said, "I jumped from the wharf," and it was so like him still, this boyish man, to fling himself about—but reckless as well. "You might have been killed," she had said, "and then where would we be?" Were those knobbed manly knees, with their coiled circles of dark hair, once shapeless boy knees? How careless the boy looked, and how ignorant of all this man knew.

Not that he knew much. She had watched him apparently devolve in wisdom. Clare was ashamed, still, to catch a cold, and asked her not to tell anyone, and barked at her if she mentioned it, as if having a cold, or a sprained wrist, or a bad tooth, demeaned him in his own eyes or the eyes of men. High of pocket, narrow of hip, he shambled; his long neck forward, his eyes snapping, he came pelting. He believed in himself unshakably; he boasted and abounded; his hopes vaunted, his innocence preened; he would outdo all the world. He had started out among Lummi families, lived a year in a stockade, took part in the struggle, helped open up and develop both Whatcom and Goshen, and urged their fortunes' rise. The Bellingham Bay Improvement Company had altered him; the pride of the city had been puffing him with pomp, and he was piddling himself away. The slouch-hatted, long-geared man shingling a roof in Minta's clearing, the free spark who courted her on horseback, who sang "In the Sweet By and By" at bonfires on the river beach and threw knives like a Mexican, now rode a bicycle in a narrow suit in Whatcom. He had purchased a topper, and hoped to run for the state legislature. Before the Goshen Normal School closed, he sat on its board. When he won the county clerkship, he passed out cigars. June saw these honors as meaningless and thankless tasks no one wanted.

In Oregon, the train crossed a long lava desert northwards, following the old Oregon wagon road. Nothing grew. Her mother-in-law had labored through here forty years ago. Ada had told June that when her wagon train reached The Dalles—where the upper Columbia shot down the ledges of Celilo Falls in the hellish desert, and every Indian person in the region was having a party—right then, a woman in their train from New Jersey lost her senses, cracked her baby's head with a stone, set fire to her wagon, and turned around walking east and was lost, until an Indian man brought her back tied on his horse. Now the Union Pacific barreled along the Columbia River, and entered the mazy Cascade Range.

They highballed down the green Pacific slope, through snowsheds, and their air brakes hissed. Their locomotive paused before a trestle so unpromising that many passengers, including June and the Honers, chose to walk, in the rain. Conducted by Mr. Tommy Cahoon himself, they spent two hours crossing the wet ravine, where devil's club caught June's skirts, and Minta and Ardeth walked close and laughed over nothing. Cahoon told them that on some local freight lines the hemlock trestles were so soft that the engineer routinely set the throttle and jumped off with all the crew. The men raced down the ravines and up them, and jumped on the moving train.

They picked up the Northern Pacific in Portland, Oregon. In the terminal, on the benches, and in the crowds rushing under the vaulted ceiling, June saw men and women dressed in working clothes, and men and women dressed in rich, supple fabrics, whose faces had stiffened, whose jaws jutted, and whose eyes grimly marked their paths and nothing else. She had seen just such hard faces on the pavements of Baltimore and in Chicago on trains and in depots; living in Whatcom, she had forgotten both how poor people could be, and how rich. In Whatcom the poorest scrapers looked worried, not angered. Whether it was toiling for others that made these people grimace, or greed, or indifference to strangers, or envy, she did not know. She would know soon, when they moved.

It was spring in Portland; the city spread to its hills and bloomed. It would be convenient, when they lived here, to have the main lines meet in town. The cold, soft air smelled like home—wood smoke, rain, fog, and bark. They boarded; the rhythm of wheels pounding rails resumed. The express crossed the Columbia River at a swoop and bore into Washington. There was Mount Adams's white cone rising from the forest; its peak poked into clouds.

Now June often brought out Clare's boyhood portrait when she was alone. She borrowed glue to mend the parted frame. When had she seen this fir forest without his towering beside her like one of the trees? After their wedding Clare and she had crossed on the Northern Pacific to Seattle—for the railroad had relented, and awarded Seattle a spur—and Clare bore her to the new house in Whatcom in a hired buggy. He set the pony at a fast trot. The buggy pitched into potholes and gravel flew. She had carried with her from Baltimore a canary in a brass cage, and the faster the buggy rattled, the more grandly the canary sang.

One morning, when she was a new bride, she despaired of a bread dough that failed; she buried it by the back door, lest Ada see. The day warmed, and the dough rose in the ground and emerged through the soil, to the wonderment of all eyes. She had learned the work, though, and could surpass at many skills the women born to them. In a cold spell she mixed her dough after dinner and took the sponge to bed with her; in the morning it was risen and light. She drew the line at the cow. Clare could not feature life without a cow. His parents had walked cows from Illinois, and got two of them to Washington Territory, and one lived. The economy jumped around so, everybody in town kept a cow, even the mayor; still, June had never entered the cowshed.

In the three months since Obenchain's threat, June thought, Clare was assuming again the stature he formerly held in her eyes. No longer the pleased, blithely unconscious boy he was during their early marriage, and no longer the piddling, unconscious, institutional man she feared he was becoming, he had wakened and hardened. He was losing his sense of his own invulnerable charm, of his own limitless spirit, boundless resources, and unique reality. He was losing, curiously, his self, and seemingly finding the world a wider place without it. She found him leaning to look at her as he had during their first courtship, when they were strange to each other. He spoke of John Ireland as if their friendship were no longer a kind of truce, as if his friend were no longer a rival for his own self-esteem, but as if he prized the pained breadth of John Ireland's thought, and his reserve, and his forced honor, for the first time. He had slowed and straightened; he thought about what people said, and developed a deliberate, attentive courtesy, like a doctor's, as if the other people were themselves all stricken and sliding into their graves, and not Clare.

Alas, he was even less likely now to yield to her simple uxorious request that he shoot Obenchain first—unless, that is, from missing her, or more likely from enjoying the absence of her constant pressure to do so, he had just recently found it in himself to kill the man and blind his trail. It had been ten days since Clare telegraphed her in Baltimore that he, Mabel, and Ada were well in her absence—they were sailing through it right smartly, he said. If he had survived the interval, Clare would be apt to think Obenchain less dangerous than before. She herself would judge Obenchain even more fitful than she feared.

She would remove Clare bodily to Portland, Oregon, and start again.

She had never cared for him more. Her ribs arched out to find him; her insides felt loose and raw as if they had been peeled. She would hold his bony shoulders soon. At the thought, the skin on her face heated in a rush of blood. She looked around. Before the curving rails, between the black trees, spread the lighted waters of Puget Sound.

CHAPTER LI

Seattle

That day, a Thursday in March, Clare Fishburn walked through the booming Seattle waterfront to meet his wife's train, and to accompany her and Minta, with the children, home on the steamer to Whatcom. It was pandemonium on the Seattle hills—like Whatcom, but more so. Shipping blackened the harbor; the saws in the shipyards shrieked, and boys hauled sawdust off in wheelbarrows to fill gulch lots. The fire of '89 had burned the business district, twenty-five blocks of it; immigrant workers piled in to rebuild the city in brick. People kept coming. Europe was stirring, America was stirring, and the people on the continents stirred like things on a swirled tray. This was the last stop, the last place in America. The past two hard winters on the high plains crushed the Scandinavian farmers and broke the cattle ranchers. If a man was moving, he was moving west. When he hit California, he found crowds and murderous prices; he rolled north by steamer or rail to wilder and better lands, to the Puget Sound country where winters were mild, where berries dropped into bowls, salmon jumped into frying pans, and a man could still make something of himself. Now tens of thousands of strangers thronged the mud streets and real estate offices.

To honor old times, Clare stopped in Mother Damnable's former southern-style two-story bordello, where his brother Glee had courted Grace with sweet talk. Grace recently complained to Clare that his brother had not said a word since: "Are you certain your father wasn't a species of clam?" Clare slipped between glossy painted vans and rough lumber carts on Alaskan Way. A woman with blondined hair, wearing a Union officer's cap, offered to tell his fortune using colored clamshells: "Hey, Low

Pockets!" A sign advertised—rather frankly, Clare thought—"Bunco and Sure-Thing Games." Another sign, lighted in red and illustrated with a broadly winking eye, touted a dance hall's performers: "The Adamless Eden Company."

The Lone Joe Saloon now occupied the former bordello's ground floor. The building was already so old, in this new country growing so fast, that Clare had to descend several steps from the street to duck through its door. Behind the crowded bar, above the mirror, he saw a professionally painted sign ten feet long and three feet high. It bore the genial motto "SKIN 'EM!"

These were stirring times, a gentleman in a felt top hat told Clare at the bar. The very frogs in the ponds sang in a chorus, "Struck it! Struck it!" He was drinking a dry martini, just as the swells did back in What-com, who met at the Birdswell Hotel.

"… We strictly screwed them," Clare heard a Southerner say. Stand-ing three rows back at the bar, he ordered a whiskey. A freckled young Englishman at his elbow tilted back his hat and shined up at him—Was he interested in any of several gratifying prospects? Would he like to acquire the titles to Lake Washington property, corner office lots, or tim-bered acreage?

The Englishman drew a map from his jacket, which stung the men on the stools to life; they made room, and he unfolded the map on the bar. On the map Clare could see blocks of streets, named in tiny script, extending out into Smith Cove and Elliott Bay. He downed his whiskey and drew away, slapping through the lake of tobacco juice that slicked the floor. A stout gentleman caught his arm, and gestured towards the crowd bent over the map.

"They want to get rich quick—" the top-hatted man confided "—without stroking a lick of work. There's a kind of evil in it, don't you agree? Are you a stranger? You must make your moves carefully." He spoke in a low, kindly voice which Clare heard easily under the high shouts of the others. The man kept his hand on Clare's sleeve.

"There is a moral approach; there's a moral approach to everything. Start slowly, lay something aside, investigate every proposition thorough-ly, and spread your risks. Live soberly, provide for your family, and do without. Put yourself in firm prospects, and enlarge your principal bit by bit. That is what life's all about."

Oh, is that what it's all about? Clare thought. He had been wondering. "That is the only way—" the top hat nodded to Clare emphatically "—to make your pile and keep it." Clare fled.

On the street he breathed again. It was drizzling, and blue and white clouds moved overhead. Below him at an intersection, a buggy and horse were stuck off the road in the mud, attracting a swarm of experts. Clare proceeded down to the depot. His long neck protruded from his collar; his graceful gait was quick, and several women with smutted-up eyes turned to look at him.

Clare drew most of his convictions from the common pot, and distrusted dissenters. Since his wife possessed the same mental habits, he never noticed them in her. What Obenchain rightly considered the chief force in most minds, including theirs—the restless urge to discover the newest opinions as fast as consensus formed them—both were insensible of, as of the blood streaming in their veins. Everyone, however, possesses original conviction, honor, and perception to some degree. His wife did. Clare had not noticed. He had become aware only recently, for example, of June's unsearchable depth.

As June had adjusted to a new life based on Obenchain's threat—sometimes, she had told him brightly, turning her round head, she caught herself wondering who would come to his funeral—as January, February, and March passed day by day and Clare survived, she still wanted to move. She had some backbone. She was evidently willing to give up the town she knew, where she had come of age, and her sister's proximity, and all her friends and their stable life, in order to struggle and scratch somewhere as a stranger, with him. She surprised him. Clare did not want to move, and they quarreled about it. Whatcom is better than Portland, he said; he chose to live and die there. Obenchain could find him in Portland or anywhere else. He knew that June saw only a new fatalism in his decision, and he wondered if she missed his old carelessness.

He had thought about these things, shakily, before her trip east and during it. In the light and changing rains he rode his bicycle to the company's office along the same streets he always used: Obenchain was not likely to gun him down in the streets in front of the neighbors, like a desperado. June had always seen things in him no one else ever saw. Of course she loved him—why was he surprised?

He saw she acted from an unmentioned source of feeling, a source that, he discovered, he tapped as well. It had been there all along. He asked himself if she was conscious of it and understood at once that she was, that she probably had been since Mabel's birth, when their courting talk had hushed and let go, loosing them to drift into the great silence. She had been waiting for him to notice it, and she forgave his doltishness in advance. Wherever he found himself, in whatever deep caves and vaulted mazes of understanding, he discovered her already there before him, her arched eyes glinting with amused sensibility, her lively, small form seeming to beckon him onward. She mocked him, guided him, understood him, and tantalized him, at every level of depth he reached. What else did she know that he did not?

Along Seattle's Commercial Street, men stood smoking under dripping awnings. Women held their dark skirts out of the mud. Two teams of black mules hauled a covered wagon from the docks. Where crowds blocked the raised sidewalks, Clare moved down into the planked street.

Marriage began to strike him as a theater, where actors gratefully dissimulate, in ordinary affection and trust, their bottom feeling, which is a mystery too powerful to be endured. They know and feel more than life in time can match; they must anchor themselves against eternity, so they play on a painted set, lest they swing out into the twining realms. He was acquiring a taste for those realms, for the cold strata of colors he saw from the beach, for the crack of thin darkness that spread behind the thick sky.

Again and again he discovered at his side, working in his own parlor and kitchen, the quick and glowing creature he first courted eight years ago in Goshen. Clare had recently arrived at this notion, then, that the ideal alone is real, and contempt is misunderstanding, and indifference is mental failure.

Clare knew that common wisdom counseled that love was a malady that blinded lovers' eyes like acid. Love's skewed sight made hard features appear harmonious, and sinners appear saints, and cowards appear heroes. Clare was by no means an original thinker, but on this one point he had reached an opposing view, that lovers alone see what is real. The fear and envy and pride that stain souls are phantoms. The lover does not fancy that the beloved possesses imaginary virtues. He knew June was not especially generous, not especially noble in deportment, not especially tolerant, patient, or self-abasing. The lover is simply enabled to see—as if the heavens busted open to admit a charged light—those virtues the beloved does possess in their purest form. June was a marvel, and she smelled good.

These weeks' long absence of June, he was not unaware, abetted this view.

What could other people know of June's courage in loss, her upwelling hopefulness, her defiant will, her quick, startling wit that made play of even ardent moments? The skin of her temple, that dipped across the hollow, and the soft ruddiness over her hard forehead bone?

Their intimacy seemed a mingling of spiritual limbs. He had rediscovered what he learned in the early days of their marriage and forgot, the life about which even the books he read were strangely silent, but which could not be new: the passion that is both possible and inexpressible, the prolongation of intimacy as a peculiar state, the touch of living skin everywhere, as if the very air and the colored world were a lover's features that bodied a soul. This seemed to him now, as he walked the gray streets, the truest state, the highest apprehension, and he strictly hoped to keep sight of it, scorn comfort, and stay awake.

Courting June, he had thought it a privilege to wash dishes with her in river sand; he thought it a privilege to hold her cutaway coat, to look at airy Mount Baker from her side; he thought it a privilege to hear her opinions over tea and watch her eyebrows rise and fall. Now, he knew it was.

He saw gulls over a department store, inflamed by the falling light. Towers were rising on every lot, four stories, five stories, six stories, of brick and stone. Seattle hackney drivers tapped up their horses and converged with him on the Northern Pacific depot; their harness bells jingled, and their wheels knocked planks. Boys in knickers wore sandwich boards to advertise restaurants and hotels. Clare imagined June's tilted brown head, her unfathomable silences. How had they found the courage to marry, when they had known nothing? Clare felt a bottomlessness in himself: he felt a bottomlessness in his attachment to June that made him teeter, and he felt a parcel of infinity between them, over which their days floated like chips.

His niece Ardeth was first to step from the train, wearing a flat straw hat forward on her head, and blind behind the five or six hatboxes she bore in a pile. Hugh, thin and sober, handed bags down to Howard. Green paused in the door and threw a folded-paper bird, which he had possibly been waiting to do for three thousand miles. Minta emerged, adjusted her plumed hat on the step, raised her heavy jaw, and blinked. Here was small June, flushed and flustered, wearing a wrinkled duster. Her eyes found Clare's at once, and their glances' touch unstrung both. They made a blind path through the crowd to each other, and Clare took her in his arms.

CHAPTER LII

Whatcom

A week later, Johnny Lee walked through the elevated streets of What-com to the high school; he bore a telegram for John Ireland Sharp. He wore a black cloth cap, a buttoned vest from which his thick shoulders bulged, and a white collarless shirt. He had rolled up his shirtsleeves to feel the air on his skin. It was drizzling, but not much. The men working on a new office building on Conley Street were in shirtsleeves, too. One of the last things Johnny Lee's brother said to him concerned this build-ing: it was going to cost thirteen thousand dollars to build, and already the owners had rented its spaces to the tune of ten thousand dollars a year. Was that not a marvel? His brother's triangular face had creased with pleasure as he spoke—Lee Chin appreciated good fortune, and loved to enumerate the signs that luck was hovering near him.

Now Johnny Lee turned his head as he passed to watch the builders scramble, and the cords in his neck stood out beside his lustrous queue. Only the back of his neck, crossed by thin, deep wrinkles, looked like that of a fifty-five-year-old man. His smooth face and hands, his robust frame, and his sure swagger made him resemble other Whatcom men twenty years younger. He had learned long ago not to expect wisdom, or even restraint, from men who looked to him like grandfathers.

He could see, in the distance below him, the old wharf where, two years before, a fisherman had found his younger brother's body. Someone had lashed Lee Chin to a piling below tideline. Part of the brothers' labor contract guaranteed that the broker in Canton would return their remains, if any, to China. Johnny Lee had untied Lee Chin—at whose lips crabs had been feeding, revealing his small, short teeth, and under whose black tunic crabs had been feeding also. He turned the wet body over to the widow, An Ho, for packaging, telegraphed their benevolent associa-tion in Sacramento, and shipped the remains out on the steamer that noon, on the day of the water fight.

Since Lee Chin's death, no man in Whatcom knew who Johnny Lee was and what he could do. He was faster with a hand drill than most men were with steam drills, and he could work suspended over a 2,200-foot drop. Some other Chinese men practiced meekness; he had given it up.

Johnny Lee had been born Lee Chow, in the village of Sun Tak, out-side Canton. In 1860, he and lighthearted Lee Chin, when they were twenty-two and twenty, immigrated to Sacramento, with eight friends from their starving district. An immigration official renamed him John Lee. An Irish rail crew boss in the Sierras renamed him Johnny Grant, for the boss liked him, and hated General Lee, who had led the army that killed his friends on the banks of the Chickahominy. In 1872, when the Crédit Mobilier scandal discredited Grant's Republican administration, a Central Pacific engineer named him Johnny Lee again. The men in his gang called him Lee Chow; his carefree brother called him *dai go*, "older brother," except when they were alone, when he called him *go go*, which meant the same thing, but sounded friendlier. His new wife called him Johnny. His employer, Mrs. Pearl Sharp, called him Johnny, and Mr. John Ireland Sharp called him Mr. Lee. His young son and heir called him Papa, an appellation he had thought he would never hear in any tongue. "Papa" was the only intelligible word the child could say at all, except "cat."

He was a basketman and a headman, out of work. All basketmen were out of work, wherever they were, because they had built the railroads until they were done; still, wherever his own twenty men were, and wherever were the crews they had worked with and lived with in the Sierra, he knew they called themselves basketmen, for that is what they had made of themselves. They volunteered. When dynamited rock cut the cords, blowing a man down into the valley with his basket, another five men volunteered. They were still young then. Lee Chin with his loose smile and short teeth, his triangular face—Lee Chin was ever imagining improbable dynamiting schemes to save labor. He made friends easily, never seemed to sleep, and shrugged off losses. Johnny Lee, slender then and stiff-necked, solemnly held and divided his crew's gold-coin wages; he enjoyed the respect of his men, who trusted him to keep them alive. He raced his crew against other crews, interpreted simple English into Can-tonese dialect and vice versa, rose quickly to defend his men in fan-tan disputes with his powerful arms and legs, and held himself apart.

It was stimulating work. They cut a roadbed for the Central Pacific in a smooth granite spur that rose straight up from the American River, in the Sierra east of Sacramento. They cut a curved, ascending roadbed in the monolith that everyone called Cape Horn. It was impossible, and they did it—five thousand men, six hundred teams of horse and oxen. Two years later, Johnny Lee and his brother Lee Chin rode a scheduled coach north over the line. At Cape Horn the engineer stopped the train; all the passengers got out to peer vertiginously at the thready river 2,200 feet below. The conductor sailed into a speech on the spot, and praised the boldness of the engineers and the courage and skill of the coolies. Some Sacramento passengers in their own car had applauded Johnny Lee and his brother, and pounded them so on their backs that both thought, they told each other later, they might belatedly fall down the cliff then and there.

Johnny Lee used to lower Lee Chin over the rock face in a woven basket; alternately, Lee Chin, laughing, lowered him. With hand drills they bored into the granite. They crimped fuse, tamped black gunpowder around it in the bore, cut the fuse, lit it with a match, jerked the rope, and, to be on the safe side, ran up the rope while it rose.

Some of the Irish bosses called them powder monkeys. They called themselves basketmen. He and his crew from Sun Tak possessed skills so refined that they played at cutting fuses of different lengths and lighting them serially, so all the charges went off in one good-luck blast. Coming across the mountainside to their tents, they found pieces of granite weighing two hundred pounds that had blown a mile sideways. Black smoke covered them; they bathed, and changed their clothes for supper. Johnny Lee, as elected headman, had cleared thirty dollars a month. He sent half home to their father, who was subsisting on grass roots and grubs when they left. Lee Chin freely spent his pay in Sacramento—"Yee Fou," they called it—impressing the merchant father of lovely An Ho, then nine, who he hoped would bring wealth to the match. Johnny Lee had disapproved of An Ho, for she was born here in Gold Mountain, and spent too much money.

Now the inbound steamer was laying a streak on the water of Bellingham Bay below, and dark crowds hung at the rails. From bare hill to hill across Whatcom, the mills sounded their whistles, like birds calling and answering. Dynamite exploded dully in the distance, where today men were blasting stumps on slopes other men would sell as business lots tomorrow. Here in front of the livery stable, two hackney drivers finished harnessing teams to polished victorias. They gave the teams smart cuts with the whip and set out high-stepping to meet the steamer. Johnny Lee approved his townsmen's effort to impress visitors. He figured to enjoy wealth as much as the next man. He wondered, however, if even the greenest immigrant would fall for the red locomotive, which was just now emerging from its northern roundhouse. The red locomotive had no other purpose than to perform antics for the steamer passengers: it ran back and forth busily over just two miles of track, and blew its whistle and raised a white plume of steam. Could not any man see it speeding into its own steam trail after it turned?

After they rounded Cape Horn, Lee Chin merrily married An Ho, who, grown, retained her melancholy, narrow face and fragile carriage. She preferred to speak only English, which became the language of the household. The brothers joined her in their shared Sacramento room every winter. Every February before New Year's Day, they took down the paper kitchen god that hung above the stove. They spread sugarcane syrup on his lips, burned him up with a match, and watched his smoke rise up to the Jade Emperor, to whom the god would speak of their household in sweet terms.

Every spring in those years Johnny Lee, Lee Chin, and his same gang of village men worked clearing right-of-way. They falled trees and blasted stumps with nitroglycerin, and here for the first time they lost a village man, and then three more—one to a short fuse, one to a falling tree, and two to stupid horses. Many seasons and deaths later, eight years ago, in '85, when they completed the Northern Pacific spur, they found themselves in Seattle at the dark of the year, out of work like everyone else. No one needed powdermen to blow stumps, or graders or fallers, let alone basketmen; nothing was building, nothing was stirring. A woman in a breadline swore filthy oaths at them. The brothers made their way to Whatcom to seek work in the lumber mills. Lee Chin was down-at-the-mouth then. He no longer invented money-making schemes, but hung his head, hungry and out of luck; Johnny Lee encouraged him forward.

Fresh from the boat, they located the Myers mill on Tulip Street, from the door of which a ragged man fired a carbine convincingly over their heads, and held it trained on them until they left. The two planned to return and settle his hash later, if they could establish themselves here at all. Within an hour, the shabbily dressed, neat-headed man who was John Ireland Sharp had hired them as houseboys directly off the street, and furnished them with a room. Lee Chin sent for An Ho. There were no children. The three set up their household in the Sharps' west bedroom, where they remained for five years. They all learned Pearl Sharp's untamed and exacting ways. They learned the hideouts of her disrespectful sons, and the crannies where she secreted plunder she brought back from stores. They obeyed, for the first two years until he lifted it, John Ireland Sharp's unexplained injunction that they never leave the house. Three years ago they moved to an attic corner in the new Birdswell Hotel.

After his brother's murder two years ago, Johnny Lee had married slender An Ho. Now, in his old age, he possessed a wife after his heart, whose feet, round as a cat's paws, he had noticed quietly for twenty-five years. No longer young, never outstandingly submissive, An Ho had slid to his bed with gales of laughter, deriving, he could only hope, from enthusiasm—and so it had proved. Johnny Lee was reborn. He began a program of disciplining his strength with exercises. Throughout each day's tasks his stirred imagination bent towards their fragrant attic room in the Birdswell Hotel. He divided his own small savings cautiously between two solid operations: a waterworks for the town of Goshen, and shares in the biggest branch bank in Whatcom. He lost interest in his gambling excursions to Seattle, where he had formerly enjoyed paying monthly homage to "His Excellency the grasping Cash Tiger." He took his bride to Vancouver instead, where she paid cash to seamstresses for satin dresses of bewildering complexity, which contained as much steel as trestles.

For her part, An Ho now had for her own husband the only man, in her trying life, she had ever loved. She had given birth to a son. They named the delightful boy Walter. One morning last month Walter took off walking across the bed, so his parents set him on the floor; until then, his feet had never touched the ground.

CHAPTER LIII

Whatcom High School was the first secondary school in Washington; it was six years old. It rose four stories tall, all white clapboard, and occupied most of a residential block on a hillside just south of the business district. People hated the sight of a tree, and even of a shrub that threatened to resemble a tree, so the high school, like its neighboring elaborate mansions, sat flat on its mud lot as if beached. A crew was grading a side street.

In a classroom, an arrogant fourth-year scholar sat down, having just heard from Professor Sharp what he already sullenly knew, that he had failed miserably at his recitation. It was Vinnie Fishburn's turn, and she rose from her shared seat and turned. John Ireland Sharp, standing in the back of his classroom, relaxed. Vinnie Fishburn did everything brilliantly, and he need not struggle to frame any suggestions for improvement. He wondered where she found the time to learn her lines. She had doubtless worked eight hours at the counter in her mother's store yesterday, and doubtless minded her brothers and sisters at the same time—John Ireland knew that much about her life. He knew that her father, Glee Fishburn, fished and was doing poorly. He did not know that Vinnie also worked entering and straightening the store's accounts until midnight, while her mother, beside her at the kitchen table, ordered from the wholesaler and paid bills; he did not know that only in the small hours did Vinnie Fishburn then turn with passion to her own schoolwork.

Vinnie lit into Portia's speech—"The quality of mercy is not &c." Her black bangs framed her earnest, glowing face. She held herself quietly, with apparently splendid control; the brown folds of her skirt were motionless, and her coarse white sleeves were still at her sides. Only the life in her pronounced features, dark and fine against her white and freckled skin, and the natural motions of her head expressed her prodigious energy and vigor. She addressed the people in the room, in Shakespeare's jammed diction, as if these were her own thoughts, which she was compelling into words for the first time.

It was a convincing performance. John Ireland knew her intelligence. Two years ago, Vinnie Fishburn entered his second-year Latin class, having skipped over the first year; she had "boned up on it," she said, over the summer. After the first week, he moved her into the third-year class—this fresh-faced young girl in a patched blouse—for she seemed already and uncannily to know the Latin language, and to need only the faintest reminders. In complexity and power, as well as in grammatical perfection and fluidity, her compositions (on temperance, on idleness, and on railroad freight charges) resembled Cicero's orations. He knew that he should tutor her privately, but he had never yet proposed it. Two years ago John Ireland had judged that this Vinnie Fishburn, fisherman Glee Fishburn's pretty black-haired daughter, had the finest mind in Whatcom. Nothing had changed his view. He stood limp under the classroom flag, with his hands clasped neatly behind his back. Vinnie was still speaking in her clear, thoughtful voice, but he was not listening. More than once he had left this classroom in her charge. Today he was tempted to leave this entire high school in her charge.

When the bell sounded, Vinnie finished. John Ireland dismissed the class of forty pupils and adjourned to his office. Things were out of hand this spring, and John Ireland lived in a cloud of resignation that never lifted. He shrank in his gabardine suit, and his finely cut head hung down. He removed his jacket and sat at his opened desk. He was sensible of his passive nature, and this was just as well, for he was powerless in any case to do his job. He saw his job, perhaps quaintly, as educating the young, and preparing them for college. His superiors, as was their greater right, saw it as enhancing the superficial reputation of the town, and providing canny young businessmen for canny old businessmen to employ. Enrollment in September had been fifty pupils. Now, in March, enrollment was one hundred and twenty! Where were these people coming from, who were rich enough to send their children to high school? Their children stepped right off the train wearing shoes.

The school could educate almost any number of pupils, if it had teachers. Space did not matter: when he presided over the lower school, John Ireland had commonly heard pupils' recitations at home in his parlor. Here he headed a staff of four: himself as principal and professor of Latin and literature; Ascher Dan as assistant principal and professor of science, mathematics, and manual training; and the two girls who taught physical geography, literature, and ancient and European history. He needed a German teacher; the city bought automatic-closing school desks. He needed a rhetoric and English teacher; the city superintendent proposed a big gymnasium. He needed a biology teacher; town council presented him with a fir flagpole and a silk American flag. He remembered how grateful he was, as he assumed his first post as principal of the elementary school, when town council donated to the school a large fir log, for fuel, which happened to be lying across High Street a quarter of a mile away.

At issue this morning was textbooks. Pupils supplied their own books, and none of the necessary books was available in the state. John Ireland began another doomed letter to his superintendent. He stopped his pen because this concern paralyzingly raised all the others. The library possessed fewer than one hundred volumes, of which fifty were copies of the Congressional Record. Almost every high school in the country offered, if no other language, at least German. His school offered no courses of instruction in any living language. A week ago, John Ireland had only sighed over his dinner when their guest Ada Tawes told him that in its earliest history, Whatcom County had elected and paid a school superintendent for three years before it had a single school.

He and Clare Fishburn—and, this year, he and Clare's replacement, Ascher Dan—planned to make theirs a model curriculum, which would provide pupils a course of study comparable to the preparation John Ireland had undertaken with Miss Jean Zumwatt at Oberlin Academy. Now the schoolbells rang almost continuously to switch mobs of scrubbed youths to classrooms where he, like the other teachers, could only, as it were, wave books before their faces: Shakespeare ... Riley ... Cooper ... Barrie. At his desk John Ireland caught himself figuring, in the back of his mind, how he might best encourage more pupils to quit. Might they not rather go fishing? Join a gold rush somewhere? For the past five commencements in the decorated pavilion he listened to valedictory orations full of errors, and wondered if his best scholars suspected the extent to which they had been shortchanged.

A firm knock at his door heralded the surprising appearance of Johnny Lee. John Ireland stood to shake hands; the men were the same height. Johnny Lee was in vest and shirtsleeves—powerful, smiling, and smelling of the fresh rain outside.

"This just came for you," Johnny Lee said, and handed him the yellow envelope addressed to Lambert Street. He could not sit down, he said; he wanted to finish early. So saying, Johnny Lee left. The bell rang, and John Ireland glimpsed the back of his head, his hair pulled tightly in its queue, as he deftly threaded the crush in the hall.

The Morgan Bank in New York had sent the telegram. John Ireland struggled into his jacket walking to his next classroom, and read the telegram while the pupils took their seats. His mother had died, a month ago, in New York. That is, his foster mother, Martha Obenchain Belshaw, had died a month ago, and the terms of her estate specified John Ireland Sharp, of Whatcom, Washington, as sole legatee. He should contact the trustee at the bank.

His pupils were looking at him expectantly. John Ireland thought of his foster mother, her familiar ready laugh, her masses of pale curls nodding in and out of the light as she chattered, approving all she saw. For two years after college, John Ireland lived with her in New York, in a three-story Fifth Avenue apartment, while he undertook his first teaching position, at the tumultuous school on the Lower East Side.

Returning through town, Johnny Lee again passed the livery stable, in the alley of which he saw a knot of men holding a wagon's corner while one man removed a broken wheel. Before him, Beal Obenchain stood in the street's mud, his arms tense; he was facing the water, his neck bulging over his shirt, his expression obscured by his hat. He shook out a handkerchief and wiped his nostrils. Just as he passed, Johnny Lee noticed Obenchain's handkerchief. He had its match: a small white square edged in blue embroidery. Johnny Lee walked on, agitated and thoughtful.

CHAPTER LIV

Throughout the rest of the day John Ireland Sharp recalled his foster mother, as he hurried between classes, paused, or leaned over his wastebasket to eat his sandwich. He saw deep-bosomed Martha Obenchain peeling potatoes in the dooryard above the beach, and rising to greet a visiting fisherman with simple grace. She ran her hands over the worn shoulders of Axel Obenchain's shirt; she hung on his least remark, and repeated his rare jests to all comers. She and young Nan carded greasy wool by the fire, talking or singing; the fire backlighted their fair heads, which glowed at the edges like clouds. They spun the wool into yarn on the back porch, where they kept the wheel after John Ireland left home.

For five years John Ireland returned to the Northwest from Ohio each summer. He came home to his foster family on Madrone Island for a few weeks to help Axel make hay. Miss Arvilla Pulver was gone from Madrone; she married a customs officer in Port Townsend. Beal had left the island for the mainland in a rowboat, and never returned or wrote. Nan grew up yet more lovely than her mother, possessing those striking warm features and enormous, misty eyes, but lacking Martha's vitality and free chatter, so that the gazes of both men and women were drawn to Martha even as she aged and Nan bloomed. Nan was serene, superstitious, competent, and content: "I can see the sunrise and the sunset from my door in any season—what more could anyone want?" Each of those summers, after he got the hay in the barn, John Ireland made his way to the Olympic peninsula. There he joined the sealing fleet out of Neah Bay, where, as part of a Quileute Indian crew on a schooner, he harpooned Pacific seals from a dugout canoe forty miles offshore, and salted their skins in barrels.

On his last trip to the island as a son of the family, he found his foster father dying. Axel's faded red hair spread around his head on a pillow. His beard tangled on his white chest, and his watery eyes roved. Martha and Nan had purchased four glass windows and installed them low by the bed so that Axel, recovering from a stroke, could keep an eye on the water and the beach. Several times a day he gestured vaguely, with his powerful, golden-haired right arm, towards the water, where John Ireland would see, and subsequently fetch if he could, a floating fir log, or a milled plank of Port Orford cedar on which cormorants were riding, or a blue blown-glass fishing float from Japan. Nan concocted dubious sandy teas of boiled flowers, which her father did not drink. Martha passed the nights fearfully in a chair at her husband's side. She held his hand, and would not let Nan or John Ireland relieve her. It was June, and nights were dark for only a few hours.

One morning Axel seemed worse; he questioned Martha unintelligibly, over and over, apparently frantic and pleading, in words that at last John Ireland realized must be Finnish. There was no one to send for who might interpret, eager as John Ireland was to quit the house on some mission. Later that day Axel improved and asked in English for each of them in turn. The streaked sky over the water outside poured changing colors over his red features. He named Martha, and laid a bearish hand on her skirt at the knee; he named Nan, and touched the bright hair on her bowed head; and he named John Ireland, and grasped for a second John Ireland's wrist before his hand fell. He said nothing more, and evidently saw nothing more in this world, for his opened eyes seemed to follow some stately inward scene, and he died early the next morning.

The next winter, during his last year at Oberlin College, John Ireland received an engraved invitation to Martha Obenchain's marriage, on Madrone Island—"Saltwater Farm"—to one Gilbert P. Belshaw, of New York City. The accompanying letter, in Martha's childishly careful hand, said the wedding reception was to be held in their barn—the small log barn into which the previous summer John Ireland and Nan had loaded baled hay, and into which years before he had peered, as if studiously, to watch Beal strangle a calf.

* * *

John Ireland knew the new husband, Gilbert Belshaw, by reputation as a partner in the beloved Tacoma Steamship Company, whose early stern-wheelers shook and sunk in rough seas, but whose improved side-wheelers stepped through any seas and made business and travel possible for the whole region. John Ireland saved his board money to send the pair a brass candleholder and a green Chinese bowl from Cleveland.

He next saw his foster mother in New York, in her dark, sumptuous apartment hung with Moorish tapestries, swagged brocades, and big paintings of Napoleon's horseback battles. He was then so young he expected circumstances to change people. During the next two years, while he lived there, he never fully recovered from his surprise that Martha Belshaw was exactly the woman she had been on Madrone Island when she had tied an opened tomato can around her waist for a bustle. She wore high-necked silk dresses and chatelaines hung with gold chains and charms; she traveled in a polished phaeton behind a matched black team with braided tails; she cleaned with a toothbrush either of two diamond tiaras to wear to the Mystic Rose dinners of Ward McAllister, whose ballroom, holding just four hundred guests, was said to determine the size of society. Nothing of substance, however, had altered in her. Gay as a pioneer at a picnic, carelessly beautiful in a shimmering dress of red charmeuse, Martha had interrupted the butler to greet John Ireland with the ceremonies only of boundless maternal feeling. She installed him in a room beside theirs, and cooked with her own hands in the kitchen the first of many relaxed dinners that the three ate by a heavily curtained window above Central Park.

She hung on Gilbert Belshaw's every word, and repeated his remarks gleefully to the butler and to guests. She cultivated roses under incandescent lamps, and kept ugly dogs. At a time when ladies wore low-cut dresses to display a smooth, jeweled surface of what they called "throat," she wore dresses that swathed her to her noble chin. She entertained, with ribbon candies or whiskey, and bright streams of kind and innocent remarks, anyone who came calling at any time of day. Belshaw's associates, who formerly met at Sherry's or Delmonico's, took to dropping in, as did the Italian building superintendent, the lonely society women whose husbands were never home, and their bored children in long coats, who climbed the furniture, and no one minded.

Gilbert Belshaw accepted John Ireland into this household as if he were his own son—he had already four wildly varying grown sons—and asked him each day, as no one else on earth did, how he was finding his work. The vivid misery of John Ireland's pupils' lives seemed to quicken Gilbert Belshaw's interest, and he sometimes jotted down names. He was a bulky, blond man with the limber air of an athlete and the amused expression of adults who like children. His dark eyebrows met over his nose, as John Ireland's own eyebrows did. He wore brushed suits with the air of a dandy, and unaffectedly clasped his palms over his knees to inquire thoughtfully, of his least visitor and his greatest, how the world was going. He never discussed his own work, apparently because he viewed the stirring and rotating of money as a duty of no interest. So far as John Ireland could determine, Belshaw had pulled out of the Tacoma steamship company in '78, at the height of that decade's depression, transferred unscathed back to New York with Martha his second bride, and now performed acts upon his money directly, with quiet distaste. The couple moved in society only infrequently, and summered in the Adirondacks, in a moldy camp cottage, on eight hundred acres.

Everything about the two amazed young John Ireland Sharp, who had supposed—since he had seen the staked Skagit Indian, lost his family in a rowboat, obtained a rich man's education by harpooning seals from an Indian canoe, and taught in a city slum—that nothing life presented could amaze him. The single most astonishing fact was that Gilbert Belshaw, Martha's husband, whom she adored, shared no qualities with Axel Obenchain, her previous husband, whom she adored. The men were utterly unlike. His foster mother's sweet ease bewildered him, because he viewed her as someone who had shot for a wide mark—a man to replace Axel Obenchain—and missed completely, incomprehensibly, and gaily wed a man whom any child, any spaniel, could see resembled Axel Obenchain in no particular.

John Ireland lived as a cherished member of this family for two years. Every morning he took a horse-drawn bus to the slum street, overflowing with trash barrels and human filth, where he worked. There by gaslight he taught grammar and read poetry to the tubercular factory workers, dressmakers, pickpockets, and desperadoes that his supervisor called, with a straight face, schoolchildren. During his last term, two boys drew straight knives on him in the new lavatory. Later, to distract his memory of how fearfully he had fled, he thought of Saint Cassianus, whose pupils had stabbed him to death with pencils. At home, at the ball-fringed table by the curtained window, beside an urn filled richly with peacock feathers, he and Martha recalled almost daily some aspect of their life on Madrone Island, which Gilbert had visited only twice before their wedding.

They knew that Nan was living on the island still, presumably in their old house, presumably raising sheep, presumably watching the sun rise and set. She never answered her mother's loving, importuning letters, but sent her a card at Valentine's Day pasted with seeds shaped into geometrical, possibly magical, figures. The Valentine envelopes came addressed to Fifth Avenue in a different hand each year; it was conceivable that Nan had lost the skill of writing. She had attended school, haphazardly, for only three years. It was not conceivable that she had forgotten how to read; the islanders were avid readers, and Nan had read Fourier and the island's two spiritualist books over and over when she was a girl.

Of Beal, John Ireland said nothing, and neither did Martha, until one spring day, as the family took tea in Central Park, she looked down with apparent dread at her gauzy rose lawn dress and asked, in the lightest voice, as if this were the most ordinary of topics, "Have you heard anything about Beal?" John Ireland had not, nor, evidently, had she. Neither ever mentioned her son again. John Ireland saw a photograph of him, though, on her marble bureau: a little long-headed hatless boy looked challengingly at the camera, holding the neck of a sitting dog.

After he left New York for his Whatcom post, he wrote Martha and Gilbert Belshaw biweekly; they looped around the country in steamships, crossing the isthmus by train, to attend his wedding. The two helped substantially, if the truth be known, to finance construction of his Lambert Street house—built on his father's old unsold lots, which Tom Sharp had abandoned in the panic of '73. Having live children of his own inflamed John Ireland's filial feeling, always freely given if given at all, towards Martha Obenchain and her two husbands, which feeling he tried awkwardly to express in letters. About nine years ago he started returning to the island for three or four weeks every summer. He attended Nan Obenchain's island wedding, and the celebration at Lee and Eliza Shorey's afterwards. The Shoreys, he learned, and probably other islanders as well, mourned the memory of Martha Obenchain. They did not know Gilbert Belshaw, and so they concluded he was shallow, and that she had not married for love.

A year ago Martha's familiar envelope came edged in black. Gilbert Belshaw, having narrowly missed being electrocuted on Wall Street by a falling wire which killed his companion, succumbed to pneumonia follow-ing a sore throat. Martha would marry again, John Ireland thought, for he had learned this about her: she married people, with cheery aplomb. Her subsequent letters, however, showed her demoralized by grief for Gilbert Belshaw, weakened, despairing, and hopeless; now she had died. Standing alone in his office at the end of the school day, scratching searchingly under his vest, he found he hated the idea of a world without her.

CHAPTER LV

When Clare Fishburn left his office that March afternoon, having sold a Skagit delta parcel to a Swedish farmer, he swung by the high school, as he often did, to visit John Ireland in his office and accompany him part-way home.

The two men started uphill through the town. Clare walked bent beside his bicycle, so they could talk. He observed his friend, who seemed even more abstracted than usual, and whose dark, wide mouth spread downward.

Early that morning, Clare said, he had seen one of the high school's best teachers, winsome and fair Miss Myrtle Ordal, botanizing along the railroad tracks in the company of slim Lee McAleer, the city treasurer, who held a silk umbrella for both. The two were courting, in other words, which both men knew to be sorry news. If Myrtle Ordal married, she would have to resign the next day, and the school would lose her tireless efforts on behalf of students, with whom she enjoyed, they agreed, an instinctive rapport. John Ireland noted to Clare that she had conducted herself well last week when flying rock and glass injured three of her pupils in geography class. Workmen were blasting and grading the street beside the school. She had patched up the pupils, shaken a fist at the workmen, nailed lumber to shutter the broken window, and carried on vigorously.

As Clare and John Ireland approached the Birdswell Hotel on Ninth Street, they saw a procession moving towards them. Legless Arthur Pleas-ants, wearing his customary scowl, was wielding his two canes at a power-ful pace to propel his wheeled platform clattering down the plank sidewalk. Pleasants wore striped suits of the softest wool or linen anyone had ever seen. He was said to possess no small talk. The town studied Arthur Pleasants, but learned nothing to shed light on the crucial question: how did an outside investor, from New Bedford, Massachusetts, know, so early, where to light? He never drank, and he spoke, unsmiling, only to his loquacious young associate, Champ Hixon, whom he summoned from saloons with a clack of his canes and the words "Mister Hixon."

Pleasants was followed, adroitly, by Lee McAleer, who politely checked his pace. McAleer, wearing a stiff white collar, a printed tie, and a pearl stickpin, carried the infamous silk umbrella, now rolled; he had the creased, soft face of a good sport, a fellow who got along, and did right well, to his apparent surprise. Clare, walking in the mud street, noticed when McAleer's roving attention picked up him and John Ireland. It was McAleer who, with Tom Tyler, had walked Clare home from the Sons of Pioneers' initiation meeting, and suggested he run for office. They had talked about it a few times since, but Clare was losing interest. Visible at intervals behind McAleer's perfectly tailored form, Champ Hixon, a snub-nosed youth, was hauling on the handle of a rattling dolly piled with gladstones and carpetbags.

When the two groups drew abreast, they stopped. John Ireland and Clare looked up to greet the high rollers on the raised sidewalk.

"Professor," McAleer said with a humble nod to John Ireland, and "My Lord," he said with a comradely smile at Clare. He had a slender frame, a high, soft forehead, and a small chin. He wore his fawn-colored suit to striking advantage. His yellow calf shoes were so fine, Clare could locate the wrinkles in his socks. Clare asked how his boat was coming. Would it be finished in time? Arthur Pleasants, low on his platform, looked bored, and held his canes at parade rest. His trouser legs, two or three inches long and sewed shut, sat neatly on the yellow pillow. Clare could smell bay rum from his pocket handkerchief.

It was widely known that Lee McAleer had hired Thor Avidsen to build for him a racing sloop to enter in the Victoria regatta. Glee Fishburn was watching the sloop take shape in the bayside shed; he kept Clare posted on his progress. Two years ago, Whatcom's own Avidsen had built the yacht *Helen* to the queer specifications of Nat Herreshoff of Narragansett Bay. It looked like a cheesebox, people said, and would slew under the weight of its sails. The yacht *Helen* proved a sensation at the Victoria regatta, however, and won the Class A trophy by a quarter of a mile. The town greeted the victorious crew with flags, bunting, and a memorable party.

This would be a smaller boat, Class B; maybe it would look like a butter firkin, Glee Fishburn had said, but he jested no more when McAleer honored him by asking him to crew. The boat's name was *Cleopatra*. Avidsen would finish the job for the regatta in June, certainly, McAleer said; he hoped to see them at the launching. "Bring the boys," he said to John Ireland, unnecessarily; the whole town would make a beach picnic of the launching even if it occurred in a blizzard.

"Are you leaving the hotel?" John Ireland Sharp asked in his rich voice. Champ Hixon piped up, "We're just taking a little trip, a little excursion—aren't we? Mister—" At this, Arthur Pleasants drew from his limp trousers pocket a gold watch, which he elevated and snapped open to consult. With the watch came two fistfuls of heavy gold chain like brass knuckles. Hixon hushed. Pleasants poled his platform into motion, released a nod, and the procession moved on.

Beyond town Clare and John Ireland climbed towards blocks of cleared ridgetop where workmen were throwing debris on smoky fires. Clare looked out at the water. He admired it, this surface of the water: it showed the wind raking over its face like fingers. It deepened and spread the shifting red and yellow above, it pulled the near blue islands down in reflections cut streaky by boats, and it repelled the misty far islands, and suspended them aloft in mirages. His eye followed the long curve of logs on the bay.

He heard a shout, an unintelligible exclamation. There were some Lummi men on the beach below. He watched one man heave a plank of driftwood high over the water, crying a cry. The other three, whose laughing he could faintly hear, shied cobbles at the plank as it fell. Everything splashed into the water. He heard the sounds later. He smelled the wet wool of his jacket, a smell mingled with mud flat and mineral salts. He saw a raft of white sea ducks and a raft of black sea ducks. Turning, he steered his bicycle's tire uphill through a shallow film of clay mud, on which it printed tracks. Beside him John Ireland walked with his hands behind his back.

It was always and everywhere exactly as real and vivid as this, Clare thought: always the planet where you belonged, the generation you hated to leave, and nowhere more telling, more saturated in meaning, than this place at this moment—not on any Galilean shore or hill, not in any parliament, nor battlefield at Hastings, Waterloo, Antietam. This is all there had ever been and would ever be, these men throwing stones, this amateur harbor, the sea, the west sky above it. The silent schooners strained towards the light in their own sails.

He had glimpsed the same fragile, fraught reality in the darkening school halls this afternoon. He had been heading for John Ireland's office. Boys and girls, their lively shoulders and knees bursting the seams of their blue and black dresses and jackets, passed each other and passed him. The boys' and girls' eyes glistened over their white shirts and bib aprons; they struggled to compose their lips, and their pale faces and red cheeks shone. The girls wore, on their plaid or dark dresses or basques, the white ribbon badges of the Christian Temperance Union, which symbolized the motto "For God and Home and Native Land." The boys wore high-buttoned vests and white shirts buttoned tight on their necks, so their flushed faces looked like escaped substances, and their red hands swelled from tight sleeves.

Two years ago, when he taught physical sciences in this building, Clare used to generate sparks on the Wimshurst machine. He cranked the wheel and made lightning crack and bang across the air between the metal balls. Sparks jerked buzzing, blue and white, from ball to ball. The scholars jumped and whooped—they always did—and he himself never twitched. "Electrostatic energy," he used to say, "is only one form of energy." In fact, he had wanted to jump and whoop himself, to cheer the many-thousand-volt force that burned the air, that pumped fresh blood in the forty red hearts in the room. He made Saint Elmo's fire. His pupils were ambitious, democratic, energetic, optimistic, innocent. What humanity they resumed, the moment he dismissed the class! They flung off obedience and attention like hoods, and moved freely and slanged one another, and smiled at him shyly, glowing, as if smiling were suddenly permitted because their class was over. Today when Clare had walked the hall, the school day was over, and Clare had seen the same clarity and mirth in pupils' faces, and the same animal grace in their turning, upright spines.

They had scattered, and Clare was alone in the building with John Ireland. Outside, he fetched his bicycle and, with the mute figure of his friend, plunged into the expanding March stillness. The pupils had vanished from the streets; gulls rose in the rosy light. A wren sang from a slash pile. A pick rang against stone. They would all die from the face of the earth plucked and howling, like motes in a storm blown to sea, and why, Clare wondered, did he find this so exhilarating? The air was a lens that focused the sky's hard glance on the earth; it ignited the forest and burned holes in his hands. Of course, he had always known he was going to die. He never, however, believed it.

Above the town, above the beach on which the four Lummi men were no longer visible, Clare said good-bye to John Ireland. He climbed onto his rusty bicycle, and sheered off onto Golden Street. It was all downhill from here.

John Ireland continued his traverse to Lambert Street. His small head turned from side to side alertly, but he saw nothing, not the smirking girl wearing two caps, the buggy whose driver checked the reins to miss splashing him, or the building frame on the hillside that showed, through its dark doorways and window cuts, slatted squares of sea.

If indeed, he thought, Martha Obenchain had contrived to leave him all her fortune legally, he would divide it equally with Nan Obenchain and Beal Obenchain. Their need was clearly greater than his own, and however frail or broken their connection these many years, they were, after all, her offspring. He knew himself to require self-respect more than mere cash. Less exaltedly, he had long considered substantial sums to be substantial burdens on natures as unworldly and indecisive as his own. He would simply have to prevent Pearl's learning of any of it.

CHAPTER LVI

March, 1893, Saint Paul, Minnesota

That night, in Saint Paul, Minnesota, a man wearing a tight dark suit and a pale top hat left his new mansion on Summit Avenue. The city of Saint Paul spread below. Incandescent lights and gas lamps dotted the darkness indistinctly. The man, Frederick Weyerhaeuser, was ordinarily asleep at this hour. Now he stepped up the sidewalk and turned in at the stone gate, entered the iron gate, and finally achieved the arched stone entryway of his next-door neighbor's mansion. The mansion was all stone—blunt, simple, and directly powerful, like his neighbor himself. Weyerhaeuser was not sure he approved of stone, however, as a building material.

His neighbor's housekeeper, Miss Veeley, apparently expected this invited guest. She escorted him through the echoing picture gallery and past many dark fireplaces; she showed him into the master's study. Weyerhaeuser was mildly surprised to find Miss Veeley still in service, for she was known to fortify herself from the spirits in the cellar, and had recently been discovered on the front porch, defending the household from all comers, crocked to the gills, and bareheaded.

He found his neighbor working at a simple cherry desk—a small, bald-headed man with a big blunt nose and a curly white Old Testament beard. The people of Saint Paul, with midwesterners' characteristic respect for wealth, referred to him as James J. Hill; he owned the Great Northern Railway. The people along Puget Sound, with westerners' characteristic back-slapping democracy, referred to him as Jim. Weyerhaeuser was one of his many associates who never noticed that he was blind in one eye—from playing Indians when he was a boy. Jim Hill rose to greet his taller guest, motioned him to a sofa near the burning fire in the fireplace, and took for himself a stiff chair. He had thick nostrils and wild white eyebrows. His wide beard was long and disarrayed; when he spoke, its waves caught the light.

They talked. Frederick Weyerhaeuser directed the largest timber enterprise in the world; he shipped Wisconsin and Michigan lumber east. Hill wanted to talk about Washington timber, the fir belt that grew from Puget Sound to the Cascade Mountains. Could he interest his neighbor?

Weyerhaeuser had anticipated this topic. He had already read a letter of Hill's on Washington timber: "It is impossible to realize the immense growth of these trees without seeing them in their native forest." The trees grew on the railroad's land corridors. Would Weyerhaeuser buy the land, harvest these trees, and use Hill's railroad to ship them east? Jim Hill would sell him 900,000 acres of trees at six dollars an acre. His railroad would ship immigrants and merchandise westward, but unless he could carry the lumber, his eastbound freights would run empty. He could guarantee him low freight rates—the lowest freight rates in the world.

Weyerhaeuser, growing sleepy by the fire, roused himself to express doubt. He rubbed both palms over his face. The state of Washington itself presented unknown difficulties; most of it had not even been surveyed. Early signs showed the transcontinental railroads in trouble; they ran up wild expenses on unsound financing. Politicians of every stripe were turning on them. Hill was enormously intelligent, and had succeeded at every endeavor, but his Great Northern line was not yet completed. He could go broke before he built the line; he could raise freight rates before he shipped a log. Then the biggest timber in the world would not pay, not if it grew in boards you could break off by hand.

"How do you propose to cross the Cascades?" These jagged alpine mountains were notoriously more impassable than the Rockies or the Sierras. On their west slopes piled the deepest snowfalls in America—one winter's accumulation measured 120 feet.

Jim Hill was waiting for the question. His quick eyes caught Weyerhaeuser's as he produced from his breast pocket a telegram. His engineer, John F. Stevens, had already located Marias Pass through the Rockies in Montana; last year Hill had assigned him the problem of the Cascades. With a pack pony, Stevens had investigated the Skagit Passes; the line could obviously cross there, run down the Skagit Valley, and up into the harbor on Bellingham Bay. The line could, alternatively, travel what people were calling "Cascade Pass," which used a Skagit tributary called the Cascade River. Stevens's recent telegram, however, proposed yet another route. Weyerhaeuser read it, sipping wearily at his port. An Indian hunter had shown Stevens a third pass, he said, farther south: it crossed the range at only 4,061 feet. It would be cheapest to build through this pass; the line could swoop down the Wenatchee Valley and into Seattle.

Jim Hill refilled Weyerhaeuser's glass. "I have good friends in Seattle," he said, "who can prevent its citizens from charging me the sun and the moon for terminal property and rights-of-way. Which is what the boys on Bellingham Bay have been trying to do. It's all sewed up—I'll end in Seattle."

Weyerhaeuser wished he were home in bed. He ran a finger under his high collar, hoping to release some heat. His trousers' worsted was so hot from the fire, he tried to keep his knees from touching it. The two men might have been different species; Hill always worked late. As he aged, he looked more and more like one of those Bavarian creatures in illustrations who dwell in holes under trees.

"The amount of merchantable lumber per acre," he was saying, "is from six to ten times as great as on the best Michigan or Wisconsin timber land." The stumpage on an average timbered acre was 40,000 feet. Weyerhaeuser found he could not imagine such lumber; it would be interesting to see it. "Come in with me. It's an immortal cinch." Hill's white curly beard moved up and down as he spoke. Weyerhaeuser knew that Hill was harsh and hurried by nature. He took charge of everything, and had even done his own contracting on this house, while building a transcontinental railroad. He was so strong that to save his papers once in a fire, he picked up his three-hundred-pound rolltop desk and threw it out a window. He was also honest.

Hill had prepared a schedule of rates; he found a paper on his desk and passed it to Weyerhaeuser. Weyerhaeuser looked at the numbers, those looping swirls of ink, and realized that Hill was cheating himself; no one could transport lumber at a profit at those rates. The man must truly hate the thought of empty cars.

"Can you guarantee me these rates?"

"I can, and do."

Weyerhaeuser stood. It was after midnight. The men shook hands. Jim Hill's fingers were short and thick—so thick, Weyerhaeuser had heard, that his wife had to wind his watch for him.

Hill pulled the electric bell pull. Miss Veeley appeared, stiff and correct, and led Weyerhaeuser out. Jim Hill remained by the fire, calculating with a pen. Since a timbered acre in Washington yielded 40,000 feet of lumber, then it compared right favorably with an acre of Dakota wheat. In fact, one timbered Washington acre would produce freight wealth for his railroad equal to 367 years' freight wealth from an acre of wheat. He looked at the figure with satisfaction. It crossed his mind that one could harvest such heavy timber but once, while the acre of wheat produced forever. He had learned at his mother's knee, however, that this is an imperfect world.

CHAPTER LVII

Spring, 1893, Whatcom County

Spring came to the northern coast. Daylight stuck a wedge into darkness and split it open like a log. Clare Fishburn was still alive, was still walking abroad in the daylight where everything changes, and holding tight to the nights as they rolled.

Hour by hour the sea ducks of winter vanished from the water, the harlequin ducks and the brant. The trees were going. All winter Clare had learned his own trees' hard branches, how they grew and twigged: the cottonwood in the yard with the sky behind it, the alder saplings yellow-tipped behind the blackberries in the alley, the slim lilacs. Now those dark lines were vanishing into leaf and disappearing before his eyes. The strong roads softened under his bicycle tires. Through the parlor window he saw the snow on Chuckanut Ridge diminish and disappear.

All that April it rained. The Nooksack River flooded its banks and coursed over Minta Honer's yard and hop fields on the plain. The youth Hugh Honer, still home this term from the university, and the man Kulshan Jim, who was bending with age, led their cows to a dry hill on the old Kilcup claim; they paddled a canoe there twice a day to milk. The *Doris Burn* canceled its runs when loose logs fouled its paddle wheel. South of Goshen, the flood isolated the Lummi reservation on Gooseberry Point. Children there continued going to school—fifteen years earlier, the Lummis established and paid for a school on the reservation, having waited twenty-three years for the promised government school. Epidemics had thinned the Lummis, and this year many of the reservation's residents belonged to Canadian tribes.

South of Whatcom, the new cemetery became a low lake where green-winged teal dabbled and dove among headstones and logs. Vinnie Fishburn, her green bonnet tied under her chin, stood with her wildcat sister, Nesta, and three or four of her brothers on a bridge over Whatcom Creek. They saw bloated cows and a henhouse tumble downstream. Through the henhouse slats they saw drowned leghorns, which Nesta tried to catch to make sure they were dead. She slipped, and Vinnie fished her out by her orange plaid dress. The roads were "slick as calf slobbers," Iron Mike told Vinnie in the store.

In the Fishburns' backyard, next to the alley, the water rose under the soil. Early one morning Ada Tawes saw, through the kitchen window, their terrier barking at a spot of ground. Taking an umbrella, she gave a look outside. The wet grass in that spot trembled, bulged, and rose. As Ada watched, bending her sore bones, the earth began to split. Something was pushing it from underneath. "Well, I never," Ada said companionably to the dog, who was both edging back on his legs and straining forward at his neck, to bark in the highest register, as if aghast.

The grasses parted, and a pale, curved form began to surface, slowly and smoothly, like a shoulder. The sod slid down its sides. When the object had emerged fully, Ada could see it was an old coal-oil can—a big twenty-gallon metal canister. She hefted it; it was empty. Ada could see that someone, probably the man who built the house, had resealed its cap. Underneath the risen object, the sod subsided, and the soaked grass lay smooth as before. The old buoyant can rested neatly on the grass, as it were triumphant.

Back inside the house, Ada found herself watching the yard through the window, as if something else from the history of the world might pop up. It all reminded her of the time her young daughter-in-law had buried her failed bread dough to hide it, and it rose in the earth quite nicely, split the ground, heaved, and emerged.

June made lighter bread now than Ada herself did. Clare could have done a heap worse—there was that puff-eyed farmer's daughter out in Goshen, for instance, made of solid afflatus, who had her heart so fixed on marrying an Englishman that Clare had sifted around for a year like a pommy, twirling a cane; he did not stroke a lick of work, and said, "All my eye and Betty Martin!" in a voice that sounded like he was holding eggs under his tongue. That one made her tail ache. June was peppery in speech, too uppish to milk a cow, and cheerfully impious, but she put Clare and Mabel before herself, and never complained. She thumped out wheezing hymns on the organ. She shifted all the washing and all the ironing; she stood between the hot stove and the ironing board, and worked the hot sadiron with her apron corner wrapped around her hand.

Now Ada set Mabel to lettering her name, with a pencil, on pieces of paper on the floor. Her own children—lacking paper, pencils, and everything else—had first lettered their names with sticks on the muddy sides of pigs. She looked down at Mabel's red head, so close to the paper she seemed to be writing with her nose. She looked from the window and saw it was still raining. The more time God granted her on this earth, the more she saw it rain, but He mustn't think she wasn't grateful, because she was grateful—only if He was giving out time, why not pass some to people who needed it?

The water table had risen halfway up the grass blades, and the coal-oil can floated off and lodged against the trunk of the cottonwood, the one tree left standing on the whole hillside. During rains like this, Ada scalded and plucked chickens indoors, in the kitchen.

* * *

When the water drained back, it was May. The earth rolled belly-up to the light, and the light battered it. The snow on the mountains—an accumulation of one hundred feet—sent up a blinding sparkle. In Georgia Strait, the first sockeye run would soon appear; men anchored reef-net gear in Legoe Bay, off the island the Lummis called Skallaham. The Lummis held a feast at each reef-net gear when the first sockeye swam over its net; they prayed. In the reservation orchards, the pruning was over and the bees were out.

In Goshen, Minta wandered from window to window patting her lace bodice, for no reason. She stood lightly on the balls of her feet. Her grand house was full of furniture, colored prints, and baseball gloves. Twice a year she ordered children's shoes from catalogues; already, it was time. Now the green grass was thick in the clearing before her, and at its edge the alders bloomed, and the singing Nooksack ran clear. Each day the light sprayed the sky like a hose. Minta found herself thinking of former times. Her existence seemed a mystery to her. She was a twig afloat on the sea; she felt the lightness of heaven, and its lift. She avoided the company of everyone but Ardeth.

Minta's son Howard's brass band practiced in a pasture for the Fourth of July. The music persisted in Howard's mind while he slept, and he seemed to swing his cornet from side to side on his pillow, to march time. Upright Hugh Honer took the train into Whatcom on the frailest pretexts, carrying a plant press under his arm; he came back silent and withdrawn as a cloud.

Kulshan Jim, his shirt straining over his belly, planted and staked new hop vines—the others drowned. He had lost his enthusiasm for new settlers. A while ago he had furnished the requisite two recommendations—from Eustace Honer and from Norval Tawes—and the state allowed him to homestead 160 acres of his own land. Yesterday in the dry goods store, a purple-faced Dutchman yelled at him for not fencing his pigs. The man lost his self-possession, showed contempt, and raised his voice across the store. He had lived here less than a year. Many newcomers despised his people. Kulshan Jim trod heavily around a seedling's base to pack soil against its roots. The Lummi reservation formerly included the Nooksacks' land at Goshen; the state took that part back when agents discovered the soil was good—took it back so that bulging trains full of purple-faced Dutchmen could tear it up.

Kulshan Jim had a mustache now; it curved down from his delicate nose, and made him seem to scowl. He worked in a white shirt and serge pants. Three years ago Skookum George, the *tyee* the people loved, fell from a tree and injured himself deep inside his enormous frame; three months later he died. That winter Kulshan Jim started participating in the old dances in the longhouse. When his song came back to him after circling the world, he sang it. The Nooksacks were hunters. The elk were gone, disgusted; the beaver were gone, embarrassed; the great and delicious bear were going. East of the mountains, some visionary chiefs like Little Wound said that if men lived sacrificially, and prayed, they could drive the Bostons out, and life would be as free as it used to be. Last year Kulshan Jim's son Frankie, who did most of the work on their place, left. His soft-voiced Aigal went with a Boston who would not marry her in the Methodist church. Of his younger children, only one could speak the language with him and with his cousins' children upstream at the forks of the Nooksack. His sister's children had forgotten the language. His wife was learning to read the Bible and seemed to derive much strength from its words, though he did not know why. She was agitating for a good school.

His sons were not industrious; they were lazy, he thought, and disrespectful. His lovely daughters held themselves too carelessly, and took seriously the doings of insignificant people. Having never been a father before, or talked to any man about these things, Kulshan Jim had no way of knowing that these were a father's thoughts, always. He hefted a peeled pole from a pile and tied four twenty-foot lengths of baling twine to one end. Struggling, he pulled and dug a rotted pole from a hole and planted the fresh pole there. He caught one of the strands of twine and staked it beside the new seedling. With a stroke of his forefinger, he looped the seedling's frail vine a full spiral around the twine. Carefully, he dusted off the six fresh leaves.

One scented evening, Minta's son Green saddled up Gossip, the barely broke yellow colt of old Peaches, and took him out on the road. The boy's tall-crowned slouch hat, like a cowboy's, held the two sides of his center-parted black hair out of his eyes. He was tall for eight, taller than Howard, who was eleven; he wore a man's galluses, if they were almost doubled. He had saddled the horse just for show. Now outside the gate he cached the saddle behind a tree trunk, caught a low patch of Gossip's mane in his left hand, jumped and swung up on the blanket, and flicked the lines.

Gossip was a bolter, like his dam before him; he made a practice of leaping into a hard lope from a standing start, as if he had turpentine under his tail. Just for that moment when he leapt and came down flat-out, stretched and speeding up the road like a demon chased—just for that—Green reined him to a stop again and again, and kicked him up again to bolt. Green ran the horse through the dust on the straight part of the road, and stopped him, and let him burst into a run, over and over, back and forth, from here to there, directly from plain life to thundering heaven. Every time, it felt like they were jumping straight through a hoop into another world.

At last a sheet on the Reeses' clothesline frightened Gossip. He reared back. Green forgot his training and tightened the reins, clinging, and when he slid off he pulled the horse over on him.

It was worth it, Green thought as he led Gossip home. Though the boy bunged his tailbone up some, sprung his ribs, and cut his head, Gossip was not hurt, and it was worth it. Wrens were singing everywhere in the woods, the berries and wild roses were in bloom, and cut hay scented the fields. Green noticed none of these things, but they were part of it.

Up on the Skagit River, at the base of the mountains, old ponytailed Elliott Yekton was dead, and so was the woman chief, Laxabulica. Laxabulica's nephew Joseph was chief now—who had felt in the lodge with his fingers, when he was a child, the boy John Ireland Sharp's hair. Three years ago a smallpox epidemic had taken almost everyone Joseph knew. The county sent in government crews to bury the dead and burn all their houses; they burned their longhouses, where they danced the winter dances. Their memories went up in smoke. The wide prairie openings where the people grew camas and potatoes were now homesteads. Tarheels from North Carolina settled along the river to log and work the mills. They came in freight cars with loose hounds and wild raccoons in cages; they released the raccoons in the woods to hunt later. This spring, upriver, Joseph logged the big firs, the silver fir and the Douglas. He made holes in the woods, down which sunlight now poured late into the evening, changing color as he watched, as the river changed color, and made him long to visit relatives he had never seen, in places he had never been.

In Whatcom, no one could believe in business; nothing got done. Only Wilbur Carloon kept on working, down at the department store; night and day he unloaded bags, bolts, and crates, and ordered new shipments, and rang up sales, his dolorous face composed. June Fishburn and Pearl Sharp spent three mornings digging clams all by themselves, and stained their shoes. Grace Fishburn combed henna into her poufed bangs, pinned on a fiercely narrow straw hat, and took a railroad excursion south to visit her cousin Henrietta. On the train she reflected that she had not really loved Glee Fishburn when she married him, and now she loved him like a schoolgirl, for his deep ways. It was a bottom fact, however, despite her hopes, that he despised her. He told her so plainly, every few months. That was the deepest part about him, how purely he despised her, and she was facing up to it.

Glee Fishburn should have mended nets and scraped his hull with a putty knife; instead he got drunk and went rowing. This summer, for the first time in the history of the world, the government was going to make rules restricting a man's salmon traps and nets. He rowed, standing, under the trestle and into the broad bay. The sky opened above him, bare and fragile; it littered the sea with its yellow like leaves, like narrow willow leaves. Glee studied the pale sideways light, and its stroking sheen on the water; he rested his eyes on the dense blue islands. From deep in the bay he could see Mount Baker in the east, holding the sunset aloft like a cone of coals after the stars came out. The sight of the mountain's rock and snow, its vaulting, swooping perfection high in the sky, was like finding the white moon in a hayfield—the white moon stuck in your own hayfield like the blade of a knife. Its mineral magnificence brooked no argument, admitted no sentiment.

That spring, the Sons of Pioneers, including Clare, got up a weekly baseball game on the mud flat. Come Fourth of July, they would challenge the Lummi baseball nine. Small Mabel Fishburn went to bed in daylight, which dispelled the sharks from the floor. She woke mornings planning to play in harmony with her tumultuous cousin Nesta, and learn secrets and tell them; a bubbling furious unnameable hope filled her chest.

Eddie Mannchen, whose mother burned to death up in Goshen, and who had moved to Whatcom twenty years ago, was a passenger on the Seattle steamer that May, when the current drove it into a rock near Anacortes and it went down. Everybody got off but Eddie Mannchen; he stayed aboard. The people in the lifeboats called and pleaded. The water rose to his waist on the afterdeck, but he stayed aboard with his arms crossed, his hat cocked back. At last the steamer sank and pulled the surface of the sea down with it, and Eddie Mannchen, and his hat. An annoyed cattle breeder fetched him out with a landing net. When she asked him what possessed him, he said he only wanted to know, for thirty minutes, "how it felt to be a vessel owner, and fabulously rich."

It was indeed the month of May, and the light never quit. People grew fitful, bold, or melancholy. They moved pianos, adopted puppies, drove buggies out to look at land in the county, staked sweet peas. New-comers honed, they said, to plant corn and tomatoes. Old-timers, out for a late stroll at ten o'clock, advised them that it was no use; nights were too cold. Ada told June that she and Rooney used to plant tomatoes on their first claim. By fall they used the green tomatoes for target practice, which is all they were good for. On the other hand, as targets they were keenly satisfying.

Time expanded. The day widened, pulled from both ends by the shrinking dark, as if darkness itself were a pair of hands and daylight a skein between them, a flexible membrane, and the hands that had pressed together all winter—praying, paralyzed with foreboding—now flung open wide.

Miss Myrtle Ordal returned from a day of teaching at the high school and told her mother the biggest little news in Whatcom: that the high rollers from Massachusetts, Arthur Pleasants who had no legs and his assistant Champ Hixon, had left town and cleared a profit of eighty thousand dollars. They were gone without a trace. Miss Myrtle found the news stimulating, but her mother, the humpbacked dressmaker, drew her apron up over her face and skipped dinner.

John Ireland received a stiff letter from a New York lawyer about Martha Obenchain Belshaw's legacy. On deposit in the Morgan Bank of New York, in a demand account in his name, was more than fifty thousand dollars. When the school year ended, he would go to the island to give her share to Nan, and to spread and exult in the privacy that settled on him there in the open. There he would live in the big, round day, the day simple as a clock face, and he would own the bright, blank hours. He would see from the beach the twilight conducting the sky like many instruments; he would sleep in a blanket on sand, and wake to the voices of gulls fanning out across water to feed.

John Ireland got to the island every summer—since Nan had married and moved, he used the old Obenchain house—and every summer the thought of it drove everything else from his mind, so that by graduation he was essentially gone. Last June a boy, not a girl, earned first place in the graduating class, and when that boy realized he would have to give the valedictory speech, he quit school, the week before graduation. His parents sought meetings with John Ireland about this matter. John Ireland, who faced making a speech himself, sympathized with the boy, and irked the parents, who notified the school superintendent. By then, however, John Ireland did not concern himself with anyone's opinion. In his mind he was out vaporizing over the stone beach and the light-shot, cold sea.

Street St. Mary, who had purely reviled the mountains in his days as a claim jumper, now hankered to see them. He took bacon, tea, and a wool muffler, and left for a hike through Hannegan Pass. He came back in ten days, having never got out of the woods, for it was too early; snow blocked the mining trails. He had forgotten, in this feckless weather, how long the snow stayed in the mountains. When he returned to his house—Mabel reported in her low, chuckling voice—he drank two glasses of corn syrup spiked with molasses, and lit into a pail of lard with a spoon.

One night Street St. Mary walked home from the Blue Moon Saloon with Clare; the sun had set, and gold light poured down the sides of buildings like slag.

"I knew a fellow once in California"—he squinted up at Clare—"who raised sunflowers, for the oil in their seeds." His voice was hoarse and high; his scalloped line of red hair—which he plastered across his forehead from above his ear—kept jibing like a sail when he turned his head, and blowing off. He caught it in the air, pressed it back, and adjusted his tack until he forgot again.

"He heard that up in Alaska, north of the circle, the sun never sets all summer; it just goes around. So he took his sunflower seeds up there and planted a crop. The first summer, you know what happened?" He gestured with his stump arm.

Clare had no idea.

"The sunflowers grew straight up in the spring, all right, and the first day the sun didn't set—they twisted their heads off."

High in her attic chamber, at ten o'clock, Ada heard Clare and Street St. Mary, raucous, coming up the alley. In March, when the days had first lengthened appreciably, Ada had quailed. She kept on her long-legged underwear beneath her loose corset and corset cover; she let her bun of white hair unravel till it was no bigger than a button. Her hipbones hurt; her hambone ground on its socket like a pestle. Like many other drenched, smoked, bookish, half-asleep, whispering people in Whatcom, she had suddenly remembered another life, remembered summer, when she lived outside all day and night and wandered loose in the immense landscape. She disbelieved that such a stretching, abandoned life was possible to her even with the mercy of God, and thought, as many younger people thought, I am not going to make it. Not this year.

Now reading her Scriptures into the night, Ada happened to feel of one of her earlobes; it was long and creased, empty, like nothing human. She was so fatigued by idleness and so bent on the half-lit, solemn works that saw her through the winter darkness, that she thought: summer may come, summer will come, but I myself cannot rise to meet it. She used to have the strength for things; she used to need it.

One summer, the summer of 1857, after she and Rooney and the boys left the stockade, Indian troubles began in earnest. The troubles culminated, as she and Rooney saw it, in the killing and beheading of Colonel Ebey. As usual, "their" Puget Sound Indian people had nothing to do with it; it was avenging northern tribes who did it, the people both the settlers and the Sound tribes hated and feared.

Nine months earlier, a crowd of Stikeens from Alaska were camped on a beach up the Sound, by a lumber mill. Among them was a man suspected of robbery. The U.S. naval steamer Massachusetts hove up to the beach and cut its engine. When the Stikeens refused to surrender the suspect, men on the Massachusetts fired naval guns into the camp. It was a massacre: they killed twenty-seven Indian people, including a woman and, especially, a chief. This summer, everyone knew, the Stikeens would retaliate. As Chowitzit had noted to Rooney, closing his eyes and speaking in the gentlest tones, the Stikeens would have to get a white hyas tyee, a very big man.

They had already tried twice, and failed. In December of 1856, fifty or sixty Stikeen men in painted canoes, half of them dressed as women, landed on San Juan Island to kill the customs inspector there. He was not, however, there; friendly Lummis had warned him, and he was gone—off like a jug handle. In April a war party came to Fort Bellingham and demanded the head of Captain Pickett; soldiers waved them away.

This August, the Stikeens had got their man. They killed Colonel Ebey, down on Whidbey Island. The settlement pitched into a frenzy. Ada and Lura had repeated to each other the killing's haunting details, and inflamed themselves.

Indian warriors in black paint had beached their canoes on Whidbey Island, where Colonel Ebey was a prominent settler and the inspector of customs. One of the Stikeens made a check: he asked a boy on the beach, "Does Isaac Ebey live in that white house?"

"Yes, he does."

"Is Ebey a very big man, a *hyas tyee?*"

"Oh, yes," said the unlucky boy, "*hyas tyee*, a very big, very important man."

There were seven people dining in the Ebey house; they all saw the Indian men, but the sight was ordinary. No one worried except one jumpy woman. When Isaac Ebey answered the door at midnight, a volley of musket fire hit him. He fell, and the raiders beheaded him—"With his own hatchet!" the same woman kept saying, "The very hatchet he just sharpened hours before!" They paddled off singing, and escaped pursuers in the mazy islands north. The news went out to the settlements.

A few mornings later, Ada was gathering driftwood on the beach. She glanced up, to see in the distance a painted dugout canoe gliding ashore. She was already nervous as a witch. She seemed to recognize the silhouettes of Lummis she knew: Striking Jim, Jack Pain, and a dozen others, all men. They hauled the canoe halfway up to the tideline and began entering the forest, single file, on the far path to the mill. They were carrying rifles. Ada no more feared Lummis than Swiss, but the Ebey killing disturbed her mind, and returned to it the category "Indians," which from time to time she almost forgot.

Ada dropped the driftwood and, with no small difficulty—Nettie was born the next week—hightailed it up the shortcut path to the mill. She would warn Lura Rush that something was stirring, for that was her duty, and there was no one else.

Felix Rush had recently hired a northern Indian man, a Haida from the Queen Charlotte Islands, to work at the mill. His name was Billy; he was a thin-faced, pockmarked, steady young widower who trimmed logs for the saw. He set up camp in the millyard with his small son, whom he treated with notable tenderness. Lura was training the boy to sweep for her, and make pancakes. When Ada got to the millyard, breathless, she saw Billy stay his ax. When she tore in the Rushes' cabin, Billy flew in behind her. Lura, in a pale calico dress, was clawing with a sixpenny nail at hard sugar in a barrel. Billy cried, essentially, "Hide me."

Before any of them could close the door, Jay Tamoree burst in and slammed the door and barred it. He seized the women, running, and pushed them before his wiry arms into the back room, where the baby slept. Immediately, they heard eight or nine shots. Lura hauled her mattress from the bed and threw it over the cradle. There was a silence.

Then the Lummis entered the back room. They were half naked, excited, solicitous to Ada and Lura, and boisterously friendly to Jay Tamoree, who had been working as a millhand, and whom most of them knew. Striking Jim's delicate features were painted black. He apologized for the disturbance. He explained in a torrent of Chinook that they had merely been lucky enough to spot earlier, and pick off now, a northern Indian, a Haida, their old enemy. To Ada's fascination, the men surrounded the cradle, pulled the mattress back, and admired the oblivious, gaunt baby. They held her up and made a fuss. Then, with cheerful, "Nothing personal, ma'am!" gestures, they took their leave.

In the front room, Billy the Haida was dead on the floor; the Lummis had shot through the cedar door. He was blown to flinders, and mixed with cedar splinters on the floor and walls. Outside in the yard his naked son was dead, too, with a pail of cracked eggs beside him. The Haidas were courageous, like the Lummis, and trained their sons from infancy to run toward trouble.

The next week, Nettie's birth temporarily changed the subject. Then, down the Sound, settlers strung up, and hanged from a pole, a Skagit Indian they suspected of murdering a surveyor whose canoe they found adrift. For this lawlessness, the lynchers went before a jury, which acquitted them. On Whidbey Island, the U.S. Army hired friendly Snoqualmie Indians to kill their northern Indian enemies, at twenty dollars a head— or eighty dollars a head for a chief. It was something wonderful, Felix Rush said, the number of chiefs' heads those friendlies brought in and bounced on the counter. The army suspected the Snoqualmies of substituting slaves' heads for enemy heads when they ran low on cash. Slaves' heads had short hair, but so did the heads of people in mourning, so it was hard to be sure. Still, some consignments of heads were about half chiefs—too many chiefs, not enough Indians.

* * *

High now in the civilized town of Whatcom, Ada pinched out the bitch light by her bed. She saw from the window the red sunset lingering in the tallest fair-weather clouds. Ada, and the other grieving and sleeping people of Whatcom, had lain winter-killed and crouched when spring found them out. Spring pried open their jaws and poured sunlight down their throats. The light picked them up and floated them as spring tides lifted logs on the beach: lightly, taking their heaviness from them, and setting them free. Some of them could not, in fact, stand it. On the first sunny day in May, Mr. Evan Vernon, a partner in the Whatcom Savings Bank, had shot himself in the earhole with a sawed-off shotgun. It happened every spring.

Still later, in her swaying chamber, Ada heard the sounds of children shrieking below in the streets. There were roaming boy gangs and girl gangs. Careless and maddened, they took life at a run. When that day Ada had looked at the children closely, she did not recognize any. She did not know that no one else recognized them either.

In four hours Ada woke again, because the finches were singing so loudly on the porch. The sky was evenly moist with light, and cranking up for another round.

CHAPTER LVIII

The day of *Cleopatra*'s launching was the third of May, a light day indeed. The sun dried the mist on the rough shore of Bellingham Bay. There, behind the gravelly beach where Squalicum Creek emptied into the bay, Thor Avidsen of Whatcom had built the racing yacht for Lee McAleer to sail in the Victoria regatta. Towards there, on the evening's high tide, the people on Bellingham Bay were wending, to admire the boat, launch it, and, especially, toast it.

Glee Fishburn stepped the mast on his fishing dory and sailed his enormous family—heaped like salmon—to the picnic. He stood in the stern, silent and watchful, and the wind pressed his trousers over his long legs and tightened his dirty shirt over his potbelly. Late last night, while Grace and Vinnie bent over the store's accounts, he had walked out to his boat to sponge her down for the picnic and fetch his net. He returned along the beach and up a trail through madrones on the cliff. By the time he got home, he had composed in his head eight lines of a poem about old times and the layer of light on the water. He had always wanted to write poetry. A man who mislikes his wife needs some enjoyment. It was a glad fact, too, that the first sockeye run had come up smiling. He would ask Striking Jim how they were doing on the reef nets.

Bunched up on a thwart, Vinnie held the baby. Nesta, who was Mabel's age, pushed up her orange plaid sleeve and surreptitiously stirred the water, looking for pipefish in the eelgrass. Glee tacked out against the northwest wind and hardened up his loose-footed sail; Grace was soaked when she got there. Her corset stays would rust and stain her white dress, but she did not mind—it was a glorious evening. Her protuberant eyes glowed. Summer high tides were the finest hours of the year; every evening before sunset, they welled up so full, the peaceful sea seemed to bulge. Grace's ordinarily pinched face opened like a child's; her shopkeeper's spirit expanded, and she hoped. Last night when Glee came in all red in the nose, he had lifted her up and swung her around, and the chair with her, to Vinnie's surprise. "Aw," Grace had said, "go chase yourself." How could she have ever doubted Glee? Before her now the flooded bay brimmed with light, and she thought, "My cup runneth over."

Beal Obenchain, sleepless, excited, and full of doomed imaginings, quit his stump and walked through town northwards to the picnic. He was barefoot; his splayed feet were hard as hooves. When he strode a raised plank sidewalk, he clopped, and the planks rang. Wilbur and Dolly Carloon turned at the sound, and their boy Simon, whom Wilbur carried, turned his raised head. They were expecting to see a horse, for it sometimes happened that a carousing rowdy tried to buck his cayuse into a saloon. It was only Obenchain, big and ragged, his mouth curved down fanatically, like a whale's carved grimace on a totem pole. He waved a convivial greeting, and his great smile reassured Dolly Carloon, who hated to see anyone looking blue.

Obenchain wore his high-crowned derby; his face was big and dished, his chest enormous, his spine long, his long legs thin, and his hands delicate: these elements combined to give him a top-heavy, careening look, although he carried his arms carefully, and walked with his wrists flexed and his fingers curled.

The mood of the town was giddy. Everywhere business boomed, and people owned they were "in the chips," except in the local real estate market, which had gone bust. The truth was that Jim Hill was locating his Great Northern terminus in Seattle, not on Bellingham Bay. When rail-road agents confirmed the gloomy rumors and pulled up stakes, lots fronting the deep water south of town suddenly rolled up worthless, and so did lots by the putative terminal. Eastern investors, who claimed to love Bellingham Bay for its sunsets, booked passage on the new Seattle steamer and never returned. No wonder Arthur Pleasants and Champ Hixon had cut the painter and made off; how did they know? In March, Street St. Mary had refused a ten-thousand-dollar bid for a corner business lot; now, in May, the same lot was what he called a dead cluck. Through Clare, he was offering it, in vain, for four thousand dollars, in order to meet pay-ments to the bank on yet more dead clucks. Two bank directors quietly left town. The plungers in local real estate had taken a licking, all right, but mostly these were outsiders, Lodisa Tamoree said—served them right—or swells who could roll with the punches.

Many local men had overstayed the market, among them the partners in the Bellingham Bay Improvement Company. Clare had spread his risk by moving some profits into the Whatcom Gas Company. Everybody needed gas. City real estate might even bubble up again. A nearby termi-nus was better than no terminus. The region was still coming, and every-thing else was jake: farmers got high prices for potatoes, loggers for logs, mills for lumber, quarries for stone. Grain prices were high following two years of crop failure in the Dakotas; farmers here were spending. Farm land was selling, especially down on the diked Skagit flats, where the soil that men wrung from the salt-marsh delta proved rich. The smallest coin in town was a short bit—ten cents. Last week the city fathers raised the school tax, at Clare's enthusiastic urging, and no one squawked. Clare remembered the old days, when some irate bachelors quit town rather than pay a school tax.

Clare and his family, with Street St. Mary, took the common route to the picnic: they walked through town to the ridgetop where a long flight of cedar steps would lower them to the beach. Ada walked with her cane. On the way they accumulated John Ireland Sharp, whose blazingly dark, alert features gave him the air of a handsome brave; his shoulders sagged like an old man's. Holding his arm, Pearl Sharp loomed resplendent in a flowered hat the size of a small dinghy. Their larksome boys alternately tossed the buggy pillows they were carrying and scratched bug bites through their black stockings.

With the Sharps were the Lees—substantial Johnny Lee, in a white shirt and a straw boater, and his small wife, An Ho, who was now forty. She wore a cinched, ruffled, and flounced blue dress, over which a yellow apron hung unfastened and askew. An Ho had tied one long apron string to the back of young Walter's galluses. The boy climbed things, and he had led her merrily tilting across town. He rarely talked; he just climbed.

When Lord Walter, as the Sharps called him, balked at the flight of steps—he hated losing altitude—John Ireland scooped him up. He bore him down to the distant beach, trailing, perforce, An Ho and Johnny Lee, all of them pleased. John Ireland, who had considered his first son a freak of nature, now preferred babies as a class to all others and, frankly, preferred horses and dogs even to babies, for their innocence was secure. He smelled the boy's dry hair, guarded his head from tipping, and watched the steps.

At the top of the steps Clare paused to look out over the water. The wind was blowing from the northwest; he could see, far away, its white scrapings blow backwards over the bay and spray the trestle. Hezekiah in the Bible had reminded God, in a canny bid to save his bacon, that it was only the living, the living, who could praise Him—as if God would save a life to swell the ranks of his flatterers, if only He could remember this simple piece of reasoning. Far out on the water, the humped San Juan Islands seemed to advance and turn green, as they did when a northwest wind dispelled the haze that made them blue and remote. Piled clouds sailed slowly and laid blue prints on the water like upwelling stains.

Between clifftop fir trunks Clare could see the Lummis coming from the Gooseberry Point reservation in dugout canoes. Lummi women in crews of six, kneeling in dresses, paddled some of the racing canoes; they were practicing for the canoe races on the Fourth of July, where not only the men but also their *klootchmen* would race their canoes over a two-mile course against the Tulalip reservation tribes. The long canoes slid lightly across rucked seas; the women dipped their oars in unison, like wings. Clare tried to remember everything. If he were down on the shore, he knew, he would hear their songs, piercing, over the water. The local favorites were the young men, who paddled eighteen-man racing canoes; now in the distance they made dark streaks, fleet, from which sunlight flashed. Whatcom people were proud of Lummi racing crews, and bragged on their speed. John Ireland had remarked to Clare that these enthusiasts, excepting a few old-timers, would no more receive a crew member in their parlors than a racehorse. Behind the men, slowly in state, came rolling long dugouts, which carried from the reservation everyone and everything else, heaped up in silhouette.

"Everyone in town will be here," Clare said to Street St. Mary. "All the old-timers." Street St. Mary, in blotchy buckskin breeches, started climbing down the log steps. He turned to address flat-nosed Cyrus Sharp, eleven. Cyrus was small, like his father, soft-faced, and ambitious. He was taking each step in the company of his yo-yo.

"Do you know what constitutes an old-timer in the Northwest?" The boy did not.

"That's a fellow who has two haircuts in the same town." Cyrus laughed, and his cap shook. He did not get it. He had smelled cloves on Street St. Mary's breath, which reminded him of something he could not place. His brother Vincent, ten, who got it, gave him a kick. All the boys ran down the steps. Mabel whirled to hand her grandmother the basket she was meant to carry, and followed the boys; two green ribbons trailed bouncing from her hat.

Clare watched the children spread up the beach; they cast long blue shadows, which bumped over the rows of driftwood trees and logs. It was another half mile to the picnic. Below him he could see Tom Tyler and the Tamorees laboring up the shingle, and other people arriving from north and south on horseback. He saw yellow-haired Miss Myrtle Ordal, in a dazzling white dress with leg-o'-mutton sleeves, and her humpbacked mother, the dressmaker, who usually spent her days traveling from house to house; she spookified the children by drinking tea with a dozen pins between her lips.

Clare took Mabel's basket from his mother and took the old red trade blanket she carried; he offered to tote her personally down the steps. Ada glanced blackly up, hitched her skirt, and started down.

"You take care of that fiddle," she said. She was barely audible inside her bonnet. Clare and June exchanged a glance. June watched Ada's every step and every placement of her cane. Ada wore a clean but plain dress of green-checked outing flannel and a knitted gray woolen shawl. Every day, June thought, she seemed less and less present. Her bones and skin were softening for her death; she was shedding the crust that shields people from eternity, the crust that Mabel was already growing at four, as she pretended to know the score.

* * *

Children were crawling over the boat, high in the canvas shed. Earlier Vinnie Fishburn caught her sister Nesta, who had picked up a hand drill, starting to bore "a little hole" in the boat's hull. Now Nesta was skylarking with Mabel and the others on deck. Her orange plaid dress would need mending; it looked like she had drilled a few practice bores through the skirt. She climbed onto the transom.

"At least take your shoes off," Vinnie Fishburn told Nesta—and at that, all the children, scores of children thick as mosquitoes, unbuttoned their shoes and threw them out over the adults' heads. The shoes popped on the canvas walls and slid down. John Ireland, examining *Cleopatra* in the shed with Glee and Clare, knew that sound of canvas popping; he had been a boy sleeping on the banks of the Skagit when fir cones struck the stretched canvas overhead. He wondered if Jay Tamoree, outside on the beach in his blue forage cap, would hear the sound and think of the Skagit trip, too. Fir cones ran over a foot long, and people said a direct hit would kill. John Ireland knew only that many nights on the Skagit, a dropping fir cone knocked a tarp pole down, and his good father rose and guyed it again in the rain.

John Ireland walked around *Cleopatra* with Clare and Glee, avoiding the children's black-stockinged feet, which dangled from the gunwales. *Cleopatra* was a thirty-two-footer with a clipper bow—that is, she measured thirty-two feet on the waterline and could race in the B class, but she had a deck long enough, and a keel deep enough, to carry ninety yards of sail. The men bent to study her shallow fin keel; she had the first fin keel on Bellingham Bay. Clare told John Ireland, who was not listening, that she would lift into a high-speed plane, so she could surpass her hull speed of eight knots. Her double-chinned builder, Thor Avidsen, was straddling a beach log beside them in the shed, wearing a white Cleveland plug hat. At this late hour, transfigured by exhaustion, he was drilling into a polished spar, screwing a fitting onto it, and evidently thinking. He accepted congratulations unhearing; his face glowed.

Also accepting congratulations was Lee McAleer, whom the newspaper was calling Commodore McAleer. McAleer had picked *Cleopatra's* crew for the regatta. He was standing now just outside the boat shed with Miss Myrtle Ordal and her mother, who sized him with apparent approval. His hands clasped behind his back, legs spread, he wore a slender pale suit, a pearl stickpin, and a straw boater banded in striped grosgrain ribbon. He greeted everyone on the beach by name, nodding, and the soft skin on his face creased. Half a dozen gallon jugs were passing through the crowd; whenever a jug came his way, he passed it on with a deprecating smile, carrying the weight and extending the handle.

The Lummi canoes had landed. Lummi children climbed the boat in the shed. Some Lummi men looked at the boat and stood by to launch her, talking with the older Harshaws. Some men smoked facing the water; some men tied to alder trunks the ponies that others had ridden the long way around the bay. They wore white or blue shirts, galluses, straw boaters, or narrow railway caps. By the canoes, women in dresses and wide hats loaded off their *itkus*: food in baskets, babies in cradleboards, old circular mill saws for fireplace grills. The Lummis would return to camp on the beach during the town Fourth of July splash, which lasted three days if people stayed calm. Last July the white Lummi tents for 450 people occupied all the waterfront, so the dry beach itself looked like a sailing regatta in full swing.

On the Fourth, the eagle would scream. People would inquire of their friends in other towns, "Did the eagle scream?" The answer was: "The eagle screamed"; it always screamed. Last year the eagle screamed in Clare's head for a week. People from all over the region came in to Whatcom for the Fourth. Twelve guns had fired at sunrise; ordnance on the naval vessel *Conley* in the harbor answered them gun for gun. At noon, 123 guns fired, and their reverberations met over forest and sea. Masses of children pretended to fall dead on the beach.

Last year four happily helling Whatcom citizens climbed up on three empty flatcars and released their brakes. The cars rolled down to the wharf and into the sea; the men jumped off. Other townspeople listened to orators, played at tug-of-war, raced the beach on foot, set their children to jumping in contests, and, best of all, watched the Lummis' foot races, pony races, and canoe races. Bare-knuckle prizefights on the beach followed the London rules. Last year John Ireland watched Joe Ajax give the out-of-town fellow a sound drubbing. The fight lasted one hundred rounds. On the celebration's second night, the entertainment chairman had to remind Clare please to play his fiddle for the Lummis, who wanted to dance, too; he did, and they did.

The next day the Lummi baseball nine played against Clare's. Glee never played; the salmon were running, and he fished. Ada always cheered for the Lummis' nine—she knew more of the players' parents.

Ada's friend Margot, from stockade days, had died of lung fever years ago. Now at the launching, Margot's two daughters, who lived on the reservation and had grandchildren, caught sight of Ada squinting out from her deep bonnet, and made their way over to her where she sat, on a buggy pillow on a log.

"Are you about ready?" Lee McAleer called into the shed. His hair was silver under his hat, and his face was pale. "Ready as I'm going to get," came a hoarse voice. "You sure you won't come aboard?"

"Thank you kindly," McAleer said, "but this is your show." Radiant Miss Myrtle Ordal looked down at her mother to see if she was taking all this in; the bent old woman nodded.

Beaming at the glowing hundreds on the beach, McAleer said in an ordinary voice, "Here we go, boys."

Within a minute, sixty or so men and women had stripped the canvas from the shed frame, shooed the children down from the boat, and jammed themselves tight around its raised hull. All wanted to take part, so they stood in file, one arm apiece raised. The hands lining the gunwale were of many colors; half the men's hands were missing fingers, for most had worked some for the lumber mills or railroads. Nearby stood another thirty men and women, who hoped they might be needed; another hundred, including all the children, lined the short route to the water. Cross-legged on deck, slightly forward, where the sail's center of effort would be if she were rigged, sat Thor Avidsen, the top of whose white plug hat was alone visible to those who touched his boat.

Steaming dry boards over vats on the solitary beach, and bending them over the course of years to fashion a boat's curved hull and ribs, was a task the people of Whatcom appreciated. If the boat was small enough, and its builder as willing as Thor Avidsen to gin up the beach, they launched it by the simple expedient of throwing it in the water.

Obenchain and Clare found themselves uncomfortably at opposite sides of the hull, like posts. Obenchain stood between councilman Tom Tyler and a man whose swept-back hair had a white streak, a man they all knew as Thomas Jefferson of Lummi, who was actually a Nooksack forced onto the reservation of his enemies by hunger. John Ireland and June flanked Clare. They all stood edgeways, closely packed. Obenchain and Clare could each see, from the corner of his eye, the other's dark form rising above the hatted heads, the way a grand fir breaks from a ridgetop line of Douglas firs and sticks its mussed crown in the sky.

Obenchain was greeting everybody. That he was deliriously enraged only John Ireland Sharp, suddenly, knew. John Ireland heard—and his heart fell—panic strain Beal Obenchain's voice. He watched his head jerk; he involuntarily looked for, and saw, the twisted mouth, and the glassy layer over his eyes which made his irises look submerged.

CHAPTER LIX

Clare had never told John Ireland that Obenchain was going to kill him. He would only stew, Clare had reckoned; John Ireland would feel responsible, as he had evidently felt responsible for the deportation of five hundred Chinese men, and he might get himself done in, too. Knowing nothing of Obenchain's doings, then, John Ireland nevertheless quailed at the sight of Beal's black rage, and wanted to flee. After all these years, he thought; he hated himself for his fear, and hated himself for being surprised. He had fancied himself free from illusion, if on no other subject, at least on that of his own courage—confusing courage, perhaps, with fearlessness.

In his New York days, John Ireland used to pass a young lunatic on a street corner. She leaned on a lamppost, wrapped in an orange rug, and said, over and over, "The Lord is my shepherd; so help me God, these people are crazy. The Lord is my shepherd; so help me God, these people are crazy." She always made him recall, with pity and terror—*eleeinos* and *phoberos*, as he put it to himself—his boyhood with brother Beal.

In Whatcom he had been able to give Beal wide berth; when grown Beal sporadically attended his high school, the two had never spoken, met, or even passed in the halls. Subsequently they nodded decently—an onlooker would have said warmly—to each other in the streets. John Ireland recognized in Beal's occasional outbursts of public speech an originality of mind that would have drawn him to contemplate, at least, any other possessor of it. Beal was, for example, one of the few town residents who saw through the patriotic cant and sham of the free-silver movement— "pure slush," he called it, in the Birdswell Hotel bar. His melancholy was appealing, too; he usually wore it well. Now John Ireland owed Beal money, as he saw it. He owed him one third of over fifty thousand dollars.

Damn him if he did not hope the man would be in better shape, much better shape, by the time he redeemed the bank notes in gold.

"Ready—" said McAleer. He had taken a spot at the bow. Directly ahead on the beach, sober Hugh Honer herded back a flock of girls and boys, all hopping, all in dresses, mostly coily-haired Carloons and young Harshaws. Hugh had allowed himself to come to town today, but he did not allow himself to occupy a place at the boat.

"Steady—" said McAleer, and the sixty people inhaled.

"Heave!"

The crowd lifted the boat and walked her over the tricky rows of beach logs. The boat seemed to weigh nothing. Each person felt he was failing to heft his share, and each put more muscle into it. Consequently the boat rose so high it surpassed June's reach, and then Johnny Lee's reach, and then John Ireland's. They dropped out swiftly lest they trip the others, who were now running the last few steps and gathering momentum to loose, to throw over their heads like a javelin, the thirty-two-foot yacht and its builder. They slung her straightways into the water—a dozen men and women pitched over when she flew from their hands—and she skimmed along, dark, with the sun low behind her.

The people cheered, the brass band piped up. That's a good enough work for a lifetime, Clare thought, to have lent a hand to launch a boat. Elated, he watched Thor Avidsen raise a paddle over his head, dip it to turn the boat, and begin running her back and forth close to shore so everyone could see her neat clipper bow, the handling and balance her fin keel afforded even without ballast, her polished decks, and the bold line of her sheer. Avidsen would rig her and ballast her later. He raised a jug for now, to ballast himself, and the men on shore cheered again, and most of the women groaned or glared.

Pearl Sharp still spoke an agile Chinook. She tried to make pets and mascots of the Lummi men whose fathers had made a pet and a mascot of her when she was a girl. They had watched her sweep and peel potatoes as if she were a play, as amazed by her blue dress and pale hands as she was by their earrings and bare thighs. Now she was the canoe racers' greatest enthusiast, and believed their skills were not practiced but innate. Pearl Sharp passed among the several hundred families spread a mile along the beach, Indian and immigrant. She addressed everyone in the jargon, smil-

ing and nodding firmly under her massive hat, and extended a poke bonnet for donations. The whole town hoped to raise funds to send forty
expert Lummi paddlers to the Chicago World Exposition this summer.
John Ireland had noted to Pearl that they were sending one paddler for
each year that had passed since the Lummis owned the whole place. She
had flashed back proudly that it would cost a lot of money, but it was one
hummer of a crew. Sometimes it wore at him to think of her teaching
school. His own superintendent had been one of her pupils in the old
days; he seemed to have learned her style of logic. Today on the beach she
got more promises than cash; it was a picnic, after all.

The Sharps, Lees, and both the Fishburn families spread their blankets together over dry cobbles. The adults took the silvered old driftwood
trees and logs as seats; young Walter Lee climbed the logs. They ate cold
boiled sweet potatoes, cold fried pork, buns, and pies. A boy limped up to
Hugh Honer; he had split his big toe on a buried log. Hugh eased him the
few steps to the water, washed the cut, and sent him on his way.

Vinnie Fishburn had pinned her black bangs up with her hair in a
loose mass that seemed to spread like a molded cornice to hold her wide
hat. Her white blouse glowed in the low red light like a paper lantern. She
wore a long dark skirt, tightly belted, schoolteacher style, and seemed to
possess more vitality and sense than she knew what to do with. When she
gathered all the knives and plates to rinse them in the salt chuck, Hugh
Honer followed. At that, Clare saw that June was giving him a brilliant
look. Of course she remembered, as he remembered, when a chance to rub
freezing Nooksack sand on greasy pans side by side was life's highest gift.
Hugh and Vinnie were stuck on an open beach now, and the whole world
had nothing to do but watch them against the blazing sunset. Clare and
June, in their day, had been lucky to cross the broad clearing to the river
under the gaze only of Mount Baker and the Sisters peaks, and to tuck
themselves down a bank in the alders. When their busy hands met accidentally in the river, they could look at each other, startled.

After Eustace Honer drowned on the logjam eight years ago, Clare
felt his friend's absence as a hole in the air—a hole that at first threatened
to pull him in, too, for they were roughly the same age, and later a hole
that became a familiar, sullen presence in the Goshen fields and forest, a
rip in the atmosphere inside which Eustace's calked boots and broad, red-
shirted shoulders, the driven set of his mouth, his small, blocky head, his
gravity and pluck, and his pipe, all disembodied, sifted around and

whirled. Now Clare dug his elbows into the sand and watched Eustace's own son Hugh. Hugh bent quietly to the task, and scoured the knives and plates with sand like Lister himself. The water shone up on his resolute, square face; it lighted his round hatbrim from below darkly, so it looked like painted gold.

When Ada tied the ends of her shawl around her, her bony shoulders drew together so she could hardly breathe, and she had to loosen the knot. The skin on her face looked soft as a blossom, spotted, and her black eyes squinting out seemed glossy and hard. She was watching her granddaughter Vinnie souse the plates with curly-haired Hugh Honer in the sea. The boy had hardened up considerable since the bad summer when everybody died on him and he seemed ready to curl up his own self. He had an upright carriage and he kept an eye out, and though she herself favored responsible young fellows with a mite more foolery in them, that kind seemed hard to find.

Ada saw that, to the north, Thor Avidsen had beached *Cleopatra*. A score of men steadied her sides, and another three held forestay and shrouds, while Avidsen stepped the mast and walked his hands up it. Her high rigging was as light as possible to carry the sail, Glee had told Ada and Clare a month ago—a fact that Clare now relayed to John Ireland as if he had discerned it on sight. The weight saved went into the keel, so she would not slip to leeward or founder overpowered. Under way she would seem to be a solid suit of sails; her little hull would string under her like a kite's tail. John Ireland seemed barely to notice the boat. The sun had set. The wind was backing to the west and easing off.

People had eaten; they rose and spread to gather wood. Beal Obenchain, and the drifters and philosophers who frequented the livery stable, sat high on a washed-up tree. They wore shirts light or dark, striped or plaid, and as many different kinds of hats as there were men. Obenchain climbed into the trunk's dried root system and settled there, spraddlelegged, ten feet off the beach. He was speaking, swelling for the boys on the subject of David Friedrich Strauss, whose *Life of Jesus* was, in some circles, all the cry. Then he saw scrawny old Iron Mike lean to mutter something about him to a handsome-looking stranger, who laughed. Obenchain clammed up. He saw that no one even noticed, although he had just started to build his argument. He stayed in the roots till they all went away.

Ada found chinless Priscilla Judd, who had been searching the beach for her. Priscilla had long since moved to La Conner—the former trading station on a Skagit delta slough that its developer, Mr. Conner, named for his wife, Louisa Ann.

Priscilla Judd was now stout, dressed in a military-looking black serge jacket and skirt; she strode the narrow beach, looking into faces. She had lost her teeth, so her lower jaw was no wider than a strap. The two women clung to each other; each saw in the other's aging face how long it had been since Rooney Fishburn and George Judd fell over dead in the well hole. Ada reckoned it was partly her fault that George, helpful coachman as he was, died trying to rescue Rooney, and left Priscilla with a new baby in a raw settlement, possessing the hapless skills of a Worcester ladies' maid, nineteen years old.

After Ada and Clare moved out to Goshen, Ada prayed for God's mercy on the woman night and day; she set Glee to looking after her back in Whatcom, and keeping an eye on the boy Samson and their pitiful stock. Then Priscilla had married a hell-raising young man from Richmond, Virginia, whose family had shipped him west to shape him up. Now he raised cabbage for seed on the Skagit delta. Priscilla had another fifteen children, and they made out fine—so wonderful fine, she told Ada, that she was able to have George Judd's coffin dug up and shipped back to Worcester, England, after all. A few years ago, Ada had heard that Priscilla was grown so stout that the only way she could get out of a rocking chair was to rock so hard she flew out.

She and Ada rested their bones on a driftwood stump. Ada inquired, Fifteen children? Priscilla noted, in her familiar, forgotten accent, that throwing off babies one after the other was a sorrow, for she had to abandon each dear child to tend the next, before either of them was ready. She could see the last baby's betrayed expression, and hear its pleas, which she had to ignore; she worried that it embittered them, one by one, too early. Her firstborn, Samson Judd, was twenty-one; he was "connected with" a dry goods establishment in San Francisco "that employed over one hundred and ten men," Priscilla said. Ada saw the satisfaction on her smooth face, and heard the pride swell her voice, and wondered again at this new thing she heard everywhere, that people fancied that a big, rich firm shed greatness on its one hundred and ten hirelings, and each was thereby worth more than a lone man, a free and proud figure like her Rooney or her Norval, not only under heaven but even in the eyes of this crazy world. Priscilla mentioned further, and more to Ada's taste, that this same Samson in San Francisco had trained a cat to carry a soda bottle.

A new Dutch fellow hauled a black Kodet and tripod through the crowds. When he got to Ada and Priscilla, he offered to take their picture; they could buy prints at $1.25 each if they liked it. They agreed, and the fellow, who had thick brown mustaches and a boy's clear face, spread the tripod and fussed, placing it here and there in the stones, in the water, and in the beach peas blooming behind the logs, until he seemed to approve what he saw under the black cloth.

Then Priscilla had a thought; she jumped up, surprisingly agile, and told Ada she needed some teeth for the picture. The photographer emerged from the black cloth, pushed back the lens, and waited. Ada saw Priscilla engaging the families south on the beach. She came back with a set of teeth, which she rinsed in the bay and popped in her mouth. Both women gave the Kodet a fierce look and held it. "Beautiful!" said the photographer. Priscilla rinsed the teeth again—Ada heard her corset stays creak—and returned them. The photographer entered their names in a notebook. He said that until recently, he had worked selling real estate all over the county.

John Ireland Sharp walked off and looked out to sea towards Madrone, which the mountainous bulk of Lummi Island hid. He would pass a month there alone this summer, as every summer, watching the tides. To the south the sky was dark blue and the clouds red. He imagined how the same sky must look from the beach by his house, the old Obenchain place; from there, he would see this colored sky above a black curve of firs.

Last summer on the island, John Ireland had helped bury Clarence Millstone, the grizzly bachelor fisherman who formerly packed the herring his bonfires drew. He lived on clams, and he used to say, "When the tide is out, the table is set." Millstone had died in a peculiar way. Lee Shorey found his boat adrift in Georgia Strait, washing towards Canada, and he found Millstone's dead body lashed to the tiller. With him in the boat was an enormous dead halibut—a three-hundred-pound halibut—still hooked to a cable. The deck was slippery with Clarence Millstone's blood; both Millstone's legs were broken, Lee Shorey discovered, and their bones protruded. There was one dead man and one dead fish in a floating boat on a quiet sea. This tableau occasioned much speculation. Most people concluded that when the thrashing halibut broke his legs, Millstone lashed himself to the tiller, knowing he was soon dead anyway; he had always hated the thought of drowning.

The island solitude was tormenting, really. It drove a man to his own resources, the empty contemplation of which sane men flee. John Ireland forgot this melancholy fact every spring, however; he studied the skies from Whatcom as if his angle were wrong and glory lay elsewhere and beyond. Now to the west the smooth sky rang down the spectrum ending with green, and the high clouds streaked it yellow and orange. Running low clouds changed shape and changed color, and the water broke the colors and multiplied them on the skin of Rosario Strait. Two swimming seals humped up and dove into the slick light on the water. They slapped their hind flippers, spattering blue on the yellow, and John Ireland heard the slaps later.

He headed down the Whatcom beach. He saw that darkness was spreading from the land. In the dark, five or six big bonfires were going. People sat lighted by flames, and from a distance the live sparks that rose over the fire seemed to emanate from the people; the yellow sparks turned red and, as they met the darkness, went out.

In a silhouetted crowd he found Clare—Clare wore his bicycle cap. Obenchain was nearby, behind Clare around the fire. When John Ireland joined them, Clare had his fiddle out, and people were singing "Throw Him Down, McCloskey." Big Dolly Carloon was holding her boy Simon, whose head always tilted up as if he were listening to the sky. This posture gave his many rushed and forced remarks the air of pronouncements, and people superstitiously repeated his words, and wished him very well. Wilbur Carloon, with a hooded glance of his heavy-lidded eyes, passed John Ireland a round brown bottle with a white label—sloe gin. John Ireland drank and passed it up to Clare. "*Bibendum*," he surprised himself by saying—the old Horatian ode Clare would not know.

Clare waited till the chorus finished, lowered his bow and his fiddle, drank, turned, and saw Obenchain, studying him, his eyes sharp in their soft sockets. He nodded curtly, and passed the bottle to someone else.

The women, low on the logs, had started up "Long Ago, Sweet Long Ago," and the men's deep voices met their earnest sopranos boldly; they all loved this song. They sang in the dark, and looked at the fire. They had seen younger faces, around other fires; they had sung beneath other skies, in other times, far away. The tide was starting out, and the wet mud reflected the fire darkly, in only the yellows.

Each man and woman had seen the old ways lost in half a lifetime, and knew there never was a generation so pushed, spun, and accelerated by change as their own, and so nostalgic for a more innocent past, however fanciful. It was their childhoods they mourned for, and the vanished times and places and people.

For June it was the lost warm colors of the Chesapeake country, where she rode with her young father between trees, a careless girl. For John Ireland it was the world before his family drowned—Viola and Vesta's domestic and eternal battling on the puncheon floor, his mother's lost voice saying over them, "I want you calm"—and he broke off singing. For Johnny Lee, standing in the dark holding Walter, it was not Sun Tak village in China, but the first forest camp in the Sierra, when he and Lee Chin hung over Cape Horn in baskets and blasted away—for they were so young then, and made of those lost days a game. For the dressmaker Mrs. Ordal it was one lost Christmas night in Michigan, when her mother wept at the sight of an orange from Spain that her father sold a calf to buy, and she, a mite in her mother's lap, had wept, too. For Street St. Mary it was egging on the lost cliffs of Isleboro, on June mornings, when he was agile, and the gannets cried around him in the air.

While they sang "Long Ago, Sweet Long Ago," Wilbur Carloon and old Lodisa Tamoree and the school superintendent thought, as they had thought before, and said, and read: fast steamers and trains, and their rush of business, have coarsened these new youngsters, and they follow the latest fashions heartlessly, and hope only to make a killing. They will never know such sentiments as beset us, who have lived in a wider and nobler time.

These new youngsters, Hugh Honer and Vinnie Fishburn, stood hand in hand in the back of the circle, the grave, curly-headed boy and the white-skinned girl. As it happened, each had never felt life's loneliness more keenly than at that moment, holding hands and singing. Each had never suffered, than at that moment, greater and more decimating loss. The strength of adult emotions was new to them. The purity and depth of their private, sourceless griefs overpowered them; the feeling was to each fearsome, unfamiliar, undiluted, unstoppable. Over the next several weeks, each would wake to this same crushing sorrow every day. Hugh, who had seen his father drowned and Lulu and Bert killed in the fire, feared insanity, because he suffered more pain, for no reason at all, at a picnic. Vinnie, pacing through her summer tasks in the store, feared insanity, too, for nothing caused her misery, and nothing eased it. Each dreaded the other's discovering it, or, barring that, the duty to tell.

Clare held the singers to the long notes, and by the end, only one man's voice and one woman's voice, both tight and quavering out of the smoky darkness, sustained the last beats that concluded the line, "On the golden shores of sweet long ago."

Clare lowered the fiddle, and swiveled his head to loosen his neck. Johnny Lee was looking down the beach, his face set grimly. Clare followed his gaze and saw Obenchain in silhouette, high hat small on his big head, approaching a distant fire. Here beside him, crouching, was John Ireland; he was fingering a small patch of sand. Clare liked John Ireland's rich, clear voice, but he had not heard him singing.

Sparks rose and wood snapped; a woman's shoe pushed in a log. A baby cried and stopped. Up the beach, Indian families were singing. The stars had come out.

CHAPTER LX

Now what should they sing? They sang "Will you go, lassie, Go to the braes of Balquhidder." Almost no one present was Scottish; almost everyone present had lost a land, and a love. Then Street St. Mary suggested "The Old Settler." A Puget Sound pioneer named Francis Henry had written this song to the old tune of "Rosin the Beau"; the Sons of Pioneers began every meeting by singing it, to loosen up. Clare figured it would stop these folks, including him, from busting out bawling. He sawed through all the verses, ending on the one they all shouted, even John Ireland, the one for which the ladies, the better to belt it, cranked themselves up from their logs:

No longer the slave of ambition
 I laugh at the world and its shams,
As I think of my happy condition
 Surrounded by acres of clams.

As the last notes ended, June heard a cheer swell from the bonfire farthest south on the beach. Then another thick cheer sounded from the next bonfire up, and some whistles. Then she heard hoofbeats, fast and hard on the cobbles by the tideline. A horse and rider were bearing down on their fire at a hard gallop; people moved out of the way. This speeding apparition passed them, heading up the beach and spraying stones. The horse pounded, spread and gathered its legs, fleet as pistons; the reins rippled; the rider's short torso eased back, and her bonnet and shawl blew out behind her. It was Ada. June saw Ada's skirt and petticoat hitched up to her hips, as she flashed by the fire; she was riding stride-legged like a man, and revealing her blue-and-white-striped stockings.

"That was your mother." June was whispering carefully up to Clare. She tugged on his arm and pointed her shadowed head up the beach.

Clare was looking out over the heads of the crowd.

"Wasn't it just?" Neither of them could think of any snappier thing to say.

Clare watched Ada pelt towards the next fire and past it, touching up the horse with her heels. Far in the distance, up by the Lummis, she wheeled inland and took a row of logs at a long, silhouetted jump. She came down smartly, and Clare lost sight of her.

Five or six songs later, Ada came sneaking in to join their campfire, her bonnet tied again around her chin, her skirt settled, the corners of her woolen shawl tied. She looked sheepish at the fuss people made—Oh, piffle, she said. She sounded breathless still, and completely exhilarated. She had walked the horse to cool him before handing him back. She explained to Johnny Lee and Pearl Sharp, "Seemed like a good night for a little ride."

Hugh Honer saw old Ada Tawes lope up the beach bareback, spraying sand, and the sight deepened his melancholy, he did not know why. She was Vinnie's grandmother, and he had known her all his life, this little pioneer lady with her bow-shaped mouth and black eyes, her thin shoes tilted like tent pegs at the corners of her skirts. People seemed so joyous tonight, yet it was the same world it ever was, and they all had forgotten. When a baby is born its fuse lights. The ticking begins, and the fire starts fizzing down its length.

It was Hugh himself who discovered Ada Tawes's husband Norval, the minister, and brought him back to her in the rain. He was about twelve then, the man of the Honer family, two years after Ardeth, Howard, and

Green joined them. That year the county had completed the twenty-mile road into Whatcom. Local men, on hire, laid corduroy—split logs fastened together—over the worst patches of mud and marsh. Unfortunately, rainwater accumulated in just those patches, and the corduroy floated like rafts, and tipped, and horses pitched off it.

In April, Norval Tawes and Ada got themselves a bay gelding named Noel. At the post office Mr. Norval Tawes told Hugh and his mother that he would ride Noel over to show them that evening even if it was raining, for it was unlikely to stop raining anyway. He never did arrive. The next morning Hugh and Kulshan Jim found Mr. Norval Tawes a few miles down the road, dead of a broken neck or drowning, in three inches of water by a raft of corduroy; the horse was gone. When they hauled his body from the water, Hugh lifted an icy ankle in each hand, and Kulshan Jim hefted the armpits. They carried him back down the road to the democrat wagon at home, and Hugh never slung a heavier load. Those icy ankles seemed to drive towards the ground, as if the man were diving in his socks, and Hugh had to fight him in the air. Holding his half of the body by the ankles, Hugh saw the length of Norval Tawes headless, because his pointy head hung between Kulshan Jim's legs like a plumb bob, and pulled his neck skin straight down from his starched collar.

Now, standing by the beach fire, Hugh remembered Vinnie's hand, and moved his to feel hers. It all seemed stingy and shabby and tormentingly sad. He always thought that when he became a physician, he would stand on two feet holding on to people and fighting with the ground's tug for their bodies. Tonight he had no heart for the fight, and wondered how he ever had. He looked out at the fixed and waterless stars. Vinnie was singing full-throated beside him, and her hand was warm. There was no doubt about it; he was abnormal.

Down at the Harshaws' fire, Mabel, her reckless cousin Nesta, and a swarm of other children were singing in the dark. At the same time, they climbed up, and jumped from, a log wide as a road, whose roots tilted it above the beach. These activities, combined, kept them awake. Mabel's hands were cold. When she bit the end of a splinter to slide it from her finger, she noticed her hand smelled something awful; the other one did, too.

"Smell your hands!" she cried to Rush Sharp, who did so in midair while he was jumping down from the log, and knocked his knees into his chin when he landed. Rush's interesting brother Cyrus had caught a striped snake hours ago, and the children had passed it from arm to arm and stuck their fingertips in its mouth, seeking to give their mothers the pleefer, to astounding success. The little bugger was peeing on their hands the whole time, Mabel thought now. She jumped down and rinsed her hands in the water, which did no good.

The parents were singing some dragging song, and someone played chords of music. Mabel climbed up the log and squeezed into a place near the roots. The children faced out towards the water; the sea's witching spread, and the deeps of the starry sky overhead, and the touch of their pressed bodies, excited them beyond bounds, and nothing would do for it but to sing "The Desperado." Nothing could ease them but singing so loudly; nothing could save them but singing "The desperado, from the wild and woolly West," and they sang it over and over—"A bold! bad! man! was this desperado, From Bad Man's Gulch way out in—Colorado!"—for they were desperate themselves, with the fever and mystery of living.

In the darkness Mabel felt a firm hand grasp her ankle through the shoe, and arrest its bounce. She looked down to see her mother's beautiful upturned face, lighted in streaks by the bonfire. "It's time to go," her mother was shouting. She felt her father lift her down, her mother wrap over her a cold blanket.

"And everywhere he went he gave his war—whoop!" she sang in her whiskey voice over her father's shoulder to keep her place in the group even as she was borne away crying "No! No!" and trying to wriggle down; "No!" and they put another blanket on her and she noticed the slow rhythm of her father's footsteps, and far over his shoulder the yellow fires, which seemed to float in the darkness.

CHAPTER LXI

That same day, on Wall Street in New York, panic broke out. The U.S. Treasury's gold reserves had fallen, for the first time in over a century, below the so-called $100,000,000 danger limit. European investors in U.S. businesses had pulled out and asked for their stakes in gold; they feared the silver-crazed country would be unable to meet the international gold standard of payments. American investors and bankers feared the same thing; they dumped their stocks and called their paper. Now the word was out. The stock market plunged. Businessmen cashed in their silver certificates for gold. Branch banks near New York ran out of gold, and their agents rode the subways into the city to carry gold reserves back to the branches in bags on their knees.

Men in telegraph offices strung across the continent tapped the story down the line. In Whatcom, the *Bugle Call* editor, Dean Whipple, heard the news come in at the railroad station, where he wandered twice a day to eavesdrop at the wire.

Dean Whipple was twenty-five years old, a big, slow-talking, thin-lipped, quick-witted man whom nothing bored. His predecessor at the paper paid a "thirsty" two drinks a day to swing by the depot's telegraph office and bring him news. Whipple did the job himself. He had worked as a transcriber in the telegraph office of the Chesapeake and Ohio to put himself through Ohio State; American Morse Code was his second fluent tongue.

At the local line's depot, Whipple leaned over the table where his friend the telegrapher, Crying Johnson, kept an empty Prince Albert tobacco can to amplify incoming code so he could hear it ring over the freight clerks' typewriters. Both men made sense of the keys' dots and dashes as fast as they heard them—and a fast "fist," as they called a man's personal style at the key, could transmit thirty words a minute.

"Secretary of Treasury Carlisle may abandon policy of redeeming Treasury notes in gold stop Wall Street panic New York banks closing early stop...." He and Crying Johnson exchanged a quick glance. They waited, both leaning, for the next signal. In the pause, Whipple saw vividly that this impulse which had crossed the nation would snap the Washington coast into the sea. The Northwest depended on the East for capital. Western banks actually held most of their reserves in eastern banks. It occurred to him to mosey on down to the Seattle branch bank, where he had deposited his $120 savings, before everyone else got there; he dismissed the idea as ignoble. His wife, Hilda, however, to whom he told the news later, at lunch, scrupled not; she abandoned the Monday washing in the yard and sprinted on down to the bank. The lugubrious teller told her to come back tomorrow.

After lunch Whipple pulled the front page, returned to the railroad station, and hung his bulk over the telegraph and the tobacco can with Crying Johnson. "National Cordage Company announces failure stop dubious practices uncovered...." The Reading Railroad had already collapsed. The Pennsylvania Steel Company had gone into receivership. The Populists were right, Whipple thought—if money were based on both silver and gold, this disaster would not have happened.

His dull face expressed no emotion, and his mind raced. There was little enough money in circulation as it was—about twenty dollars passed through each American's hands a year, and even less here in the West, where politicians made these facts known. Western farmers cried for a money system based on both silver and gold—which would double, pure and simple, the money in circulation. Eastern bankers, moguls, and monopolists blocked them. They insisted that coining money does not create wealth; they pointed out that economies were international now, and the United States could not stand alone with a system other nations rejected. Surely theirs was an unpatriotic view, Whipple felt. Since when could the United States not stand alone? It grated on a young man who loved the West and lived by his wits.

Now banks would drive farmers off their land, and widows and orphans would sleep in ditches—as Whipple put it to himself, running his hands over his big face—and breadlines would form again in the East. Whipple was not a student of economics. He subscribed to local sentiment sincerely, and called it wisdom, which is why people bought his paper. Still, he felt another's hardship as his own. Come to think of it, if merchants stopped buying advertisements, and if the county and the town had fewer notices to publish, his publisher would shut down the newspaper. Well, he could fish. He liked the idea of making monthly mortgage payments in sockeye.

Whipple had brought a sandwich of smoked beef and some strawberry pie; he returned to the *Bugle Call* office, where he knew he would compose copy and set his own type all night. His wife, Hilda—after she finished the week's washing in the yard and ironed his shirts and collars, and ironed her petticoats, skirt, blouse, and dress—brushed some cornmeal through her hair to clean it, and went to the boat launching to tell the world, riding their bicycle to the top of the steps.

A Tulalip switchman, whose canoe rode the tide north, had hit the beach first with the news—him, and Crying Johnson. Clare and June Fishburn heard it when they paused halfway up the wooden steps to rest, Mabel on Clare's shoulder. Jay Tamoree and Lodisa passed them on the left, and Lodisa asked, in her boiler-plated, imperturbable voice, without breaking stride, "Have you heard? The stock market has failed, and another panic is on. It's going to be hard sledding."

"The houndish dastards!" Street St. Mary put in, so violently his streak of hair fell out of his hat. In the dark they could hear Lodisa Tamoree up ahead, saying now to Ada Tawes, and to Hugh Honer, who was leading Ada and the Sharp children home, "Have you heard? The economy has collapsed again, and we're in an awful fix."

John Ireland Sharp and Pearl were stopped behind the Fishburns on the steps; John Ireland carried sleeping Rush, who was four. Rush had painted his face and neck in stripes with pokeberry juice, as had all the Sharp children, but no one would know it until tomorrow morning, when Johnny Lee woke them for breakfast. By then Johnny Lee's mind, and the minds of Pearl and John Ireland Sharp, were distracted by fear and dread, and the piping, striped children, who wanted to resume a picnic life on the beach, looked like strangers.

BOOK VI

PANIC

CHAPTER LXII

1893, Whatcom

Three months later, in August, the town of Whatcom was on its beam ends. Every single bank in the county had failed and closed. Ignorant bank officers, who looked singularly sober, had loaned out townspeople's deposits to plungers and speculators of the wildest stripe, whose ruining schemes all went belly-up, and there was no money to be had. The panic was general. Although Jim Hill and his Great Northern Railway hung on, both of the earlier overland lines, the Northern Pacific Railway and the Union Pacific Railway, suspended dividends and fell bankrupt into the hands of receivers. Across the country, 15,000 banks failed. Of the 158 national banks that failed, 153 were in the South and the West. In Whatcom, people were poor as snakes.

The Birdswell Hotel had electric elevators; they stood idle, for no one came to town. The crushing fact was that steamships no longer called in Bellingham Bay. Freighters from San Francisco had dropped Bellingham Bay from their runs; Whatcom had the passenger steamer, but was otherwise cut off, like a fingertip that would die. Consequently every last wholesaler closed. The bankrupt trolley line reduced its runs; the bank that owned it could not foreclose, for what did it want with a losing business that owed money? Trolley fare was fifteen cents; fifteen cents was also the trolleyman's hourly wage, and the company could not pay it. Farm prices fell so badly that peas sold for two cents a pound. Potatoes sold for fourteen dollars a ton. Everyone had potatoes; potatoes were the common crop. A man could insulate his house with them. Farmers defaulted on loans and taxes; many farmers, like many merchants, simply walked away and vanished. Other farmers hung on and cleared land, hoping to meet payments later when times improved; they were confident, and rightly, that the eastern banks that held their mortgages would not foreclose on worthless lands saddled with debt. It seemed as if all of America was spinning down a drain, Whatcom first. How could these boastful, we-can-do-anything people think of themselves, if America's rise to glory was already over?

Clare Fishburn straddled a cedar shakebolt in his backyard and split shakes. Of the $35,000 he had invested in the Improvement Company, of the approximately $100,000 it had become a year ago, and of the approximately $20,000 that was left by the morning of the boat launching in May, nothing remained but $1,000 of Whatcom Gas Company shares he had purchased for $5,000. The Seattle American Bank had closed its doors, and its certificates, such as those the partnership held, were value-less. The partners' chief holdings were of course local business lots, residential lots, timber acreage, and farms. These assets might as well have been seawater. The lost money was mostly June's—her wedding present and legacy.

Senator Randall had never said so, but he had made it plain, that he judged Clare a wretched proposition of a man. June had never said so, but her Baltimore circumstance had made it plain, that she could have found a suitor to match her fortune, not lose it. Clare's simple pride before men, that a rich and beautiful young woman should have lighted on him, had long since changed to shame before men, that his wife was so rich. Now he and June were scuffling for themselves like everybody else. In the hot yard he tapped the frow, and the shakes popped off the bolt. No one went to the office; nothing sold, the partners were away, the agents dismissed. Clare was, if nothing else, his own man again.

When the market hit bottom, Clare dreaded June's contempt. Ordinarily he would have quailed at the worse possibility that she might hide her contempt, thereby demonstrating that she felt her very life to be a calamity entire—he would have quailed, that is, except that he could barely fix his mind on any aspect of the loss. He chided himself: What was a man's duty but to provide for his family? What species of scoundrel would lose all his wife's money? He felt himself, however, more substantial than before.

A new baby in the house gave it an air. The panic was showing all Whatcom what people could live without. No one would knock on the Fishburn door at midnight and threaten to take away anything they need-ed—Beal Obenchain had already done just that, and nothing had come of it. Clare had never clapped eyes on piles of gold; he had only signed papers, and brought papers for June to sign. He had done nothing more with the money than buy June an organ with it, and imagine buying a boat or two, and a horse, and a carriage. He had prized the money as evidence of his rise. Now he found he rather liked falling; there was some solidity to it. A man knew where he was bound. On the other hand, it was June's money, and if Obenchain killed him now she would have nothing to shift with.

He told her about each loss as he learned of it, and she was not best pleased, but the new baby distracted and invigorated her despite its uncertain future. He had seen her as her family's molded creature, when perhaps she had never been; the Randalls had made a deeper impression on him in a week than they had on her in thirty years. Until recently he doubted she chose this life freely; perhaps, he thought now, he doubted because he himself would have chosen luxury, in a trice. June was eager to pitch in, she said from her childbed; she raised her high brows. The skin on her face was puffed and red. She gave out rather more of her usual ironic brand of affection, and never blamed him. She really was a daisy, he thought—for those were all the words he found for his increasing sensation of participation, of glory, even, in a world of flux.

That August afternoon, John Ireland Sharp had a drink with Clare in the empty hotel bar. With surprising vigor, John Ireland mentioned that his principal's salary of seventy dollars a month, in money, was going to become sixty dollars a month, in scrip; the town was broke. John Ireland knew Clare was broke too, but neither man could dissimulate his own good cheer. His tie undone, drumming his fingers, John Ireland looked amused. And why should John Ireland not be cheerful? Clare thought. John Ireland would get by, and so would he; he had a cow.

CHAPTER LXIII

In July, Clare and his brother Glee had shifted Ada from her attic bedroom into the parlor under the tall south windows that gave out on Chuckanut Ridge. Ada lay with her legs apart on her feather-bed, on a cot so narrow the red trade blanket pooled on the floor on both sides. Her wind was failing; moving her pillow wore her out. Throughout her life, Ada had skinned off her suit of underwear for the summer on the day she saw the first snake. This year she kept it on. She wore a yellow dress of sprigged calico, unbuttoned in the back, and a shawl. Her hands swelled, and their backs were dark blue just under the skin.

It seemed to Ada right friendly to live in the parlor, under the circumstances, but when the new baby came, June passed her ten days' confinement in the bedroom upstairs. Then June developed the milk leg, and kept in bed another two weeks, with the baby, and Clare danced attendance. Only torpid Mabel kept her company downstairs, though Clare had to duck through the parlor on his way upstairs from the kitchen—which was sometimes a blessing, but sometimes a burden when she pined to twine away into her thoughts. Her granddaughter Vinnie helped out, often in the company of upright Hugh Honer from Goshen, now seventeen and a college boy, who used to be two years old on his mother's knees, like everybody else, and who had carried her Norval home by the ankles with his head hanging off.

Her insides stopped working and her belly grew tender so she could not endure the blanket. June stirred out of bed and got back to work; Clare rigged a padded cradle for the baby and set it by the organ stool. Ada perceived events clearly. She heard Clare's mallet tap the frow in the yard. Every spare minute, he split shakes, for a dollar here, a dollar there. It was the only work in town. The laying waste of Whatcom she thought a fitting retribution for its waywardness. Whatcom was eaten up, broken up, trodden down. "Therefore hell hath enlarged herself, and opened her mouth without measure," Ada noted composedly, "and their glory, and their multitude, and their pomp, and he that rejoiceth, shall descend into it."

Dying, with time on her hands, she recognized in her thoughts the same familiar, inescapable self she had been toting up hill and down dale these sixty-odd years. With a jolt she realized that the dying must often feel this way—steaming along just fine, while on ahead someone has torn up the rails. Years ago, when a load of slate slid off the coal mine roof and cut Chot Harshaw into two pieces across the middle, Rooney was among the men who sailed in to dig him out. "Don't trouble yourselves, boys," Chot Harshaw's top half had called out in a normal tone. "I'm just fine, just fine." He repeated it all in Chinook to the Lummi workers.

Ada could not turn in bed this morning. The dog was sleeping on one side of the blanket on the parlor floor, and the cat on the other. Her spine had jabbed through the bed's feathers, and she lay in a hard trough. When her father was giving out in Illinois, his head pained him confoundedly, and he said he wanted to "stick his spoon in the wall"; he wanted rest, but when it came right down to dying, he was not ready to leave, after all, and he fought it, and lost, of course, and finished his circle, right on this feather-bed, where they put him.

Ada heard Clare's tapping on the frow blade cease. After a pause, it resumed. She heard June, inside, mocking the baby to itself. Through the tall window by her cot she saw two blue shadows slide down Chuckanut Ridge quick as otters, but she could not see the clouds that made them. Her mouth was dry. Like Chowitzit in his blankets, she was feeling *mela-moosed*. She felt she should be mourning and roaring, and looking for sal-vation, but instead she watched the stiff trees on the ridge, whose tops the wind stirred, and found that restful.

She drifted off, and when she came around again the parlor was dark and the window showed some stars over the black shape of the ridge. The household was asleep, and so was everyone in the town outside, asleep like children.

Under the open skies at the boat launching this summer, Ada had found Priscilla Judd, and the elegant Mrs. Clara Tennant, Chowitzit's daughter, who had married John Tennant years ago and was a powerful and admired Whatcom matron, and who had turned herself out for the launching all in white, old as she was. They were about the only people left on the bay from the old days—they and the Tamorees, who were not her sort, and Iron Mike, who came and went, and of course some of the grown children, like the Tennants' son, who was a lawyer, and Pearl Sharp. Grinding the toe of her shoe in the sand, she complained first to Mrs. Clara Tennant, and later to Priscilla Judd, that they were the only ones left. "The rest are all gone." She pronounced this commonplace with sorrow in her voice then, and more fear, and yet more pride.

Now, lying in the Golden Street parlor this midnight late in August, she repented the pride. She purely missed every major figure in her life, starting with her mother and father in Illinois, and thought the world was going to perdition without the likes of them, and the likes of her, too, if the truth be known. The people remaining were not serious; they suc-cumbed to the world's secret enticements, and its plain ones. "The wicked walk on every side, when the vilest men are exalted." Even the new live-stock lacked heart. The good hogs, that you could reach an understanding with, were dead, and so were the good cows, like you never see anymore.

She must have struggled, for she opened her eyes again to find yellow lamplight, and the doctor kneeling there by the cot. She looked at him for a bit, panting, then ignored him. She judged she had lived a good life—a strenuous one and a lucky one. For she had truly felt God's power. Charley got killed in the rut. Nettie died, whose initials she wore in her braided-hair ring. She buried two fine husbands.

It was not everybody got so deep into the battering and jabbing of it all, got in the path of the great God's might. She moved across the burning plains, crossed two mountain ranges. She saw from the western shore with her own eyes the mild islands rolling off in the light, the way they must have looked at the foundation of the world. She called Lummi and Nooksack women her *tillicums,* and they called her *tillicum,* which who would have guessed. She lay under mats in the bottom of a canoe once during the Indian troubles, and Rooney told the Haidas she was clams. Lived in five or six different places, including a stockade. She felt her freedom. Reared two boys to manhood, busted open this wilderness by the sea, buried the men on their lands. She saw a white horse roll in wild strawberries, and stand up red. She took part in the great drama. It had been her privilege to peer into the deepest well hole of life's surprise. She felt the fire of God's wild breath on her face.

Now June in her chemise, her brown hair unpinned, was opening the gas jet on the wall; it hissed. She touched a match to it, and it popped into flame. Ada tore her gaze from the pleated tin reflector behind it. The doctor looked to be but a mite older than Mabel. He said, addressing Clare, that she had about an hour to live, possibly two, so when morning light cleared Chuckanut Ridge and poured in the window, she found the whole world sitting in the parlor pretty much triumphant, as if she had produced a baby, and not just opened her eyes. Her pain was gone. There was nothing to breathe. The road before her was clear. After a while Vinnie went into the kitchen with June and the baby. Clare was upstairs, stuffing Mabel into her clothes. There was Hugh Honer on the organ stool—curly-haired like a dark lamb, only square-headed. He was wearing overalls and a necktie. She met his pale, solemn eyes, then sifted off.

Hugh Honer was used to the dense, necrotic smell of Ada. He noticed it only when he first came into the house. Back in Goshen, he doctored most people's stock; he knew the stink of hoof rot on sheep, of abscess pus, of cattle-bloat gas. This was the smell of a person dying in old underwear.

Now he saw Ada's eyes roll up under their hairless brows; her eyelids closed and she strained as if to see. Her mouth eased and took on a bow shape; she drew a great breath and called out into the distance.

"Up, Maude," she called.

"Up, Bright."

Her features bunched forward. The mystery was being accomplished once again before Hugh's eyes. He could hear Clare's footsteps on the stairs, the women running out of the kitchen. Ada called out, "Up now, up. Up!"

CHAPTER LXIV

On the afternoon of the day Ada died, Beal Obenchain sat next to his stump on the thin cherry chair he had drawn outside. His long feet were bare and white save for streaks of orange callus where his trouser cuffs scraped them; his high-crowned derby eclipsed half his brow. He pulled from his mouth an orange crab leg, which he bit delicately up its length, then upended and sucked. High overhead, fir and cedar needles shredded the sunlight till it was gone. In August the forest was as dry as it ever got. The moss, lichens, and ferns that grew on the deep reddish folds and phalanges of his stump house were yellow and crisp. Here the forest lay flat. Only to the west could Obenchain see, as he gazed downhill through the trunks and fir tops, some blinding strips of water and sky.

The panic touched Obenchain but slightly. He had toyed with the notion of living this winter in the Birdswell Hotel basement and tending its furnace, for his shoes and boots were expensive, and so were the jars of sourwood honey, the tins of peppered Danish bacon and thin English cookies, and the rounds and bars of French cheeses he liked to buy in Victoria. The Birdswell Hotel, however, had no money, and its owner doubted he would fire up the furnace at all. To the south in Fidalgo, a hotel owner filled his empty lobby with white leghorn hens; Beal saw the hens milling about in the lobby like drummers. Here in Whatcom, most men were reduced to splitting shakes from cedar stumps for cash or scrip. Townsmen entered Obenchain's neck of the woods; they built a rough flume down his embankment and used it to slide shakebolts to the beach.

He lay low. The train's coming through the woods woke him just before midday, and he hastened out to greet it in his fashion; half an hour later he heard it rattle out on the trestle.

In July, Obenchain had worked on the Olympic peninsula. He directed a team of one hundred Quinault Indians, who, taking the place of sixteen oxen, hauled logs for masts out of the forest. His employer paid him in scrip, so he quit. Now and then he trapped octopus. He could always join Iron Mike selling high wine and watered rum outside the Lummi reservation; running a booth there was an old enterprise of his that he sold to Iron Mike when he had had a bellyful of rowing eighteen miles to work. He could join, cynically, any of the crews surveying the North Cascades, yet again, for a road. Every time the region's sock ran dry, people awoke and discovered they were a million miles from nowhere—the which Obenchain could have told them—and they reinvented the striking plan of a road east, towards money. Obenchain reckoned a road through the Cascades' mess of peaks would be impossible to build for another four or five generations. He was not yet so flat he would take any pay to break his back on a losing venture and listen to men's absurd hopes.

Earlier that afternoon, Obenchain had rowed out and found a big male Dungeness crab and most of a smaller male in his crab pot. He reset the pot with dogfish skin and carried the crabs by their hind legs up the embankment and into the woods. Now he was eating them. The boiling vat lay on the needled ground beside him. From time to time he shook the broken shells from the tops of his feet.

It had not worked with Clare Fishburn, whose life he now knew. "You are going to die," he had said, and this simple townsman believed him. He seemed, however, singularly unaffected by it. In the first months, Obenchain knew, Fishburn avoided the south side of town and the deep timber. He stayed out of the Birdswell Hotel bar all winter and early spring, and hauled his bed away from the upstairs window. Beal had scared him out of his own garden once. He wore a sidearm outside. Obenchain even knew that the man's wife was badgering him to move.

He knew also that, despite these alarms, the man was not yet ontologically dead. He persisted in thinking his own thoughts, and Obenchain was uncertain what those thoughts might be. The panic failed to panic him. A boyish, unchastened stupidity had left Fishburn's face—that was good. The face, however, had not merely flinched or emptied. When he walked or bicycled in town, he no longer searched the streets and glanced behind him, as he had last winter. His gait had wakened, and he looked sharp, but not strictly in fear. It was no longer a pleasure for Obenchain to surprise Fishburn in the street; the subject failed to react. Now Obenchain hated him, when he recalled him.

He rose and bent to a pan of dough on the ground. He punched the dough down, slid the pan over the gray dirt to a patch of sunlight that had moved, and sat back.

He had meant to observe and preside over the corruption of a man's spirit. He meant to dramatize to an ordinary man, by the threat of death, the spectacle of his own cowardice. He meant to reveal to the man his own lifelong ignorance and self-satisfaction, and to vivify and display both his helplessness and his insignificance. He meant to murder Fishburn without leaving a corpse—to own him by possessing his thoughts, to kill him legally, by the power of suggestion. The suggestion had failed. Fishburn was not tormenting himself with uncertainty. His self-satisfaction had, if anything, apparently increased. At *Cleopatra*'s launching in May, Fishburn carried himself on the beach as if he knew something, although he knew absolutely nothing. Fishburn set his teeth and bore forward following his sharp nose, apparently confident of his mastery. His self-deception overpowered any truth. It exceeded even Obenchain's contemptuous measure. Limber but not slack, Fishburn looked as though he owned all the time in the world. In open mockery by the bonfire, he had passed the jug to someone else.

Obenchain cracked crab legs in his teeth. There were many things on his mind this August. An artist, a painter of shipwrecks, had come to town; he was an insignificant personage—what could more properly be termed a booger—whom everyone from Iron Mike to the newspaper editor worshiped as a god, and who was seeking to destroy Obenchain's reputation as an intellectual. There was a rich book collector, too, in La Conner, a book collector of delicate sensibility and decidedly youthful appearance, whose fortune insulted him and whose image appeared in his mind. Finally there was Fishburn, a shrivel of a man, who would not give up the ghost.

A week ago he considered blackmailing John Ireland Sharp, whom he knew of old for a spineless freeloader and bilk. He had often seen John Ireland's vaunted wife squirrel away merchandise in the store. Obenchain's threat of making her thievery known would induce John Ireland to obey his order to abandon his friend and increase Fishburn's distress.

He liked the idea of kicking the struts away from a man one by one, so the false front fell. The spectacle of his decline would be a kind of moral display for the town, if the town could see it. Accordingly, he had called on the Sharp household on Lambert Street. The Celestial houseboy answered his ring; his evil look narrowed. He said impertinently, "Mr. Sharp is out of town"; he shut the door. Now Obenchain reflected that blackmail could always wait. Possibly it would prove even more useful in a future setting. Here it might be redundant. In fact, a provocative new idea was taking root in Obenchain's mind.

What Obenchain considered, crumbling crabs, was this. Although Fishburn was afraid, he was not destroyed. Likely fear alone could not deliver a man into his hands, not if it presented a clear challenge. Perhaps uncertainty alone could destroy. Perhaps, he went so far as to presume, perhaps the Chinaman tied to the wharf had not suffered at all as he waited for the tide to rise and drown him—because he was certain the tide would rise. Perhaps his own weapons were, hitherto, crude. If uncertainty was the last hope of destroying Fishburn, then he would furnish him with more of it.

He would take it all back. He would tell him he was by no means going to kill him. Tell him it was a joke, or an experiment, something finished. Then—what would Fishburn do? Would he be acute enough to reckon the experiment just begun?

Since Fishburn was alive so long after he told him he was going to die, he had reason to doubt Obenchain, and disbelieve him. He might think Obenchain was an inveterate liar like one of the Cretans in the epistle to Titus—"always liars, evil beasts, slow bellies." A liar who told you he would not kill you actually meant to kill you in earnest. Fishburn might think Obenchain sometimes lied and sometimes spoke the truth. Obenchain could say, "What I told you in December was a lie, and now this is the truth: I am not going to kill you." In these uncertainties, Fishburn could stew. Obenchain was losing interest in Fishburn, but he would allow him this last chance to furnish diversion.

Obenchain determined, then, to find Clare Fishburn tomorrow, and tell him this new thing. He stood up, and fine sand and triangles of orange shell fell from his pants. He moved the dough pan again. He poured the crab water over the bracken ferns by the door.

CHAPTER LXV

The next morning on Golden Street, Clare Fishburn pushed up from the table. "That," he said to June, "was a meal fit for the gods." They had breakfasted on bacon and oat mush, as they did every morning. "… And I was glad the gods didn't get it." The man was a born after-dinner speaker, June thought distractedly. The baby in June's arm was jaundiced and light, but her head smelled good. They named the baby Ellen. Her unseeing eyes and closed lips gave her an otherworldly look. Mabel appeared not to have noticed her yet, though once she referred to her—clearly to her—as "Neil."

Mabel looked darkly at her bowl. Her limp reddish hair had already slipped its ribbon. The gods could get this, in her view. Sugar was so expensive that her mother held her to only a pinch on her mush. She had nothing to live for. Her cousin and best friend, Nesta, was moving to Seattle. Her grandmother had died, who was nicer to her than her mother. She herself was too young yet for school. "You sorehead," she said to the cat blinking under the stove.

Out in the yard, Clare straddled the shaving horse and got to work. He wore his yellow plaid bicycle cap, his old suit pants, and a collarless shirt, from which his long neck protruded and bobbed. Beside him was a heap of red cedar shakes. He picked up a shake, and the whole pile slid about with a dry sound. He secured one end of the shake under the shaving horse's head, picked up the draw knife, and thinned the shake's free end in a few skilled, splintery strokes. Now the shake was a shingle, a little item for which the paying market in the Northwest was nil. He released the shiny-bottomed shingle, dropped it at his side, and began on another shake. Behind him, spread on dead grass by the chopping block, two shakebolts—wide wedges two feet thick—were all that remained of a wagonload of bolts representing a cedar stump, which Clare was trying to turn into money.

He had started in May. The week after the launching, when all the banks had closed, when the senior partner J. J. O'Shippy had embarked on an extended visit to California, and the Bellingham Bay Improvement Company decided to sell its carpets and a few chairs to pay the rent, Clare Fishburn took to the woods, looking for cedar. How else could he fill his days? Other men gathered at the dock early every morning to see the

Seattle steamer depart. A round-trip ticket to Seattle cost two dollars, and they were curious to know who had it.

In a series of ten-hour days, Clare had worked all summer with his friend Tom Tyler. He had admired the bulky, toothy, walrus-mustachioed city councilman ever since he pulled a gun on the boys at his initiation and fired blanks. Tom Tyler was both reckless and skilled, a combination of virtues Clare especially prized, never realizing that this was the splendid combination everyone in the region prized, and he was just following the crowd. In his twenties, Tyler had bought a herd of thirty-two dairy cows in San Francisco. He accompanied the cows north, saw thirty of them drown crossing a river, and sold the remaining two for so much money he made a profit on the whole venture, which took six months. Then he paddled a dugout canoe to Alaska, carrying a load of ladies' hats and picture frames. Now his many teeth spread radially in his mouth, as if his internal power blasted them outwards.

The spotty fires of '85 had burned out the fir in the woods and left charred cedar stumps. Clare and Tom Tyler sawed these stumps into rounds with a ten-foot saw, and split the rounds into bolts. Clare swamped out a path through the young fir to the road. It had rained most of June while they worked. Tom Tyler dragged the bolts by stoneboat to the road, and both men loaded them on the wagon. Together they could make up one cord of shingle bolts a day. Before the panic, a shingle mill would pay a silver dollar for a cord of bolts delivered, but now there was only one mill going, and they did better by hand. Both men's jaws and necks bristled up dark; they paid a barber every two weeks now, instead of every week.

After they chewed through all the stumps they could find, they resorted to downed cedar logs. They had to rig levers to roll the logs and hold them raised to saw, because neither man owned a peavey. A cedar log could lie mossed over in the soil for hundreds of years and the wood inside would be sound. With chokers they handled two logs forty feet around. A big log was worth five or six dollars, once they added a few weeks' work to it. Sensible men made up the shakes right there in the woods, but by July—a month ago—Clare reckoned he wanted to shift at home: his household was due for a birth and, it looked like, a death. It cost a dollar a day to hire a team to pull the wagon to his house, where he could split the bolts into shakes in the yard. He and Tom Tyler heaped the bolts high as hay on the wagon, and random children rode the load to town.

Now, in August, the cottonwood leaves hung dry on the backyard tree. No finches sang from the blackberries by the alley, and the cliff swallows' second brood over the back door had fledged. The Fishburns' yellow cat caught at least two fledgling swallows that Clare saw, right after his mother died. Then in the hot afternoons the cat started catching snakes by the middle, and looking up at him where he sat tapping the long-bladed frow with a mallet. The snakes twisted symmetrically in the cat's still muzzle.

June came out with her sleeves rolled over her elbows; she brought him a cup of tea. She made coffee sometimes with burned bread crusts, for a pound of real coffee was worth your life. This was watery tea without sugar, and the two passed it back and forth. She brought the alarmingly floppy baby out and set her on a sheepskin in the sun, which the doctor said would cure the jaundice. It stimulated June to have a baby, and already she wanted another. "... for Ellen to play with," she told Clare now, her high brows lifted. He allowed that when this creature could boost up her own head and stir on her pins, the Lord might sling a playmate at her; it was out of their hands.

June went back indoors as if reluctantly; she said she loved the sharp scent split cedar released in the sun. Clare knew she would find Ada's cot gone from the parlor, and the floor swept smooth where she had lain. June and Clare were surprised that expecting Ada's death, and planning for it and around it, was no proof against either its grief or its shock. Clare had observed that when someone died, the world hushed the matter up. The living swarmed over the gap and closed it; the hole in the mud swelled shut. His mother, however, had left a hole, a space in the air like a space at the table, into which bits of living thoughts flowed and were annihilated. They buried her, as was now customary, in the cemetery instead of in the yard.

Clare set the shaving horse aside, for he had finished the pile of shakes. He set on edge one of the last shakebolts, and split it in two with an old crab-apple wedge that was his father's. Then, holding the frow's straight handle, he set its heavy perpendicular blade in position along one billet's grain, and tapped it with a mallet. A shake split off as if goosed. He moved the frow blade a notch and tapped again. The red shakes crackled at his feet. He worked through both bolt halves whistling, and trimmed those shakes into shingles. Then he turned to the bolt he had sat on all summer and reduced it to a clatter of shakes. He shaved those shakes with the two-handled knife. Now he was kneeling at the horse, for he was too tall to work the knife bent over. It was not yet nine o'clock in the morning.

In the alley the wagon was already full of shingles he had woven and tied into square packets. Clare would weave up these last shingles and load them. Then there was nothing more he could do but wait until this evening, when Wilbur Carloon was sending out, into the farthest yonder, a rail shipment for the whole town—shingles and potatoes, mostly shingles. It was the common hope of every adult in town that some broker over the mountains might part with cash money for shingles and potatoes—which would not fetch a nickel here, if anyone had a nickel. No one in Whatcom County could find any other paying work, and farmers with land were clearing forest just to kill time.

Clare stood and flexed his back. He surveyed the littered yard; would he learn if the grass reseeded this fall? He had taken to looking at things as if for the last time. This practice caused him to see them as if for the first time: yesterday John Ireland's white and freckled forehead, now the baby asleep on the sheepskin, the frow leaning on the back step, sunlit, and the crab-apple wedge beside it. The wedge top was furred from blows. It looked to be outlined in the blue shadow that streamed behind everything; the crab-apple wedge held its shape for now, vivid and stubborn against the current, as he did.

The baby woke on the sheepskin, and June came out and got her. There was not a cloud in the sky. It seemed to Clare that a man in his situation, on such a day, in such a possible world, had just plain ought to go fishing.

CHAPTER LXVI

At the same time, Pearl Sharp took a big step and stood on a chair in her dining room. Mrs. Ordal, bent, began to crawl circles around her feet. This morning was Pearl's first fitting for a winter dress coat—a lustrous gray cutaway coat that would be edged with a band of black lamb's wool. She and Mrs. Ordal were determining the coat's precise length. Its hem should just skim over the red leather tips of her shoes—she was wearing those shoes now—and it should neither show any more of the shoes, nor drag in the mud. The coat must seem to swoop, without bulking or creasing, over her gown's magnificent bustle and the gathers and scallops beneath it, and over the triple puffings and ruffles of its sleeves.

Pearl had worn to the fitting the black silk gown; below her, over three chairs, spread the low-backed brown velvet gown the coat must also accommodate. She had never seen so many dances and card parties—during a Panic, what else was a town to do?—and the coming winter season promised many more. Navy officers, many of them expert dancers from back East, were still available to be entertained. Nevertheless, she had worries. She was troubled about her son Cyrus. He had moved himself and his yo-yo to the beachfront north of town, and he was only eleven—thin as a chicken bone, flat-nosed, with twigs caught in his hair. Surely, however, she could maintain her gaiety, and comfort herself, and encourage others.

"Have you heard?" she said to the flat top of Mrs. Ordal's head. The town of Everett, on the Sound, was "holding what it calls a Hard Times Ball. And guess what the door prize is."

Mrs. Ordal emitted a noise. Her mouth, Pearl reflected, was full of pins.

"It's a sack of potatoes! Isn't that wonderful?"

Mrs. Ordal made another sound. Pearl realized the dressmaker was crying. She climbed down from the chair, put her arm around Mrs. Ordal's firm humpback, and eased her to her feet and into a chair.

"Whatever is the matter? What is it? I will see what I can do to fix it. There, there. You needn't ..."

What was the matter, Pearl discovered as she stood delicately looking away from Mrs. Ordal's disconsolate recitation, was grave indeed, and there was nothing she could do to fix it. Miss Myrtle Ordal, the dressmaker's only child, with whom she lived, had eloped. This daughter—whose pale and lively beauty, soft heart, paid position as schoolteacher, and infinitely fair prospects were all her mother had in the world—had leaked out of the landscape without a word. Yesterday afternoon Mrs. Ordal had a telegram from San Francisco, she said, and added at once, "Or maybe was it Cincinnati?" Myrtle had eloped with Lee McAleer.

"Oh, Mrs. Sharp, you know about Mr. Lee McAleer." Mrs. Sharp did not. She had not seen the newspaper.

Mrs. Ordal took the pins from her mouth and was falling to pieces into the second of several handkerchiefs with which she had prudently supplied her calico bodice. Pearl ducked into the kitchen, wearing half a bolt of wool cloth over her evening gown, and bade Johnny Lee bring tea to the dining room.

It came out over tea, and Pearl learned yet more from the *Bugle Call* after Mrs. Ordal, having finished the fitting and consumed half a dozen deviled eggs, left. The state of Washington had indicted Whatcom's town treasurer for misappropriating funds—"larceny," the attorney general called it, though the term seemed harsh to Mrs. Ordal—first to the tune of $5,000, then, overnight, to the revised tune of $500,000. Plunging freely into the town till, and borrowing in the town's name, McAleer had been riding a spree. He paid his own campaign debts, purchased controlling shares of a logging operation up the Skagit, set up a partner in a gold mine on Ruby Creek, bought from Clare Fishburn the two high building lots on Golden Street where he was erecting what the town approvingly called his "mansion," and paid Thor Avidsen to build *Cleopatra*. So far as Mr. Whipple at the paper knew, McAleer had fled to Wyoming.

Yesterday, Mrs. Ordal had said, she was "just stoning a peck of plums," when she heard steps, and her door knocker sounded. She found on the porch a crowd of men in black hats—"at least four"—who were looking for Lee McAleer. The black-hatted men were contractors who were building his house on the hill. The nicest one explained, begging her pardon, that they were collecting unpaid bills; conversation downtown "over a cup of tea" aroused their suspicion, and they had paid a convivial call upon town hall, where they found the treasurer's office cleaned out to bare walls. Then they rode the trolley to Happy Valley, where McAleer's landlady showed that he had pulled up stakes, and he owed her six months' rent. The landlady suggested they try asking Miss Myrtle Ordal, and another well-lubricated trolley ride brought them here.

"I didn't know what to tell them," Mrs. Ordal told Pearl. "They all seemed so nice. They only wanted to talk to Myrtle." Pearl nodded. She had taken a chair and settled in. Mrs. Ordal's face had grown mottled and red, and her eyes looked like pinheads in a cushion.

"So I left the men there on the porch, and I called out for Myrtle. I looked for her in the kitchen. I looked in the cowshed. Then I looked into the bedroom. And there she was—gone!"

Early mornings it was cold in the Sharps' dining room; Pearl brought Mrs. Ordal a shawl.

"She was just too softhearted," Mrs. Ordal pronounced, as if Myrtle were dead in the ground. In her telegram she said she "could not abandon him in his hour of need." There existed on earth another kind of girl altogether, who might take a fellow's dishonor and disgrace as a signal to reconsider his suit, if not in the light of his reputation, at least of his character. If her Myrtle, however, had been this other kind of unforgiving girl, Mrs. Ordal owned, frankly, she wouldn't miss her so much and here she broke off again.

Pearl's heart went out to her. After she left, however, it snapped right back.

CHAPTER LXVII

Just before noon that same August day, Mabel Fishburn, her puttylike face sunburnt below her eyes, returned from her cousin Nesta's house and was sitting on the front porch waiting for her mother to prepare lunch. A man came along the front alley and stopped at the foot of the porch steps. He was as big as her father, and wider. He wore no shirt or coat. He smiled at her and said, "Where is your father?" Mabel tried to remember. She rotated her feet in their hot shoes.

"Gone fishing," she said, looking away. People were always trying to get her to look in their faces.

"Where has he gone fishing?"

Mabel rose and went inside. She returned in a minute, with her stockings pulled up; she sat again on the edge of the porch and said, "On the river."

"Which river?"

Mabel rolled her eyes at the botheration to which life ceaselessly subjected her. She went inside and returned to stand in the doorway—she had no intention of sitting any longer on the porch—and said, "The Nooksack."

John Ireland Sharp, returning home in his shirtsleeves for lunch, checked behind the cougar skull on the shelf above his study desk. It was here that Johnny Lee left for him, by an arrangement three months old, any letters or telegrams addressed to him. Today he found the stiff envelope he had been expecting.

When the panic broke out in May, there never was a run on New York banks; the bank that held John Ireland's legacy from his foster mother neither failed nor closed its doors. During the monetary crisis this summer, however, New York bank officers had taken the extraordinary measure of refusing to cash checks even for their own depositors, except in proven emergencies. John Ireland's was no emergency. Last June, in a similarly stiff envelope that he had found behind the cougar's skull, a letter from a bank officer assured him, in black script on heavy bond, that the bank would "presently be on its feet.

"President Cleveland will indubitably call a special session of Congress to repeal the popular and"—here the bank officer apparently forgot himself—"stupid Sherman Act, which, as you undoubtedly have taken cognizance of, requires the U.S. Treasury to purchase silver in notes redeemable either in silver or gold." Repealing the Sherman Act, the officer wrote, would "renew public confidence in money" and in banking, and—in John Ireland's translation of his flowery abstractions—they ought to be able to pay up sometime in August.

At that time, rereading this early letter behind the closed door of his study, John Ireland had resolved to believe the bank officer, and forget about it. If the usefulness and value of money depended on such a superstition as "public confidence," he was over his head. The more he considered it, the more unwilling he found himself to undertake the several years' study of economics that would enable him to assess the situation for himself. He had long ago concluded that he possessed only one small and finite brain, and he had fixed a habit of determining most carefully with what he would fill it.

Now, in this last week of August, he saw it had been a good decision. The officer had just written to say the bank could now honor its certificates. John Ireland shed his hat and sat at his study desk. He had spent the morning in his office in the quiet high school building, exasperated. Miss Myrtle Ordal had eloped with Lee McAleer when that worthy absconded with his bad debts on the Whatcom treasury. Now John Ireland was calm and pleased: his judgment was not all bad. He could have wasted the summer troubling his spirit about money he never earned. He could have grown attached to it like many a better man, he thought, and proprietary about it. He returned the letter to its envelope and threw it away.

Lunch was a lively affair. To begin, Pearl appeared in the dining room in an evening gown. Her black mass of hair was in disarray, and she wore a black fur muff pushed up on one wrist. Her gleaming, wrought expression took the edge from John Ireland's short-lived calm. The two sat with Vincent, Rush, and Horace; Cyrus was absent. There were two summer salads on the table—greens and fruit—and a platter of deviled eggs. Johnny Lee began serving salt pork.

"Have you heard?" Pearl burst out. "Lee McAleer—"

She stopped when John Ireland nodded. He had heard. He had spent the morning interviewing applicants for Myrtle Ordal's position; the news was all over the county. He turned away both men and women who needed the work, and some of them wept. He made the mistake of telling Pearl that he had known yesterday. She rose half out of her chair—"Then why didn't you tell me?"—and startled Horace, who began to cry. John Ireland remarked that he did not know she would be interested. Now Pearl was really on the prod; she stood and expressed her sentiments for a long time, standing; her white throat worked, and her hands trembled. Her teeth were not as good as they used to be.

"Why must you everlastingly come to the table looking like a grizzly bear?" Horace ran into the kitchen. John Ireland liked silent meals.

He had never really favored her high voice, and privately considered it a triumph when she retired from the home-talent stage. Presently Vincent and Rush left, each with a handful of pork. Johnny Lee, silent in the kitchen, was doubtless waiting to clear. Pearl worked her way through his other failings of the past few years, while John Ireland looked at the mysterious pile of pins by his plate. He listened for an opening in his wife's discourse into which he might insert the sudden charming and disarming news of thousands of negotiable dollars. He would omit from his account the actual sum, and conceal his intention to divide it with Beal Obenchain and Nan.

It was Cyrus, Pearl said suddenly, softening, who had her so agitated. She was sorry. She sank to her chair and fixed her brown eyes on John Ireland.

"Cyrus." It seemed he never saw the yo-yo boy anymore. The last time he noticed him, he was under the wharf, chewing tobacco and reading a book, which proved to be *Allan Quatermain*. He made the boy turn over the rest of the tobacco plug, which he had been running into in his pants pocket ever since.

"And how might Cyrus be serving the Lord these days?"

This was another mistake. Pearl claimed she told him last evening,

right here at this table, that Cyrus had built a birdhouse—a very big birdhouse—on the beachfront north of town, and was living in it. He had
moved out of the house. He said he was not going to school anymore.
Now she was crying furiously; she walked back and forth in front of the
window and let her tears drip on her gown—the drama of which, she tried
to point out, was escaping John Ireland, who did not know how wonderfully silk spotted, which apparently enraged her further.

John Ireland did recall, clearly, Pearl's mentioning after dinner that
one of his high school scholars had shown Cyrus how to build a birdhouse. He had noticed her accusing tone—one of "your" scholars—but
dismissed it, for surely there was no harm in an older lad's teaching a
younger lad to build a birdhouse. Building a birdhouse in the fall term was
part of his high school's domestic arts curriculum. Fall term would begin
in a week, John Ireland had thought, and he was distressingly short one
fourth of his trained staff, in the person of Miss Myrtle Ordal. He had not
heard the rest of it.

"What are you going to do?" Pearl turned from the window.

This was a grave turn Cyrus's interests had taken. John Ireland needed
time to absorb it. "Do?" he said. What was he going to do, about any of it?
He had not the foggiest notion.

Later, after John Ireland had given his wife an opportunity to collect
herself, he found her upstairs in their draped and swagged bedroom, collecting instead, into a hatbox, photographic prints from a drawerful that
she had spread on their bed. She was wearing now a dark skirt, a white
blouse with a lot of shoulder to it, and her most heaped-up hat. He had
taken the precaution of barbering his own face.

"My darling," he said correctly from the doorway, "I have good news."

She took it very well.

He had reflected in the postprandial interval that Pearl needed a project. A project would refresh her spirits. The town's plan to send Lummi
Reservation paddlers to the Chicago Exposition, which endeavor she
oversaw, died the day the banks closed and tied up over $800,000 of
townspeople's funds. Pearl subsequently proposed to the Whatcom County supervisors that they send instead—this raised a rousing cheer—a piece
of bark. Consequently Whatcom County paid to exhibit that summer in
Chicago a piece of bark sixteen inches thick, from the sight of which

imaginative fairgoers could extrapolate the sort of daisy timber Whatcom County citizens saw all day without thinking a bit about it. The bark derived from a log that had in fact scaled 12,125 feet of lumber, as Pearl had printed prettily on the card that accompanied the exhibit—thirty times the yield of an average Wisconsin or Michigan log.

That flurry was over. The recreational larceny that enlivened Pearl's winters was possibly over, too, as Grace Fishburn was closing her store and moving with Glee to Seattle to run a rooming house with her cousin Henrietta; rooming houses fared better now than hotels. John Ireland himself would miss Grace's civil calls. Pearl would have to switch to Carloon's. A human being with Pearl's creature kindness could not live for parties. When school started, and the rains began, she would have time on her hands. Projects interested her keenly. Surely with $16,000 and more in her reticule, she could think of something. He had entertained himself in his study after lunch, while his wife composed herself, by reckoning on the back of a magazine the magnitude of the pleasure with which he would soothe her blighted spirits. Their share of the legacy alone amounted to 210 years' salary. It would be like having 210 husbands. He intended to produce this latter pleasantry, thinking Pearl would enjoy it, and yield up one of her pealing, tight-mouthed laughs. She did.

It was only an hour later that Pearl, stepping out to tell June Fishburn of her good fortune, passed Lee McAleer's unfinished mansion on the Golden Street hill. The town would seize this property and the boat *Cleopatra*; the town would attach all that McAleer left behind, down to his inkpots and laundry. Pearl saw the turreted house in all the black disgrace of its emptiness, and, as insight rushed her, she envisioned it in all the sunlit joy of its promise. She climbed to its high porch to examine the gleaming prospect of bay and islands afforded by its leaded windows. She removed her hat to press against those windows. Inside she saw unpacked crates; she saw brass window frames leaning against a wall, and a white piano. The floors and wainscoting were dark redwood. The stairway's curved banister was in place. She knew the house had indoor plumbing, seven bedrooms, and seven fireplaces; it would probably go for a song. Another two or three songs would complete it to fit her household's especial requirements.

CHAPTER LXVIII

That afternoon, Clare Fishburn came walking over the Nooksack plain. He was returning after his solitary outing on the river north of the reservation. He carried a fishing pole and a knotted sack containing one cleaned two-pound trout. He followed the lazy dirt track that traced the Nooksack down from Goshen and swept out towards the bay. The river lay low and sleeping; the poured plain lay slow and flat as the river, and the sky lay monumental over the world.

Miles away at the eastern rim of the plain, the snowed mountains lighted their portion of sky. Mount Baker, the Twin Sisters, and the Canadian Coastal Range peaks appeared to rise and spread behind the very bank of the river, the plain was so smooth. In every other direction the fields gave way directly to light; the farmers' yellow flax fields and green hayfields curved beyond sight. Clare walked towards the train tracks to town. It was afternoon; overhead the sun was ample. Above the earth rode fifteen or twenty tall clouds. Clare watched the clouds—clouds like rocks you could chip, edged with light, caked in grit—and never saw them change, but when he looked away and looked back he saw that they had changed. They bulged and piled. In the distance he saw a rank of clouds whose bright bottoms reflected shine from the water—so that, if he had been a stranger on the plain, he could have guessed from the clouds' sheen that water lay westward and south, even though he could not see beyond the fields.

Beside him a dense hedge of berries darkened the lip where the fields met a delta meander. Goldfinches were feeding in the hedges—wild canaries, his mother used to call them. As Clare moved across the plain the goldfinches swept before him, burst by burst, then flew behind him after he passed. He flushed flock after flock; they looped down the riverside before him.

He was walking home and remembering a Sunday last spring, a day after his wife returned from her father's funeral. In the drizzle after church, children were playing in Clare's backyard.

Mabel and her cousin Nesta, and flat-nosed Cyrus Sharp, and his youngest brother, Horace, were tying each other to a tree. They had found a length of line and were tying each other to the cottonwood tree. Clare watched from the kitchen. He had forgotten this piece of information: children tie one another to trees. Children find wild eggs, treasure, and corpses; they make trails, huts, and fires; they hit one another, hold hands, and tie one another to trees. They tied Horace Sharp to the tree; he cried. They tied Mabel to the tree; her flat beret fell off, and she could not break away.

Clare had looked out past the pie safe. Here is a solid planet, he thought, stocked with mountains and cliffs, where stone banks jut and deeply rooted trees hang on. Among these fixed and enduring features wander the flimsy people. The earth rolls down and the people die; their survivors derive solace from clinging, not to the rocks, not to the cliffs, not to the trees, but to each other. It was singular. Loose people clung in families, holding on for dear life. Grasping at straws! One would think people would beg to be tied to trees.

Mabel stood, dubious in her blue-trimmed dress and shawl, lashed in manila rope to the wet cottonwood trunk. She looked up and saw him in the window. June, her sister Minta, Grace Fishburn, and Vinnie were in the kitchen, preparing a big dinner. If the children tied him to the tree, Obenchain could shoot him. How soft-shelled she was, with her bones inside her! She could break, burn, suffocate, puncture, or freeze, this Mabel, for whom everything had been made so smooth. His mother had come bending around the house to the back door in her worn church finery; the children were calling her. "No," she said from the doorway. "I am too old."

Today Clare had walked all afternoon. He saw a marsh hawk riding the air slopes low over the plain. The big clouds brightened; the sunlight shone yellow now on their bossy sides. What could be unthinkable? When the river curved Clare left its banks and cut westward past pea fields north of town. He flushed the finches and the finches flew; the sky colored up and a killdeer ran calling. Presently he saw patches of forest ahead—the uncut railroad right-of-way on the bluff past the trestle—forest, and a forest-broken lighted band of water. After another mile his path joined the railroad track. It entered a strip of timber where cows ate ferns, and burst out on the railroad grade up to the shore.

Clare lowered his hat, looking out at water. White gulls dropped cockles on the roadbed and lumbered down to feed on broken bits. The sun was low. The tide was in; water covered the beach below past the cobbles, where the mud began. Clare shifted his sack and pole, changing arms, and started up the tracks towards the trestle. Looking ahead, he saw Obenchain almost at once.

It looked like Obenchain. The man lounged inert on the point of the bluff where the trestle's log foundation met its ties. His body pointed out toward Georgia Strait, and his head lay sideways, resting on naked shoulder and arm, facing down the track towards Clare. It was certainly Obenchain, from his size and his hat. His shoulders were bare. Clare could not see if he had a gun. Clare had no gun; he had a knife and some fishhooks. If Obenchain also had no gun, he would simply throw Clare from the bluff. His back would break, or his legs, and he would drown. He sifted his options without emotion. If they tangled on the bluff, could he use his knife? Should he open it now? He decided he should not open his knife. Obenchain could point any weapon Clare held in any direction Obenchain preferred. He would, slightly, rather drown in cold water than get stuck by his own knife.

There was no one else near; no farmboys bringing in the cows, no crewmen inspecting track, no men in boats on the water. Obenchain alone was in sight, and Clare was in sight of Obenchain and the yellow clouds. Obenchain looked for all the world as if he was expecting Clare and waiting for him.

So Clare carried on up the tracks towards Obenchain. Obenchain raised his head from his arm; he made no move to stand. Clare came pacing the roadbed cinders towards Obenchain, his legs moving in rhythm, because Obenchain sat in his path.

As he walked from the long habit of walking, he felt wide and aerated as the sky. He knew he was walking as if he were opening the air as a canoe bow opens the river. He himself was being opened as if Obenchain were a table saw. He was a clod of dirt that the light splits.

When Obenchain stood and stopped him—his face thickened under his hat—and told him he was not going to kill him, he was not going to die, Clare looked out over the trestle and down to the water, where gulls flew without bending their wings. Obenchain was offering him a view he had to reject. The tide on the bay was slack at the flood. There was a plank walkway on the trestle by the rails. Clare moved onto the walkway, nodding and serious; he held his breath as if he were diving. The trestle quit the shore, and Clare stepped out over the bay and the strait in a socket of light. Sky pooled under his shoulders and arched beneath his feet. Time rolled back and bore him; he was porous as bones.

"No," he said to Obenchain—but Obenchain was already far behind him on the bluff, his head swaying up like a blind man's. No, indeed. The sky came carousing down around him. He saw the sun drenching the green westward islands and battering a path down the water. He saw the town before him to the south, where the trestle lighted down. Then far on the Nooksack plain to the east, he saw a man walking. The distant figure was turning pea rows under in perfect silence. He was dressed in horse's harness and he pulled the plow. His feet trod his figure's long blue shadow, and the plow cut its long blue shadow in the ground. The man turned back as if to look along the furrow, to check its straightness. Clare saw again, on the plain farther north, another man; this one walked behind a horse and turned the green ground under. Then before him on the trestle over the water he saw the earth itself walking, the earth walking darkly as it always walks in every season: it was plowing the men under, and the horses, and the plows.

The earth was plowing the men under, and the horses under, and the plows. No wonder you are cold, he said to the broken earth, he said to the lighted water: you kicked your people off. No generation sees it happen, and the damp new fields grow up forgetting. He would return home and see his cedar shingles off on the train. Clare was burrowing in light upstream. All the living were breasting into the crest of the present together. All men and women and children spread in a long line, holding aloft a ribbon or banner; they ran up a field as wide as earth, opening time like a path in the grass, and he was borne along with them. No, he said, peeling the light back, walking in the sky toward home; no.

CHAPTER LXIX

Down at the depot, Wilbur Carloon and Tom Tyler finished loading the two cars. By sunset, half the town was there. Unshaven men in white shirtsleeves, straw hats, and dirty trousers surrounded Wilbur Carloon, to make sure he recorded precisely their shares of the load. Carloon was writing in a ledger propped on Tom Tyler's broad back. Carloon had pushed back his hat, revealing the pale coils of his hair in rows; his wide mouth pressed tight as he reckoned and wrote. Across the street the Depot

Restaurant was boarded up, and a barbershop and a real estate agency were boarded up; no one had removed the bright advertising signs.

The diminutive An Ho had carried Walter to see the cars off. Wearing a tall hat, she milled about in the twilight with the storekeeper Grace Fishburn, whose spirits were low, with Grace's big, active daughter, Vinnie Fishburn, who restrained young Nesta, and with Pearl Sharp, who never missed an occasion. Now An Ho lifted her brown skirt and petticoats to step over a set of tracks—the same set of tracks on Railroad Avenue across which the disgraceful water fight had occurred two and a half years before. She peered in a melancholy way at the open boxcars. Reddish packets of made shingles, in stacks, filled both boxcars from floor to ceiling, except for a corridor near the doors, which men were loading with dusty and toppling sacks of potatoes. An Ho smelled the fragrant cedar shingles; she envisioned the shingles' transmutation into handfuls of greenbacks and premium gold coins. She had been disappointed before. Johnny Lee worked in the woods every spare moment all summer; tomorrow he would start again in the cedar, although no one knew if there was any market on earth for the shingles, or if any such market would last.

Johnny Lee, his close-set eyes softening, saw his wife inspect the cars. Down the track, she joined a bunch of children looking over the rusty locomotive. Johnny Lee was waiting for a chance to speak to Wilbur Carloon, whose coiled yellowish hair and downcurved nose he could not look at directly. Johnny Lee's savings were gone. He had bought shares in a waterworks in Goshen; it failed in July. He held certificates in the biggest bank in Seattle; it closed its doors in May, and would not pay. The bank's Whatcom branch forfeited the cash in his demand account; already, alder saplings were sprouting between the bank's steps. Johnny Lee had attained manhood in China despite a dizzying sequence of droughts and famines; he saved to forfend such emergencies, and now, the emergency having come, his savings had gone. John Ireland Sharp held his wages steady; still, at day's end he took to the woods to cut cedar, and brought his son. He knew the woods. Both here and in the Sierra, he and his brother Lee Chin used to find snails and mushrooms on the forest floor; Lee Chin dug bracken fern roots excitedly, boasting and scheming, and his face widened when he smiled.

Clare Fishburn strode from the knot of men around Wilbur Carloon to join Tom Tyler in front of the warehouse. Tom Tyler's mouth always looked to possess an unnatural number of teeth, those spreading teeth, which forced him to smile. An amused young man on a dun pony rode up, and Tom Tyler and Clare walked beside him. Tyler, who served on town council, was cheerfully owning that the town was washed up; it could not collect any taxes.

The amused young man drew rein and dismounted. Clare took out his pipe and packed it, settling a shoulder against the warehouse doorway; he was "right fond," as he put it, of this natty fellow. He was George Bacon, a live spark of a Whatcom booster, who had been to college. He jiggled his hands in his pockets and greeted Clare. He was the mortgage agent; he loaned eastern banks' money to Puget Sound farmers. These days he was carrying those farmers through the panic, and begging them—he told Clare and Tom Tyler—to hang on and pay a little interest now and then. The indebted farmers were delighted at the sight of him, he said—they held their heads up, whistled, and walked tall. They knew he would not foreclose and saddle his eastern clients with profitless farms that owed taxes. Bacon's thick mustaches trembled; he liked to hold down his smile for the humor of it. His flat hair above his high forehead parted in the middle. On the other hand, he said, lately if he happened to see a fellow he owed money to, that miserable fellow would lower his head and slink around a corner, lest he slip him a deed and hang property around his neck. These were plain peculiar times. One of his partners paid his tailor today in building lots. The tailor shook his fist.

George Bacon had been out of town, he said. Twice a year he visited his New York clients. A week ago in New York he took in National League baseball; he watched the Boston Beaneaters take the New York Giants to the cleaners, Kid Nichols pitching. That same night he attended one of Hoyt's Comedies. Now he would be back at work tomorrow, riding his pony, Pedro, into the timber forty miles up the Skagit River to see a farm, with all of America behind him.

George Bacon could not be said to be truly abreast of what was afoot; he had missed the local news men were analyzing at the dock. He had not heard that the deputy city clerk was under investigation for forgery. Forgery! Just like the big-time cities. He had not even heard about the Seattle madam. Clare told him. It seemed that last spring a Seattle bank president had personally signed a certificate of deposit for a local madam. The certificate was for fifty thousand dollars, the biggest he had ever signed. Now the madam was—this story pleased Clare—"ruined."

The blue light in the sky was fading; the clouds were red, and the gulls were gone. A white owl flew from a broken window in the warehouse behind them. Clare heard Wilbur Carloon close the boxcars' doors and throw the bar. "Prayer meeting's over, boys," George Bacon said. Clare started across the street to talk to Carloon, suspecting that he had had a longer day than any man here. The earnestness of the men who had crowded around Carloon's ledger afforded only the mildest fun; they all had shingles in this load, including George Bacon. The price of shingles had fallen to one dollar a thousand. Even this pittance, however, could not be had. Wilbur Carloon offered seventy-five cents on the dollar, but he could not precisely pay it. He issued scrip, negotiable at his store, in denominations of five cents, fifteen cents, twenty-five cents, a dollar. It was some of this scrip—"shinplasters," they called it—that Clare Fishburn, relieving Carloon, began handing out now from a cigar box.

Men from all over Whatcom County formed a slow line. Tom Tyler held a lantern; men counted their printed papers of money. Clare checked the ledger and disbursed the scrip. A potato farmer slowed the line by counting his under the light, flipping it, and counting it again. "Isn't that right?" Clare asked him. The farmer grimaced. "Just barely," he said.

With shinplasters, people could buy flour, sugar, and bacon at Carloon's store, at current prices. Grace Fishburn used Carloon's shinplasters at her store, too, before it went under, and Dean Whipple at the dying *Bugle Call* accepted it for advertising. Mrs. Ordal hovered in the crowd, holding a dark shawl over her head; if Junior Minton sold his shingles, his wife could pay her the eight dollars she owed. It was becoming apparent to everyone that Wilbur Carloon's enterprise was keeping the town alive; only a few people hated him for it.

The rusty locomotive ejected a white plume of steam. She blew her whistle to clear the tracks. Her light came on. Children jumped back; the crowd surged toward the rails and spread. The engineer waved, and the steel wheels' connecting rods began to rise. The single locomotive and the two cars started down the track towards Seattle and points east. Horace Rush commenced to cry. If the cars of shingles and potatoes found a buyer in Saint Paul, Minnesota, or in Chicago, Illinois, forty dollars or so of cash money would arrive in town, accompanied by cheers and bunting, and Carloon could honor the balance of his accounts.

That night Clare lay in bed with June and the baby Ellen between them. Recently Mabel had objected to this arrangement. "Why do I have to sleep in bed by myself?" "Because," Clare had told her, amused, "you are an American." It seemed to satisfy her—at least somebody knew why. Now he felt his tiredness.

I am asleep, he thought; it felt good. In fact, he was awake. To feel time beating you senseless—it seemed to him—that was the great thing, to feel time beating you off the beaten track and down to the beaches, where the tide sucked at the bluffs and the guillemots dived in the surges—that was the great thing.

After the freight cars left town, Clare had stopped by the beach; he helped Glee pull up his boat in the dark. The sockeye runs were fair, but they were ending; coho runs were starting, pinks and chums. Glee's second son was nine; this summer he shot, with a rifle, a twenty-pound salmon from a cliff. Glee and his family were moving to Seattle. Nothing, he said, was stirring here. To Clare it seemed that everything was. Today he had pleated a worm on a hook and caught a brown trout. By the tracks this evening, he had seen full-bodied Tom Tyler hold the lantern while he counted scrip; Tyler's red beard glowed in the light the way Clare's father's used to. By the Nooksack this noon, he had seen a turtle eat a bud.

CHAPTER LXX

1893, Goshen

Still later that August, during the first year of the panic, the good women of Goshen staged a tree-planting ceremony in the schoolyard, to beautify their world. The children, the mayor, and other townspeople assembled to plant two big-leaf maples, a linden, and—someone's supreme inspiration—a Douglas fir. They were disappointed that so few men attended. The men, for their part, who had exhausted their youths and manhoods, crippled their backs, and sacrificed flesh, digits, and limbs at the task of clearing trees, marveled at the women's zeal at planting trees, and reflected, not perhaps for the first time, that their partners and helpmeets seemed never fully to grasp the nature of their joint venture.

"They're down at the school planting trees," Welshy Bovard said to Elmer Pike, leaving the post office that noon. He put the faintest warm emphasis on the word "trees." Elmer Pike replied, "I know it." The two men's glances met deeply, on the edge of amusement, for a fraction of a second before they parted for their respective farms to continue their tasks.

The next morning, Minta Honer woke to find a crowd of men, women, and children encamped about her yard. She looked from her window: they were people she had never before seen. They climbed from their blankets on the grass and put on shoes, even the children. Minta dressed in something, hooked on her dingy spectacles, and neglected to arrange her hair. Then, as the sun warmed the side of the house, she sat with Green on the porch steps and talked to the people. They had walked all yesterday to the hop ranch from Whatcom to pick hops. There was no cash on the bay, a vigorous young Swede explained, no cash in the state except on the Skagit delta farms, so far as they knew, and they had heard she was paying a dollar a day cash. And ten cents a day for children. Was it true? Well, Minta said, she guessed it was true. She rubbed at her face. She had already hired all the Nooksacks who wanted to pick, and the Lummis, some families from the Tulalip reservation, and what seemed like half the Indian families in British Columbia.

Minta possessed, however, if she looked at it in a certain light, all she needed and more. A bank in Baltimore administered her share of her father's estate and remitted her checks when she asked. The depression had soured most of the estate's holdings, but certain manufactures in steel and textiles continued to pay dividends. Last year hops fetched a dollar a pound. She was the biggest hop grower in the county. With horror she heard herself say, "Would you all like some coffee?"

The next morning she discovered another crowd in the clearing, carrying their lunches, and the next morning there were more. There were families from the islands, families from Birch Bay, Anacortes, and Blaine. The women wore faded skirts, fitted basques, and flat-brimmed hats; the men wore jackets and collarless shirts, or overalls. The girls had stained their aprons with berries they had picked on the way. Minta had forgotten the world contained so many strangers. Rusty-haired Green showed them his pet gosling, which bit. They were experienced pickers, the people said. The growers who usually hired them were not picking this year. They did not stress this point. Minta knew the other growers were letting the berries shrivel on the vines, for the price was down to twenty-five cents a pound for hops picked, dried, bagged, and hauled. She herself had no choice, she thought. She hired them all. Anyone would do it.

On the third day, after breakfast, Minta was picking green beans in the garden with Ardeth. Ardeth had tied her sunbonnet so tight it looked like a rifle barrel; she worked low, kneeling on her apron.

This morning all the beans in the garden, of every variety, had evidently ripened at once. Minta and Ardeth moved down the rows, filling baskets with green beans, and filling soap jars with black and yellow slugs. Ardeth wore gloves in the garden, for which vanity Minta twitted her, all unknowing how highly the girl prized pallor. Above their bent heads, over the yards and pastures, over the fields and woods, shone the solitary, glossy peak of Mount Baker, whose snows the sun edged as it rose.

Ardeth had Queen of the May's long face and Charles Kilcup's strong teeth; her engaging enthusiasms and alarming despairs kept Minta fascinated. She could come back from an hour's trip to the bakery heated up with stories to last a week. Minta, for her part, felt she had never enjoyed a finer friendship than with this unexpected young woman of fifteen; where no love was required, it flourished, and she thought Ardeth her better half, her darling, the sharer of her heart. Almost everyone she knew leaned on Minta. Minta, for her part, leaned on God, and on Ardeth. She sometimes thought she favored Ardeth over all her children living and dead. She thought the same of Hugh, Howard, and Green severally and in turn, and of Bert gone-before, and Lulu as well, just as often, and never noticed.

As the years passed, Ardeth had imperceptibly parted from her brothers and joined the adults—Minta and Hugh, and Jenny Lind. Her uncle Kulshan Jim was the man of the place, but he did not linger; he hunted ever higher in the mountains, and stoutly worked his own Boston-style homestead. Her mother—technically her foster mother, but who minded?—and Jenny Lind made room for her at hurried teas on the Honer porch, or in Jenny Lind's furnished parlor after church. Over tea both women derived a grim enjoyment from speaking of themselves as old and done with. Ardeth snorted and remonstrated, for this was expected. Jenny Lind's physique, as Ardeth said, was youthful, and her visage, as Ardeth said, was splendid. (Goshen was growing into so populous a town that the appearance of persons began to matter, as it did not in villages.) Minta was only forty-two years old, Ardeth went on—had not Mr. Street St. Mary of Whatcom proposed marriage to her just last month on the street? This always broke their reserve and set them off. Privately Ardeth puzzled over their amused repetition of this theme; they were indeed old and done with, so where was the drollery?

Ardeth's enrollment in the normal school's preparatory course had persisted through last summer, when the school folded. Her favorite schoolteacher had stayed in Goshen; he lacked the funds to move. He joined the survey—there was always a survey—and appeared at odd moments in church. Her friend Mina Reese also liked him, and she had red hair. Ardeth brushed and fashioned this red hair into beau-catchers for her friend, as Mina roached and pinned and crimped Ardeth's hair for her; they felt they had much in common.

Now in the garden two blue shadows fell across the vines. Minta turned to see her sons Hugh and Howard, back from the fields. They stood a minute. Small Howard tucked his red thumbs in his galluses and spread his legs, and Hugh—wooden-faced and slender, wearing a tight jacket and boots—composed his thoughts.

Hugh wiped his wide hands slowly down his trousers. "Mama," he noted mildly. "... Down at the fields now every berry has—well—every last old white berry has ... its own personal picker. Kulshan Jim wondered if you knew." Hugh frowned, and Howard beamed.

Minta rose and said that tomorrow she expected those same pickers and more, and the next day yet more. She explained that there was no cash on the bay. After absorbing that for a minute or two, Hugh nodded and returned to the fields. He would begin his next term at the university in three days. Howard beamed again and followed; he squinted behind his clear spectacles.

Picking time was wild for everybody, and the children loved it. Howard's school would also resume in two days, and he would be practically alone in the classroom for the first three weeks, till the hops were picked. On the other hand, when he got home all those other children would still be here. At night the serious Canadian Indian men gambled at the bone game. They knelt in two long lines behind peeled poles; they wore handsome straw boaters and vests, and some wore neckties. The women watched, cheered, exclaimed, and brought out blueberries and licorice. Some made light of Minta Honer's munificence, nearsightedness, and improvidence. These nights there were more children, awake and playing by lantern light, than either Howard or Green knew the world contained.

The whiskey seller Iron Mike camped in his wagon nearby, and when Minta drove the man off he came right back, so she gave up.

"Is whiskey so much worse than beer?" Howard heard his mother say one night to his sister, who looked alarmed. "My husband took a drink, and so did my father, and these men work every bit as hard." Long-faced Ardeth looked like she might swoon into the sink; she shut and locked the door to her room, and Green had to sleep on the horsehair sofa. The Dorrs and the Reeses pitched fits, too, when they saw the whiskey wagon, and said, scientifically, that the Indian people were like children. It was something in their blood; they could not stand up to drink. They raised hell and put a chunk under it. Kulshan Jim and Jenny Lind did not like it either. They forbade their children to go near there. So did Minta, on pain of whippings. They were all good children, who, however, knew their own interests; they slyed out to play with the children and took the chance.

That afternoon Hugh met an old friend whose wagon had busted. He was returning along the forest road from the hop fields when he saw Angus Reese leading a horse and a wabbling wagon towards the village. Angus was his schoolmate since childhood, a broad-faced, quick-witted youth, class salutatorian, who starred in home-talent operettas and founded an alpine hiking society. The wabbling wagon was the muffin wagon. Mr. Virgil Reese, Angus's father, had bought it from the Dutch minister two months ago, for four blueberry muffins.

As the muffin wagon neared, Hugh saw that one of its wheels was clean off the ground. Angus hailed him and started talking without slowing. The front axle broke in a hole, he said; he was taking cream to the creamery, and had no time to lose. He had roped his wagon's broken axle to the high corner of its own frame and carried onward. Hugh saw that the jury rig worked; the rope raised the down corner, and the muffin wagon rolled on three wheels. Angus pulled evenly on the lead rope; the old cayuse's walk was slow.

"Do you know where I can get an axle?" Angus asked Hugh over his shoulder, conversationally. "... Or oak to carve one? The cream must go in tomorrow, too, and every day."

Hugh turned and caught up with him.

They had an oak log he could have, he said. It was garry oak from a grove on Charles Kilcup's old claim. He told him where it was in the barn.

Angus Reese and Hugh's friend Josie Dorr were hoping to marry in three or four years, but the depression had forced both of them out of the university in Seattle. In three or four years' time, Hugh knew, they would still be working to meet their parents' mortgage payments, not their own. Josie Dorr was taking in laundry. Angus's father clerked until recently at the dry goods store in the village—"the establishment," he called it— which had disestablished itself into the hands of a receiver in July. Now Virgil, his wife, Lottie, and their many children were putting up a second crop of timothy hay for eight new cows, two of which neighbors had donated. They possessed a two-story frame house and eighty acres partly in ditched marsh. When the dry goods establishment failed, Angus and his sister Mina were forced to leave the university. They set to separating cream and driving it to the creamery. They would need eight or sixteen more cows to live on cream winnings. Welshy Bovard, who also sold to the creamery, did all right, but he milked thirty cows himself.

Hugh bade Angus farewell and turned back towards his house; he scratched the curly hair under his hat. Hugh alone, of all his friends in Goshen, could afford to continue his university studies in these hard times. There was no question of Vinnie's matriculating; her savings from lunch would help the family start in Seattle. Last week the Whatcom *Bugle Call* reported that of the four girls and three boys who had planned to matriculate from Whatcom this fall, only two, a boy and a girl, could actually go. The others were presumably splitting shingles, or trying Seattle like Vinnie's family, or moving to California, as people did when they lost hope and threw in the towel, or when they surrendered themselves excitedly to wild fate.

Hugh turned up the carriage road and stopped in the field to check on Gossip, on Peaches, and on the new horse, Caspar, a meticulous, philosophical sorrel gelding who was the pet of the place, because he had white mustaches.

Tomorrow Hugh would take the train into Whatcom, stay with his aunt June, and spend an evening and a morning with Vinnie Fishburn before the early steamer sailed for Seattle and the university. Hugh knew his mother hoped he would complete his studies and return to run the farm. She had been training him for it since she gave him his first bee colony to raise on fireweed, and a dozen blue medicine bottles in which to sell honey. Instead, in a year, he was going back to Baltimore. It must look to her as if her whole emigration and enterprise had been a wide detour.

By the pasture gate, Hugh ran his hands down the horses' hard legs. Caspar followed his movements, his mustaches dripping. Hugh found farm life messy and talky. A farmer had to chat up the workers and the buyers, if not the whole legislature, all the while watching his step on the logs. He saw his mother compose three lists a day before breakfast, and rise from the breakfast table to add to those lists, frowning through her greasy spectacles. He held no brief for agricultural idylls.

Of course he wondered, deep in his unrelievedly earnest mind, whether, given his lugubrious history of seeing people die and discovering their bodies, medicine was not perhaps the last profession he should pursue. He seemed, however, to doctor livestock in Goshen without undue mishap. Goshen had its first doctor now—a woman—but no veterinarian except Hugh, who was, he said, "no better than willing." He tied calves to castrate or dehorn. He shaved a powder of blue vitriol—copper sulfate— from the glassy blue stone he kept on a window ledge. He used it as a caustic. He treated cattle poisoned by wild parsnips; he punched cows' bellies with a trocar, or a knife if he had to, to let out gas, and those wounds never festered; he hoped to learn why. His brother Green once lighted the rushing gas with a match; it burned every kind of pretty color, but it scared the cow so she rushed a fence and broke a leg.

Since to the villagers a man willing to wipe off newborn calves and trim horses' hooves was practically a physician, they importuned Hugh in their own emergencies; he bound wounds with court plasters he made by soaking cotton in glycerin adhesive. He drew the line at birthing babies and jumping Virgil Reese's teeth. At Johns Hopkins, he hoped to embark on a white-shirted curriculum composed chiefly of shaving useful palliatives from colored stones.

He packed his *itkus* in the room he shared with Howard. He would ultimately doctor the children of the deserving poor, he thought, and only rarely request payment for his services. He had seen enough of education to suspect, however, that another six years of schooling on the East Coast would alter his notions in unguessable directions; he might end up anywhere, doing anything, and tell himself he had meant to all along. Further, he was just beginning to understand that Vinnie Fishburn hoped, in the depths of her dear, girlish heart, that he would become a physician to the rich. The rich, after all, had ailments, too—grievous, interesting ailments. She let this drop one day in the store. She would keep his accounts, she added, all aglow. They would live on Lake Union, in a big house filled with children, nursemaids, and canaries.

CHAPTER LXXI

Whatcom

A man's greatest treasures, it seemed to John Ireland Sharp, are those things about which he cares nothing. How rich, how invulnerable, is that man indifferent to the fate of everything he owns, even his life! He sought to rout vainglory from the field, and emulate Hyperbolus, of whom Plutarch said, "having no regard for honor, he was also insensible to shame."

Late on the first of September, on Lambert Street in Whatcom, young black-haired Vincent Sharp was deploying iron soldiers over the red parlor carpet. Pearl Sharp was looking at the Sears Roebuck catalogue. She moved the china lamp across a table draped and fringed in beads, and her long-throated shadow grew and loomed impressively on the wall. John Ireland Sharp, wearing carpet slippers, was picking his way through the parlor to his study. He paused to glance at the catalogue pages opened in his wife's lap: he saw engravings of electric stoves edged in brass, and gas stoves the size of locomotives, possessing three stories and two ovens.

Pearl detained her husband in the parlor; she had something to show him. She hastened up the stairs, her skirt swashing. John Ireland bent his neat head and picked up the catalogue. It fell open at a well-thumbed page picturing maidens in corsets, where, he presumed incorrectly, his oldest son, Cyrus, was pursuing his studies—surely not Vincent, Rush, or Horace. He turned the pages and saw pneumatic tires for bicycles, cast-iron muffin pans, bow ties, foot scrapers, plumb bobs, apple corers, top hats, stickpins, and pipes.

"How many things there are in the world," he thought, "of which Diogenes hath no need!" It was a story he used to tell pupils, back when he cherished hope for pupils: Diogenes visited a county fair. He marveled at the swords, cloths, pots, combs, shoes, flasks, mirrors, pillows, and all the rest, and remarked, "How many things there are in the world of which Diogenes hath no need!" It was Diogenes too—wasn't it?—who shaved off one side of his hair, so he would not be tempted to stir abroad among men and listen to the day's passing excitements. John Ireland thought that he himself could live tranquilly—could live gloriously—on the island with half his hair, forking potatoes from coals on the hearth. He did it every summer. What was keeping him?

Pearl returned to the parlor bearing three sheets of stiff paper: plans for the new house, the former McAleer mansion. She flushed to her hairline; her tight, animated smile was as wide as it could be, lifting her cheeks into spheres. John Ireland moved the lamp again and spread the sheets on the table. Pearl had toured the house today with An Ho, she said, who found its solid splendor and airy prospects as enchanting as she did. Johnny Lee and An Ho had consented to join the Sharps there, in the five rooms on the third floor. She herself missed having babies underfoot. The Lees' little Lord Walter was full of tornado juice, and would answer for a world of babies.

John Ireland studied the plans. When Pearl threw herself into things, she excelled. She had drawn each floor pretty much to 1:10 scale, and labeled the rooms in a fair copperplate hand. Cyrus, she explained, could have the west tower to himself. The tower was really a heated "birdhouse sort of place," from which he could view the sea and the islands; when the rains came he might very well prefer it to the beachfront where he was living now. The east tower could go to Vincent, who was too old to bunk with Horace. Vincent, from the floor, cheered; he did not rise to look. Their own bedroom faced west; just beyond it, her dressing room, lined with mirrors, would absorb clutter. In the plans John Ireland could see Horace's bedroom, facing south and east; it would be warm, and he approved. Maybe Horace cried so plenteously because he was cold. A sewing room, by Horace's room, would give Mrs. Ordal space to cut fabric without tying up the dining room.

On the next sheet, John Ireland saw the new house's wide entrance hall and curved staircase, occupying much of its ground floor. The kitchen and the pantry were large. If they opened the wall between the enormous dining room and the parlor, Pearl noted, they could hold dances in the winter, and have fires burning in the fireplaces. People of their rank were expected to hold dances. A nook under the stairs with a frosted-glass door would go to Rush; he liked his privacy.

Where was John Ireland's study? Well ... Pearl caught his eye. Her black hair rose straight from her white temples and curved out like a brim. She thought he would want to seclude himself from uproar, and spread out. On the back of the sheet she had penciled in the basement. His study could be walled in virtually anyplace he chose. It could be as snug or as ample as he wished, and furnished with, of course, shelves. From there he could keep an eye on the furnace, too, when he was home. Then they could economize on a furnace man's hours.

"I will think about it," John Ireland said, needlessly, and rose.

What, indeed, was keeping him? In his study he lighted the gas lamp and stood spread-legged in the center of the room between two sloping piles of magazines. He scratched under his shirt and rested his hands in his pockets. His head tilted to the left, for a singular thought was opening a passage deep in his mind. He could, someday, buy his way out of his own life. What good was money, if a man could not purchase with it the life he desired? He could settle his share of the money on Pearl and his sons; he could go. He could throw in the money and, after it, the towel.

He stepped beside his dark desk, unseeing. How would this heartening proposition look to the cold eye of reason? Wherein lay duty and honor? In fact, duty and honor lay here, but he had done his time, and he would not, apparently, be missed. The high school would be enrolling many fewer students; people were quitting the region, and those who remained needed their sons and daughters to work. If he himself were—hypothetically—to go, Professor Ascher Dan could possibly be named principal; Ascher could handle the school, and relish it. If the board refused to promote Ascher Dan, perhaps Clare Fishburn could be persuaded to return. His company was failing; he was cutting shakes and shaving shingles for cash; he had seemed to enjoy the work of education, consuming as it was. Clare was thick with Tom Tyler and town hall. He had boyhood cronies in the state legislature, too, men elected when Bellingham Bay had a future they would not easily relinquish. As principal, Clare would be in a position to urge the location of a normal school in Whatcom.

Recently John Ireland had been losing interest in Whatcom. Standing now in his dim study as if on the gleaming beach on Madrone, he saw Whatcom as it seemed from the island when he had to return: as a shore town behind the forest, on the other side of the island, across a deep passage where black-and-white whales breached, on the far side of another wide, wooded island, and north towards the Strait of Georgia, which the

Arctic wind blew down and the salmon swam up, on their way to the Fraser River in British Columbia. He found he no longer cared a whit if Whatcom got a normal school. That was a treasure right there, something to cling to.

It was because he suffered most keenly on the island, he now thought, that its shores drew him. There he had first discovered that he was alone, and nothing the gulls did gainsaid it. That island's north beach was the world's rim, mineral and geological. The heavy clockwork spooling of tides—clearing the mud or wetting the doorstep—and the perpetual airy swingings of the sun around the sea, which told the years, and the moon that illumined the pea patch, and the stars that moving together slid to the water—this was the brainless company he would join. He would witness, not perform; he had never yet done anything, and he never would. He berated himself: he was a moral putterer. The strapping high school student Vinnie Fishburn had a finer mind; his own frivolous Pearl had a broader sympathy; and even his youngest son, Horace, had a braver heart, for although the tiny boy bawled piteously all the time, he bawled in the middle of events, or running towards them—not, as John Ireland felt himself inwardly to bawl, from the sidelines.

Now he would at last permit himself to give up on himself entirely. In the past eight years he had returned to his first and clearest view, which he formed with the memory of the staked Skagit fresh in his imagination: that life in time was a freezing bivouac, and the world's people forever cruel. He had changed this view under the influence of Miss Arvilla Pulver and the Oberlin professors. The massive economic evils he saw in New York he thought he could help alter. Although he had been only a boy on the Skagit, he felt implicated in the evil. He had wanted to redress his earlier passivity. That morning on the Seattle dock eight years ago, however, when he saw slim Mary Kenworthy jump on a crate in triumph and wave a hat full of cash to expel the Chinese, he apostatized again. Now he thought: if I cannot learn, how can I teach? This question, in this phrasing, had sounded in his head these past eight years like a song, nonsensical as it was.

It was in John Ireland's nature to pile on the agony in a dignified manner, and exaggerate his honest failings and normal fears; it was in his nature to shrink from the viciousness of men, as he put it to himself, and to punish himself on the familiar hardness and emptiness of nature. That living alone and useless on the island would torment him, he did not doubt; he had done it. He had learned that bare beauty and truth left him heartsick, like everything else. For what crime would he torment himself? Why, for deserting his family—even for having wanted to desert his family for so long. It was tidy. It was cowardly, but it was his duty.

Tomorrow he would consider further. He knew himself for a conservative man who lived soberly, passively, without imagination or hope. It could be that when he jumped, he jumped far. He had jumped only twice before in his life—from the island to Oberlin, Ohio, at Miss Arvilla Pulver's pressing, and from bachelorhood to marriage, possibly at Pearl Rush's pressing. Could he find it in himself to act on his own hook, to pick up his stake and walk? Did life stir in his fragile bones yet, and will? There was no hurry, unless this impulse which so invigorated him as he stared into the shadowed corner of his study, which so quickened his pulse and his breath, should weaken and faint from dread.

He heard Vincent bagging his soldiers, and Pearl climbing the stairs to bed. He sat to his desk. He folded his small, freckled hands. Before he spoke a word to Ascher Dan, and before he spoke a word to his school superintendent, he must find Beal. He had telegraphed the Morgan Bank to open an account in the name of Beal Obenchain, and to transfer one third of Martha's legacy there. Beal must needs learn about his fortune, and in person, too, for the gesture of it. Then he would settle her share on Nan. If he stayed, he would write Nan a letter to the island. If he left, Glee Fishburn's dory could carry him to the island one last time, and he would tell Nan himself.

Nan Obenchain was thirty-one now. When he saw her this past summer, her heavy blond hair tumbled down her back; her wide eyes were growing light with the years. She had married a hermit from tiny Lingcod Island, a sullen giant named Will Ruffin. After the wedding they left by war canoe for a camping trip. Now they had three ruddy round-headed children, who roamed the forest and shore like deer. Nan blew on a trumpet of bull kelp to call the children to dinner. They grew quinces and plums. They burned coal that had washed in when a coal-bearing ship broke up on the reef by Lingcod Island.

John Ireland had no use for Will Ruffin, and neither had the Shoreys, who gave the pair a nightlong wedding party in their house. The next morning they told John Ireland at breakfast, from the height of their position as long-settled worthies, that they had hoped the fair and endearing Nan would make a finer match.

It was said that Will Ruffin washed the family laundry by trailing it by a long cord from his rowboat. That did not seem right to the Shoreys; washing was meant to be hard work. Lee Shorey—a wiry, mild man who wore a slouch hat—had often glimpsed Ruffin on Lingcod Island, where he lived alone from boyhood. John Ireland knew that island as, mostly, a sandstone ledge that storms pitted. There red-billed oystercatchers and seals fished, and there, Shorey said, Will Ruffin lived in what looked from the water like a puffin burrow, enlarged and roofed. One Fourth of July years ago, Lee Shorey told John Ireland, he was sailing his family home from a picnic at Birch Bay when they passed Lingcod Island. The Shoreys saw Will Ruffin just after sunrise: a hardy young man was climbing the ledge with a firing piece in one hand and a steamy cooking pot in the other. When he got to the island's highest point, thirty or forty feet up, he primed his firing piece and, whooping, shot it off at the sky, to celebrate the nation's independence. Then he folded his legs under him and ate whatever was in the cooking pot. Shorey, over breakfast indoors, folded his hands against his vest, as if he had proved, and now rested, his case against the damned.

John Ireland acknowledged he held nothing against the man—he rather admired any oddities of behavior that scandalized worthy families and set them cackling. He was not certain he tolerated him sixteen thousand dollars' worth, however. Ruffin glared at people, and often failed to respond to friendly comments. Nan smiled emptily whenever he loomed near her; she worried about him, which enraged him, and she seemed to think he hung the moon. He would control the legacy. John Ireland wondered what he would do with it.

An impulse to celebrate seized John Ireland in his study, although he had yet done nothing. He knew for the first time how Pythagoras felt when, pleased at his discovery of the mathematical nature of right triangles, he went out and sacrificed a bull.

John Ireland set forth just after dawn the next day to track Beal Obenchain down. He might be anywhere. John Ireland started by walking south of town along the trolley tracks. Ahead he could see the height where the railroad right-of-way entered the woods. He was wearing a wool worker's cap and a tight jacket, in a pocket of which he carried the last letter from the Morgan Bank. His empty hands he bore limply at his sides, and his arms barely stirred with his short strides.

It was curious to seek the man he had avoided for so long. For several years John Ireland had regarded Obenchain as a closed man who lacked all ease, who jerked himself along by a series of acts of will. "I will never again drink milk," he had said as a vengeful, trembling boy. ("But you love milk," his mother had said, bewildered.) "I will have nothing further to do with Clarence Millstone"; "I do not read American books." Sometimes he behaved well—when he joined the company of men to raise an island roof, when he joined the men at sheep penning every spring, and helped townspeople launch *Cleopatra*. These acts, too, John Ireland considered the product of Beal's vows. Indeed, overgrown Beal made vows so consciously, and with such strain, that he seemed to fancy that he alone of all people felt any responsibility to the world, and he alone made moral choices. From his earliest years, John Ireland thought, Beal disdained the world's people morally as well as intellectually. His manner, even as he strangled a calf with a crowbar in a barn, was that of a patient saint finally provoked beyond human endurance by continuous attacks. His approval of his own virtue, if he had retained it, was really a species of gift. John Ireland could not imagine what sixteen thousand dollars would do for Beal. Beal had never prized wealth that John Ireland could see—at least not so much as he prized freedom, which the town called laziness—but the sixteen thousand dollars were his, if not by right, then by John Ireland's decree. Handing the money away would do a world of good for John Ireland himself; it would be like cutting half his hair.

It was early September, but in the forest aisle the day was cold and dark. The fall of the year could not come so early, John Ireland thought; not yet. September should be fair, would be fair. Premature night, however, was already intruding into the evenings, and he had been growing uneasy and sorrowful, the way people here did in the fall when they first felt the winter blackness tighten about them like a noose. Pliny described what he called a happy death. A comedy actor named M. Ofilius Hilarus was entertaining guests at his birthday party. On a whim he put on his comic mask, and happened to die within it, which was not discovered until the person sitting next to him said, "Your soup is cold." John Ireland felt like Hilarus.

The fir trunks were dark with moisture, and on them the lichens glowed green, like phosphorescent animals underwater. The air was so wet John Ireland felt that if he were to raise his voice in the forest to call "Beal! Beal Obenchain!" the air would liquefy around him heavy as the sea that drowned and held his parents and sisters and brothers. He did not call out; he followed the tracks deep into the trees.

CHAPTER LXXII

A little later that morning, on his day off, Johnny Lee walked into the woods south of town, looking for cedar. He carried only an ax, holding it near the head. Walking with the substantial man was a short-legged boy. Walter wore a red jacket, high-buttoned baby shoes from Victoria, and blue cotton pants open Chinese-style along the seam, obviating the need for diapers. The forest was hazy with mist; innumerable dead twigs on fir trunks crisscrossed the mist and divided and dispersed the light infinitely in the middle distance.

The going was rough. When he could not get around a blowdown, Johnny Lee carried Walter up steps of branches to the top of one trunk to gain footing for the next trunk, which lay across it, and on to the next above that, so he was thirty or forty feet off the forest floor before he started down. He headed south and west, towards flat ground. When the boy stopped to finger an Oregon grape or to peel moss from a log, Johnny Lee searched the dark trunks in every direction for a reddish, smooth trunk. A cedar stump left by fire would be fine, and so would a deadfall, and so, especially, would a tree. He saw where men had already found cedar, and recently; fresh chips surrounded cut stumps the size of threshing floors. When Walter wandered to climb a log, his father looked for his red jacket and called him back. The tall trees soaked up the sound.

A wren jumped silently in rough slash. High overhead Johnny Lee saw a dozen dark birds, small as dots, soundlessly working firs' lowest branches. Now he could see that to the west the trees gave out into emptiness, at the top of the embankment. There, a footpath through moss ended where light hit, at the top of a rough flume down to the beach. At the cliff edge, twisting madrone trees, looking like flayed muscles, grew low under the fir trunks.

Where had Walter gone? Johnny Lee saw his red jacket, and his round head with its thin queue, disappear around a cedar stump of just the sort he had been seeking.

This cedar stump, however, had a roof and a chimney pipe. It was a house. When Walter did not appear around the other side, Johnny Lee walked over there. No smoke came from the chimney. On a gray bench outside was a water pail, cup, dishes, an overturned basin. The plank door was open. Inside, Walter had climbed from a chair onto a desk; he was trying to get something from a set of packing-crate shelves. Johnny Lee hauled him down, and wiped the boy's dusty footprints from the desk with his palm.

"Come on," he said. "Let's go." He swung him outside and glanced around quickly before he shut the door. There was sooty bedding in there, a stove, a lamp, a candle in a turnip, bright cans, books, a plank floor—all within the wavy red cedar walls. The only light inside was the green and watery light of the forest. He set the boy on the ground and said, "Shame on you," lightly, then reached for his hand to hurry him away.

Something was in Walter's hand; he had taken something from the house. Johnny Lee peeled it from the boy's fingers. It was his own brother's cash tiger—the orange porcelain figure, posed springing, which grasped a coin in its jaws. The coin was black porcelain, and had a square hole in it. Lee Chin had the cash tiger made for himself thirty years ago in Sacramento. In their Sacramento room he kept "His Excellency" on the windowsill. When the brothers went out working on jobs, and here in Whatcom, Lee Chin wore the tiger in a drawstring bag around his neck.

Johnny Lee took a deep breath and looked all around. He left Walter picking lichen from a trunk, and went back into the house. The orange tiger's glaze was cracked, and completely familiar; its black stripes narrowed smoothly where its maker had lifted a round brush. The tiger's brow frowned, its muzzle spread, and its long torso stretched up, as if it had just jumped to pluck the coin from the sky.

Beal Obenchain had his brother's embroidered handkerchief; Johnny Lee saw him use it in front of the livery stable last spring. Was this stump Beal Obenchain's house? He leaned his ax against the desk and examined the dusty papers there with both hands. He opened some books on the floor; he found nothing. Outside, however, he found an octopus trap—a fir box with a hole in it, an eyebolt, and a weedy line—and burned into the box, OBENCHAIN.

He put the tiger in his pocket. "Come on," he said to Walter. His accented English was melodic, its consonants soft. "Time for you to go home." He shifted the ax, picked the boy up, and moved out.

Beal Obenchain, his heels numb in gum boots, looked for clam holes in the mud. Near him were five or six pigs, loose from the town, which were also clamming this tide; the pigs used their snouts. Their snouts left runnels in the silt. The runnels, with the pigs' deep hoof tracks, and the broad tracks of the man, marred the mud flat's colorless sheen with brown ridges and coils.

It was early morning. Twenty feet out from the shore, the tide had turned; the water itself was invisible in blowing mist to the west. Obenchain walked vaguely northward. Sleepless, he had been reeling on the flats for over an hour. The pigs accompanied him shrewdly, just out of kicking range. Beyond the contours of his bulking figure, the trestle pilings were visible, out of water down to the rock piles that anchored them. Behind him the three town wharves ran out over the flats and met the trestle before it curved into deep water. Winter ducks, already down from the Arctic, were calling in their grievous voices, invisibly, out on the swells.

By habit Obenchain watched the mud by his feet. Two holes in the mud, swollen at their edges and linked by a crack, marked something alive and buried in the substrate—a horse clam whose neck stretched up, or a red jointworm, or a stinging proboscis worm. Obenchain crouched at one of these holes. He lowered himself slowly, for his green hip boots, held by suspenders, came up to his midsection, and the stiff rubber resisted. The pigs saw him crouch and, murmuring, ran over to wreck his hole. The big one rooted in up to its eyes and brought forth a horse clam. The clam's brown neck was too big to retract; it hung from the pig's muddy jaws and swung when the pig edged away. The pig watched the man from one low, small eye; it cracked the clamshell and swallowed the mouthful. One of the other pigs, rooting in the hole, recoiled and ran away with its tusks bared.

Obenchain did not particularly care for clams. He was walking to escape the dread that had been overpowering him for a week in his house in the forest. It was early September, and winter was already pooling at his heels. His feelings had rotated under him; the force of his life had turned on him overnight.

The sight of tallow candles against the red cedar walls, the thick door, the tin of tasteless bacon, the dripping trees, exhausted him. His life he considered vile. The memory of his own fitful enthusiasms rebuked him. Nothing had come of them, and he could never believe in himself again; everything was draining away into a basin of loathing. He had known he was heading for it, and now, over the course of this past sleepless night, he was collapsed in it.

He walked unseeing, over black snails and stringy egg masses. Fingers of water moved up the low mud-flat channels. If he was not, as he did not now feel himself to be, the exceptional and superior man, then he was no man. He had wasted his life, his supreme own and only life, to which he had bent the singular force of all his power and hope. Although this had happened to him before—his last belief had emptied and left him sealed with demons—this time was the most murderous, he thought, and he would not recover. Over the past year his brain uncovered undeniable systems of hopeless truths. Now in the September morning, in the light before the year turned inward, he recognized again that there was no delirium to his thinking, nothing fanatic, emotional, or false. His vision was clear. No assertion of the worthlessness of living any life could be denied by reason at any point.

Fog wet his derby, and eelgrass trailed from his boots. It seemed to him—it had seemed to him all his life—that he could feel a precise point, at his neck below one of his ears, from which his fluid soul was making its escape. He could feel the pressure bulging at the muscles there and the skin.

The colorful men and women of the world distracted themselves in all the old familiar ways, and babbled in families over the daffodils. They created in a million tongues a sentimental league to shield, deny, soothe, and deceive each other from knowledge of their own spilling numbers, of the foolishness of their many local preenings, and the piteousness of their helpless condition. Obenchain was too honest to subscribe to these deceptions. He had vowed long ago, and renewed his vow frequently, that if holding hands in a circle and singing hymns, as it were, was what it took to make life endurable, he would rather die. He had endured life, barely, without such clamorings and comforts up to now. There was no question of his apostatizing to embrace them under any circumstance.

The silt underfoot grew soupy and cold, and his boots began to stick.

He passed a clump of oysters and preying ghost shrimp on a rock. Under the morning mist the tide moved in. The pigs were gone, back south, and the discolored water hid their tracks. Obenchain had rarely been abroad at this hour; the spectral light seemed to disperse from the wrong quarter of sky. He headed towards shore; the trestle would take him back home across the bay. From here the town spread neatly under the forest. Nearby, the water was rising up the barnacled trestle piling. Just under its surface, a flesh-colored octopus moved out between rocks. Obenchain gained the stony beach. The fog was moving onshore, and to the west, behind his back, some islands were emerging, dripping, as if they had just risen from the sea.

When young Cyrus Sharp had awakened that morning in the dark of his birdhouse by the northern beach, he found he was powerfully hungry. He had looked from the round window in the door and saw the day under way; Mr. Beal Obenchain was already clamming the flats. It was Saturday. On Johnny Lee's day off, his mother made pancakes—raspberry pancakes, this time of year—and served eggs in silver cups, and two kinds of sausage, a peppery one and a sweet. He pressed his hat down, put on his shoes, wiped his flat nose, and attached his yo-yo string to his third finger. The quickest way home was the shore road; if he was lucky, he could catch the milk wagon.

He was lucky, and the milkman let him off at Wharf Street, at the corner by Carloon's store and the bank. There he saw Johnny Lee, outfitted for chopping wood, who hailed him and asked him if he knew Beal Obenchain. When he told Johnny Lee he had just seen him north of town, Johnny Lee took off downhill on the double. Then he met his father apparently heading homeward, and enjoyed for a moment the sweet peace of thinking he had not missed breakfast. When his father caught up with him, he, too, asked him if he knew Beal Obenchain. Had he seen him around town this morning? Knowing Beal Obenchain by sight had never before occasioned any noticeable popularity in Cyrus, and so he speculated, climbing the porch steps alone, that perhaps his building his own house, however small, had already made him some sort of man among men.

CHAPTER LXXIII

Early the next morning, Hugh Honer and Vinnie Fishburn were botanizing along an abandoned tram railway south of town. Courting couples all
over the region were keen on botany, especially the botany of this forsak-
en tramway, where fresh, young alders grew, and thimbleberries, and
mountain ash. Many times over this summer, walking hand in hand
behind Vinnie's house up to the old logging tracks, the two had passed
other young men and young women deep in conversation together like
themselves, who also from time to time stopped to pluck and press the
flowers that sprang up in the strip of sun. They found lady's slippers in the
spring, trilliums, sweet cicely, and wild roses. This morning they had cut
sprays of trailing myrtle, and eaten raspberries off the vine. Hugh pushed
his hat back; it almost, but not quite, made him look relaxed. His wide
mouth had a wooden set to it, and he held himself like a sentry or guard;
as long as Vinnie had known him, he had an air of soldiering on.

They turned back. Vinnie, sturdy and graceful, was holding her hat by
its ribbons. Today Hugh carried, instead of a plant press, a valise. He had
to catch the steamer *Kathy Anderson* to Seattle, to start his term. The
steamer sailed overnight from Seattle, and reached Whatcom at eight
o'clock. Their parting would not be so wrenching as last year's, for Vinnie
and her family were moving to Seattle in a week or two. The lively memory of last September's parting, however, tinged this one with sentiment.

Nothing will ever be the same again, Vinnie thought; she tried to
lean her head on Hugh's sharp shoulder as they walked, which proved
impossible. It was true that her long hope of further schooling was dashed.
It was true that she and Hugh would likely never again walk this abandoned tramway. Their courtship would transfer to some heartless spot in
Seattle, and Whatcom itself—the scene of all their first happiness, whose
dark, plunging shores and bright waters were all Vinnie knew—would
drop from their lives. How was it possible to endure the losses one accumulated just by living? Sentiment based on fact was the most grievous
sort, she thought, for the only escape from it was to shrug off the fact—
that babies died, say, or that people lost lands they loved, that youth aged,
love faded, everybody ended in graves, and nothing would ever again be
the same. She pounded herself to tears with these melancholy truths, as if

to ensure that she would not betray herself by forgetting them—which, however, she knew full well that she would, as all other grown persons have done, to their manifestly improved mental balance.

The two came out of the woods talking, picked up the trolley tracks, and descended towards the harbor. Hugh wanted to shift his valise, but he did not want to intrude it between them, especially with Vinnie's touching his shoulder from time to time with her precious head. Moving around her seemed overbold, so he struggled on, and tried to banish his impression that a certain set of muscles was starting to cramp. High overhead the solid cloud was reflective in a metallic, scoured way; the sky shed a true light on the painted houses they passed, on the warehouses down at the depot, on the planks in the wharf and the mud flat the wharf crossed.

They were early. It was quarter to eight. From the wharf they could see the *Kathy Anderson* approach between islands far to the south, laying its plume on the water. Below the wharf, on the mud, a whitewashed rowboat stood by to ferry passengers to the steamer, which had to anchor out on a few low tides a month. A big Lummi man used to carry passengers through the mud for a dollar, but he died over the winter. Beyond the rowboat, migrating black brant were feeding on eelgrass. A salmon jumped out of the water. Hugh maneuvered around Vinnie, left his valise by the gangplank, raised his sore arm around the waist of Vinnie's fitted jacket, and drew her out on the trestle footpath. She tied on her hat, an everyday hat of yellow straw with a sharply curved brim. Her black bangs below the brim repeated the arc of her forehead; her eyelids were swollen.

"How is the irrepressible Nesta?" Hugh said to distract her. He was eager for this university term, as he had missed last spring, and Vinnie's evident sorrow made him feel like a cad.

Vinnie's wide eyebrows shot up. "Just the same," she said, springing to life. Nesta came in last night "so skinned up, she looked like the U.S. flag." With full vigor, her broad, ruddy cheeks glowing, she embarked on the tale of her sister's most recent mishap, and Hugh reflected that she distracted from her sorrow almighty easy. The two matched their footsteps to walk close on the narrow footway that curved between sea and sky—or, on this tide, between mud flat and sky.

When they turned back, Vinnie saw that the *Kathy Anderson* was still making up the strait. A few figures had gathered on the wharf ahead, and a cart, and a dog. She stopped and turned to the handrail, facing out to sea, as if to put the world behind her. She took Hugh's hand and stared at the blue, mountainous island whose far shore her father fished every autumn but this one. On either side of the island the water spread and joined the sky beyond in a blur of slush-colored light.

Hugh watched a black eagle descend on the wing; its path took it towards them and down. He glanced at the mud flat and looked again. The crabs were at something on the mud by a piling. There must have been a dozen of those big Dungeness crabs that were pests alongshore. They were scrabbling in an inch or two of rising water. Suddenly he saw that what they were on was a hand underwater, a neck leading to a torso in a jacket, a damaged face, a man.

"It's a man," Hugh said, and took off towards the wharf. Vinnie looked for it, saw it, and felt her breath leave her. Without knowing, she covered her throat with her hand.

It was not more than twenty feet beyond her on the mud flat, slung around a piling's rocks. She headed back along the trestle towards it. An eagle was walking up to it on the mud side, the way a fish crow walks, as if it had all the time in the world. When Vinnie drew up just above the body, the tan crabs were climbing over each other to flee the wading eagle at the belly. She peered through the refracting water. When one crab climbed down across the temple she recognized Beal Obenchain's pale forehead, the close placement of his eyes, and his massive neck, which seemed to flow straight from his chin. The ear on that side was gone. It was indeed Beal Obenchain. She herself had sold him those green hip boots on special order, because his feet were so big.

She tightened her shawl. She had heard of people's drowning in hip boots. Her own mother had a horror of them for that reason, and begged her father not to wear them, but he did; shoes were too expensive not to. Silt drifted over Obenchain's dark clothes, and strands of sea wrack. His body bent near, but not on, the piling's rocks. The torso twisted so the back was down; one of the arms was flung, and the head skewed stiffly up. The head was hatless, and the underwater mud around the body was smooth, pocked with snails. One of the suspenders seemed to shake under ripples, and appeared now broken, now whole. A small red crab came out of the hip boots. Vinnie's detachment ended when she saw both of Obenchain's arms move, as if he were struggling to rise with his face full of crabs. Then her heart jumped. Still, she steeled herself to watch, and saw that the movement was only the tide, which had opened his sleeves and stirred them. Rigor mortis held his arms, the way it held dead salmon. The tide lifted and swirled the body's hair.

She looked down the trestle to the wharf and saw Hugh coming back, his slender figure small under the sky, hastening, but composed; he was carrying a coil of rope. With him were two men carrying the gangplank ladder. On the water side, someone was bringing the rowboat around.

BOOK VII

AFTERWARDS

CHAPTER LXXIV

1893–1897, the Washington coast

Ruinous times continued in the region for four years. In June, 1894—nine months after Hugh Honer discovered Obenchain's body—an unprecedented flood swelled up in the coastal rivers, up in the Columbia, the Nisqually, the Skagit, and the Nooksack. The flood wrecked farms and drowned crops. The price of oats had already fallen to $6.50 a ton, as steam power replaced horses and oxen. Dairy farmers in Goshen, and up the river in Burnett, had begun making Whatcom the leading dairy county in the United States, but prices were off. A team of analysts from the U.S. Department of Agriculture declared that the reclaimed marshes of the Skagit delta "possessed the richest soil on the globe." Most farmers there, however, and in Goshen, had no cash to buy seed.

Whatcom's lively George Bacon rode his pony out to encourage farmers; his New York mortgage holders would carry them without payments, if they would hold on. Some did—especially, as he saw it, the Scandinavians. They had nothing to grow, and nothing to sell, so they cleared land in the hope that prices would someday rise. They falled the big firs with crosscut saws and with fire; they scaled the trunks with axes and saws. They bucked the logs with axes, fire, and dynamite. They yarded and moved the bucked logs with steam tractors or donkey engines if they had them, or with crews wielding peaveys, and with oxen, horses, mules, chokers, and chains. They floated and milled some and burned many more in heaps. When they found cedar, they made shingles and shipped them east for a few dollars. A Finnish farmer down on the Skagit built a two-story house from a single log, and also sided a barn. He harvested some hay every summer, and hung it like laundry on fence rails to dry. George Bacon, slender-headed and wearing thick brown mustaches, walked out with the farmer along the fence rows, and came into the house to tell stories over a lunch of dried-apple pie.

In Seattle every dark enterprise flourished underground, and gamblers slipped protection money to the police. "It's a wide-open town," people said. Glee Fishburn found the term rang false; he tended bar in an underground saloon, and felt close-hauled. He was tall, thin-limbed, and stooped; his trousers rode high over his potbelly. When the bar owner told him to water the whiskey, he refused so gently that he kept his job; customers liked him, quiet as he was. Certain of his regulars supplied him with books. To simmer down at two in the morning from the rush of the bar, he read by lamplight in the bed he shared with Grace—Elisha Kane's Arctic travels. He rose at noon, left the family's hillside lodgings, settled in a dark corner of the bar, and wrote what had become a three-hundred-page narrative poem in which men fought pack ice and polar bears.

There was tuberculosis in the city, and Grace wondered why she had moved her brood. In 1896 a Japanese steamer company chose Seattle for its terminus, and the town rolled out the red carpet for Asian immigrants.

In those lean years, mining alone prospered, and families quit Puget Sound for Colorado and Idaho. Men struggled up Ruby Creek in the Cascades, where a miner found a vein of gold, and up Thunder Creek, where a prospector found silver. Other strikes petered out, and old Jay Tamoree found himself shooting a mountain goat to live on during the long pack trip back. When Frederick Weyerhaeuser started buying timber lands in earnest, however, land prices started up.

Clare Fishburn had owned one of the first bicycles with detachable pneumatic tires on Bellingham Bay. Pneumatic tires endured blows well and cost little to replace. Since it was cheaper to pump tires and pedal yourself than to feed and stable a horse, townspeople unloaded horses and bought bicycles. By May of 1896, these same townspeople, or some just like them, owed Whatcom $96,283 in delinquent taxes. Neither the city, the county, nor the state of Washington had a nickel to spend fixing muckholes in roads. The county had paid all its works from the two hundred dollars it taxed fifty saloons every year. When people left, saloons closed. The cyclists complained of the roads. Street St. Mary claimed to have seen, on the Goshen road, a large sockeye salmon, swimming upstream.

Now more than three years had passed since crabs worked over Beal Obenchain's body in tidewater under the trestle. The Whatcom police had investigated the death and established a likely suspect, who could not be found. Young Cyrus Sharp told police, who questioned him in his big birdhouse, that he had directed both his father and his family's servant, Johnny Lee, to Obenchain the morning in question. John Ireland Sharp told police, in confidence, that he was looking for Obenchain to give him sixteen thousand dollars, the provenance of which he explained. Johnny Lee, with An Ho and little Walter, had left town. John Ireland gave police a forwarding address in Seattle. In fact, the Lees had moved back to Sacramento.

The Methodist minister Broadbent King, a half-starved Scotsman who ran himself ragged performing acts of charity, had resolved, over some opposition, to give Obenchain's body a Christian funeral and burial. At John Ireland's request, Broadbent King delayed the late-summer funeral for four days, to allow Glee Fishburn to sail out to Madrone Island and back.

On Madrone, Glee informed Obenchain's fair sister Nan of his death and began to fetch her and her husband, Will Ruffin, back to Whatcom for the funeral. While they were sailing on their first day out from Madrone, the manila forestay parted with a twang, and the mast and boom dropped into the boat. Glee made a rocky landfall on empty Lingcod Island, Ruffin's former empire, and there he and Ruffin jury-rigged another forestay—a feat not in itself remarkable. Then, however, a storm kicked up and pinned them on Lingcod for two days. Glee told the two, who were not interested, what little he knew of Beal's life and death. When they got under way again, contrary tides and winds caught them, and added another two days and nights to the trip. Nan Ruffin, her face drawn and fine, her calico dress dirty, could be seen in the boat working her lips over some sort of spell, which she repeated day and night—Will Ruffin explained to Glee proudly—for the protection of their three children back on Madrone.

The funeral at last took place in mid-September in the graveyard on the bluff south of town. Both Clare and June Fishburn were in attendance, to general surprise. John Ireland Sharp was there, freckled from the sun, his lips cracked and pale. Pearl Sharp was there, a black gauze veil hanging from her hatbrim; she had a marked proclivity for watching funerals. Bald Iron Mike was there—who had been the sole proprietor, for six years, of Obenchain's old whiskey-selling business at the reservation's edge, and who, giving the coffin a very wide berth like everyone else, nevertheless cried his eyes out.

Obenchain's death had excited June wildly, and when she learned of it she had broken out dancing and beating pans. In the following days Clare could not persuade her that Obenchain's death did not free him, or anybody, from the threat of death. She did not care. At the graveside June was first in line to drop a resounding clod on the box, and when she passed Clare, dusting her hands, she whispered, "Hurrah, boys." Though he loved her, Clare did not like it; one box was like another, after all.

In the cemetery John Ireland moved to scruffy Will Ruffin's side and mentioned that since Beal Obenchain had died intestate, the state would doubtless award his estate to Nan, his sole survivor. Nan favored John Ireland with a melancholy smile, which clearly meant, And what shall my family of five do with a hollow stump on the mainland? John Ireland let it go. Nan and Will Ruffin sailed back with Glee at once.

Over the years, many of Clare Fishburn's friends had died, like Eustace Honer and Chot Harshaw long ago, or moved away, like his brother Glee. Most of his partners in the improvement company had scattered. Increasingly he spent time with George Bacon, who was a McKinley gold bug, but an amusing sort anyway; he enjoyed recounting the expedients that he and everyone else used to get through the depression. In August of '96, Clare and George Bacon, with Tom Tyler, mounted an expedition to the mountains. Tom Tyler had tried to climb Mount Baker the August before, but after eight days' travel to its base, and another day's climb, snow squalls turned his party back. Only three expeditions had climbed Mount Baker in twenty-eight years, though many had tried; one of the successful ones included a woman, a painter named Sue Nevin. Tyler persuaded the group to set their sights lower.

They poled shovel-nosed canoes up the Nooksack from Minta Honer's hop ranch. They were a varied trio: Clare tall and thin as lath, George Bacon slight and garrulous, and beefy Tom Tyler, his mouth full of teeth. They poled past the banks where the logjam had blocked navigation until it was cleared. At Nooksack Crossing they passed the misty farmlands where Kulshan Jim and other Nooksacks homesteaded. They portaged and poled upstream to the forks of the Nooksack River. It was eleven years ago that Clare had met the *tyee* Hump Talem, who was wearing a bearskin cloak and a mink hat. Hump Talem presided over the forks of the Nooksack, where eagles spent the winter hunched in the firs; he presided over the height and breadth of the mountains the three forks drained. Now many of the Nooksacks who remained at the forks of the Nooksack were loggers. They wore their pants legs unhemmed and stagged high on their shins, so no slash caught and tripped them. They had recently wrung from the state the right to live where they lived, in their village.

From the forks Clare could see Mount Baker looking like Captain George Vancouver's familiar description of it from the Strait of Juan de Fuca—masses of glowing opal, a detached island separated by a line of mist, and floating above the dark forest. They poled canoes another day on the north fork, and Clare reacquainted himself with the big fir trunks of his childhood, and the bearded lichens that hung from them in strands. After four days of what Tom Tyler called "cussed and unspeakable" forest bushwhacking on elk trails to snowline—which Clare thoroughly enjoyed— they climbed between two green frozen lakes, and traversed a steep meadow hip-deep in wet blossoms. They skirted a snowfield, climbed, and, as they put it, conquered, an unnamed peak.

The men of the first party to ascend Mount Baker, in 1868, had been so moved they broke into the Doxology: "Praise God from whom all blessings flow...." On the summit of their unnamed mountain, Clare, Tom, and George broke into the rum, but not before admiring the bunched and jagged peaks around them, and the raw glaciers their black and red pinnacles broke through. The mess of rock and ice peaks rose up like waves all around, the men agreed, like a fearsome tumult at sea. Here, however, the troughs fell through torn clouds and down thousands of feet. Just beyond the nearest black-and-white peaks, the mountains were in British Columbia. Clare was astonished to gaze down a corridor in the crags and ramparts to the west and see the glazed waters of Puget Sound. There lay the peaceful blue islands he had been looking at all his life. He was only about thirty-three miles from his house. Was there ever a country like this one?

That summer Pearl Sharp had a telephone installed in her turreted mansion on the height of Golden Street. She and Dolly Carloon established a foundling home downtown and hired a staff to run it. Two times recently, Cyrus answered the doorbell at home and admitted a woman with children who asked to see Mrs. Sharp; both women asked her to take their children at the foundling home, as they could no longer keep them. "I'm swashed up," one said. "I don't have a tail feather left." Both said they would come for their children when times improved. When would times improve? Whatcom had shut off its gaslights. Pearl saw people now in clothes worn to rags, who could not buy fabric with which to sew dresses, jackets, and pants, let alone pay a dressmaker and pay a tailor, as she did; clothing was expensive, and poverty plain to see. One day from a buggy she spied Street St. Mary, who had made forty thousand dollars in the boom, shoveling, with one arm and his stump, peaty coal from a poor seam on land he could not sell. "Well, my coffeepot's run dry," he called out to her in high good humor. "All I've got is my butt and my hat!"

The distraught mothers left Pearl shaken. After she settled the second batch of children in the home, she soothed her restless nerves by making off with a coatful of goods from Carloon's store—headache powders, clarinet reeds, an alabaster inkpot, and a pair of cast-iron ice tongs.

June Fishburn, too, had a telephone; she could connect to the trunk line and ring up Clare in Olympia when the legislature was in session. Clare had run for the Fusion Party, as they called it—those fused Populists and Democrats who opposed the gold standard. They swept the county and the state in '96. He mounted a simple campaign when he got back from the mountains, calling himself a Poplocrat. Later he told June the party "could have run a yellow dog" that year in Washington and seen it win, a remark June had heard biennially since she was four.

None of it came easy. George Bacon's genial reasoning was wearing at Clare's dearest beliefs. Whenever he returned to town from Olympia, George Bacon was there, a smile parting his mustaches, telling stories at the Birdswell Hotel. Bacon had lived back East and passed through four years of college; Clare knew he cahooted with both farmers and bankers. He maintained that it was European investors' fear of silver madness that caused the panic and hard times, not eastern bankers' greed. Maybe western silver miners were the greedy ones. The more Clare thought about it, the less he said on the topic. Even more perplexingly, Clare now found himself reluctantly sympathetic with the socialists' views, with their hope for universal justice, or at least for lower freight rates—the very views Clare previously despised, and in which John Ireland Sharp had lost interest years ago. Arthur Pleasants and his eastern ilk sowed not, but reaped; they took the money and ran. The farmers of the West had played by the rules, worked hard, and now saw themselves ruined by a "system" that, Clare was beginning to think, men had made, and men could improve.

He brought it up to John Ireland once over a dish of ice cream; his old friend shook his head sadly. His mind could still not distinguish socialism from the expulsion of the Chinese. Clare brought it up to George Bacon; his new friend was appalled. Clare's thinking went forward. No bill, however, came before the legislature "to redistribute wealth." It might take time.

His chief task in Olympia, as he saw it, was landing a state normal school for Whatcom. This was neither so simple nor so gratifying as he had reckoned on when he promised himself and the voters to do it. Seven or eight other dying towns had the same idea, for the same reason, and he found he must either bed down with thieves, on one hand, to magnify Whatcom's prospects, or, on the other hand, drill holes in the seven or eight other towns' men, poke embers down them, and let them knock themselves over. Consequently he bedded down with thieves. It was not pretty work. He wondered if any town on earth amounted to a hill of beans. He determined to return to teaching at the high school when it was over, lest he lose his bearings when the currents caught him—though the high school could spin a man around almost as quickly as the statehouse could. He would not have guessed a man his age would have to keep reminding himself of what he knew was true and constant, but in his particularly sorry case he tended to drift and slip if he did not set himself straight every day—even every hour. He possessed, he said to himself, his own death, as Chowitzit hunting in the mountains possessed fire in a gourd lashed to his skin, but he kept letting the tarnfool thing go out.

In July, 1897, Clare was forty-seven. His nose and ears had lengthened; his knees in his long suit pants turned in. The summer was proving mild, and its skies were as deeply colored and changeful as any he could remember. There were many church suppers and picnics; Clare played his fiddle as if there were no tomorrow. He carried the new infant Lee home, its head the size of an incandescent bulb heating his shirt. June shepherded Ellen. Mabel, whose limpness the years had elongated, stayed behind with friends by the beach fires in the dark.

CHAPTER LXXV

July, 1897, Madrone

Late in July they took a sailing trip to the islands. Pearl Sharp chartered *Cleopatra* from the town. Clare brought his family, and Pearl brought her four boys. June's nephew Hugh Honer, back with his mother, Minta, for six weeks from his medical studies at Johns Hopkins, came along, as did his sweetheart, Clare's niece Vinnie Fishburn from Seattle. Thor Avidsen served as mate.

As they rounded out of the bay, Thor Avidsen squinted under his white plug hat. Building *Cleopatra* had broken his health, he told Clare at the helm; she cost him "too much more than every last bit he knew." Four years ago, when they launched *Cleopatra*, she had sailed away with the B class trophy in the Victoria regatta, but the town had lost interest. Although *Cleopatra* was, to Avidsen's trained eye, a far finer boat than the Class A–winning sloop *Helen* he had built two years earlier, the townspeople greeted that first homecoming with bunting and flags, and shrugged off *Cleopatra*'s success as no news. She had been Lee McAleer's boat, so the town had claimed her; now the town could not sell her. He rubbed his face. He had an idea for a spoon-bowed racer, short on the waterline, broad and powerful, which would carry acres of sail. He took off his hat and scratched his scalp, as if to sting himself to long life. He was Clare's age; he had two grandchildren.

Cleopatra was plenty fast enough for Clare, who reduced her sail; he was grateful to young Cyrus Sharp, who caught on fast as crew. The wind blew Cyrus's hatbrim back and showed the softness of his flat-nosed face. At home Cyrus no longer lived in his birdhouse, and he no longer spun a yo-yo. He attended high school, wrote absurdly short epic poems, and played basketball, which wearing sport was all the cry.

Hugh Honer kept an eye on all the children and took tricks at the helm. Thor Avidsen navigated a series of dogleg courses to miss bad tides. They made south and west for Madrone. Loaded with people as she was, *Cleopatra* still rose and planed on the runs. The first night they anchored in a tight bay and bedded down on Daleo Island. The next morning they reefed her down to beat, so that the doleful Horace Sharp—whom a jib sheet had pinned briefly in a strangulation hold on the low side when they got under way—would not blubber or jump ship. Now they were skirting shoals where seals lolled and gulls squawked over hissing seas.

Robust Vinnie Fishburn rode at the bows, wetting her skirts, and watching the green island shores. Her short black bangs, cut in an arc, outlined the soft curve of her skull; her vivid eyes were perfectly circular under flat dark brows. She was twenty-one years old, and generally felt herself to be growing duller as Hugh grew sharper. She would have blushed to learn that Professor John Ireland Sharp had ever considered that she possessed the finest mind in Whatcom. Every day for the past two years she had posted Hugh a letter, and received from Hugh a letter—every day, except for these fine few weeks in late summer when he came home from Baltimore. Composing those letters, she seemed to have nothing to relate. In Seattle she worked seven days a week in her mother's rooming house. The scrapes and escapades of her family's bachelor boarders constituted her days' diversion, but she could not risk burdening a busy medical student, who lived in splendor among educated people, with such rough tales. She wrote, as Hugh did, in a state compounded of mental vigor and bodily exhaustion. After she wrote her letter, she read borrowed books into the small hours. She read books as one would breathe air, to fill up and live; she read books as one would breathe ether, to sink in and die. She outlined for herself brave courses of study in poetry and in ancient history, in preparation for what she did not know—nor did she know how she would obtain the necessary books. She also corresponded with Minta Honer in Goshen.

Hugh apparently found the study of medicine absorbing, but he could not say why. He apparently found a lively friend in his classmate Louis Philip Hamburger, but he could not say why. Together the two had followed the great British medical man Dr. William Osler on rounds, which privilege, he confided in a letter, was the high point in his life. His written expressions of esteem nevertheless grew less wooden every season. The marks of affection he had shown Vinnie this July were affecting. Drawing in the sand with a stick last night, his pale eyes alight, he had explained to the company how Koch's rod-shaped bacillum caused tuberculosis, and Vinnie envied him and loved him. Now she gathered her cold skirts under her and lay supine under the loose-footed staysail. She spread her arms to hold a shroud and a cleat. She felt the deck tilt and pound, and watched the mast stir at the skies.

The day was late when they struck the sails and anchored. All the children, dazed, looked out; the silence rang down on their heads like something dropped. The island lay motionless before them: pale logs lined the curving gray beach, and behind the logs, strips of marsh and clearing gave way to the vaulting trees. The thin water surface was blue, and they could hear it lap on the hull; the sky was blue and still also; and the children seemed to notice, now that they had stopped, that they had been sailing, and were loath to quit. Onshore a figure dragged a green rowboat a few feet to the water and rowed out; they could hear the oarlocks creak and water splash.

John Ireland Sharp greeted his family, whom he saw no more than a few hours a year, with what might have been reserve. His brown face bent into a dozen creases, his smile expanded, and his bare arms wrapped hard around Pearl and the boys, but his voice was a whisper. On the beach by their crates and rolled blankets, he looked over their shoulders at nothing they could find. Clare had seen him five or six times over the years, when John Ireland rowed into Whatcom to visit, to eat bowls of ice cream, and to lay in beans, salt pork, and *Police Gazettes*. He also bought and borrowed dense books on every subject to lend all over the island, for most of the islanders were learned thinkers and readers, he told Clare, though he himself was not.

Now they ate dinner together on the smooth, barkless beach logs. The sky and sand were blazing hot, the air dry. Clare noticed the freckles on the backs of his friend's hands, and the freckles on the bony curve of his forehead, and the white stripe of skin just above that his hair shaded. His hairline was receding; so was Clare's. John Ireland's alertness had softened and gone. His black eyes, glassy, gazed out over the water. His slackness was gone, too. His limbs had tightened, and the cords of his back made a deep cleft the length of his shirt. He said there was a pond in the woods on the island, where he would take them bathing later that night.

John Ireland's house was plank cedar—the old Obenchain house, just back from the beach. His wife Pearl's skirt and triple-puffed sleeves filled it. At home in her vast house on Golden Street, she had baked him four dozen sugar cookies. She laughed now when he offered them round at once and the children ate them all. John Ireland showed Clare and Vinnie the journals in which he recorded, twice a day, the speed of the wind and its quarter, the temperature, and the height of the glass. He showed Hugh, Pearl, and his sons the old hand microscope he used to study mosses: he impaled the moss on a pin and screwed the single lens down to bear on its parts. After trying it, Hugh said, "The single lens works"—apparently amazed—but nobody heeded him. Grease and soot from fir smoke stiffened John Ireland's pants; he lived on porridge, milked a cow, and whispered, as if the size of the sea and the sky overwhelmed him. When he opened his door, sunlight shot the length of his room and blackened its corners. Outside, gulls circled and raised their urgent voices.

Clare and June, Hugh and Vinnie, and Pearl sat with John Ireland on a yellow log before his house. The tide rose; it lowered the sky's light to their feet. They watched the children straggle down the beach. They watched Avidsen row out to Cleopatra; his wake cut green streaks on the water. Vinnie took June's baby, Lee, on her shoulder; the baby held her chin, and she wagged it. They looked out at islands—the blue backs of islands now blinding as the sun hove down. Vinnie shifted the baby over to Pearl, who sighed.

Last winter, John Ireland said, someone had planted a log on the high beach and carved a rough head in it, so it appeared from the distant houses to be a person, perhaps a person coming to pay a visit. This log figure so raised island people's hopes and dashed them, so deceived them a dozen times a day, and especially so revealed to them undeniably that they glanced down the beach a dozen times a day watching for a figure—it so magnified their loneliness and mocked it—that someone beheaded the log with an ax, and split it, and knocked it down. John Ireland laughed. His voice was airy, and he coughed.

At that moment, down the beach, an otter slid from the water; it had something in its mouth. Its thick dark tail undulated with its backbone as it started for the marsh. At the instant Clare noticed the otter, John Ireland had already sprung to his feet and was running after it. He ran hard and purposefully, kicking up fast bursts of sand. The otter turned its flat head and glanced back at the water; John Ireland met it before the marsh and chased it over the logs. It dropped the fish and ran, a waving dark streak. Clare watched John Ireland pick up the fish and turn back. Light-bodied, a swift silhouette, he was running now at an easy lope along the slope of sand and cobbles. He came up to them smiling, and spread the flat fish with both hands before Pearl's face.

"Flounder," he said.

He was not winded; he gazed up the beach as if he would like to run once or twice more around the island. He wiped sand from a log, slapped the fish on it, and brought out a rusty pocket knife. "If you catch your otter just right," he said, looking Clare straight in the eye, "it will clean your fish for you."

They spread their blankets behind the line of logs, in the dune grass where John Ireland said his foster mother used to grow her roses and polyanthus. Then he took them to meet Nan Ruffin and Will. The Ruffins lived down the beach, on the spit. There the sun set behind the braided line of wave that lay on the sea like a lapped seam; there Beal Obenchain had fought John Ireland, when they were boys. Vinnie and Hugh lagged behind, bending to pick up stones and shells.

Will Ruffin met them on the shore; he was almost as tall as Clare. He wore a cracked straw hat that formerly, he told Cyrus and Mabel, belonged to a mule. His own three children paid no attention. He had a thin goatee, which wagged off to one side when he gestured to show Avidsen the expanded size of his land. Clare found Ruffin perfectly amiable, and reckoned that his reputed sullenness, if any, began, perhaps, at his kingdom's borders.

Now Ruffin, however, grimacing with what looked like sudden rage, told Clare that he opposed the new "barefoot schoolboy" law—which stipulated public education for all. They were standing on the beach, looking out at the water. Ruffin shouted and declared his intention to defy the law, and "educate his children at home"—which meant, he explained when asked, that Nan could do it. He seemed to think he was baiting Clare, as if Clare, as a government man, were in effect the truant officer or sheriff. Since his election to the legislature, Clare had grown accustomed, if not reconciled, to being treated, no longer as a man, but as the useful holder of a rank. He had not realized, before he held it, that his office would taint his every meeting with men and women. Ruffin raised his thin goatee at Clare in a challenge, and appeared satisfied that since Clare let it pass—since Clare did not try to scrape up his unschooled children and haul them off to Olympia—he was an inferior man, after all.

Nan glanced at John Ireland, apparently proud of Ruffin; she untied her bonnet when the sun set, and the red sky inflamed her cheeks. She looked at the visiting children and muttered. Mabel stared at her, and so did June, for she was herself a giant, whom some melancholy seemed to have stilled: her features were large and striking, her head perfectly oval, and her hair a heavy pile of light. Her voice was weak, and she rarely spoke. Her long throat, her high ears, and the whiteness of her hairline above her ears gave her an air of straining, of unworldliness. Pearl, who knew Nan from many summers as unworldly indeed, walked around the fenced garden and turned to look at the loose cows and pigs. Hugh and Vinnie appeared arm in arm, black against the gleaming sea. John Ireland had not spoken to Vinnie at all; perhaps he did not recognize her.

The adults settled on the Ruffins' porch. By the door was a heap of cedar logs, which John Ireland looked at in dull recognition. The bucked logs were old and silver, except for their red fresh-sawn butt ends. They were the walls of the old Obenchain barn, which Will Ruffin had just taken for kindling. There were still old cow tail hairs stuck in splinters, and the odd bent nail for hanging lanterns.

Had they heard the news? Ruffin, settled on a log seat, suddenly seemed to remember there was news. That day he had rowed out to a village on Orcas Island, where he bought the newspaper. He rose, rustled around in the house, and came out with the Seattle *Post-Intelligencer*. There was truly news: rich gold strikes in the upper Yukon. Pearl tipped the newspaper into the twilight. Hugh read the story aloud, over Pearl's shoulder, to Vinnie and Avidsen, and Clare followed it over Pearl's other shoulder. The find was on a Yukon tributary called the Klondike. On July 17—a few days ago—the steamer *Portland* docked in Seattle. It carried sixty talkative miners back from the Klondike, and about $800,000 in gold dust.

There was no discussion on the porch; everyone's mind was working. The region's fortunes had swung over again, hard. Vinnie would be needed at home. Avidsen would have paying work all winter. Clare's real estate holdings would be worth something; they could buy food. "That's that," Pearl said. "Let's go home, troops. Hard times is over."

June thought that a bit rich of Pearl. Pearl had just added a furnace man and a second maid to her household; she possessed a new landau and a sleek matched team. June and Clare, by contrast, were sorely behindhand; they had not met a mortgage payment in two years. She herself did not have enough clothes left to dust a fiddle. Clare had to wear a decent suit to Olympia; round-trip fare on the steamer was $2.50. His position cost more than it paid. She fed the lot of them on milk and potatoes. She milked the very cow, and liked it. At first, milking, she wondered what her mother would think. Her mother was dead and in heaven, presumably—up to her wing bones in people who had milked cows. It must be awful for her.

Standing half off the Ruffins' porch, they agreed to go at first light.

Clare enjoyed night sailing, but he held his peace. June wanted to wait till morning, because she was eager to try bathing in the dark, in the pond in the woods; so was Vinnie.

Pearl wanted to sail all night, although there would be no moon. The gold find was a winning for Whatcom. Shipping would return; wholesalers would set up shop; prices would fly up like skyrockets. Pearl wanted to "get in early," she said. She had cash; she had kept her eye on certain lots, including a piece of her parents' old claim by the mill. She could make five different down payments—or ten—and watch the equity swell. She could stake a wholesaler: she knew that a retailer selling supplies to miners would strike it merely rich, but any wholesaler would make a whole killing. It was all a great game—the only game, she said—and this time she would play. Hugh studied this market strategist steadily. Clare glanced at her; excitement made her florid. Death would fetch Pearl away like the rest of us, Clare thought, and her piling up things now did not mean she did not know it, but meant that she did. For now, she began collecting her younger boys from the beach to bed them down. It was almost two hours after sunset, and the sky was dark blue.

Clare strained at the print in the paper. The exuberant story said "one man has worked forty square feet on his claim, and is now going out with $40,000 in dust." Passengers showed anyone "sacks stuffed tight" with gold. In one day, one miner brought out $24,480 in gold from the gravels near Dawson. "Well, well," Clare said, and for a second he wished he were younger. Now he was the kind of man who said, "Well, well," and let the world wag as it would.

Later John Ireland led Clare and June, Pearl, Vinnie, and Avidsen away to the pond for the midnight bathe. There was a long rope swing in the woods that would give the occasion a reckless, celebratory air. Cyrus and Vincent Sharp, who were fifteen and fourteen, got to go, too. Swinging out on the rope would be unsafe for little ones. June put Mabel in charge of Ellen and the baby, and settled them in the blankets in the dune grass near young Rush and Horace Sharp, then set off with the company, behind the marsh and into the woods.

Hugh Honer rowed out to *Cleopatra* to fetch Vinnie's daybook. From the water he heard the Sharp boys hooting in the woods; their voices receded. He himself was not fond of bathing, but he would go. In his childhood he saw many people dying, and people dead; he lighted the fire that consumed Bert and Lulu. At Johns Hopkins he studied anatomy in bits, and failing tissues, and portions of people harboring disease-bearing organisms that kill. Here in the northwest summer during his holiday, here with spirited Vinnie, whom he would marry, he found life abundant. Rowing back, he lifted glowing streams of phosphorescent microbes from the water. He dragged the rowboat up, and it struck stones. The cold water had released its mineral scent; it mixed with the sweet smell of planted land. The night was clear; there was no moon.

Barefoot, Hugh felt his way up the cold sand to the dune grass, where he inspected the sleeping children, lighting matches to find the holes in the grass where they nested. He loaded his pipe, and looked over the water westward, where the multiple contents of the sky were easing down. He took a lantern, and set off alone on the path through the woods.

The forest floor was soft and familiar underfoot; the papery, pitchy fir cones stuck to Hugh's bare feet as they had when he was a boy in Goshen. The dense welter of trees hid the sky completely. After a long walk, he heard the voices. Will Ruffin called to him, Vinnie called to him, and he held the lantern up to find the fir trunk down which their voices fell. He climbed the tree one-handed on many rungs, emerged at a high platform, and pulled himself up.

Hugh found a dozen unrecognizable people on the platform, and heard unfamiliar voices. Cyrus Sharp was there, taller than Aunt June. Hugh held the lantern aloft and saw it illumine the stiff boughs of trees; he set the lantern down. He stripped to his union suit, and somebody handed him the heavy, knotted rope. He could feel Vinnie low beside him, shivering and excited in the dark. Her wide skirts and many petticoats nudged his bare ankle once, then twice, and a pang ran through him. Before his eyes in every direction he saw nothing: no pond, no ocean, no forest, sky, nor any horizon, only unmixed blackness.

"Swing out," the voices said in the darkness.

"Push from the platform, and when you're all the way out, let go."

When? he thought. Where?

The heavy rope pulled at him. He carried it to the platform edge. He hitched up on the knot and launched out. As he swung through the air, trembling, he saw the blackness give way below, like a parting of clouds, to a deep patch of stars on the ground. It was the pond, he hoped, the hole in the woods reflecting the sky. He judged the instant and let go; he flung himself loose into the stars.